GABRIEL

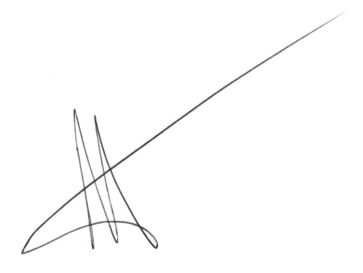

Gabriel R. Ballard

CHALK PORTRAIT · LATE 1862 – EARLY 1863

GABRIEL

A Novel of the American Civil War

MATTHEW J. WATROS

Book design by The Troy Book Makers
Printed in the United States of America
The Troy Book Makers • Troy, New York • thetroybookmakers.com

ISBN: 978-1-61468-598-2

AUTHORS NOTE

I remember I was in 9th grade. I had always been very interested in history, specifically the American Civil War, and after dabbling some with genealogy, I became curious to know if I had any ancestors that fought in the war. My grandfather, Lynn Watros, was unsure if we did, but suggested I call up his cousin, Bob Watros, and ask him what he knew. So, one night I looked up Bob's number in the phone book and gave him a call. That was when I first heard about my great-great-great grandfather.

The next morning, I remember going into the school library, before my first class, to get on a computer and look him up to see what battles his regiment had fought in. I was beyond excited and intrigued and afterwards had a deep desire to learn more about him. Luckily, over the next few years, while I was still in school, I was able to find out a lot. I got in touch with some distant relatives of mine from Canada, Ballard cousins, who like myself were direct descendants of Gabriel. They astonished me by sending transcriptions of four of his journals from 1863, 1865, 1868 and 1871. They also sent me a digital copy of his wartime portrait and his enlistment papers. I was blown away by their kindness, but still I wanted to learn more. I combed over his journal entries, read books on General Sherman's late war campaigns and even forced my family to visit two battle-fields he fought at, on the way to a summer vacation in Myrtle Beach. Senior year, my mother took me to Washington D.C. as a graduation present and I visited the National Archives in search of additional information on him.

While I was in the Marine Corps my research slowed, but after getting out in 2010 it picked back up again. It was around that time that I found out about his court martial, after a quick Google search of his name. I was shocked to say the least. I found his story incredibly interesting though, and after compiling all that I had, I decided to put it all together and write a short biography on him.

Through construing his biography, I found that I enjoyed writing and put together several more family histories, and a few articles for the local papers and some historical society periodicals. Always keeping Gabriel on the back burner, I eventually thought I might try my hand at writing a novel on his time in the war. It took me several years of writing in my downtime, between work, other projects, and helping my wife to raise our three children, before I had a completed manuscript.

To write the book I relied heavily on primary sources: Gabriel's journals, his court martial record, notes on a letter he wrote in 1862, and dozens of letters written by two other men in his company. The Official Records of the War of the Rebellion were also a great help, along with the 143rd New York's regimental history, and countless other nonfiction books on the Civil War. I was writing a novel of course, but I wanted it to be as close to the facts as possible. To do so, I took what facts I'd learned on Gabriel, his family, his company and regiment, and the times he lived in, and fashioned a story around them. The whole process was a lot of fun for me, especially coming up with some of the fictional filler. For that I simply relied on my imagination, various life experiences, and was without a doubt influenced some by the works of my favorite fiction authors, guys like Kenneth Roberts, Bernard Cornwell, and Larry McMurtry, just to name a few.

In keeping with my desire to write a historically accurate and honest novel, I also felt that it was important I didn't gloss over or steer around the reality of northern politics and society of that era. For that reason, the reader will find that there are several characters in the book that don't exactly have what would be considered a modern perception of race and equality. In a few instances in the book some even use outdated language, that was openly and commonly used at that time. This I must state is not meant to offend. It is also not meant to be edgy, political, or controversial, and is certainly not representative of my own thoughts or beliefs, other than my belief in the honest, accurate and impartial telling of history.

Sure, I could have written a novel where all my characters were radical abolitionist, or had a modern day perception of race, but that in my opinion would have been a lie, a misrepresentation of reality and an injustice to what actually happened. I think it also would have been a downplaying of the African American struggle for me to falsely portray that it was all "peaches and cream," for them in the north, when in reality northern ideas of racial equality weren't all that much different than those of the south.

Again, that all being said, above all else, this is a novel about my ancestor and his experiences during the American Civil War. Due to modern day politics though, I thought it important to explain my decision to include some of the language and different stances that I did. I did not and do not want that decision to be misunderstood or misinterpreted in any way.

Matthew J. Watros

*This novel is for my children, Bracen, Colton, and Zara,
but is dedicated to the memory of my grandmother,
Nancy Lee Watros. A great storyteller in her own right,
Grandma introduced me to the study of history
and taught me the importance of books.*

BASIC CIVIL WAR
ARMY ORGANIZATION

(FROM SMALLEST TO LARGEST)

COMPANY
(approx. 100 men)

REGIMENT
(approx. 10 companies)

BRIGADE
(approx. 3 to 6 regiments)

DIVISION
(approx. 3 to 5 brigades)

CORPS
(approx. 3 to 4 divisions)

ARMY
(1+ corps)

BASIC CIVIL WAR
ARMY RANK STRUCTURE

PRIVATE

CORPORAL

SERGEANT

(Sergeant, First-Sergeant, Ordinance-Sergeant,
Quartermaster-Sergeant, Sergeant-Major)

2ND LIEUTENANT

1ST LIEUTENANT

CAPTAIN

(typically commanded a company)

MAJOR

LIEUTENANT COLONEL

COLONEL

(typically commanded a regiment)

GENERAL

(Brigadier-General, Major-General, Lieutenant-General)
(*typically commanded brigades, divisions, corps and armies*)

Part One

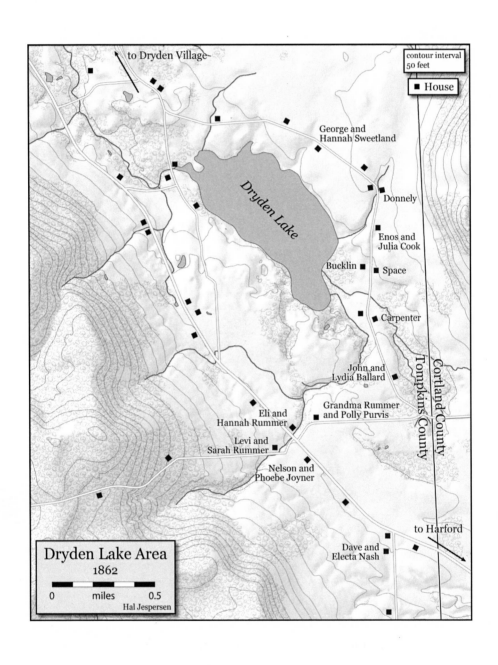

to Dryden Village

contour interval
50 feet

■ House

George and
Hannah Sweetland

Dryden Lake

Donnely

Enos and
Julia Cook

Bucklin ■   ■ Space

Carpenter

John and
Lydia Ballard

Grandma Rummer
and Polly Purvis

Eli and
Hannah Rummer

Levi and
Sarah Rummer

Nelson and
Phoebe Joyner

Cortland County
Tompkins County

to Harford

Dave and
Electa Nash

Dryden Lake Area
1862

0   miles   0.5
Hal Jespersen

CHAPTER ONE

The sun had been up for an hour before the rooster's crow finally woke him. Gabriel Ballard had slept in this morning, and it wasn't from a late night spent in town. In fact, he had gone to bed early, just after dinner, but had trouble falling asleep. He felt anxious and conflicted. He had been for the past couple months, actually. The war, which had been consuming the country, had also been consuming Gabriel's thoughts lately and playing tug of war with his conscience. How could he be at home he wondered, when other boys, some even younger than himself, were off fighting and dying to preserve the very nation he called home.

He had expressed these feelings to his parents, hoping they would consent to his wish of enlisting, but his mother would hear nothing of it.

"It's a fool's war, Gabriel," she had said, "and I will not send my oldest son off to die because some turkey-brained politicians in Washington can't get along. Besides, your father and I need your help on the farm, especially now. The harvest will be here before we know it."

Gabriel's father, John, wasn't much help to his cause either. Secretly, he himself longed to enlist, but a farming accident two years prior made that dream all but impossible. "I agree with your mother," he had said, and that was that, or so they thought.

Even after his parents rejected his plans to join the Army, his desire to do so didn't go away, if anything it only grew. In reality, he was 19 years old and could sign up without their consent, but going against his parent's judgement was still something he was reluctant to do. It took some hard thought and self-convincing, but after several hours of tossing and turning in his bed late the night before, he had come to the conclusion that he would enlist anyway, and do so the very next day.

"So what if Mother and Father don't want me to go," he had thought. "Once I do sign up, there'll be nothing they can say and surely they will warm to the idea when they see me in the blue uniform, and I start sending them home my pay." "Maybe," he thought, trying to reassure himself with his decision, "maybe Mother truly does wish I'd go off and fight for the Union, but thinks it's her Christian duty to outwardly sue for peace."

As he was dozing, Gabriel congratulated himself on his decision and made it a resolution to visit Martha Marsh on his way into town in the morning. It would be a Friday anyway, and Martha's sister Hannah and her brother-in-law George Sweetland would be in Dryden as they were every Friday morning. They said they did so to exercise their carriage horse, but Gabriel knew it was just an excuse for Hannah to snoop around the village for the latest gossip and pass on her own tidbits of half-truths.

As he rolled out of bed, Gabriel let out a big yawn and after standing, bent over and tried touching his toes. He stretched out his arms and his legs and back, as he knew he had a long walk to town ahead of him. He pulled on a clean pair of trousers, a clean shirt and pair of socks, too. "No sense in giving the recruiter a bad first impression," he thought to himself. "Rill won't want me rolling around with her in filthy trousers anyway." Rill was Gabriel's pet name for Martha Marsh. Her full name was Martha Marilla Marsh, after her mother, but he liked calling her Rill for short.

His mother Lydia was up. He could smell she had been frying up some bacon and spuds for breakfast, and had made pancakes, too. As he walked downstairs, it occurred to him that his days of enjoying her good home cooking were numbered. He would miss it for sure, he thought to himself, but sacrifices had to be made.

Lydia was still busy cooking when he came into the kitchen. His little brother and sister, Sam and Mary, were eating at the table, and Gabriel's oldest little sister, Sarah, was busy feeding their baby brother George. Sarah was less than two years younger than Gabriel, and the two of them had been adversaries for most of their childhood.

"Your father was out on business last night and has yet to make it home, Gabriel," his mother said as she turned from the stove with a heaping plate of food for her eldest child. That meant his father John had been out drinking with his brothers again.

"Sit down and eat up now, I've got a list of chores for you and your father to do, and Lord knows when he'll be home to help."

John wasn't an alcoholic, but when he went out, he usually went all out, and sometimes he'd be gone for several days afterwards. Once, he and his brother William had gotten drunk at a friend's house over in Caroline and stumbled into an unlocked railcar that was stopped on the tracks. As they slept, the train took off and by the time they finally awoke they found themselves halfway to New York City. That had been when Gabriel was much younger, though. It wasn't until his accident in 1860 that John's binges started to become more numerous. John had been threshing wheat at his brother-in-law's one day, and the threshing machine clogged. He stuck his arm in and easily cleared the debris, but the machine started running before he could pull it out, and all the fingers on his right hand got lopped off.

Lydia was a petite and pretty woman, and even after birthing five children had managed to keep her figure. She was short and thin about the chest and torso, with dark brown eyes and hair that, at 38, was beginning to show signs of graying. She was also smart, at times demanding, and although a woman, the true head of the family farm. When she and John were married in 1842, Lydia's father, Gabriel Rummer, parceled out a portion of his estate to his daughter and son-in-law as a wedding present. It was comparatively small, being only 50 acres in size, and they were poor, but Lydia was determined to give it a cleanly appearance and efficient reputation.

As Gabriel ate, his mother sat down at the end of the table and spoke to him. "Now Gabriel, I don't mean to be pushy, but you know what kind of state I'm in when your father's been out all night. I get so nervous for his safety. He's getting older you know and those pesky brothers of his, your uncles, pressure him into doing the most reckless of things."

"Yes, Mother, I know. Would you like me to have a talk with him?"

Gabriel asked her, as he stuffed a hunk of bacon into his mouth.

"No, I suppose not," Lydia said, "it just worries me dear and I need to vent my frustrations. I've been on edge ever since you brought up that nonsense of joining the Army last week and now with your father out…, well doing Lord knows what, I'm starting to feel overwhelmed."

Gabriel's siblings sat silent. He could tell his mother had been venting to them all morning, too. He said nothing, so she got up from the table and returned to the stove.

"I'll make him a plate, but if he's not home in one hour I'll feed it to the hogs, and he can chew on dry corn kernels for all I care!" she decried in a wave of frustration.

As Gabriel got up from the table, his sisters, Sarah and Mary, started clearing it. It was the girls' job to wash the dishes and clean up the kitchen after breakfast, while his brother Sam took George to the water pump out back to wash up. As Lydia was making up his father's plate, Gabriel tried sneaking out the back door with his brothers without her noticing.

"Now hold on, Gabriel. Don't be taking off just yet. You can't do your chores until I tell you what I want done, can you?" she asked.

"Well I was hoping to walk down to the lake and get a bit of fishing in before it gets too hot out," Gabriel said.

"But I was counting on you cleaning out the chicken coop this morning and mending the fence in the pasture. Can't you go fishing in the afternoon after your chores are done?" his mother pleaded.

"No, because the fish won't be biting in the afternoon, and all the boys from here to Dryden will be jumping in and swimming around my spot by then. I'll be back soon enough anyway, and I promise I won't go to bed tonight until all my chores are done."

Lydia was a strict proprietor, but she sometimes struggled when it came to disappointing her children. She also realized that Gabriel would more than likely be married someday soon and thought she might as well let him enjoy his carefree life while it still existed.

"Alright, you can go and do your fishing, but I want you back by noon and not a minute beyond."

Before she finished her sentence, Gabriel was running out the back door and around the house to their front gate. As he reached for the latch, though, Lydia stepped out the front door.

"Aren't you forgetting something, Gabriel?" she asked, while eyeing his new cane fishing pole he'd purchased in the village the week before at French's Hardware. It still lay propped up against their front porch.

"Oh, yes, Mother. I almost forgot. Thank you."

He trotted up to the house, and she handed him the pole as his sister Sarah walked outside to join them with a look of innocence on her face. Gabriel wasn't fooled, though. He could see a hint of the devil in her eyes. She had always been a thorn in his side, as well as a tyrant to their younger siblings and she waited for him to get on the road before finally piping up.

"Dressed awful nice for fishing isn't he Mother?" she said in an inquiring tone that was loud enough for Gabriel to hear. Fed up with her constant antics, Gabriel's face grew red with anger and he whipped around to confront her.

"Shut your snotty little trap you little witch, its none of your affair!" he said, and turned to walk away. Lydia put her foot down, though, and halted him.

"For heaven's sake, Gabriel, I will not have you speak to your baby sister in such a way!" she scolded. He wasn't bothered though. He didn't care. He was sick and tired of Sarah's prying.

"Mother, she's 17 years old. She's no baby. Lord knows, she could have one of her own by now, if she weren't so miserable. No man wants to put up with that. Besides, my affairs are my affairs and none of her concern."

"Oh my word, Mother, did you hear what he said about me?" Sarah whimpered, trying to play the victim, but Lydia was having none of it.

"Get inside, Sarah," she said. "He's right about one thing. You do need to mind your own business," she added, before focusing back on her son.

"Hold it right there a second, Gabriel. I want to talk to you."

Gabriel sighed and stood in the road, looking annoyed. Sarah stepped into the house but crouched to listen in the shadow of the doorway as Lydia walked out to their front gate.

"I hope you're not going to visit that Marsh girl again. Remember the last time her sister caught you poking around while she and George were out? She told the whole town that you barged into their house even against her sisters' protests."

Gabriel shook his head.

"Mother, you know that wasn't so. I told you, Rill saw me walking by and asked me in to help her fix their stove. The pipe was clogged and smoking their whole house up. Besides, Hannah Sweetland's a liar, and a prying gossip and you know it," Gabriel said.

"I know perfectly well what Hannah Sweetland is and isn't, but you still don't need to be giving her any more of a reason to spread rumors. It's embarrassing. Lord knows what they say about your father, I don't need them whispering lies about my son too." Lydia went on. "Promise me you won't go to Martha's, will you, Gabriel?" she begged.

"Mother, I said I was going fishing and that's what I'm doing. I haven't changed my clothes in a week that's why I'm wearing clean ones. If you want, I'll go put my soiled ones back on to set you at ease."

Lydia stood quiet for a moment in thought, before letting out a slight sigh. "No, no. I trust you. You can go. Just remember, not a minute past noon. God willing, your father will be home by then to help out," she said.

Happy to have shaken her suspicions, Gabriel took off.

"Yes, Mother, I know," he called out over his shoulder.

The sun was already bright and hot in the sky, and his plodding steps on the old dirt road were kicking up enough dust to parch his throat and coat his fresh pants. As he was just about out of sight from home, he heard a commotion behind him, and turned see that his father had arrived. It looked as if John was riding almost sideways on his horse, and his mother, he could tell, was hysterical, scolding his father while at the same time barking orders to his sisters and brother Sam to help him down before he hurt himself.

Gabriel felt bad for his father but was happy to not be in his shoes, as he knew John now had a morning full of endless nagging to endure. Before his mother caught sight of him and called him home, Gabriel quickly turned and high-tailed it out of view.

CHAPTER TWO

The lake, Rill's house and the Village of Dryden were all north of Gabriel's home, so it was in that direction he headed. Just before the Carpenter farm, he took a left off the road and into a standing field of corn. It was his normal route to Dryden Lake, so he headed that way so as not to raise any suspicion. Rill's house was just a few farms further up the road. She lived with her sister and brother-in-law on their farm at the north-east side of the lake.

Rill and her sister Hannah had been born in Harford, a town in Cortland County that bordered Dryden. In fact, the back of John and Lydia's property was on that border, and John had been brought up there as well. Most of Gabriel's Ballard relatives still lived in Harford. The Marsh girls had family in the area, but after their mother died, they moved with their father to New York City. Hannah was miserable in the city, especially after their father, James, remarried. Their step-mother, Victoria, was only 12 years older than Hannah, and the two girls detested each other. To ease the tension at home, James sent Hannah back upstate to live with his brother Augustus. Hannah ended up marrying a Dryden boy by the name of George Sweetland in 1859, and it wasn't long after that James sent Rill up to live with the newlyweds, for she too had begun complaining of mistreatment at the hands of her step-mother.

Gabriel carefully made his way through the corn to a stream on the far end of the field that fed into the lake. He followed along its bank, trying his best to keep his boots out of the mud. Near the shore he entered a thick patch of young willow and underbrush that bordered the lake there. He decided he ought to take a quick plunge and clean up some before he went to see Rill. Stripping off his clothes, he hung them on a branch and waded in. Just off the shore he could see fish taking big gulps at the surface where their breakfast of flies and other insects were trapped on the water. For a moment he thought about casting in a line, he was sure to get a couple bites, but decided against it. He had more important business to attend to: Rill and then his enlistment.

That reminded him, he was on his way to enlist. All the trouble he'd had getting out of the house that morning made him briefly forget the true purpose of his outing. He felt slightly nauseous at the thought of it now. The deed was fast approaching. In only a couple hours he would be in Dryden filling out the necessary paperwork. Harrison Marvin was slated to be in the village all day recruiting to fill a company of soldiers from the town. David Ferris had passed by Gabriel's place the day before and told him so. He said he'd be going too, and that if Gabriel was man enough, he'd sign up with him.

Gabriel dunked his head under the water and combed his sopping hair back with his fingers. He didn't have any soap, but this would do just fine. Gingerly, he made his way back on shore and to a large rock under one of the willows to sit and dry. The sun was big and bright, and there was a slight breeze. It caused a ripple on the surface of the lake and fluttered the thin willow leaves above him. It didn't take long for the wet to dissipate. After getting his clothes back on, he picked a small mirror out of one of his pockets to make sure he looked presentable. There were still a few bits of bacon in his teeth, so he used the inside cuff of one of his sleeves to scrub then clean. He grabbed a handful of mint that grew along the shore too, to gnaw on and freshen his breath.

As he made his way along the eastern shore of the lake, Gabriel picked a handful of black-eyed susans for Rill, hoping they'd butter her up. If it worked, and she consented to his advances, he decided that once they'd finished, he'd tell her about his decision. If he did it in that order, he figured he'd get everything he wanted.

Reaching the point on shore behind Rill's, he followed an old cow path up through the pasture and snuck into the hedgerow that led to the backside of the Sweetland's barn. It was there where he tossed his fishing pole aside for safe keeping. He knew that Rill would likely be inside, busy with her daily chores. She did her fair share, too, for her sister always seemed to be suffering from some sort of imagined illness. In fact, already that morning Rill had milked the cows, made breakfast for the family, cleared the table, washed the dishes, scrubbed the kitchen, and bathed and dressed her nephew. As Gabriel approached the barn, he could hear Rill. She was in there alright, singing softly as she often did while at work.

As he walked into the side door, he could see she was plopped down in a pile of fresh golden straw with something in her arms. She had on a crimson dress with black lace trim and a long line of black buttons running from her neck to her waist, that Gabriel couldn't wait to undo. One of the many gifts her father sent up from the city.

She looked up when she heard him come in and once she saw who it was, flashed him a warm and inviting smile.

"You brought me flowers? How sweet," she said in surprise.

Gabriel smiled back and walked over for a closer look. She tilted her head toward the bundle she was cradling, and Gabriel could see at once that it was a newborn lamb.

"Look, Gabriel. Isn't it adorable? She's an orphan, like me. Her momma died last night giving birth to her, and George found her when he came in this morning."

"Poor thing," he said, reaching down to scratch the soft tuft of wool on its head. Rill was always nursing or playing mother to some sort of impoverished creature. Truthfully, though, he could care less about the lamb at the moment. All he could think about was scooping Rill up and carrying her off to someplace private. Just being in her presence made his insides go wild; she was intoxicating. He loved her dainty little figure, her shiny dark hair and the barely noticeable line of freckles under her glittering hazel eyes. He loved, too, how her visible skin, on her face, neck and hands was dark from working long hours in her sister's vegetable garden, while underneath her many layers of garments it was soft and milky white. It showed that she was up to the task and willing to pitch in, and he found that very appealing in a mate.

What he loved most about Rill though, was not her beauty, but her easy-going nature and her sweet and caring disposition. Rill always made everyone around her feel welcome and wanted, and even under the most stressful of circumstances she remained calm and cool-headed. She had to, too, for living with her sister was no easy task.

To Gabriel's pleasure, Rill set the lamb into its pen and began focusing her attention on him. After standing, she brushed a few pieces of clinging straw from her bottom, then gave him a hug.

"I was hoping you'd come," she said, as she buried the side of her face into his chest. The top of her head just slightly touched Gabriel's chin, and he couldn't help but smell the scent of lavender in her hair. He kissed the top of her head before she looked up into his eyes, gave him a quick smile and moved in for a long and affectionate kiss of her own.

"Where do you want to go, into the corn or up in the hayloft?" Gabriel asked her. His heart was pounding so loud he thought Rill might hear.

"Slow down," she told him, "not so hasty."

Taking his hand in hers, Rill began to lead him out the sliding barn door toward the back of the Sweetland's house.

"Follow me," she instructed, but realizing where they were headed, Gabriel let go and refused to move another step forward.

"Not in the house, Rill. Are you out of your mind?"

She giggled at his trepidation.

"Don't worry, Gabriel, my sister and George said they were going up to McLean today. They won't be back until mid-afternoon at the soonest. We'll be alright." Taking his hand in hers again, she turned back around and tugged him along behind her. He still felt uneasy about venturing inside but held his tongue and obeyed. He knew it may very well be their last time alone, and he didn't want to upset her.

* * * * *

In age, Gabriel was a year older than Rill, but due to her life experiences she was far more mature. The death of her mother and the somewhat strained childhood she had in residence with her icy step-mother had taught Rill many of life's lessons early. Living in the city prematurely educated her on many of the true facts of life as well. Before she was ten, she had seen several men hanged, and another get his brains beat out by a club-wielding thief on the street in front of her home. On a daily basis, she saw poor whites and blacks dressed in little more than filthy rags, and half-starved children who would fight almost to the death over a crust of bread.

Moisy Cunningham was an Irish girl that had worked in her home for a while when Rill lived with her father. It was Moisy's job to help Victoria with her younger siblings. Rill was the eldest child in the home at that time, though, and would often ask Moisy of her life in Ireland before coming to America. She told fascinating stories of the old country, its stone lined fields, ancient castles, manor houses and her trip over the Atlantic. What shocked Rill the most was the time Moisy confided in her of her work as a prostitute during her first years in New York. That is how Rill was introduced to the workings of sex.

She wasn't experienced in it by any means. Gabriel was her first and only partner, but through Moisy's stories she knew more about it than most young ladies her age. When she first moved back upstate, she had a hard time fitting in. The other girls in town, Sarah Ballard included, were jealous of her fancy clothes and good looks. Her friendly personality meant little to them. Gabriel was the first one to take notice of her and treat her with compassion. He was her first real friend after moving home, and he was still almost her only one. He would come by often and work for her brother-in-law George, and his friend Enos Cook, with whom they shared a home at the time. Once Rill's sister Hannah noticed the two were becoming attached to one another, though, she forbade Gabriel from coming over. After that, Gabriel and Rill had to secretly meet down along the lake or in Dryden if they could arrange to be in the village on the same day.

The two hadn't become intimate until earlier that spring. It was on a Friday like today, and Gabriel dropped by after Hannah and George had passed him on the road heading for the village. Gabriel found Rill in the barn doing her chores, one thing led to another, and it happened. It wasn't their intention for it to happen, it just did. Afterward, Rill felt awful guilty but consoled herself with the thought that she would eventually marry Gabriel someday anyway. Gabriel was quite the opposite. He was beyond overjoyed when he left the Sweetland's farm and was busy the rest of the day pondering how to get some more alone time with Rill.

* * * * *

A while later, after the deed was done, Gabriel and Rill lay in her bed together. It was a rope bed with a straw tick mattress, and too small for two people, but they didn't care. They were just happy to be with each other. Gabriel had never been in Rill's room before. In fact, he had never been on the second floor of the house.

"It's a nice little spot you've got here Rill," he told her.

"It's much better than my room at Papa's house, that's for sure. I know it's small, but at least I have it all to myself. Victoria always forced me share mine in the city with Moisy or whatever help she had at the time. Once, she even had her uncle stay there with me when he came visiting. He was a nice enough man, and slept on the floor in the corner, but can you imagine, Gabriel, making a twelve-year-old girl share her room with a bachelor in his fifties? It makes me sick just thinking about it. Why Papa let her get away with such things, I haven't a clue."

Gabriel chuckled. Rill was all sorts of kind, but bring up her step-mother and she'd get all worked up.

"Well, I think I have a couple ideas why," he jokingly responded, with a smug-looking grin.

"Not funny, Mr. Ballard," Rill said, and poked her dainty little knuckles into his ribs.

"Ouch!" he cried in jest, attempting to give her some satisfaction.

"I'm going to miss this, Rill. Spending time with you is what makes me most happy. I swear it," he said, then cringed. He hadn't wanted to bring up the fact that he was enlisting until just before he left.

"You mean when you join the Army?" Rill asked, calmly. "I'm going to miss it too, Gabriel, but you'll be back home before long and then we'll have the rest of our lives to spend together."

Gabriel was shocked.

"What, you knew?" he asked. "But how could you know? I didn't know myself until last night, and I haven't told a soul."

"How could I know? How could I not?" She sat up in bed and looked down at him. "I know you too well. I knew you couldn't sit around when half the other men in town have gone off or are going off to fight. I supposed it would happen sooner or later, but then David Ferris stopped by here yesterday boasting how he was going to sign up in the morning and…" "Hold up," Gabriel interrupted. "What was David Ferris stopping here for?"

"Well he didn't stop exactly, he was just passing by when I was out front, playing with Monroe." Monroe was her two-year-old nephew. "He said that he was going to enlist and then he said that he tried to get you to go along too, but thought you were too yellow and wouldn't."

She giggled, but Gabriel was upset.

"Yellow? That bastard!" he said, as he leapt out of bed and went to pull his clothes on. "I'll show him yellow. I've whooped him so many times I've lost count. Yellow! He's more than yellow. He's a God-damned coward!"

"Gabriel Rummer Ballard, sit down this instant and quit that cussing," Rill scolded him. "We don't have much time left together, and I'm not going to let you ruin it by going off to chase down the likes of David Ferris."

Gabriel was heated but came to his senses. He sat down in a chair in the corner of her room, as she continued to try and talk sense into him.

"I am all for you defending your honor, just not at a time like this," she explained. "I obviously didn't believe him anyway. I knew he was wrong and that you wouldn't let him outdo you."

Her mood had returned to its usual cool, and level manner. She got up out of bed and started to dress herself. A rare cool breeze was blowing through the window and it fluttered the white lace drapes she had in the sunlight.

"So, when are you leaving?" she asked.

"Well, I don't suspect I'll be leaving for a few days yet, but I was planning on going to the village after I visited with you."

"Were you going to tell me before or after you signed up?" Rill asked, as she pulled up her long stockings.

"I planned on telling you when I left here."

"What do your parents think?"

"Don't know yet. I suppose I'll find out soon enough, though." He smiled sheepishly.

"Your poor mother, Gabriel. She's going to be heartbroken."

A puzzled look crept over his face.

"Hey how come you don't seem so distressed? Shouldn't you be fighting me and telling me not to go, crying and carrying on like a good lover would?" Gabriel asked, half in jest but also slightly concerned.

She gave him a scolding look at his question and reached over to nudge him with her fist.

"Your lover?" she said, and Gabriel smiled. "Please don't call me that. It makes me sound like a trollop, but I'm anything but the sort. I consider myself your future wife, and to answer your question, no, I'll not be making a scene. I won't stand in your way. Sure, I don't want you to go but that's for you to decide not me. Besides, I know you're going to be fine."

"What do you mean you know I'll be fine? How can you know that?"

"I'm not sure how I know. I can't explain it, I just do. I have this feeling that's all - this premonition that everything is going to be alright. I don't know how I have it, but I do."

It made Gabriel happy to hear her say such things. The two remained silent for a moment, listening to a pair of red cardinals chirping outside her window. Rill sat back down on the bed, fully clothed. Only the line of black buttons on the front of her dress remained undone. The little hairs above her ears and on the back of her neck were slightly damp with perspiration, reactivating the pleasant smell of her lavender perfume.

"I'm sure your sister will be happy I'm leaving," Gabriel said with a smirk.

Rill smiled back at him and leaned back on her elbows.

"You want to hear something funny?" she asked.

"Sure, what?"

"George told my sister he wanted to sign up the other day, too."

Gabriel laughed.

"Oh, and what did Hannah have to say about that?"

Rill sat up and threw her voice to sound like her sisters.

"She said, George Sweetland if those words pass through your lips again in my presence, I will cut out your tongue and poke out your eyes, so that not even an army of imbeciles would enlist you into their ranks. Do you hear me?!"

The two of them erupted into laughter at the telling of the encounter.

"I bet old George shut right up, too. Didn't he?" Gabriel questioned her, as he wiped tears from his eyes.

"No, actually, he didn't," Rill said.

"What did he say?" Gabriel asked.

"I don't recall, really. Something about "duty", and then my sister said "Duty? Duty to what, a filthy bunch of slaves. Papa says this war is about nothing more than freeing them and my husband's not going to leave me destitute for something so foolish."

"Freeing slaves? Is that what Hannah thinks this war is about?" Gabriel asked.

"That's what my Papa says."

"Well that's not what I'm fighting for, Rill. I'm going to stop the South from destroying us. This country is the best thing this world's got going, and we can't just sit around and let them break it up because they lost the election. Besides, I thought your father was all for the war?"

"Well, he was at first. Ever since last summer, though, after some of his friends from the city got killed at Bull Run, he's all against it now. Says it isn't worth the trouble, and he reminds us of his opinion in every letter he sends. I wish he'd stop to tell the truth."

Suddenly, the sound of steel-rimmed wheels rolling down the road out front could be heard, and Rill peeked out her window to see who was going by. When she saw who it was, she slid back out of sight and turned to Gabriel.

"My sister's back, Gabriel. Hurry up and get out of here, or we'll never hear the end of it."

Gabriel went white and jumped out of the chair.

"I thought you said they'd be gone all day?"

"I don't know what happened. It's too late to fret about it now, though. Go on, and get," she said, but as he turned to run, she grabbed him by the arm. "No, wait."

He turned to face her, and she wrapped her arms around him and squeezed with all her might. Then they kissed one last time.

"Now you can go," she said, and like a frightened hare, Gabriel bounded out of the room, down the stairs and through the kitchen to the back door. It was his only chance at escaping unnoticed.

Before going outside, Gabriel listened to make sure they hadn't driven the carriage behind the house. Usually, George would stop out front to unload everyone before he pulled around back to put the horse and carriage away, but Gabriel wasn't taking any chances. He heard nothing, so he quietly unlatched the door and slipped outside. He was beginning to think he might just get away, but then he noticed something strange. Something was off. It was too quiet. He thought he should hear the carriage wheels crunching gravel, the horse, or Hannah and George talking, but he heard none of that.

Slyly, he crept over to the back corner of the house to make sure the coast was clear before running for the barn. As he poked his head around the corner, though, he was startled to see Hannah, George, and little Monroe seated nice and proper-like in their horse-drawn carriage. George still had the reins in his hand, and Hannah was holding a parasol above her head. They were still as statues.

"Oh boy," Gabriel said, and with that the silence erupted into chaos.

Hannah let out a blood curdling scream, that made Gabriel jump back, and George fall out of his seat and onto the ground. The baby started crying, and like a Spartan warrior with its trusted javelin, Hannah collapsed her parasol and slung it at Gabriel. He stood a good 20 feet in front of her, but her aim was true, and she hit him square in the stomach. Instinctively, he bent over at the waist and clutched his hands over the wound.

"What the hell!" Gabriel shouted after catching his breath. The missile had temporarily knocked the wind out of him.

George stood up off the ground and started brushing himself off. He had a smile on his face, because although he knew Hannah was going to be miserable for the rest of the day, he always enjoyed seeing her unleash her anger on someone other than himself. It wasn't that he was a sadist, it was more of a relieved happiness.

"What the hell!" Hannah shrieked. "The question is what the hell are you doing at my home? If I've told you once I've told you a thousand times, you aren't welcome here."

Gabriel tried to respond but couldn't come up with a good lie fast enough.

"Yes, Hannah, I know, but you see I was just walking by and then, ugh, then…"

"Then nothing," Hannah interrupted. "You're here to corrupt my sister and nothing more. I know what's on your filthy little mind and let me tell you what, you'd better go looking elsewhere because the next time I catch you here I'm running for my gun."

Gabriel was tongue-tied, but like a guardian angel sweeping in for the rescue, Rill stepped through the back door and around the corner.

"Oh, Hannah, you mustn't blame Gabriel. He didn't want to come in, honest, but I insisted, you see," Rill said.

"Insisted for what, Martha?" Hannah grilled her in a disbelieving tone.

"Well Gabriel's going off to enlist today, and I thought it only proper and patriotic to ask him in for something to drink, seeing how hot it is out."

Hannah gave her sister a suspicious look, but Rill continued.

"Hannah, you should have seen it. He was walking past the house red as a tomato and soaked to the gills in sweat. I thought he'd pass out if I didn't get him under cover and something to drink."

"I would have loved to have seen it," Hannah replied to her sister, then let her gaze fall back on Gabriel and shot her venom at him.

"Going to die for the slaves, are you, boy?"

"No, ma'am, going to preserve the Union," Gabriel said to her defiantly, as he straightened out almost to attention.

"Ha, ha, right, another reason equally as ridiculous," Hannah mocked. "My George here got it in his head that it was his "duty" too or some sort of nonsense, but I put a stop to that right quick. Isn't that so George?"

George didn't answer. He quietly walked in front of the carriage and to the corner of the house, as if he were headed for the back door. Instead, he walked straight to Rill and whispered.

"Buttons. Check your buttons, quick."

Rill looked down. "Oh, no," she thought to herself. In her haste to fasten her last few buttons on her way downstairs, she had shifted them out of alignment, and her collar was completely uneven. She turned around and went back into the house to fix her mistake before Hannah took notice.

Hannah was too preoccupied slaying the two men in her yard, though. Baby Monroe had stopped crying and was sitting obediently in the carriage, so as to not draw attention from his angry mother. He was a quick learner.

"George, George! What are you whispering over there? What did you say to Martha?" George turned around.

"Nothing. Oh, nothing, dear. Yes, yes, I'm sorry. Yes, the war. Stupid, stupid affair. Gabriel, it's a waste of time," he said.

He made his way back to his side of the carriage but gave Gabriel a quick wink.

"A waste of time, indeed," Hannah agreed, "but a good place for the likes of you, I think, Gabriel. I'll be happy to see you go. Good riddance to you, and now I will ask you to please leave my property for the final time."

Hannah stood up.

"George come over here and help me down. This unpleasantness has upset my stomach. I'll be heading to bed. Tell Martha to bring me something to drink, and then she can watch the baby."

George walked around to Hannah's side of the carriage to let her down, as Gabriel walked past them and headed for the road.

"Oh, and Gabriel," Hannah said reproachingly, "a bit of advice before you head off to play soldier. You might want to get some thicker skin. How do you expect to march into battle if you can't even walk the quarter mile from your house to ours without overexerting yourself?"

Gabriel paid her no mind, though. It showed she had bought their lie, and Rill wouldn't be getting into any trouble with her. Surely, Hannah would spread more rumors, but that didn't bother him, either. He was just thankful that he got to spend the time with Rill that he did. As he made his way back onto the road, he heard a whistle coming from the house and looked up to see Rill hanging out her bedroom window, waving goodbye. She blew him a kiss.

"I love you, Gabriel Ballard," she said.

Gabriel smiled and waved back.

"I love you too, Martha Marsh," he called out to her, and was on his way.

CHAPTER THREE

As Gabriel made his way into Dryden, he could see that the village was in its usual hustle and bustle. There were men unloading goods from wagons, and couples rolling by in their carriages. A group of boys was chasing a stray cat through a back alley and a sleepy old hound was lounging under the front porch of a house on South Street. Its elderly master was rocking in a chair on the floor above him, sipping a glass of applejack and nursing an ember back to life in the bowl of his burl pipe. Almost all the houses and buildings in town had patriotic red, white, and blue bunting hung under their windows, above their doors, or across the veranda of their porches. Many flags were fluttering in the slight summer breeze as well.

Gabriel wasn't exactly sure where the recruiting was going on, but he thought he ought to check Harrison Marvin's boot and shoe store near the south-east corner of Main and South Streets. That's where he found it. Marvin was in a partnership with his father-in-law, Otis Murdock. He and his wife took care of the sales and paperwork while Mr. Murdock made the footwear and did repairs.

When he approached the store, Gabriel saw a banner over the doorway that read 'Volunteers Wanted' in big bold letters. He could also see a collection of men milling around the entrance out front. They were standing under a canvas fly that was being used to keep the sun off the prospective recruits. He recognized several of them. Harrison Marvin was standing proud among them. He had on a New York State issued officers frock coat, with a black felt Hardee Hat sitting on top of his head. The hat had an ostrich feather fastened to its side for extra flair. His big black beard was nicely trimmed all the way down to the center of his chest and he wore a red sash wrapped around his waist.

He wasn't a commissioned officer yet, so he wore no bars on his shoulders that denoted rank. The state recruiting officials had given him the fancy garb anyway, in an attempt to entice more recruits.

Sitting in a camp chair next to Marvin was old Mr. Fortner, one of the town's last surviving veterans of the War of 1812. He was also in his military uniform, but his was considerably aged and ill-fitting. He was in his glory nonetheless, and had been recounting the many stories of his service, fighting "injuns" and "lily-livered lobster backs" all day thus far. Also standing out front was David Ferris, Socrates Schutt, who Gabriel knew well, and another man who he recognized, but couldn't put a name to. There were several others about, and a handful of children as well.

When David Ferris noticed Gabriel approaching, he called out a little jeer.

"Afternoon's half over Gabriel. Little late for your first day on the job aren't you? Socrates, Bielby and I have been here since Mr., or a…, Captain Marvin opened up shop."

David laughed at his own joke and looked to Marvin for approval, but he got a slight reprimand instead.

"That's Mr. Marvin, Ferris, I haven't been commissioned yet," he said.

Gabriel was annoyed. He was hot and tired from the walk he had just made in the scorching sun, and the last thing he wanted was to be berated by a blowhard like David Ferris. Socrates noticed his displeasure.

"Don't fret none, young Gabe, I'm sure Mr. Marvin would be happy to sign you up at any time of day or night. Isn't that so, Mr. Marvin?"

"Quite right, Socrates, quite right. We have a quota to fill, and it must be completed as soon as possible."

Looking at Gabriel, Harrison Marvin spoke to him.

"So, Mr. Ballard, is that why you have come to my shop then? Are you here to sign up to fight for your country?" he asked.

"I suppose so, Sir," Gabriel responded bashfully. He felt uncomfortable with so many eyes focused his way.

"Well, then come on inside and let's see what we can do," Marvin said, as he held out his hand inviting Gabriel toward the door.

Gabriel had been to Marvin's store many times before, and it all looked about the same as usual, except for Mr. Murdock was working at a makeshift table at the back of the store behind the displays. He noticed Gabriel eyeing him.

"They took over my workshop," he said as he nodded to the door beside him. "Needs it, they tells me, so that the doc can look at your privates," he added with a raspy chuckle.

Gabriel gave Marvin a concerned look, and Marvin's wife Kate, who was standing behind the sales counter, blushed but pretended not to hear.

"A complete physical examination is required before enlistment, Gabriel. Nothing special. It's all part of procedure, I assure you."

"Well if I've got to, I suppose it's fine."

"Excellent. Just go straight through that door then and close it behind you. The doctor is in there waiting,"

Gabriel walked through the door and slowly shut it. The room looked just about as it always had, except Mr. Murdock's big work bench was clear of its tools and replaced by a snoring individual. He was lying flat on his back with a cap over his face and a thick roll of shoe leather balled up under his head as a makeshift pillow. Gabriel smiled at the sight before walking over to the doctor and poking him on the shoulder.

"Yikes!" the man shouted, before rolling off the table and to the floor below like a falling sack of potatoes. "My God, boy! What were you thinking?" he said to Gabriel, as he got to his feet. He was a middle-aged man, and unhealthily large, with several days' worth of stubble on his face. A strong stench of liquor permeated the air around him. Harrison Marvin poked his head into the doorway of the room.

"Everything all right in here, gentlemen?" he asked.

Without looking at Marvin the doctor responded. "Yes, yes, Mr. Mervin. Everything is quite all right. Thank you very much."

Satisfied, Marvin closed the door and returned to the front of the store, while the doctor picked up a pile of papers from under the workbench and set them in front of himself.

"Age?" he said.

"What?"

"Age, son. What's your God damn age? How old are you?" said the doctor in an annoyed tone.

Gabriel was taken aback by his rudeness. "Oh. I'm 19, Sir", he replied.

"Okay, and what's your name?"

"Gabriel Ballard, Sir, or Gabriel Rummer Ballard that is, after my mother's father," Gabriel said cheerfully.

"I didn't ask for your life story," replied the doctor angrily. "Spell it out for me."

Gabriel obeyed, and once he was done, the man looked up at him and started talking to himself out loud as he wrote.

"Five feet nine and a half inches tall, brown hair, a fair skin complexion and blue eyes," he grumbled.

Gabriel knew he was taller though and felt slighted by the doctors guess. Size was important to a young man and although his barely post-pubescent body hadn't quite filled out yet, he was still taller than most, and so felt the urge to speak up and set the record straight.

"Actually, Sir, I'm five eleven," Gabriel corrected him.

Predictably, the doctor wasn't pleased.

"I didn't fuckin ask you, did I? Who's the God damned doctor here anyway?!," he shouted, and slapped his hand on the table.

"Ugh ... you are Sir," Gabriel answered.

"That's bloody right, 'me, Sir'. I'm the bloody fucking doctor, and I don't appreciate you telling me how to do my job. If I say you're five feet nine and a half fucking inches tall, then that's what you are. Got it?"

Gabriel nodded his head in the affirmative.

The doctor went to work writing again, and once he had finished the last couple notes on Gabriel's paperwork, he handed it to him.

"Now, here. Take this out front to Mervin, while I go back to sleep," he directed before going about balling up his shoe leather pillow again.

Gabriel was surprised how fast it had taken and worried that the doctor, if he truly was such a thing, had forgotten something.

"What about my physical Sir? Don't I have to get undressed or be examined in any way?" he nervously inquired.

The doctor threw up his arms in disgust and the piece of leather went flying across the room.

"Take off your clothes? What kind of a question is that? I don't need to see your little pecker, nor do I want to. That was your physical, damn it. Now get the hell out before I rip those papers to shreds and tell Mervin you're unfit. I need some sleep, for crying out loud," he shouted.

Faced with being declared unfit, Gabriel declined to protest any longer. He hadn't even learned the doctor's name but found him to be perhaps the angriest man he'd ever met. Oddly, though, for Gabriel, his anger was to the point of being almost comical, and he left the room more amused than offended.

As Gabriel approached the sales counter, he handed his paperwork to Marvin wondering if he had heard all the doctors shouting. If he had he didn't show it.

"All set then. That was quick. I take it you're fit enough to be a soldier?" Marvin asked. "That's what the good doctor tells me," Gabriel replied.

"Excellent, now we just need to add the date, 15th day of August 1862, and then your signature right here, and we should be all set. Sound good to you?" Marvin asked.

"Sounds good to me," Gabriel replied.

When they were done putting pen to paper, Marvin led Gabriel out the front of the store where everyone was still waiting from when he went in.

"Is he one of us now?" Socrates asked when they emerged.

"He is," Marvin replied and then everyone except for David Ferris let out a cheer.

"Congratulations, young man," old Mr. Fortner said to Gabriel as he joined them. Gabriel shook hands with everyone in attendance and then the four enlistees directed their attention to hear Harrison Marvin give them their instructions.

"You men listen up now," he said from the steps of his store. "You're free to go home. Spend your time wisely though, don't get into any trouble, button up any unfinished business, and above all enjoy the company of your loved ones. William Moffat, myself and a few others will be around town in the coming days on recruiting duty. Chances are we won't be leaving until we can get enough men to form a company, so if you know anyone who shows any interest, send them my way. The sooner the quota is filled, the sooner we can all head out. I don't know yet where we're going, or to what regiment we will belong. That information will come in time, and when I am informed, I will notify you. Stay at your homes or there about until you have heard from me or one of my representatives. If you live nearby the village and can check in every day or so, that would be helpful, then I won't have to send a message runner to your home. I would like to thank you men on behalf of the Town of Dryden and your Country. It takes great courage to do what you did here today, and I, for one, will be proud and honored to soon serve alongside you."

When Marvin finished, the crowd dispersed, and Gabriel began his journey home. He had done it, he had finally enlisted, and his mind was awash in a plethora of thoughts and emotions.

* * * * *

It was late when Gabriel finally made it home, but the summer sun was still hanging above the horizon. His family had already eaten their evening meal and his baby brother George and sister Mary had gone to bed. When he walked in the house, his mother and sister Sarah were washing dishes, while his father and brother Sam were playing checkers at the table. Before his mother could scold him for his tardiness, he made a pre-planned announcement to the family.

"Mother, Father, I have something to tell you… I enlisted today in the village."

There was a hush in the room, and everyone stopped what they were doing and looked to Gabriel in a shocked disbelief. Gabriel's mother opened her mouth and looked as if she might say something, but no words came out. Instead of talking, her eyelids began to flutter, and she fell to the floor with a thud.

Sarah shrieked, "you've killed her, Gabriel!" and fell over her body and began to sob.

Gabriel, Sam and his father walked over to Lydia and lifted her up off the ground.

"She's only fainted, Sarah. Go get her a cup of water," John Ballard said to his daughter.

They set Lydia in a chair at the kitchen table and John asked her, "are you all right, my dear?" but Lydia said nothing, even though her eyes were now open, and she looked to have regained consciousness. She seemed dazed. Then, feebly, she let out a whimper, followed by a sob and then a loud moaning cry. Sarah brought her mother the water, but she wouldn't touch it, so she pulled up a chair next to her and gave her a hug.

"Mother, don't cry," she said.

Gabriel, who had been standing silent beside the table, tried talking to her too. "I'm sorry Mother. I never meant to hurt you," he said, but Lydia was inconsolable. Large teardrops were already flooding her face and then she began to wail.

"Why, why, why, oh why, Gabriel. Why would you do this to me? How could you do this to me? How could you go against my wishes?"

"You know why, Mother, because he's selfish and only thinks of himself," Sarah said.

Gabriel heard, but ignored his sister.

"Because this is something I have to do," he said.

Gabriel felt bad for his mother, but was slightly annoyed with the scene she was putting on. He felt that she wasn't respecting the fact that he was grown up now.

"Mother, this country needs me. It needs all of us now more than ever. Don't you understand the South is winning? Our army out west barely survived at Shiloh. McClellan got whipped outside Richmond, and Stonewall Jackson made a mockery of our troops in the Shenandoah. I can't just sit around here like a coward with the women and old men and let it happen without lifting a finger. Even if we lose this war, at least I'll be able to say I tried, that I'd done my part. I'm going, Mother, and that's final."

Nothing had gone as Gabriel had hoped. He'd never seen his mother so emotional. After he said his piece, he walked to the front door and went out on the porch. His father and brother followed, while Sarah sat with Lydia and held her as she cried.

"I'll never leave you, Mother," she told her, "and I would never go against your wishes."

Outside, Gabriel and his father sat in the chairs on the porch, which were set to either side of the front door. Sam sat on the steps and his father John pulled a pipe out of his pocket and handed it to Gabriel to pack with tobacco. He still hadn't mastered doing so with only one good hand. It embarrassed Lydia to no end that John had taught their two sons to do it for him instead.

After Gabriel had passed his father's pipe back to him full and ready to fire, John sent Sam inside to get him a light.

"You know you shouldn't be so hard on your mother, Gabriel," John said when Sam had gone.

"I know that, Father, but she needs to understand that I'm not a child anymore, and I need to make my own decisions."

"I know, Son, I know. She's just worried, that's all. You also might want to make sure your mother's sitting down the next time you have something big like that to tell us," John said with a smile.

Gabriel chuckled, and agreed he would, before asking his father his own opinion on the matter.

"Well, to be honest, I'm worried too, of course, but like you said, I know I can't tell you what to do forever. Don't go telling your mother I said that, though."

"I won't," Gabriel told him.

"You know, when the Mexican War broke out, I wanted to go in the worst way, but I never did. Granted, my situation was a little different than yours, I had a wife and children, but still, every so often, I feel a little pang of guilt that I never went. I don't want you to have to live with that guilt too. Especially considering that this war is so much bigger and important than the last one. I think you've made the right and noble decision, and I'm proud of you for that."

Gabriel felt awkward. It was uncommon for his father to be so serious and open with him on such matters.

"What about now, Father? Why not come with me? Mr. Marvin said he's looking for more men, and we need a wagon driver. Surely your disability would allow for that."

Before he could answer, Sam came back with a glowing sliver of kindling. Clenching its stem between his teeth John lit his pipe and then snickered.

"Are you kidding me? You think they want a teamster with only one good arm? Those men don't just drive, they pack up and unload the wagons, fix them when they need mending, and care for their mules. Sure, I could do the job, but not at the speed they're looking for. Besides your mother would shoot me before she let me go, and that's no joke. In fact, I'd watch your back if I were you. She's liable to do it to you. Won't kill ya, but she'll go for an arm or leg, so they'd have to leave you behind."

"Thanks for the advice," Gabriel said, wide-eyed, "I think," and shook his head.

"So did I hear you mention Marvin, that who signed you up?" John inquired.

"Yes, right in his store, too. Four of us did today: me, Socrates Schutt, David Ferris and some fella named Bielby Starr. He sent us home for now, until he gets enough men to form a company."

"Huh, Socrates signed up, did he? He's a good man. I heard Enos Cook was thinking about it, too," his father said.

Gabriel was happy to hear that, and hoped it was true. Enos was a friend of his father's that lived up the road and Gabriel liked the man a lot. He was kind, and generous and a hard worker. His son James was one of the first boys from town to enlist back in '61. Enos was also a friend of Rill's brother-in-law George Sweetland, and when Rill first moved upstate to live with her sister, George and Hannah were living with Enos and his wife Julia.

"That Marvin give you a free pair of boots for signing up, did he?" Gabriel's father asked, but Gabriel shook his head.

"What about a discount, tell me he gave you half off at least?"

Gabriel shook his head again though.

"No," he said, "why would he?"

"Why along with a good trigger finger, a soldiers' feet are his most important appendage. Even I know that. You think he'd want his men to be well equipped as far as footwear goes, and that's something he can remedy."

"Well Father he's not exactly in charge of us yet and I think the government will give us shoes anyway," Gabriel said.

"The government," John scoffed, "don't count on what the government gives you, Son. It's made by whoever gives them the cheapest quote, and that means most of it is about as good as a stud with no balls."

"Well he's got mouths to feed at home, too, Father. He can't be giving away all his stock. Anyway, we haven't left yet. Maybe he'll surprise us."

"Ha! Slim chance of that. He's always been cheap," John replied, clearly not one of Marvin's biggest fans.

The three of them sat in silence for a while longer enjoying the cool evening air, while occasionally Lydia's sobs could still be heard from within the house.

"Father, don't you think you should go in and check on her?" Gabriel asked. He was feeling a bit guilty and also slightly concerned.

John shook his head though.

"A woman's comfort is what your mother needs right now. If I go in there all her sadness will turn to anger, and somehow, she'll get it in her head that this is all my fault. No, I think I'll just stay out here with you. Your sister is doing a fine job as far as I can tell anyway."

Sam, who had yet to say much, spoke up. "Gabriel, you think they're looking for a drummer boy in your outfit?" he asked.

"I don't know, Sam. I'll have to ask," he answered, but John quickly squashed the idea.

"You most certainly will not," he said with another chuckle. "You boys hear your mother in there? She can't handle one, much less two, of her boys goin' off to war. Besides, Sam, I'm gonna need your help more than ever, with your brother gone."

"Father's right, Sam," Gabriel agreed. "We've all got a duty to do, and yours is here to help take care of the farm. Father can't do it all one-handed." Sam looked disappointed, but he realized that there was a job to do at home and was happy to help the family in any way he could.

They sat out front until it turned dark and the peepers were singing away. Sarah had finally coaxed her mother to bed, where she cried herself to sleep.

"Well, boys, it's time I were off," John declared as he stood up and stretched.

"Father, I don't think you should be drinking tonight, not after what happened this morning," Gabriel said.

"Boy, I'm your pop, you needn't be worrying about me. Besides, I ain't goin drinkin'. I've gotta go down and tell Grandma and Grandpa Ballard and your uncles that my Gabriel's going to be a soldier," John said. "Don't be waitin' up for me, neither," he added.

"We won't. I've still got some chores to do, though, so I'm going to get a couple lanterns lit and get them done," Gabriel said.

"You mean the fence, and cleaning out the chicken coop? I already did it," Sam informed him.

"You did?" Gabriel asked surprised.

"Yes, I did it this morning after you left," Sam answered.

"You see, Gabriel, he's already filling your shoes," John complimented his younger son.

"Well, I'll just head out to the barn and saddle up Prince. I'll be back, though. Night, boys."

"Goodnight, Father," they said simultaneously, and went inside.

It was dark in the house, so Gabriel lit a candle. They weren't tired yet, so they decided to play some checkers, and ended up doing so until the candle had burned down to a nub. Even their father had come home and gone to bed by the time they finished.

"I think our times almost up, Gabriel."

"I'm getting sleepy anyway. Besides, Mother would be angry if we lit another," Gabriel said, and yawned. "I've got to ask you a favor first, though, Sam."

"Anything. What do you want?"

"I want you to watch over Rill for me while I'm gone."

"Sure, I can do that." Sam agreed.

"Thanks, Sam. Just make sure no one gives her any trouble, you know, and give her some company from time to time. You're young enough still, so her sister won't run you off like she does me. Rill doesn't have many friends up here to speak of, not other young people that is and I don't want her to be lonesome," Gabriel explained.

"I understand," Sam said as he rolled the checker cloth up.

"May need you to deliver some letters to her too, can you do that?"

"Yes, I suppose I can, but why not just address them to her?" Sam asked.

"Because if her sister saw a letter in the mail from me, she'd get rid of it before Rill even saw it. She'd read it, too, and I don't need her nosing into our business any more than she already does."

It was a big weight off his shoulders knowing that Sam had agreed to look after Rill. His greatest fear of going away, wasn't getting shot or killed or taken prisoner, it was losing her. Rill was a good girl and would stay faithful. Gabriel knew that, but there was no telling how much longer the war would last. It could go on for years, and years was a long time to ask or expect anyone to wait.

As he lay in bed, Gabriel's thoughts shifted to the wonderful time he had spent with her that day, and he wondered if it was going to be the last time he ever saw her. Hannah had caught them together again. It wasn't the first time she'd run him off, but he suspected that she wasn't going to let Rill out of her sight until he had gone.

CHAPTER FOUR

Deep down, Gabriel had known his mother was going to be upset, but he never could have imagined her having the complete mental breakdown that she did, and it was a shock to him. Other folks in his family took the news of his enlistment differently, though. His uncles, for example, saw it as an inspiration, for after they found out, three of them, Bill Neeley, and Richard and Joseph Ballard, marched down to Harford and enlisted as well. At first, Gabriel was pleased, because he thought they'd end up serving in the same regiment, but it wasn't so. The Tompkins County enlistees were being sent down to Binghamton, while the Cortland County ones were getting shipped up to Hamilton. Gabriel had enlisted in Tompkins, while his uncles had done so in Cortland.

About a week after Gabriel signed up, his father decided to throw a going away party for his brothers and his son. He approached Gabriel one morning while he was washing up at the pump out back.

"Gabriel," his father said, "we're gonna have a little get together tonight for you and your uncles. I'd like you to go over to Grandma Rummer's after you've washed up and invite her and Aunt Polly. You might as well ask your uncles and Aunt Phoebe to come with their folks, too."

Polly Purvis, Phoebe Joyner, Eli and Levi Rummer were Gabriel's mother's siblings, and they all lived just down the road, as did their mother Ann. Their father, Gabriel Rummer, had just recently passed away in January. Gabriel wasn't too keen on the idea of having a party, though.

"What? A party? No Father, I don't want that, I don't want to be the center of attention in front of all them people," Gabriel said.

John insisted, though.

"Gabriel, this is a big event, and it's not just for you. It's for your uncles, too. To be honest, this may be the last chance everyone gets to see each other, and I think you owe it to your family to let them come and say goodbye to you proper."

Gabriel had to admit his father had a point, if something were to happen to him or his uncles this could very well be their last chance to all be together as a family.

"Okay, Father," he relented, "lets have your party then."

"Good, I'm glad. It'll be fun, trust me," John replied. "I'm headed over to Harford in a couple minutes to invite the rest of the Ballard clan. Tell everyone that they needn't worry about bringing anything, this isn't a dish to pass, I've got it all taken care of. Oh, and Gabriel, might better invite Dave Nash and his family. I'm sure his wife and kids could use a good meal, and if Andrew Farrell's there tell him he's welcome too."

At the mention of Dave and Andrew, Gabriel rolled his eyes. Like him, they had both signed up with Harrison Marvin, and would be going along with him when the time came. Dave Nash lived just south of his Aunt Phoebe's, and his 22-year-old Irish born drinking buddy, Andrew Farrell, could usually be found there as well. Dave was 38 and had a wife and kids of his own. He supported them as a laborer, and often worked for Gabriel's parents during planting season. Dave was one hell of a hard worker, but he drank whiskey like a fish drinks water, and there wasn't a day went by that he wasn't drunk by noon. His family was one of the poorest in town, but not from lack of work on Dave's part. They were poor because he spent nearly every cent he earned on booze. Once, Dave's wife Electa went around and told everyone that Dave was not to be paid in cash anymore, but in goods. That way he couldn't spend his pay on whiskey. Dave wasn't fooled, though. When people started giving him chickens, or meat or bushels of fruits and vegetables for his work, he took it to the village and traded it for liquor with whomever was willing.

Gabriel wasn't gone too long on his errand because he didn't have to go very far. When he reached his Grandma and Aunt Polly's place, he found Dave, Andrew and Aunt Polly out front. The men were filling washouts in the road with gravel while Polly supervised them from a chair in the lawn. Gabriel passed on his invitations, and then Aunt

Polly sent Andrew to Phoebe, Eli and Levi's places to invite them as well. Gabriel was back home less than half an hour after he left. He spent the rest of the day with Sam, helping to clean out the house and yard, while his sisters were busy cooking. His mother just sat around the house, though, with an expressionless look on her face.

Lydia sobbed for three whole days in bed after Gabriel had signed up. Her eyes were so red and swollen from the tears that she could hardly open them. John got so worried about her state of mind that he even sent to town for the doctor. "Women get this way from time to time, John," Doc Montgomery had said after examining her. "Best to just let her ride it out." She was done crying now, but had hardly said a word to anyone, especially not to Gabriel. It was almost like she had forgotten how to talk. When his father got back from Harford, Gabriel confronted him about her.

"Father, when's Mother going to start acting normal? Everyone's going to think she's crazy when they get here for the party."

"She'll be alright," John said.

"Well, why's she doing this? Does she think she's actually going to guilt me into changing my mind?" Gabriel asked in frustration.

"No, I don't think so," John said. "She knows your mind's made up, and that's probably what scares her the most. You know it's not like you're moving down the road. You're going off to war. She's scared, Gabriel. I'm scared. You've got to remember, too, you're our first bird to leave the nest, and the first bird is always the hardest to let go."

That evening, the house looked immaculate. The sky was clear, and the temperature outside had cooled some to everyone's relief. Gabriel and his brother had carried the kitchen table to the side yard, and his two sisters completely covered its top with pots, pans and dishes full of food for the party. The first guests to arrive were Aunt Polly and Grandma Rummer, seated in his grandpa's old carriage. It was still strange for Gabriel to see it without the old man at its helm. Aunt Polly did just as well, though. Uncle Levi and Eli were next, with their families, then Aunt Phoebe and Uncle Nelson, followed by Grandma and Grandpa Ballard shortly after, with their daughter Margaret Neeley and son-in-law Bill. His grandparents sat on the front porch, the old ladies drinking tea and politely chatting, while Grandpa Ballard smoked his pipe and playfully taunted anyone that walked by.

Dave Nash and his family came, too, with Andrew Farrell tagging along. Of course, Dave was three sheets to the wind already, and Andrew wasn't that far behind him. Both men came toting big earthenware jugs of cider to share with whomever wanted a taste. Gabriel's Ballard uncles, William, Joseph and Richard were quick to oblige them when they showed up. They all came with their families in two buckboard wagons from Harford. They brought their sister Jane's husband along with them too, Moses Deyo and his two boys James and Simon. His Aunt Jane had passed in '55, but they still invited Moses to all the Ballard family get togethers.

"A most honorable and courageous decision young man," Moses said to Gabriel, after he made his way into the yard.

"Too bad, Gabriel, it looks like we won't all be going together like we'd hoped," his uncle Richard said to him.

"So I hear," Gabriel said.

"What do you think about William?" Richard asked.

"Uncle William?"

"Yes," Richard said. "Haven't you heard? He claims he's going down to Harford to sign up, too. Can you believe it? All three of us brothers and Bill serving together, we'll have a hell of a time. They made Billy a corporal too so we figure he can lead us."

Richard's news felt like a kick in the gut to Gabriel.

"Guess I should have tried to coordinate with you guys instead of going off on my own," he said, feeling left out.

"Oh nonsense," Richard responded, "it just wasn't meant to be, that's all."

Richard was his uncle, but more like an older brother or cousin, as he was only born two years before him. He patted Gabriel on the back and headed toward his brothers, who were both taking swigs of Dave and Andrew's cider. Even Grandpa Ballard was over, having his full share. "Why don't you laddies let an old Irishman show you how it's done?" Grandpa Ballard said in his Irish brogue, as he elbowed his way into the drinking circle.

Everyone was enjoying themselves at the party, socializing and eating. Some were talking solemnly of the Union's most recent defeat at 2nd Bull Run a few days before, and what they though should be done. "Just wait till they let us Ballard boys at 'em," Gabriel's uncle William boasted. The children at the party were running amok. The girls were playing hide and seek, and the boys were fighting a hard-fought battle with invisible Rebels in the barnyard. Gabriel's mother had yet to show herself, though, and she wouldn't. "I won't celebrate my son's death warrant", she had said to her husband. It was the most she had spoken all week and she remained in her room the entire night.

Some of their neighbors from up the road showed up, too - the Carpenters, the Spaces, the Bucklins and the Donnelys. The last family to arrive were the Cooks. Enos Cook had brought his wife Julia and his daughter Nancy.

"I didn't know you were coming," Gabriel said to Enos when he arrived.

"Your brother came over this morning and invited us."

"Well, good. I'm glad, Enos."

"I still haven't heard anything about orders, have you?" Enos asked.

Just as John Ballard had heard, Enos Cook was planning on enlisting and did. He was leaving with Gabriel.

"Not a word. I sure am ready, though."

"I am too, but I don't know about them two," Enos said as he pointed to Dave Nash and Andrew Farrell. The two men could barely stand now, but they were leading the rest of the party in a drunken rendition of "Rally Round the Flag".

After Enos went to mingle with the other guests, Gabriel hovered around at the front gate by himself, and kept watch for any other surprise attendees. Sam noticed him, and knew what was up, so he walked over to talk to his big brother.

"This is it, Gabriel. She's not coming," he said, as he came up alongside him.

"She? Who are you talking about?" Gabriel asked, playing ignorant.

"You know, Gabriel. Martha Marsh. I'm sorry, I tried. I went over to her place this morning after I stopped and invited Enos and the others. George met me at the door, though, and said that they appreciated the invitation but couldn't. Said that they all had colds."

"Colds? In the middle of this heat wave?" Gabriel interjected. He couldn't help but feel frustrated because he knew what was really going on. "The only one with a cold in that house is that cold hearted bitch Hannah Sweetland," Gabriel said. "God, I hate her."

It took Sam all he had, not to laugh over his older brother's sudden outburst.

"I figured that, too," he managed to say.

"Hannah's had Rill locked up in that house tighter than the noose around John Brown's neck, since last week," Gabriel added. "But I'll tell you what, Sam," he went on, "I've been thinking it over, and I'm gonna have the last laugh. When I get home, I'm gonna marry her sister whether she likes it or not. Then I'll buy the farm next door to her and George, and we'll screw so loud at night, Hannah will have to tie two pillows around her head to drown out the noise."

With that mental image of Hannah in their heads Gabriel and Sam fell to the ground laughing. They had tears in their eyes when their father John walked over.

"Come on you two goobers, it's time for dessert. Your sister Sarah's made peach pie for everyone," he delightedly told them.

"Of course she would," Gabriel muttered to himself as his father and brother went to get in line. "She knows I hate peaches."

* * * * *

It wasn't too long after the party before word was sent that they would be leaving. Daniel Hollenshead, who was to be a corporal in Gabriel's company, came by the Ballard farm one day while Gabriel was out front splitting wood for the kitchen stove. He appeared disheveled and out of breath, and spoke quickly, without any greeting.

"Harrison Marvin says we are to meet in the Village of Dryden at 8 o'clock tomorrow morning, Gabriel. Some of the men in town are to take us up to Cortland by wagon. From there, we go by train to Binghamton. He also wants it known for all men to bring enough food to feed themselves for the day, and that they are to bring nothing more than the clothes on their backs, and perhaps a little spending money. He says that other than that, everything we need will be provided for."

"That it?" Gabriel said.

"It is," Daniel responded. He stopped for a moment to catch his breath. "I apologize, Gabriel, for my poor manners and appearance, but I've got another dozen men to hunt down before the day is done, and I'd like to get it over with as soon as possible. I'd rather be spending my last few hours at home with my family, if you can understand."

"Of course I understand," Gabriel said. "You know, Daniel, I wouldn't mind going around to some of the boys if you'd like."

"Would you, Gabriel, truly?" Daniel asked, surprised by Gabriel's offer.

"Sure, I've got nothing going on," Gabriel said.

"Boy that would be a great help, Gabriel, it truly would. Thank you so much."

Daniel pulled out a folded list of names from his front pocket and looked it over.

"How about Dave Nash and Andrew Farrell?" he said. "Could you hunt them two down for me, and pass everything to them that I just told you? That way, you won't have to go far."

"Yep, they're both just down the road, Daniel. You can count on me."

Daniel turned his horse around.

"I know I can, Gabriel, I certainly do. I am indebted to you. We'll see you in the morning, then," Daniel said. Then, he slapped his reins on the horse's rump, hollered "get," and took off down the road in a cloud of dust.

Gabriel liked Daniel, and he was happy to help. Daniel was one of the carpenters in town, and had helped his father build their house when Gabriel's parents were first married. He was much older than most of the other men who signed up, but Gabriel was grateful to have him coming along. The older men, he thought, guys like Socrates

Schutt, Enos Cook and Daniel Hollenshead, would be good examples for the younger men in the company. If there were any exceptions to that rule though, Dave Nash was it.

As Gabriel was gathering up the wood he had split, his father John walked out the front door of their house.

"Who was that, Gabriel?" John asked.

"That was Daniel Hollenshead, Father. Says we're to meet in the village tomorrow morning. We're leaving, he says. Mr. Marvin sent him."

"Oh," John said. He looked a little disappointed but then tried hiding it with a weak smile. "Well that's good, Son, good. You've been pacing around the farm far too long now, waiting for that word. It must be a relief finally knowing?" John said.

"Bittersweet, Father. It's bittersweet, but I've got to be going. I offered to pass on our instructions to Dave and Andrew."

"That was nice of you," said John. "If you're headed that way, though, how about asking Grandma and Aunt Polly over for dinner?"

"No, Father, please. Not again. I thought that's what our big party was for the other night. Honestly, all I want is a quiet night at home. Nothing special." Gabriel could tell his father was getting a little choked up. He nodded his head in agreement.

"Okay, Son, if that's what you'd like, that's what we'll do," he said. "It's your night."

Gabriel thought he may have detected a hint of moisture in his father's eyes but pretended not to notice. He had been acting strangely toward Gabriel ever since he'd enlisted. It made him uncomfortable, so, trying to avoid looking him in the face, he said, "Thanks Father," and left to notify his two friends.

That night, other than Enos Cook stopping by, Gabriel got his wish for a quiet time. Enos came to ask Gabriel if he wanted a ride into town in the morning. At first, he was hesitant to accept, not wanting him to go out of his way, but Enos said he'd be passing by to pick up Dave and Andrew anyway, so he accepted.

* * * * *

Gabriel had a fitful night of sleep. He was anxious for what the morning would bring and depressed at the thought of leaving without saying goodbye to Rill. He'd walked by her house just about every day since he last saw her, just for a chance at catching a glimpse of her. She was never in sight, though, and Gabriel started to wonder if she was avoiding him.

"Is she mad at me?" he thought to himself. "Maybe she just doesn't like me anymore. There's no way Hannah's got her locked up in there that tight," he worried.

On top of that, his mother had started crying again late in the night, which didn't aid much in his falling asleep. He could hear his father trying to comfort her, but it was no use. Eventually she cried herself to sleep again. She still hadn't said a word to Gabriel since the day he enlisted.

When he rolled out of bed around five the next morning, Gabriel went outside with only his drawers on and went to the outhouse to relieve himself. His stomach had been churning in anticipation of what the day had to offer. He washed himself up at the pump in the yard and came inside. His sister Sarah and father were up getting a fire going in the stove to warm up some food for breakfast. Gabriel went upstairs and got dressed in his Sunday best. He had on a neatly pressed white shirt with black pants, and a black vest and coat.

"You look good," his father said when he came downstairs.

The rest of the family was up by then, and they all enjoyed a quiet meal together at the kitchen table, excluding Lydia who was still up in her room. Soon Enos and his wife Julia pulled up to the house in their wagon and it was time to go. To feed him for the day, Gabriel's sister Mary packed him up a hunk of smoked ham, a wedge of cheese and some apples, in a cotton sack.

"Here you go, Gabriel," she said as she handed him the bag.

Everyone was out front of the house and they all had tears in their eyes, including Gabriel. Even Sarah was standing in the front doorway trying to hide the fact that she was crying, too. Gabriel gave everyone a final hug goodbye. When his father approached him for his farewell he wept openly as he hugged his son. Gabriel had never seen his father cry, even when he lost his fingers in the threshing machine, he hadn't shed a tear.

"I guess Mother's not coming down, is she, Father?" Gabriel said. John turned around to look up at his bedroom window to see if his wife was watching.

"No, Gabriel, I guess she's not."

"No bother. I suppose I'll see her on the day I come home a hero," Gabriel said in a bad attempt at cockiness. He was trying to compensate for his embarrassment at being seen blubbering in front of everyone.

Just as he climbed up into the wagon, Lydia at last showed herself by running out the front door and past his sister Sarah.

"Wait, Wait, Wait, Gabriel!" she shrieked, "don't go, please don't go before I can say goodbye!"

Gabriel hopped down off the wagon and met his mother at the edge of the road where she fell into his arms. He hugged her. She was crying hysterically at first but then calmed down enough to say a few parting words.

"You be a good boy, Gabriel", she told him, "say your prayers and trust in the Lord, and he'll bring you home to me safe and sound."

"I will, Mother," Gabriel said back to her with tears rolling down his face. They hugged some more, then his father came and helped ease Lydia back, almost pulling her from their son. When he was finally free, Gabriel climbed back into the wagon.

As he did so, Lydia Ballard looked up at Enos.

"You watch over my boy, Enos Cook. If anything happens to him, I'm holding you responsible," she said.

"Yes ma'am, I will do my best," he told her with a tip of his hat.

"You'd better," Lydia added.

Enos nodded he would, then flicked the reins and started to pull away.

"Goodbye, everyone," Gabriel said as he waved from his seat in the bed of the wagon. Everyone said "goodbye," and waved back, except for his father.

"It's not goodbye Son, it's see you later," John called out, as they rolled out of view.

* * * * *

When they pulled up to the Nash place everyone was still asleep. Gabriel and Enos went in, while Julia waited in the wagon outside. Dave's house was a ramshackle, old, one-room log home. It had a plank floor inside, but the family slept in a loft that was suspended over half the room. They had no stove but cooked all their food and got their heat from a big old open-hearth fireplace. When the two men walked inside, they found Andrew and Dave sprawled out on the floor in front of the fireplace, where they had evidently passed out after a little going away party of their own. Gabriel could see that Andrew's pants were soaking wet in the front.

Enos walked over and nudged them with his foot.

"Hey, you two, wake up. We've got to go," he told them. Andrew groaned and turned over, but Dave sat up from the floor and let out a big yawn and stretched his arms above his head. He cleared his throat and spit the results into the coals of the fireplace.

"Time is it?" he asked in a raspy voice, while wiping the sleep from his eyes.

"It's ten of seven," Enos said, "and we've got to hurry if we're going to be in Dryden on time."

"Not even seven yet. We've got plenty of time," Dave said as he stood up. He went to the door and stepped outside. Andrew started to rouse himself when the light from the open door shined in on his face. Dave noticed Julia sitting in the wagon out front, so he greeted her with a quick, "mornin' ma'am," then turned away and proceeded to empty his bladder at the corner of the house. Enos stood in the doorway and shook his head.

"Thanks for turning away from my wife when you do that," he said to Dave.

"Oh, not a problem," Dave replied, ignorant to Enos's sarcasm. After buttoning up, he made his way back inside where Andrew and Gabriel were waiting. Andrew was having great difficulty staying on his feet.

"You've pissed your pants, Andrew," Dave noticed out loud, greatly amused.

"So I have," Andrew said looking down at his trousers. "No bother, they'll dry on the ride to town."

Dave walked over to a hewn log that was suspended over the fireplace and served as a crude mantel. Gabriel saw him snatch a metallic object down from it.

"Don't you want some breakfast before we take off?" Gabriel asked Dave.

"Breakfast? Hell, no, I don't want breakfast. Most unhealthy meal of the day, if you ask me. How can you expect a man get to work early with a belly full of food? Nope, I just take a little nip of this."

Dave held up what Gabriel now saw was a flask that he had pulled down from the mantel.

"Yep, a little nip is all I need to start my day."

Gabriel stood with a look of disbelief on his face as Dave opened the flask, took a swig and then tucked it away into a pocket he had stitched on the inside of his coat.

"Only thing my pappy ever gave me," he said. "What about you, Andrew?" Dave called out, "You want breakfast?" Andrew didn't respond in words, his face turned a slight shade of green at the thought of food, and he ran outside and emptied his stomach in the front yard.

"Suit yourself," Dave said as he, Gabriel and Enos shuffled outside, and shut the door behind them.

"How about lunch?" Gabriel asked. "Marvin said we were to bring food to last us the day."

"To hell with Marvin, we'll find somethin' along the way. Come on now, Andrew, hop in," Dave said as he climbed into the back of the wagon.

"Don't you want to say goodbye to your wife?" Enos asked Dave.

"What for? She knows I'm leavin' today," Dave answered him gruffly.

Enos chuckled as he took his seat next to Julia. Andrew was still in rough shape, so Gabriel helped him up and then climbed in behind him.

* * * * *

When they rolled into the village, the group of new recruits were just lining up into a sloppy formation at the four corners, where Main, South, and North Streets all met. Harrison Marvin was standing in front of them, calling attendance from a list of names. Enos parked by a home on South Street and, except for Julia, they all got down and headed over to fall in. They were quite the contrasting little group. Enos and Gabriel looking groomed and dapper in their Sunday best, while Andrew and Dave, still half drunk, stumbled to the formation in the same unwashed chore garb they'd had on for a week. The group of recruits were dressed about to the same ratio.

On the sidewalks surrounding the intersection, there was a large group of loved ones and patriotic citizens standing by. They had come to say their goodbyes and see the men off. There was one little boy there dressed in a miniature blue Yankee uniform. He was marching up and down the street, leading a group of other boys armed with stick rifles and swords.

Behind the formation of recruits were eight wagons complete with drivers and teams, ready to haul them away. Surprisingly, all 79 enlistees were on time and present for duty, which delighted Harrison Marvin. In his head, he congratulated himself on their perfect attendance, before turning to address them. When he started to speak, everyone hushed to hear what he had to say. He relished the attention.

"You men," Marvin called out, "have gathered here today to embark on a noble crusade to save our great and glorious nation. Every one of you is here on your own accord. Through great personal courage, you have all willingly volunteered to fight and destroy those who seek to destroy us and trample the beliefs that we hold so dear to our hearts. Sadly, this struggle will not end without great sacrifice and there is likely be some amongst us who never make it home. Gentlemen, it is for that, that I, your nation, and your town, our lovely Dryden, salutes you."

For effect, Marvin gave the men a dramatic salute. It got them all worked up and along with the crowd they let out a loud and raucous cheer. It excited Marvin, too, and for a moment he envisioned himself leading them sword in hand, in a gallant charge towards the enemy. Once the cheering died down, he refocused and continued.

"In exactly ten minutes we will be leaving, and I want all of you men to be loaded up onto the wagons behind you. Until then I will permit you to say your goodbyes. Dismissed."

The formation quickly scattered. The few men without families present milled around or got directly into the wagons, but most, like Enos, went to be with their loved ones.

Gabriel and Andrew Farrell chose to sit in the second wagon in line because its driver had been kind enough to lay a fresh bed of straw down for the men's comfort. William Moffat was standing next to the driver's seat and was consoling his crying wife Matilda.

"I will send for you as soon as I can, darling," Gabriel could hear him tell her.

Gabriel knew the couple quite well. William was a friendly, but sometimes worried man. He had helped Marvin as one of the company's recruiters, and was to become its 2nd lieutenant when they finally mustered in. Gabriel knew his wife Matilda better, though. She was a Sweetland, and was first cousin to Rill's brother-in-law George. She was friendly, too, but had a reputation for being very needy.

Enos soon showed up and climbed in. His wife was standing on the sidewalk, ready to watch them go. As the company loaded up, Gabriel realized he hadn't seen Dave Nash since the formation had broken.

"Hey, have you two seen Dave?" he asked Enos and Andrew.

Enos shook his head and Andrew shrugged before catching sight of him in the crowd.

"There he is," he called out and stood up to wave his arms in the air for Dave to see. "Over here Dave. We're in number two," Andrew shouted.

Dave heard him and hobbled over. In his hand was a brown bottle of liquor and his coat was missing. He got to the wagon and jumped in over the side as Marvin was shouting, "Forward!". The wagons began to roll, and the men cheered. Most of the women and children left behind on the sidewalks were in tears and waving handkerchiefs or little flags, while the old men shouted encouragements. The boy with the miniature uniform marched his formation in cadence alongside the rolling wagons, and the men let out another cheer for them as well.

Things started quieting down once they'd left the village, and the men settled into their seats.

"Where were you Dave, we were getting a little worried?" Gabriel asked him.

"Gettin' lunch," Dave said holding up his new bottle. "Told ya I'd get my meals along the way," he added.

Gabriel and Enos smiled and shook their heads.

"What happened to your coat? It seems to be missing," Andrew asked, knowing damn well where the coat had gone.

"It ain't missin', I traded it for this here rot gut," Dave said as he took the cork between his teeth, pulled it out and spit it to the roadway below.

"What, do you expect to down that all in one sitting?" Enos asked.

"Cortland's a long ride in these old wagons, Enos. Besides, I need to get rid of this bottle if a want to get a new one for the train. That's what this is for." Dave said tugging on his vest.

"You'd better be careful, Dave, or you're gonna show up in Binghamton naked," Enos jokingly warned him.

"So, what of it? Army's gonna give us new clothes anyway and I sure as hell ain't luggin' these rags all over creation. If I send them home, that'll cost me money. Money that I could spend on this." Dave said holding up his bottle before taking a long first pull on the contents inside.

* * * * *

Around halfway to Cortland, Harrison Marvin called the wagons to a halt and informed the men that they had a short time to eat and go to the bushes if needed. Be it nerves, or the knowledge that his liquor may not be as easy to come by where they were going, Dave Nash had imbibed a little too freely at the beginning of their journey, and by the time Marvin called his halt, had long since drained his so called "lunch," and was unresponsive in the back of the wagon. Gabriel and his friends were uncertain what to do with him, but William Moffat made the call and decided to leave him be while everyone else went into a maple grove off the road to stretch and eat in the shade.

The men all ate, even Andrew Farrell who borrowed his meal from Gabriel and Enos. After about fifteen minutes, though, Marvin told the men to pack away their food and load back up. Gabriel was the first to reach their wagon and, expecting to see Dave Nash still sleeping, was rather surprised to find no one there. Socrates Schutt was right behind him, so Gabriel turned to ask if he knew where Dave had gone.

"I haven't a clue, he was just here a few minutes ago," Socrates replied.

"Well, he's gone now," Gabriel said.

As the other men showed up, Gabriel asked around, but nobody knew where Dave was. Soon, the other wagons were loaded, but noticing how the men in the wagon behind him were still milling about, Harrison Marvin called out to them.

"Wagon two, load up. We're waiting on you."

"Sorry Harry," William Moffat said, as he approached Marvin. "It appears Dave Nash has gone missing."

"What!? Missing? That fool. He's probably run off. I knew this morning was too good to be true!" Marvin shouted, and kicked the side of the wagon in frustration. Its owner said nothing, but gave him a rotten scowl. "Load them up anyway. We'll have to mark him as a deserter. We don't have time to chase him down, William. We've got a train to catch," Marvin decided.

Moffat was shocked to see Marvin give up on Dave so quickly. He pulled out his watch to check the time. They had plenty to spare.

"I understand we've got a strict itinerary, Harry, but we're far ahead of schedule, and Dave hasn't deserted. At least I don't think he has. He was extremely inebriated, you see, and the men are concerned that he's wandered off. They want to find him before he gets hurt. Don't want the man stumbling into a bull pen or falling into a pond or Lord knows what else," Moffat said.

"Un-fucking believable!" Marvin shouted, drawing the attention of everyone in earshot. "We haven't been gone long enough for a pie to bake and that idiot does this. God damn him William. Damn that man!" Harrison Marvin paused a moment to think before finally consenting.

"Alright then," he said, "send out the men in your wagon, but I will give them ten minutes to find Nash, only ten, and if they can't in that time frame, then we'll have to move on. I don't care if his absence was intended or not. The idiot should have known not to get drunk. You should have known too, William. Why didn't you leave a guard on him if you deemed him that intoxicated?"

"I'm sorry, Harry, the men couldn't even wake him twenty minutes ago, and we weren't but fifty feet away. I didn't think it was necessary, but obviously I was wrong. I'll send the men out, then," Moffat said.

"Ten minutes William, that's all the time you've got," Marvin reminded him, as the men from wagon two spread out to search.

Luckily ten minutes was all the time they needed, for Bielby Starr found him in five. Dave was face down in the ditch about an eighth of a mile down the road, but to Bielby's misfortune, Dave hadn't a lick of clothing on, and he had to drag him about 100 yards by himself until Gabriel came along. When they made it back to the wagons their waiting comrades erupted into laughter at the sight of Dave.

"You need to keep better track of your friends there, Gabriel," David Ferris taunted from the rear wagon as they stumbled by. It infuriated Gabriel, but he was too worn out and preoccupied to respond.

When Marvin noticed what the big ruckus was about, he shouted to Gabriel and Bielby as they were lifting Dave up into the wagon.

"Where the hell are that man's clothes?!" He bellowed.

"We don't know, Mr. Marvin," Gabriel said, "Bielby found him like this laying in the ditch. We looked on our way back, but couldn't find a scrap of clothing anywhere."

Marvin rolled his eyes. He couldn't believe what he was hearing.

"Well, throw him in the wagon and cover him up with some of that straw. We don't have time to be looking for his clothes too. William if you see any garments on a line along the way, see if you can acquire some for him. We can't be taking him into Cortland like that."

"I agree," Moffat said.

It wasn't more than a mile back into their journey before they were able to get him some off a farmer for free. Moffat tried paying, but the farmer wouldn't accept.

"Take them. It's the least I can do for a man headed off to war," he said. "No matter what the circumstances of his situation may be," he added with a grin.

* * * * *

In Cortland, the men were surprised to hear that the train wouldn't arrive for a few hours yet. After the incident with Dave Nash, Harrison Marvin wouldn't let anyone leave the station though.

While they waited, Gabriel and Enos tried sobering Dave up.

"Here drink this," Gabriel said as he handed Dave a tin cup of water.

Dave, who was still very intoxicated, slurped it down quickly.

"What the hell was that?" He said after, cringing in disgust.

"Water," Gabriel answered.

"Never touch the stuff," Dave said. "weakens my drunk."

"Well that's the point," Gabriel told him.

"Don't get smart with me boy," Dave growled. "What I need is my flask. God damn Marvin, what was he in such a hurry for anyway? Train ain't even here yet. It wouldn't have taken five extra minutes to find my belongings."

"Here, Dave. Eat this," Enos said, handing Dave a hunk of bread that Julia had packed for him. "It'll soak up whatever liquor you still have sloshing around in that stomach of yours."

"Well, I don't want it doin' that, but I suppose I should have some solids," Dave said before taking a bite. "Took a shit in that privy over there a few minutes ago, and it come out like a flood, all water."

After a while, a train pulled in from the north and Marvin walked out of the station office where he had discreetly been having a drink or two of his own with the ticket man.

"This is ours, Dryden. Load 'em up!" he shouted to the men before turning to William Moffat, who had been waiting patiently outside the office door.

"Mr. Moffat, make a roll call. I'll be in the front car. Let me know when we're up and I'll pass it on to the engineer that we're ready to go."

"Consider it done, Harry," Moffat obediently responded.

Secretly, Moffat was annoyed with Marvin, though, and had been thinking over the situation since they got into Cortland. Moffat was a fair man and recognized that Marvin was unaccustomed to his new duties, but they'd left Dryden with plenty of extra time to make their scheduled train. It had been planned that way in case anything did happen on their journey, but at the first suggestion they go looking for Dave he'd gone berserk and had been flying off the handle at every little annoyance he encountered since.

After taking the roll call and making sure the men were settled in, Moffat sent word to Marvin that all were present and accounted for. A few moments later the train let out a few whistle blasts and the cars went into motion. When they did, Gabriel found himself sitting sandwiched in his seat between a snoring Dave Nash and Andrew Farrell. Dave and Andrew had fallen fast asleep shortly after taking their seats and Gabriel closed his eyes and tried to join them. Before dozing off, his thoughts were of home and the last time he had seen Rill.

"God knows I love her," he thought to himself, "I just hope she still feels the same way about me."

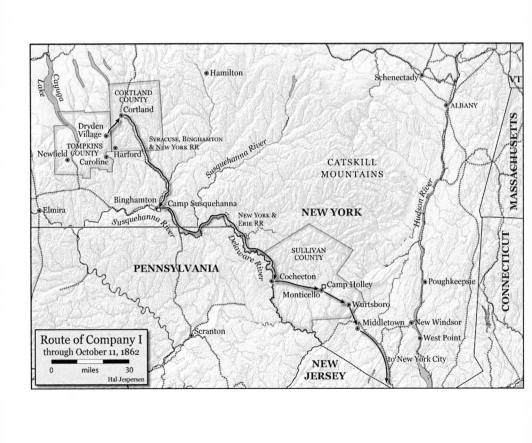

Route of Company I
through October 11, 1862

0   miles   30

Hal Jespersen

CHAPTER FIVE

Camp Susquehanna, located along the Susquehanna River in Binghamton, was to be the rendezvous point and training location for the new regiment the Dryden company was to be assigned to. Binghamton was a relatively short train ride to the south of Cortland, and Gabriel was happy to have slept most the journey.

Their first morning in camp started off easily enough. After breakfast and morning roll call, they had a short class on Army etiquette, how one should address their superiors, what a proper salute looked like and how to stand at attention. That afternoon though, drill, drill, drill became the order of the day, and it remained that way for the days to follow. In that time, they were in constant motion, but the instruction moved swiftly and soon they were marching about in formation as a company on the camps large and open parade ground.

They were issued their uniforms in the first few days at camp as well, along with the various other accoutrements that they would need for their new life as soldiers. The coat that they were given was the standard issue New York State Volunteers jacket, which was made of dark blue wool, with light blue piping sewn in along the seams and a shiny row of 8 brass buttons that ran down the middle. Gabriel had seen it worn many times around the village in the past year by men home on leave or recently discharged. He always looked up to those men and was proud to now have one of his own.

The trousers they were issued were also dark blue, along with their cap, referred to as a 'kepi'. For footwear, they were given black leather shoes called 'brogans', and two pair of socks. A black leather waist belt was also issued, with a brass buckle marked SNY, for State of New York. To carry their rations, they were given tar-covered canvas bags called 'haversacks', with a steel bullseye canteen for water, and a tin cup and plate to eat with. To haul everything else that couldn't be strapped to them, they were given a tarred canvas knapsack with leather shoulder straps. The knapsacks had two large pouches that folded and were secured together as one, with straps on the outside at the top to hold their rolled-up blanket and rubber ponchos.

Initially, upon their arrival at Camp Susquehanna, Gabriel and his companions from Dryden were in high spirits. They were eager to learn and proud to finally be attired in union blue. Not long into their stay, however, it was announced that there were more men present than the regiment was authorized to have. At first there was talk of forming a new regiment, then rumors began to swirl that the extra men were to be shipped to another regiment in the state. Still others held out hope that all present would be allowed to stay together. The uncertainty of the situation laid heavy on the minds of everyone, especially that of Harrison Marvin, who, as expected, was made captain of the company. Marvin realized that if there were to be any companies left out when all was said and done, it probably wouldn't be the best companies that were sent away. To his credit, he tried very hard to prevent that from happening to his men.

"We must be second to none," quickly became his go to phrase. Compared to the other companies in the regiment, however, they struggled, and the problem was not with the soldiers. It was with Marvin. Plainly and simply put, he was bad at drill. He lacked coordination, and had trouble calling and remembering his commands. Worst of all, he blamed the men and took no ownership of his own mistakes. If he gave an incorrect command and the men were confused by it, or made the wrong movements, he would take his frustrations out on them, even though he was to blame.

Colonel David Ireland, the commander of their regiment, was a fair man, but known for adhering to strong military discipline. After a dozen days or so of struggling on the parade ground, Marvin saw that his company wasn't progressing at the pace of the others. So, he surmised that if he couldn't impress the colonel on the drill field, he may be able to do so through discipline. With that in mind, he started parading his company after their evening meals, while the other men of the regiment had been turned to quarters. The extra training actually started to benefit Marvin, and as a result the company's performance improved. He didn't let up though, and the evening sessions continued. Many of the men began to resent him for this, and they made their concerns known to the company's lieutenants.

"What do you mean the men want a reprieve?" Marvin said one night after evening drill. Lieutenants George and Moffat had just brought up the men's grievances with him.

"Well, Sir, the men are upset. They think that they've gotten much better over the past week, and they'd like to have their evenings back like the other companies," Lieutenant George explained.

"That's right, Harry. Some of the men's families visited from Dryden this week, and they were barely able to see them," Moffat added.

Marvin was very annoyed, but he bit his tongue.

"Well, what do you two think?" he asked his two subordinates, testing their loyalty.

"Well, Sir," Lieutenant George said, thinking he was making headway with Marvin, "to be honest, we would like some time off. I mean, the company has gotten better, Sir. I'd say we're just as good as anyone else now."

That wasn't the answer Marvin wanted to hear, though, and he erupted at them in retaliation.

"I don't want to be as good as everyone else. I want to be the best!" he shouted. The lieutenants stepped back in astonishment. "First impressions are everything, you idiots, and we were the worst when we first got here! It takes a long fucking time to change a first impression! More than the week that you jackasses seem to think it does. I don't care what you or they think. We'll drill every evening until we're shipped south."

After Marvin was done with his tirade, it was quiet for a moment in the room. Only his angry and heavy breathing could be heard, as he savored the empowering feeling of control he thought he had over his two lieutenants. Moffat wasn't ready to back down though, for he had something to lose in Marvin's decree. His wife and daughter were coming down to visit the following day and now it looked as if he wouldn't get to see them. As he processed the consequence of Marvin's words his anger boiled over.

"Who do you think you are, Harry? Them boys out there have worked their tails off to compensate for your lack of coordination and memory since we got here, and now that they've finally helped you along to mediocrity, you're going to stick it to them?"

Marvin shot out of his seat like a rocket at Moffat and roared back with his index finger almost poking his opponent in the eye.

"Shut your fucking mouth, Lieutenant. I am a captain in the United States Volunteers, and I will not be spoken to in such a way!"

Lieutenant George eased away from the confrontation until his back was up against the wall of the room. Moffat didn't flinch though, he was seething with anger, but toned down his words.

"You're not a captain yet, Harry. We're all just civilians here until we get mustered in."

Moffat turned around and walked out before he did something he'd regret. Marvin almost ran out the door after him but controlled himself. He knew that if he caused a scene in front of the regiment it would look bad on him. Colonel Ireland would think he'd lost control of his men. He wouldn't forget, though. He'd get back at them tomorrow, and not just his lieutenants, but the whole company.

The following day, after everyone else had been cut loose, the Dryden boys were at it again on the parade ground. They marched left and right and wheeled about, and the men were impeccable in their movements, even Captain Marvin was flawless, but just as the sun was going down, David Ferris tripped and dropped on one knee out of formation. It was just the mistake Marvin had been waiting for, so he called the men to a halt.

"You men obviously need more instruction," he said. "I want everyone up an hour prior to reveille for remedial drill. See to it, Lieutenants. I will join you after breakfast. Dismissed!"

As Gabriel and his cohorts were processing what had just been said, Captain Marvin trotted away before anyone had a chance to challenge him or protest. Reluctantly, they obeyed his orders, though, and were all up an hour prior to the other companies in the regiment. Their dislike for the captain was quickly growing into a hatred. Previously, he would get up with the men, but now that he had them waking an hour early, he claimed he wouldn't be joining them until even later than he had before. He had just lengthened their day, while at the same time shortening his own.

Unbeknownst to Marvin, though, his little plan for retaliation was about to blow up in his face. Due to their overworked schedules and shortened sleep, the men were terrible at drill the following day. Suspecting that they were rebelling against him, Marvin renewed their early reveille as punishment. Not surprisingly, their performance at drill got even worse. Marvin now realized his mistake. The men were exhausted, but he felt that he couldn't back down from the precedent he had set and ordered another early reveille. Things were snowballing out of control, and it appeared that after all the progress they had gained, they were quickly reverting back to square one. Consequently, it couldn't have come at a worse time.

Colonel Ireland was no dummy. After watching Marvin's company perform over the past few weeks in camp, he knew where the problem lay. Had he been able to keep all twelve companies under his command, he would have simply gotten rid of Marvin, but the State had come down with their final decision that he could only have ten, so he chose to keep the company whole and move it along. The news that they were to be sent away was a terrible blow to the men's already diminished morale. Over their time in camp they had grown attached to the regiment and its commander, but now they felt as if they were unwanted. Overlooking his own shortcomings, Marvin, of course, blamed the men.

* * * * *

The other company from the regiment to be sent away with the boys from Dryden was also from Tompkins County, and was commanded by Captain John Higgins. Together, they left Camp Susquehanna on the 27th of September. By rail, they traveled to the south and east of Binghamton to the town of Cochecton along the Delaware River. After spending the night there, they boarded several wagons the next morning and travelled east for about 22 miles to the Village of Monticello, in the Catskill Mountains. They arrived late in the afternoon and were marched just north of the village to Camp Holley, the training location for a regiment of men from that area. The regiment was undermanned, and the two Tompkins County companies were to fill it to capacity.

Upon their arrival at the camp, they were met by their new comrades and given three hearty cheers. The Tompkins boys returned the favor. Camp Holley was located alongside the shores of a small body of water known as Pleasant Lake. Sullen and tired from their journey, many of the Dryden boys, Gabriel especially, found comfort in the lake as it reminded them of the tiny lake in their own town. They were also pleased when they found out that much like Camp Susquehanna, they would be quartered in newly constructed plank barracks.

"I suppose things could be worse, we could be in tents", Dave Nash had said when he walked into their building for the first time.

For some, though, the anxiety and frustration felt in the past few weeks became too much. The treatment they had been receiving from Captain Marvin was one thing, but the move to another regiment was the icing on the cake.

"I see the writin' on the wall already boys, and this is shaping up to be a rotten time," said James McDermott, after their arrival in Camp Holley. James had enlisted to be a corporal in the company. On the following day, Captain Marvin asked for four men to go on a detail to the west of camp to pick up supplies for the regiment and intercept several late arrivals, who had been on leave when the company left Binghamton two days before. McDermott was quick to volunteer himself and three of his pals, John Nugent, Robert Tomlinson and James Welch. Captain Marvin was pleased, and complimented them for their enthusiasm, but the four men returned his favor by deserting. Marvin never asked for another volunteer again. From then on, when a chore needed to be done, the men were voluntold.

On the day they arrived in Camp Holley, the men from Tompkins County were given their companies' designations. The command under Captain Higgins was to be Company D, while Captain Marvin's men were to be Company I. It also became glaringly apparent, shortly after their arrival, that the boys from Tompkins were seen as outsiders, as the rest of the regiment were from Sullivan County. It was because of this situation that Harrison Marvin again saw it his duty to try and outperform the other companies of their regiment. Rightfully so, he wanted to prove their worth, but foolishly chose to do so using the same grueling training schedule that had overworked the men out of their old regiment in Binghamton. He also continued to sleep in and not show up until after breakfast, at least two hours after his men had been awake. Some of the men suspected he was drinking in the evenings, but nothing had been proven yet.

* * * * *

"God damn that son of a bitch," Dave Nash said as he kicked open the door to Company I's barracks.

The men had just gotten done with one of Marvin's evening drill sessions and tempers were flaring.

"We've been the best fuckin' company in the whole regiment since the day we showed up, but that bastard Marvin treats us like we're the worst of the worst."

As the other men filtered in behind him, Dave strode over to his bunk in search of the bottle he had rolled up in his blankets. He had actually been somewhat sober in Binghamton, but under the current circumstances he had returned back to his old ways.

"Calm down Dave," Enos Cook said, as he and Gabriel made their way into the big room. "No sense in getting yourself worked up over things that are out of your control. Besides, you'll be happy when the Rebs are shooting at you and you're part of the best trained company in all of the 143rd."

Word had been passed to the men that evening at formation that they were to be known as the 143rd New York Infantry, and that they would be shipping out any day now for parts unknown.

"Rebs, hell," Dave shot back. "We ain't going to fight, Enos. They ain't even issued us rifles yet."

"You really think we won't fight?" Gabriel asked, sounding concerned.

"We'll fight alright, Gabriel," Enos encouraged him, as they stripped off their sweaty uniforms and prepared to bed down for the night.

Some of the Dryden boys didn't even bother doing that, they just threw themselves onto their bunks and went straight to sleep.

"The State's got so many regiments forming now, I bet they're just having a tough time distributing all the supplies they need to issue. We'll get our guns soon enough. They'll let us fight, so don't let Mr. Negative over there discourage you," Enos added.

"Horseshit," Dave snarled, as he popped the cork on the bottle and took a nice long chug.

Truthfully, Enos was just as frustrated as the rest of them, but he knew that complaining would only make things worse. He also knew that a lot of the younger recruits looked up to him, so he always tried to put on a happy face, so as to not bring their morale down any lower than it already was.

Suddenly, there was a knock at the barracks door. As the knocker let himself in, the men looked up fearing Marvin was back for a surprise inspection. They were relieved to see that it was only Lieutenant Moffat. He walked in with a cotton sack slung over his shoulder and a big smile on his face.

"Mail's here!" he cried out.

The men jumped up from their bunks and ran to the doorway in good spirits, as if their rotten day had never happened. Not since Lieutenants George and Moffat had confronted Captain Marvin back in Binghamton, had the company received any mail. It was a frustration the men had blamed on the railroad, as it was suspected that they had lost the mail or mistakenly sent it to some other regiment in the state. As it turned out, that wasn't the case at all. As he passed out the letters, Lieutenant Moffat explained.

"Well, boys, I was in the Captain's room tonight, getting my daily tongue lashing I might add, and I happened to notice this here sack tucked away under ole Marvin's bed with the word MAIL printed on it in big black letters. 'What's that?' I interrupted him, and he said none of my damn business, so I walked over and had a look for myself. Turns out he's been confiscating our mail for the past few weeks now, but as he puts it, we don't deserve it on account of our lack of motivation. I almost struck him I tell you but thank God some sort of divine intervention held me back and I just walked out with the bag instead, so here ya go."

The men were shocked and furious at what they were being told, but most of them decided to ignore Marvin's treachery for the moment. They were too eager to read what their loved ones had to say. Gabriel had received a letter and Enos got two, but Gabriel was a little disappointed, as he could tell it was from his parents and not Rill as he had been hoping. He decided to stay up near the door and hear what else Moffat had to share. Dave Nash did, too. He didn't get any letters as his wife Electa was illiterate.

"Somethin's got to be done about Marvin," Dave said to Moffat.

"I know, Dave, I know," he said. "Trust me, I've been getting it from him as bad as the rest of you boys. He's lost his mind. I don't think he can handle all the stress and responsibility."

"He can handle it just fine," Dave said. "He just enjoys orderin' us around."

Moffat pulled the last few letters out of the bag.

"These are for Lieutenant George and I," he said, and looked as if he were ready to go.

"Nothing there for Captain Marvin?" Gabriel asked, genuinely perplexed as he knew Marvin's wife could write.

"Hell no, Gabriel," Dave butted in. "Marvin probably opens all his letters the day he gets them, the pig-headed piece of shit."

"Hey, hold your tongue there Private," Moffat scolded Dave. "I know you're frustrated with the man, but he's still your captain, so don't be calling him any names. You can leave that to me. At least don't call him those things when I'm around to hear you, that is. And one other thing. The whiskey's got to go, Dave. If he catches you with that, we're all going to pay for it, and Marvin will be within his rights to do whatever he pleases."

"What whiskey?" Dave asked with a grin.

"You know what whiskey, Dave. You smell like you've bathed in it, so sober up," Moffat ordered.

"Bill," Dave called Moffat by his first name, "you know I have to drink. If I don't, I can't walk straight much less march, and then we'll all be in trouble anyway."

Moffat was on his way out.

"Not my problem, Dave. Figure something out. If Marvin were to walk in here right now and got a whiff of you, he'd have us out drilling all night and you'd be in the stockade."

As he trotted down the front steps of the barracks to leave, David Ferris and Andrew Farrell were on their way inside, and seeing the lieutenant seemed to startle the two privates. Moffat noticed their apprehension and grew suspicious, so he stopped them.

"Evening, boys. What are you two doing out so late after drill?" he asked. They were slow to answer, though, so Moffat kept prodding.

"Are you practicing your marching? Shining your brass? Or is it that you're out getting a bottle for old Dave Nash up there standing in the doorway?" he questioned them.

"Aw, shit," Dave muttered under his breath.

Gabriel turned away because he saw where the situation was going and didn't want any part in it. Ferris and Farrell stood there with their heads bowed and their eyes staring at the ground, knowing they had been caught red-handed.

"Well, give it up," Moffat said, holding out his hand.

The boys hesitated for a moment, but then they both moved to unbutton their blouses.

"God damn it," Dave said from the top of the steps, "not both you idiots, he wouldn't have expected you both to have bottles."

"Shut up, Dave!" Moffat yelled.

As the boys removed their coats, he could see how they had planned on smuggling the bottles into camp undetected. Each boy had a piece of twine looped around his neck and hidden under his collar. On the other end of the twine there was another loop fastened around the neck of the bottle, so that it hung like a pendulum under their ill-fitting coats. Moffat shook his head and chuckled.

"Nice try, boys," he said, as they handed their booze over to him. "Remember now, you two must be up an hour prior to the company, who will be up an hour prior to everyone else. Get the coffee brewed and haul a dozen buckets of water up from the lake for washing and shaving."

Poor David Ferris and Andrew Farrell had already been in trouble earlier in the evening and earned that chore for their mistakes made during drill. Luckily, Moffat was kind enough not to add to their punishment. Instead, he told Dave Nash to join them in the morning for putting them up to it.

"I'm trying my best to help you boys with the Captain, but you've got to help me help you," he told Dave before he left.

Ferris and Farrell had had enough punishment lately. Since coming to Camp Holley, Ferris was always the one to screw up at evening drill, ensuring an early reveille the following morning. He wasn't malicious by any means, just a late bloomer, and the hours of constant activity during the day wore him out. By the time evening drill came along he could barely walk, much less march. Usually, he would trip and fall forward into the man in front of him, and the two would end up in a pile on the ground. Unfortunately, Andrew Farrell was the man in front of David Ferris in formation, and consequently the one who always ended up in the heap. Captain Marvin was too thick to realize it, so he punished Andrew as well.

The other men in Company I felt bad, but they were also happy to have Marvin's attention directed away from them, so they never said much in their support. Gabriel could tell that the daily punishments were taking their toll on the poor boys and he felt bad too, especially for his friend Andrew Farrell, but he didn't have the slightest idea on how to remedy the situation without drawing the wrath of Marvin.

* * * * *

Gabriel made his way back to his bunk next to Enos and opened his letter. There was nothing much to it really. His mother just explained what they had done on the farm since he'd been gone, and his father wrote to tell him that that his uncles' regiment was called the 157th New York Infantry, and that they were being shipped south any day now.

"What do your parents have to say Gabriel, everything okay on the old homestead?" Enos asked.

"Everything seems to be about normal. Father tells me that my uncles are a part of the 157th, I guess, and are headed south soon."

"Perhaps we'll get put in the same brigade or division as them." Enos suggested. "You'd like that, wouldn't you? I bet a lot of the boys in the company would be pleased. Quite a few others have friends and relations in the same company your uncles belong to."

"I suppose so," Gabriel said. He looked discouraged, and Enos read him like a book.

"Oh cheer up, Gabriel," he said, while reaching over to give him a reassuring pat on the back. "You really think that girl hasn't tried or wanted to write to you?"

Gabriel looked up, not even attempting to pretend he wasn't disappointed about not hearing a word from Rill. He shrugged his shoulders.

"Well of course she has," Enos said. He held up one of his letters. "Listen here what my wife writes about her."

"Poor Martha Marsh, she has been heart-broken I hear ever since Gabriel left with you. Her sister Hannah keeps her on a tight leash and has someone always watching the girl. Hannah told me herself she does so to prevent her from running off to find you boys. She says that she caught George trying to post some letters to Gabriel for Martha, but that she tossed them in her stove. I'm sure George regrets getting caught. I thought it strange she has chosen to confide this all in me because she tells everyone else that her sister has been unwell. I suppose it may be that she fears Gabriel has been telling you the truth of the matter."

Gabriel leapt up from his bunk and tore the letter from Enos's hand.

"Let me read that," he said with excitement.

"What's the matter, don't trust me?" Enos laughed.

Gabriel read over the letter twice. It warmed his heart to hear anything about Rill, even if it was sad news. He was just happy to hear that she was thinking about him and was trying to write. Gabriel handed Enos back his letter.

"Thanks Enos, this is the happiest I've been since we got here," he said with a smile. "Don't thank me, thank my wife."

"I will, Enos. Tomorrow night, I'm going to write to Rill by way of my brother Sam and I'll also write a thank you note to Julia too for keeping me informed."

"Well, that'd be nice and all Gabriel, but why write her when you can tell her in person?"

"What do you mean?" Gabriel asked.

"Well look here in my second letter. This one was written on the 25th, before we left Binghamton. Marvin must have just gotten it today. She says that they heard a rumor from Mrs. Marvin, who had just visited our camp that day, that once we reached our new regiment it wouldn't be long before we were shipped south. Apparently, Marvin told his wife he estimated we'd be leaving sometime around the first or second week in October. She says that once they hear a more definite date she's coming down with our daughter, and that she's going to kidnap Martha into coming along too".

"Wahhooooooo!" Gabriel shouted and shot up off his bunk as if he were fired from a mortar. He leapt onto an unsuspecting Enos, and the two men rolled off his bunk onto the floor.

"Thought you'd like that," Enos said.

Some of the other men who had already dozed off, were woken by Gabriel's uproar and were none too pleased. They called him a few choice names and told him to "shut up," but he paid them no mind as he was far too excited to care.

Gabriel and Enos got back up off the floor and sat across from each other on their bunks again. Gabriel tried being more considerate, though, and instead of shouting whispered.

"First or second week in October, Enos. It is the first week in October. I guess they weren't lying to us this afternoon after all," he said.

He'd already learned to take Army rumors with a grain of salt.

"No, I guess they weren't," Enos agreed.

"Boy, I sure am thankful to Moffat for taking our mail from Marvin. I would have loved to have seen his face when Moffat walked out with it," Gabriel said.

"I'm happy, too. I just hope it doesn't cost us in the long run. Marvin's already hard on us. Once fellas start openly rebelling against him, though, I think things might get real ugly."

"I guess I didn't think about that," Gabriel admitted.

"The way I see it, Gabriel, is being an officer is a lot like parenting. Take Julia and I, for example. Back when our kids were little, if I ever told one of them "no" for some reason, then Julia would always stand by and support my decision, and vice versa. I would always support her rulings, too. We may not have necessarily agreed with each other, but we supported each other's decisions in front of the kids, because if we didn't, it would have undermined our authority as parents. The kids would have started losing respect for the both of us. It's the same way with our officers. Once they start badmouthing each other in front of their men, like Lieutenant Moffat did tonight, then they start to lose the respect of the men. When a company loses respect for their officers, then the company falls apart. Don't get me wrong, I'm happy I got my letters, but Lieutenant Moffat went about it the wrong way. Even if he did have an argument with the Captain, he should have just passed out the letters and said nothing of it. Hopefully, the other boys don't take it as an open invitation to disobey him, too."

Gabriel sat silent, digesting all of what Enos had to say. When he'd finished talking, they both made up their bunks and went to sleep like most everyone else had already done. There were a few other side conversations going on, but even they ended shortly after Gabriel and Enos called it a night. It had been a long day, and it would be another early morning before they knew it.

* * * * *

The days following the news of Rill's possible visit seemed to drag on incredibly slow for Gabriel. One would assume that time would have flown by, with Captain Marvin's remedial drill sessions taking place every morning and night, but Gabriel's thoughts were elsewhere. Most of the time he was daydreaming of Rill and wondering when she was going to show up, as Julia Cook had never given a definite date for their visit in her letters. His daydreaming proved hazardous, too, as he made several mistakes during evening drill and found himself getting up extra early in the mornings to make coffee and haul wash water for the men. Gabriel had finally found a way to help out his buddy Andrew Farrell, but it wasn't exactly the solution he had been hoping for.

On the 6th of October, his situation took a slight turn for the better, though. Evening drill was cancelled on account of a regimental formation. At the formation, the Colonel informed his men that they were to be officially mustered into U.S service on the 8th. He also told them that there was to be a ceremony and festivities the following day, and then on the 10th they would start their journey south by way of New York City. What pleased Gabriel the most was that at the end of the Colonel's speech he informed the Tompkins County men that two bags of mail had arrived for them that morning, and asked Captains Marvin and Higgins to send a soldier from each of their companies to his headquarters to retrieve them. David Ferris was sent from Company I.

The Dryden boys were happy because they knew there was no way Marvin could withhold their mail this time. When Ferris got to their barracks with the bag in hand, Lieutenant George was there waiting to distribute its contents. Gabriel was disappointed when he didn't get a letter of his own but was relieved when Enos did.

"What does it say?" he asked Enos immediately after he opened his envelope.

Enos ignored him, though, and read on until he finished, then handed it over to Gabriel.

"Julia says they received word from Mrs. Marvin on our schedule, and that they'll be leaving Dryden in the morning on the 8th. They're to go by train all the way to Cochecton, like we did, and then take the stage to Monticello, where they hope to arrive sometime in the night. She says they'll make their way out to our camp on the morning of the 9th with some other folks from Dryden."

Gabriel listened and read the letter over once to see for himself. "Thank God," he said in relief once he'd finished. "Just in time to see us off. I've been worried they were going to rush us out of here before the girls could make it down."

"I could tell," Enos said, referring to Gabriel's recent absentmindedness.

"Frustrates me some, though," Gabriel said. "Seems like Marvin's wife knows more than we do and days prior to us at that. I don't understand why the officers can't just tell us, too, when they're blabbering it to their wives anyway."

"I suppose you've got a point there, Gabriel," Enos agreed. "But think of it like this. If Marvin wasn't telling his wife what he knew, then the girls at home wouldn't have known in time to come down and see us off. You've got to look for the good in everything my friend, especially in the Army."

At the head off the barracks, Lieutenant George cleared his throat, to get everyone's attention, and the men stopped what they were doing and listened for what he had to say.

"Okay, boys, consider yourselves lucky. The Captain gave you the night off. I'm sorry to say he wants you up early in the morning, though. You can thank Private Farrell for that. Captain says he saw his eyes closed during the Colonel's speech this afternoon."

The men began to grumble and some of them directed some insults towards Andrew from across the room. Gabriel felt sorry for his friend, but then Dave Nash piped up from behind him.

"That's funny I never saw no eyes in the back of the Captain's fuckin' head," Dave said, sticking up for his old drinking buddy.

"What are you getting at, Private Nash?" Lieutenant George quickly responded.

"What I'm gettin' at, Sir, is how the fuck could Marvin see if Andrew's eyes were closed, when he and everyone else was turned around facin' the Colonel the whole time?" Dave shouted.

Some of the other men grunted their agreement and Andrew Farrell seemed to gain a little pride back into his demeanor.

"I don't rightly know," George said, "but orders are orders. You boys know that. I'll see you bright and early."

After that, Lieutenant George stepped out, and headed back to the officer's quarters, trying, on his way, to figure out for himself just how the Captain could have seen what he claimed.

CHAPTER SIX

The last little bits of time leading up to the regiment's departure, were entirely devoted to preparation. All items still unissued were passed out by the regimental quartermaster, while the sergeants and corporals were tasked with inspecting their men, making sure they were squared away and weren't missing any of their issued equipment. Captain Marvin seemed to forget about drill for the time being, as he and his two lieutenants were kept busy filling out the company's muster sheets and other associated paperwork. Instead of drill, he ordered the sergeants to lead their men in sprucing up their uniforms for the upcoming ceremonies.

"Second to none Sergeant, we must be second to none in our appearance. I want the Sullivan County folk to remember the day that the outsider, Captain Marvin, marched his company off to war. We must stand out above the rest," Marvin told John Copley, Company I's first-sergeant.

"I'll do my best, Sir," was Copley's reply.

In the few days leading up to October 9th, the boys from Companies I and D were awash in feelings of anticipation and excitement. Unlike the other men of the regiment, who were locals, most of the boys in those companies hadn't seen their families in over a month and for nearly all of them it was the longest they had been from home in their entire lives. They were very eager to see their loved ones once again, and rumor had it that there was quite the large cluster making the trek from Tompkins County.

Gabriel himself was initially excited, but after mustering in on the 8th, he began having second thoughts and envisioned the worst of circumstances. He worried that Hannah would find out about Julia

Cook's plan to bring Rill along, or that if Rill did get away, she would miss her train, or something of that sort. Nearly the whole night he tossed and turned, a nervous wreck, just managing to worry himself to sleep an hour or so before reveille.

Morning brought a change of mood in Gabriel, though. He told himself that whatever happened would happen, and that he'd just have to accept the outcome. As Enos often said, "there's no sense in being concerned about things out of your control," he reminded himself.

The men had their breakfast and coffee and afterwards started getting ready for the flag presentation ceremony that was to be held later that morning. According to Lieutenant Moffat, there were to be a couple speeches, and then the citizens of Sullivan County were to present the regiment with an American Flag, their "colors". After the ceremony, the men were to be dismissed and allowed to visit with their families. The men without relatives visiting were free to do as they wished, but everyone had to be back in camp for roll call by 10:30 that night, as they would be leaving in the morning.

Around 10 A.M., Company I started to form up for the ceremony. There was excitement in the ranks, especially after one of the boys from Company D ran over to say that there was a large mob of Tompkins folks gathered at the corner of the parade ground. This information caused quite the stir in the men, but Captain Marvin quickly snuffed it out by telling them that their visiting privileges would hinge on their performance at the ceremony. There were a few grumbles to the Captain's remark, but then out of the blue someone in the formation yelled.

"Fuck off, Marvin."

Nobody moved or said a word. They were shocked to silence, most not quite believing what they had heard. At first, even Captain Marvin didn't know how to respond. He just stood at the head of the company in a stupor. Then an angry look crept over his face and he shouted.

"Quiet in the ranks!"

But then that same mystery voice from before mocked him by calling back.

"Quiet in the ranks!"

Now everyone was sure what they heard and started looking around to see who it came from. Captain Marvin was none too pleased of course. He started yelling at the top of his lungs at the company, as he paced up and down the ranks.

"Who the fuck said that?" he yelled, "Who the fuck said that?"

While he was screaming the other companies started to march off though, and Lieutenant George called out to notify Marvin.

"Captain Marvin, it's time."

Marvin turned around and noticed that Company I was the last to go. Panicked, he forgot all about the mystery heckler and ran to the head of the company and called to the men.

"Company, attention! Right face! Forward march!"

The jokester hadn't had his fill though, for when Marvin said "march" the man let out a loud and obnoxious impression of a cow's moo, "Mmuuurrrr!". The men obeyed the Captain's orders, but after that sound the whole company erupted into laughter, even the lieutenants couldn't contain themselves. Marvin, at the head of the company was boiling over, but the crowds of civilians were just a few yards away, so he bit his tongue and held his composure so as not to betray the air of dignity and arrogance he was trying to give off.

As Gabriel marched along, he tried to look lean and mean and stand up as straight and tall as he could, to impress Rill if she was indeed in attendance. His eyes were staring straight forward as they were supposed to, but he tried desperately to scan the crowd for Rill with his peripheral vision. He wasn't able to get a good look at anybody, but he could have sworn he heard her voice calling out his name. Then to his right he heard someone whisper to him. It was Enos. Enos marched right beside Gabriel and he sounded concerned.

"What's wrong, Enos?" he asked.

"It's Nash, Gabriel. He's terrible drunk. Look at him."

Gabriel scanned the men marching in front of him for Dave. It didn't take more than a moment to pick him out. He was barely marching, just walking really, but in a zig-zagging manner, and he kept running into the men on either side of him.

"Good Lord," Gabriel said to Enos out of the corner of his mouth. "What are we gonna do?"

"Nothing," Enos said. "Just pray that he makes it through the ceremony without causing a scene. That was him back there shouting all that nonsense."

Enos was right. By now, the company was almost in position, and in just a few yards Captain Marvin would halt them and call them to attention. Gabriel said a prayer to himself. He didn't want anything preventing him from getting to see his precious Rill, especially one of Dave Nash's drunken stunts.

The ceremony seemed to take forever, as the main speaker was especially long-winded. Union, patriotism, bravery, Constitution, duty, honor, glory, loyalty, liberty, fidelity. He regurgitated all the typical phrases Gabriel had heard time and again at home during the war rallies in town. The flags were finally turned over and then Colonel Dewitt approached the podium and said his piece. For the most part, Dave had stood remarkably still throughout the whole procession, a fact that delighted the men in his company who could tell what kind of condition he was in.

Just as the Colonel was finishing up though, it happened. Dave, his senses finally overcome, passed out while standing at attention and fell onto the ground for all to see. Once he hit the dirt, he was startled awake and tried standing but the degree of his intoxication was too great, and he fell again onto the ground. To make matters worse, once the spectators saw what was happening, there was a great eruption of laughter from the crowd. What was supposed to be a dignified occasion had now turned into a laughingstock and Captain Marvin lost his mind. He ran over to Nash like a tiger after its prey, picked him up by his collar and began shouting insensibly. Fortunately, Dave was too drunk to put up any resistance. He could barely keep an eye open much less engage in a war of words or fisticuffs with the Captain.

Having presence of mind, Colonel Dewitt dismissed the regiment in short order, attempting to draw the crowd's attention from the fiasco coming from Company I. He then sprinted over to ground zero, with Major Taft at his heels, to investigate. When they reached the scene, the

Captain was spitting venom at the company, while Levi Dodge and Sergeant Hemingway where standing on either side of Dave Nash helping to stabilize him as best they could into the position of attention.

"Captain Marvin," Colonel Dewitt snapped. "What's going on here?"

Marvin spun around on his heels to face the Colonel with a crazed look in his eyes. He gave him a quick salute and then opened up. He looked rabid and spit flew from his mouth as he raved.

"Drunkenness, Colonel. Drunkenness and disobedience. Heathenry, my God, Colonel." Marvin stopped for a second to catch his breath, then resumed.

"Colonel. Please Colonel, I'd like your permission Sir to cancel my men's liberty for the day. Their behavior has been abominable, a disgrace, and I wouldn't want to reward it, Sir."

Colonel Dewitt and Major Taft gave Marvin a queer look.

"This man is off his rocker," the Colonel thought to himself.

"Captain," he said, "I know you're disappointed, but I won't allow you to punish your whole company, not to mention their families, for the shortcomings of one man. I will not grant that request."

Marvin, frustrated in the Colonel's decision tried to interrupt but was quickly rebuked.

"I am not finished yet, Captain!" the Colonel scolded him. "You may cancel the liberty of your drunken soldier, leave one of your officers with him if you like, but the rest of your men must be turned over to their loved ones, and I want it done at once."

Marvin held his tongue, gave the Colonel a nod of acknowledgment and turned to reface his nervous troops.

"You heard the Colonel, you're dismissed. Anyone not back by 10:30 will be disciplined accordingly."

Marvin called the company to attention and dismissed them. As the men were dispersing, he called to Lieutenant Moffat, who was speaking with Lieutenant George before he went over to find his wife and daughter.

"Lieutenant Moffat, get over here!" he shouted.

Moffatt walked over to the Captain. Lieutenant George came over too.

"Lieutenant Moffat," Marvin said, "You're in charge of Nash for the day. I want you to have him brought over to the barracks. Keep him in there and don't let him out of your sight."

Moffat was taken a back and tried to protest.

"Captain, my family is here, they've come down all the way from Dryden to see me."

Lieutenant George tried to intervene as well.

"Captain, I can watch over Nash if you'll allow. I've got no visitors and was planning on spending the afternoon in quarters anyway."

Captain Marvin smiled, ignoring Moffat's pleas.

"Lieutenant George, you can go along and take your nap or whatever you had planned on doing. Lieutenant Moffat will follow my orders whether he likes them or not."

After dismissing George, Marvin turned his gaze to Moffat with a slight smile, clearly enjoying the displeasure he was causing him.

"Was it not you, Lieutenant Moffat, who I put in charge of curbing Private Nash's clear dependence on alcohol on the day we left Dryden? This little event here today was your fault. You failed to follow my instruction and so now you will pay for disgracing me in front of all these fine people, in front of the whole damn regiment."

* * * * *

After they were cut loose, Gabriel didn't stick around to watch the confrontation between Marvin and Moffat. He took off across the parade ground with everyone else that was expecting visitors. They headed straight for the crowd. As he ran, Gabriel begged God for Rill to be somewhere among them. Although he thought he heard her call out his name, he wasn't entirely positive it had been her at all. Enos was on his toes and he was scanning the crowd, too. He saw them first.

"There they are Gabriel!" he shouted with excitement. "They're standing by the podium, and it looks like they're looking for us too."

Gabriel looked where Enos had directed. He was right, it was them. Rill was standing with Julia Cook and her daughter Nancy. About the same time Gabriel caught sight of them, they saw him and Enos, too.

"Over here," they shouted, and waved their arms.

The boys were sprinting now. When they reached each other, everyone was laughing and hugging. There were other guys from the company meeting their families all around them, too, and they were doing the same. Many folks were in tears. It was a tremendous moment.

For lunch, the Dryden families had brought down food from home to feed the men. They packed plates and utensils too, and because it had turned out to be an unseasonably warm October day, they decided to picnic outside along the shore of Pleasant Lake. While the women unpacked the food, the men piled up their equipment, where some of the men without visitors had agreed to watch it for a home-cooked meal. The sun was shining, the birds were chirping, and the children were skipping stones in the water while the adults sat to eat and talk. Gabriel and Rill sat with the Cooks and shared in the goodies Julia and Nancy had prepared.

While they ate, the girls were happy to relate their journey down, and they also told how Julia was able to get Rill to come along. As it turned out, her brother-in-law George Sweetland had played a main role in the scheme. Julia had told him of her intentions one day to take Rill down to Monticello with her. She knew he had already tried posting Rill's letters to Gabriel, and thought he may be willing to help in another way. He was hesitant at first, but eventually agreed.

How it worked out was on the day that they were supposed to catch their train, George had a load of firewood to deliver to Doc Montgomery's office in the village. When he was loading the wagon with the wood in the morning, he pretended to have smashed his hand and asked Hannah to let Rill help him make the delivery. The ruse worked perfectly, Hannah agreed and once she was back inside and out of sight, he went right onto the road instead of left and dropped Rill off at the Cooks' place, before taking the longer route around the western side of the lake into town. When he got home in the afternoon, he was supposed to tell Hannah that Rill had run off in town, for by then she would already be safely on the train.

After eating, the boys told their many stories of camp, and of all the trouble they had been having with Captain Marvin. By then they had heard about what Marvin had done to Lieutenant Moffat after Moffat's wife and daughter came over crying about it during lunch. The boys showed off their uniforms too and all their new soldiering equipment. The women commented on how shiny and new everything looked, and the boys replied that it didn't all get that clean on its own.

"Well, it's about time you men learned how to do your own laundry," Julia Cook teased them.

As the afternoon progressed, the group of Dryden folks enjoyed their time chatting and visiting along the lakeshore. Even the boys without families came over to see some familiar faces from home. Some of the folks were surprised to see that Martha Marsh had made the trip, especially when they saw who she was sitting next to all day. Gabriel caught a lot of playful teasing from the other men. They couldn't help themselves, but to come over and put their two cents in.

"Last I heard from your sister, this boy was causing you all the trouble in the world, ma'am. Would you like me to haul him away?" some of the boys would say. Rill played right along with them though.

"Oh, no, I've changed my mind," she would tell them, or "No, he's not troubling me now, but I'll be sure to call for help if he does." Gabriel loved that about her. He thought her quick wit and sense of humor where some of her best qualities.

Toward evening, everyone was getting restless because they knew that their time together was drawing to a close. Some of the men gathered wood for a fire and they planned to have a dance by its light. The Cooks noticed that Gabriel and Rill hadn't had any private time together, so Enos said that he was going to sneak Matilda and Ellie Moffat over to see William at the barracks. Julia said she was coming along too and that she was going to take a plate of food to Dave Nash as well.

"What if Marvin finds out?" Gabriel asked.

"I'm usually one to play by the rules, Gabriel, but keeping a man from his wife and daughter is downright despicable. I'm willing to risk the consequences. Captain Marvin's off with his family in Monticello anyway. I hear they're spending the night in a hotel and won't be back till morning, so we should be fine."

Gabriel was surprised at Enos. He usually tried hard to follow the letter of the law, but this was something he obviously felt strongly about, and Gabriel couldn't blame him. He couldn't imagine what he would have done if Marvin tried telling him he couldn't see Rill.

"Would you like Rill and I to come along too, Enos?" Gabriel asked.

"Absolutely not. No, you sit right here and keep that girl warm and happy," Enos told him.

Gabriel smiled and reached for Rill's hand.

"Thanks, Enos," he said. "We've been talking though, and I think we may just take a little stroll down the lake if you don't mind."

"That's a wonderful idea," Julia Cook said as she and her daughter were helping Matilda Moffat gather up a basket of food. "You kids go have some fun."

Gabriel and Rill couldn't wait to get away. They had been practically glued to each other all day, but didn't have much of a chance to say what they wanted to. The shore of the lake was beautiful, and the sky was turning into a romantic blue twilight.

"Oh, Gabriel, I'm so happy to finally be alone with you. There's so much I want to tell; I just don't know where to begin."

Gabriel didn't say anything. He just smiled and kept walking with her, hand in hand, as she rubbed his palm with her thumb in a soothing sort of way. The light from the campfires behind them slowly began to fade as they made their way down the shore. When she thought they were out of view, Rill had Gabriel stop so she could lean up and give him a kiss. It was what Gabriel had been waiting for all day. He kissed her long and hard and then, like the day he had come to tell her he was enlisting, she took him by the hand and led him away to somewhere more private.

Gabriel dutifully followed behind her as she took him from the shoreline into a stand of timber. It was mostly beech, red oak, and sugar maple, and the forest floor was covered in a thick and cushioned bed of dry leaves. Once they had gone in about 100 yards, Rill spotted a massive downed log with an indentation in the ground on one end where its ancient root ball had been pulled up from the soil during a violent storm many years before.

"This is a perfect spot," she said. "Nice and comfortable, and if we lay into it right, we'll be almost out of sight."

Letting go of his hand, she got down onto her knees and then leaned back into the soft little depression. It was quite dark in the woods, the branches of the trees blotting out most of the light from the moon and the stars. There was just enough however, Gabriel noticed, to make Rill's brilliant almond hazels glow.

After getting situated she motioned for him to join her. He did and they held each other and kissed for a long time until Gabriel could hold back no longer. Near panting he sat up and pulled off his hat and coat and threw then to the side. Then, Rill helped his suspenders down off his shoulders and unbuttoned his trousers too, and as he was tugging them down over his waist, she lay back again into their bed to pull up her dress and give him access. Gabriel got into position between her thighs and Rill grabbed ahold of him and gently guided him in. When they'd finished Gabriel leaned in fully on top of her and out of breath. She kissed him on the cheek and neck and ran her fingers through his hair a few times before he rolled back off her and got dressed again.

He felt cold and figured she'd be feeling the same.

"Why don't we go back by the fire now, Rill, where its warm," he asked her.

She looked disappointed. "No, let's just lay here, Gabriel. We only have about an hour to go and I'd rather spend it alone. If you come back down here and hold me, we'll be plenty warm enough together."

Gabriel agreed and snuggled in beside her. They just lay there on their backs together looking up through branches at what stars they could see and whispering anything that came to mind. A couple of times, they heard rustling in the woods around them, but the sounds faded, and they soon forgot about them.

Gabriel told Rill more stories about camp, and about some of the boys from Sullivan County whom he'd befriended, while Rill caught him up on his family. She told how his mother had been very depressed, but was managing since he'd gone, and how his brother Sam had been working hard to fill the void his absence left on the farm. Gabriel asked her about how her home life had been and what she would do when she got home.

"Will your sister let you back?" he worried.

"I think so and if not, I can always go to stay with Uncle Gus or Roch in the village. Uncle Roch has always said he could find a place for me in his home if worse came to worse."

Gabriel felt reassured.

"Well good, Rill," he said, "I guess I won't worry on that anymore. Sure wouldn't want to be your brother-in-law right now though."

Rill giggled.

"No, I guess I wouldn't either, but when I get home I'll take all the blame. Did you know that when he asked me to help him to town, I truly believed that's what I was doing? I had no idea I was coming to see you. It was all their plan, Julia and his. I didn't think much of it when he went right instead of left onto the road, I guess I figured he had some other errand to run first, then he stopped the wagon in front of the Cook place and said to get going. I didn't know what he meant and then he told me to just go in and talk with Julia and I would find out. I had no idea, absolutely none. When Julia told me what we were doing I didn't believe her at first. I was still unsure until we got to the train station and all the other families were there. That's when I knew it was true. I couldn't help but cry, Gabriel. I was so happy."

Rill had some bad news to pass on, too. Enos and Julia's son had been captured by the Confederates.

"My God when did it happen? Where?" Gabriel questioned her in rapid succession.

"Somewhere in Virginia last month, that's all we know. One of James's friends wrote Julia. The letter came a few days ago. It's so sad Gabriel, I hope he's okay."

"Me too, Rill. Me too. When does Julia plan on telling Enos?" Gabriel asked her.

"I think she was going to tell him at the end of the night. She wanted him to enjoy their time together," Rill said.

James Cook was about Gabriel's age, and they went to the same schoolhouse when they were kids. He had always been a nice boy, but mostly kept to himself. Everyone else at the school thought he was a bit of a pansy, which made it all the more surprising when he was one of the first from town to join up. Rill knew him well, too. They shared the same house together when she first moved up from the city. Hannah and George had lived with the Cooks at the time. He was always too shy to talk much with her, though.

Before they knew it, it was time to start getting back and Gabriel was leading Rill out of the woods to the lakeshore again. Funny thing, though, as they reached the shore, they saw several other couples making their way out of the woods, too. They all had a different excuse for what they had been up to. One couple said that they had "gotten lost," and another that the gentleman's hat had blown off his head and into the woods and they were trying to find it.

"Strange, I didn't feel a strong wind did you, Gabriel?" Rill asked him jokingly.

They all knew what each other had been up to but couldn't bear to admit it.

"Must have been all that rustling we heard," Gabriel said.

CHAPTER SEVEN

Saying goodbye to Rill that night was difficult for Gabriel. It hurt and made him feel physically ill knowing they'd be parting again for the foreseeable future. Seeing how well Enos handled the news of his son inspired him, though, and he was almost able to say farewell to her without shedding a tear. Many of the families, especially the Sullivan County ones, stuck around until the regiment marched away the next day, but Rill and the two Cook girls took off on the morning stage for Cochecton.

"I just don't think we can handle seeing you boys march away," Julia Cook had said, "so let's just get our goodbyes over with now." Julia was also anxious to get home. She was still waiting for word on her son and it worried her that it may have already arrived and was waiting for her in Dryden.

For some of the other Dryden boys, saying their goodbyes a second time was too much for them to handle. George Wright and James Wait decided they'd had enough and deserted after the flag ceremony. They were long gone by the time the 10:30 roll call discovered them missing.

When the regiment finally left camp on the 10th of October, they did so on foot, marching all the way to Wurtsboro the first day and then to Middletown the next. It was their first taste of campaigning and for the most part everyone made it through okay. Dave Nash was the only one from Company I to have any trouble, but it wasn't because of any physical weakness on his part. Near lunch time on their second day's march to Middletown, Dave passed out of formation and fell into the roadway, his body seizing and contorting itself every which way. Colonel Dewitt who happened to be marching alongside Company I at the time, quickly stopped to help the convulsing Dave.

"Get this man some water!" he called out as he placed Dave's head in his lap.

Several men reached for their canteens, but before they could hand them over Andrew Farrell shot out of the formation with a small pocket-sized bottle.

"Don't give that man any water, he needs some of this," Andrew said holding up the bottle for all to see.

He knelt down and carefully emptied the mysterious contents into Dave's mouth. It wasn't a moment before Dave regained consciousness and rose to his feet as if nothing had happened.

"Thank ye, Andrew, my boy," Dave amicably said as he found his place back in formation. "Longest I've been deprived since I was a youngster," he informed them.

Colonel Dewitt, thinking he had witnessed a miracle, stood up himself and congratulated Andrew on a job well done.

"Remarkable work young man," he said as he took hold of Andrew's hand and shook it vigorously. "May I ask the name of the elixir you've just administered?"

"Elixir? Oh no, Sir, that's no potion. That's just corn whiskey," Andrew said, tossing the empty bottle aside. As he rejoined the marching ranks, he left his perplexed colonel to his lonesome on the side of the road, scratching his head.

In Middletown, the regiment boarded a train for New York City. They were packed in like sardines, and after a half day's march from Wurtsboro, they smelled not much better. When they arrived in New York, seeing the city was quite the shock for the Dryden boys. The immense size of it was unlike anything they could have ever imagined. Never had they seen so many people or buildings, especially buildings as large as the ones in the city. Most of them found it rather intimidating. After departing the train station, they were marched to City Hall Square and quartered in the barracks there. The square was heavily guarded and due to their very limited time in residence no one was given permission to leave unless, under special circumstances, they were given a pass by their company commander.

By the time they reached the barracks, it was well into the evening. Once they were dismissed by Captain Marvin, the boys from Company I quickly made for their bunks and stripped off their gear. Being that they were still green troops, their bodies weren't quite conditioned to move about for so long with all that weight strapped to them. Everyone was rather exhausted, and it wasn't long before they were all fast asleep. That is, everyone but David Ferris and Andrew Farrell. As had regularly happened at Camp Holley, David Ferris lost his balance and fell into Andrew on the march to City Hall Square. Unfortunate for the two boys, Captain Marvin was quick to notice the blunder and in consequence he gave them the lamentable task of guarding the company's gear all night.

The next morning the soldiers bellies were grumbling and to their displeasure they got their first taste of Army cuisine, hardtack and salt pork with a little coffee to wash it down. Hardtack was a square flour and water cracker and was to be a mainstay in their diets in the months and years ahead. It was roughly three inches square and a half inch thick in size, and about as hard as a grindstone. Salt pork was just a piece of pig meat that was highly salted for preservation. Watching the men get this first introduction was a comical scene.

"I think it'd be better to shoot this hardtack to pieces rather than crack my teeth trying to grind it down to swallowing size," one of them had said. Some men tried crushing it between two stones, while others had some success breaking it apart with a hammer they found left behind in the barracks. As for the salt pork most just fried it or closed their eyes and choked it down raw. Some of the men from Company I complained when their ration had no meat to it at all, just fat, while Company A got a rancid barrel of the stuff and were given a double portion of hardtack in compensation.

Retreating to the outside wall of one of the barracks, Gabriel and Enos sat down to inspect their breakfast.

"Well I've found if you soak the hardtack long enough in your coffee, you can just about turn it from stone to a more chewable leather," Enos shared.

"I suppose so," Gabriel said, "but I can't eat this pork."

"Sure you can, just take a bite and swallow."

"No, you don't understand Enos, I can't eat it," Gabriel said, holding up his piece for Enos to see. It was basically just a hunk of fat attached to a thick piece of pigskin with bristly white hair still sprouting from it. Enos's face contorted in disgust.

"I'm sure they'd let you trade it in," he suggested.

"I think I'll just pass," Gabriel decided.

Seeing his two friends mulling over their meals, Dave Nash trotted over to them in a jovial mood.

"Top of the mornin' to ya boys. How's your breakfast?"

"We've had better," Gabriel grumbled.

"Where's yours?" Enos asked.

"Eaten," Dave said. "I'll tell you it's not so bad after you've had a few."

"When have you ever eaten this stuff before?" Gabriel asked.

"I haven't, I mean a few drinks, it goes down easier after you've had some whiskey," Dave said.

"Oh," Gabriel responded, slightly embarrassed at his naivety.

"Now how were you able to find whiskey in a place like this?" Enos asked Dave incredulously.

"Are ya kiddin' me, Cookie? This place is awash in it. Just about every one of these guards has a canteen full lyin' around. I just walked up to one when he was lookin' the other way and traded mine for his."

Gabriel and Enos laughed.

"You're something else Dave Nash. You're something else," Enos told him.

"You two hear about Farrell and Ferris yet?" Dave inquired.

They both shook their heads in the negative.

"Well they're in trouble again. Marvin caught Ferris nappin' at his post last night, so now he's got them watchin' our gear all day long too."

"When are they supposed to sleep then?" Enos questioned him.

"They're not, as far as I can tell," Dave said. "At least not until this evenin.'"

Once again Gabriel felt terrible for Andrew Farrell. He didn't care much for David Ferris of course, but Andrew, albeit a drunk at times, was a good friend, and didn't deserve to keep taking the rap for Ferris's mistakes.

"Boy, I wish there was something we could do for Andrew," Gabriel said.

"I agree," Enos chimed in. "I wish there was something we could do for both of the boys. That's just madness. Captain Marvin has to know there's no way they're gonna make it through the rest of the day without dozing off."

After shooting the breeze a while longer, Dave decided to move along.

"I think I'm developin' another thirst," he said, scratching his chin as he walked away.

Gabriel and Enos continued to lounge about alongside the barracks. It was sunny there now, and it was a welcome warmth as the mornings had been getting chilly. They sat and discussed what to do with their day. Colonel Dewitt, their regimental commander, had given them the day off to roam their temporary confines, because there really wasn't enough room around the barracks to parade about.

"Sure wouldn't mind taking a stroll around the city," Enos said. "Not a chance of Captain Marvin giving us a pass though."

"I know," Gabriel agreed. "I wouldn't mind going out either. You know Rill gave me her father's address the other night when she heard we were making a stop down here. I figured there was no chance I'd make it there, but I just played along and told her I'd try, to please her."

"Really?" Enos said. "That would be something, he visited a couple times back when the Sweetlands lived with me. He's a bit odd, likes to talk, but exceedingly nice and a gracious guest. He brought gifts along for James and Nancy when he came. I wouldn't mind stopping by to return the favor."

Lieutenant Moffat, who happened to be sitting nearby enjoying his coffee and the morning sun, came over to Gabriel and Enos and invited himself into their conversation.

"Excuse me, gentlemen," he said all prim and proper like, "but I just happened to incidentally overhear your conversation. As it turns out, I too have some errands I would like to attend to in the city and I was wondering if you'd like to join me."

Enos chuckled. "Well, Lieutenant, we'd love to oblige your invitation, but you know as well as us that there's no way the Captain's gonna be giving out passes to any of us."

"Private Cook, your skepticism offends me," Moffat said half-jokingly. "Follow me, boys, and I'll prove you wrong," he added, before turning away in the direction of Captain Marvin. Marvin was standing not 100 paces distant conferring with Company D's Captain Higgins. Enos and Gabriel looked at each other and shrugged, then got up and followed, both curious and thinking they had nothing to lose by tagging along.

The surprisingly cocky lieutenant made his way to the two captains with Enos and Gabriel behind him. He gave them both the proper military salutes and greetings before turning directly to Captain Marvin to speak.

"Captain Marvin, could I trouble you, Sir, for three passes for the two Privates and myself?" he said gesturing to Enos and Gabriel. "I have got some special errands I need to attend to in the city, and I would like to have them along to assist me."

Captain Marvin looked slightly annoyed at the request, but he answered in the affirmative.

"Certainly, Lieutenant," he said, as he reached for a small notebook tucked away in an inside pocket of his frock coat.

Enos and Gabriel stood silent, but inside they were overcome with joy and disbelief. When he finished composing the notes, Marvin handed them out to each of the men and called out their names as he did so.

"Here you are Private Ballard, Private Cook, Lieutenant Moffat. These are good until this evening, I will advise you be punctual though, as there is a possibility we may be shipping out of here tonight."

Before stepping away, Enos and Gabriel thanked Captain Marvin graciously and then followed Lieutenant Moffat to the nearest gate. When they were out of earshot of Marvin, Enos spoke up.

"You two know me, I usually don't swear, but how in the hell did you just pull that off? What is it that you've got on him, William?" Enos asked, briefly forgetting he wasn't talking to a civilian anymore. Moffat didn't seem to mind though.

"Yes, Lieutenant," Gabriel chimed in, "what just happened?"

Basking in the glory of his recent victory over Marvin, Lieutenant Moffat decided to enlighten them with the tale.

"Well boys, last night after we got here, I went up to the officers' quarters in search of my trunk, as the supply wagons had just arrived and were being unloaded. I was lucky to pass Private Ferris along the way and he informed me that he had just unloaded my things and had placed them next to my assigned bunk. Upon reaching my bunk I went for my trunk in search of a change of shirt, as mine was considerably soiled from our journey. I saw that my trunk had been unlatched, which I thought quite queer, as I am the only one with the key. I quickly flung open the lid fearing I had been robbed. When I opened the lid though I realized that it wasn't my trunk after all, but someone else's. Mine, as it turns out, hadn't been unloaded yet. It was Marvin's, and it was nearly bursting with liquor, each bottle wrapped in one of his various clothing items for protection."

"How did you know it was the Captain's?" Enos asked.

"Yes, and how didn't you notice it was someone else's?" Gabriel added.

"Well," Moffat explained, "I knew that it was the Marvin's, because when he came in the room shortly after I opened it, he ran over, slammed the lid shut and accused me of rifling through his belongings. I thought that the trunk was mine because it was identical to the one Matilda purchased for me from a traveling salesman in Dryden. Evidentially Marvin purchased his from the same man."

"Unbelievable," Enos said.

"Oh, believe it, my dear Enos," Moffat told him.

"Well that still doesn't tell us why he's being nice to you Lieutenant, shouldn't he be angry?" Gabriel asked.

"Well he is angry with me, but that's not the point. The point is, he shouldn't be toting around the amount of liquor he had stashed away in there. Why, if Colonel Dewitt found out, he could have him cashiered. They don't want to have drunks in their officer corps, especially greenhorns like us who haven't seen any action to possibly even warrant us washing away our sorrows. With the amount of liquor in his chest, he has clearly got a problem."

"I suppose you're right," Gabriel admitted.

After showing their passes to the gate guard and being let outside, Lieutenant Moffat parted ways with Gabriel and Enos.

"Alright, boys," he said, "lets meet here at 6 P.M. I don't want us showing up to the barracks at separate times. I'm going to go and buy some things to send to my Matilda. You two can do what you like. Go find Mr. Marsh. Maybe he'll be able to feed you something a little more substantial than hardtack and sow belly."

"We can't thank you enough, William, or uh… I mean Lieutenant," Enos said.

"Yes, Lieutenant, thanks for everything. We owe you," Gabriel added.

"You two don't owe me nothing, Gabriel. If you want to thank someone, you can thank Private Ferris for directing me to the wrong trunk."

* * * * *

Gabriel and Enos were certainly naive to think they could just walk out into New York City for the first time and find a random person's residence on their own. They had lots of luck on their side though, for after conferring with one of the camp guards who was familiar with the area, they found out that Mr. Marsh lived not that far away. The guard was able to direct them to the correct neighborhood, and then once there they asked a passing policeman if he knew where the home of Mr. James Monroe Marsh was located. As it turned out, the officer they asked was very familiar with Mr. Marsh. In fact, he said he had once rented a room from him for a time. He then walked the two men to the Marsh home and before leaving shook both their hands and thanked them.

"My little brother, God rest his soul, is buried under Malvern Hill," he confided, then tipped his cap to them and walked away.

The Marsh home was a wood framed duplex. Very simple, but taken care of. They lived in one half and rented out the other. Enos walked up to the door the officer had pointed to with his club and taking hold of the brass knocker, struck it several times and stepped back to wait for an answer. They stood for only a moment before they heard the locking mechanism being undone and the door opened to reveal an attractive, but conservatively dressed woman inside. She had raven black hair, dark brown eyes, and a very dark gray dress on that was tightly buttoned up to the notch in her neck. Her face, although very pretty, was severely lacking in emotion and when she spoke, she was brief and to the point.

"What do you want?" she said to the two soldiers outside.

Enos removed his hat from his head and spoke up first.

"Good morning, ma'am. My name is Enos Cook and this here is Gabriel Ballard. We're both from up to Dryden and we've been told this is the home of Mr. James Monroe Marsh."

"Yes, it is," said the woman.

"Well, ma'am, we were wondering if we could see him if it isn't too much of a bother?" Enos inquired.

The woman stepped back and opened the door wide motioning for the men to come in. As they did so, she shut it behind them, locked it and said to them, "follow me." It was somewhat eerie inside the home. All the doors were closed, the walls were void of anything but their gray wall-papering and the only furniture in sight was a single rigid looking chair next to the entrance. Gabriel stuck close to Enos as they followed the woman beyond the main staircase to a door at the end of the foyer. She opened the door and led them into what appeared to be an office, much more lively, unorganized and lit than the other portion of the house they had seen. In the back off the room sat a paper strewn desk, with a sunlit window behind it. In between the window and the desk sat a man reading a newspaper.

"Two ruffians from Dryden," the woman tersely announced before slamming the door shut behind them.

The bang of the door caused the man to leap out of his chair, and with a shout he tossed his paper into the air from fright. As the paper fluttered to the floor, it revealed the face of a startled man. His hair was brown, his eyes blue and mouth wide open in astonishment. He was slightly shorter than Gabriel in height, wore an unkempt and open green corduroy coat, with a maroon vest, a floral-patterned puff tie, and plaid pants. Once he regained his composure, a smile quickly grew on his face and then he began to speak.

"Who is this? Two boys from Dryden. Two soldiers I see. Wonderful, wonderful. Do I know you? Yes, I believe I do, I do. I do know you. You, Sir," he said pointing towards Enos. "You're Mr. Cook, the friend of George, my son-in-law. His landlord when I visited a few years ago, are you not? How are you, Sir? What brings you to New York?"

Enos tried to answer, but Mr. Marsh kept talking. He was very energetic, and Gabriel found him most entertaining. His smile was infectious, and Gabriel couldn't help but smile right along with him.

"Oh, who am I kidding, you're both with the Army of course. Passing through on your way to Washington, no doubt. You must forgive me; I am so absent-minded at times. And you, you, yes, you. Who are you, young man?" He was pointing at Gabriel now.

"Gabriel, Sir. My name is Gabriel Ballard. I'm a friend of your…"

"My daughter, Martha. Yes, yes, I know you, too. I know your father. Good man. I know your grandfather as well, your uncles even, all good men. They like to have a good time, don't they?"

Gabriel nodded his head in the affirmative, as Mr. Marsh kept talking and answering most of his own questions.

"My Martha, she's quite smitten with you, isn't she? My Hannah, though, she is not. She says you're the Devil's disciple. A heathen, a no-good scoundrel even, ha, ha, ha."

Gabriel's face turned sour, but Mr. Marsh set him at ease.

"No, no, Mr. Ballard, don't get the wrong idea, Sir. I know my girls, ha, ha. Martha is my angel and Hannah…well, Hannah is…well, ha, ha, ha, ha… lets just say she's not my angel, ha, ha, but I love them all the same. I do, truly I do. Martha, if you must know, she takes after my first wife, the girl's mother. Martha as well, the kindest of souls, but Hannah, well, she does not. She is more like her step-mother, ha, ha, but please God, oh my goodness gracious, no, no, no. Oh, please God, don't tell her I said that. If she were to find out, she'd have me shot and stuffed and put on display in her parlor like a wooden Indian."

Mr. Marsh was suddenly very concerned and clasped his hands together in a pleading manner. The worried look on his face quickly grew into a new smile though and he returned to his talking.

"Yes, the girl's step-mother, my Victoria. Yes, you've just met her, you did. Did you know? Yes, oh no, well no, no, yes, no how could you have known? She's the one who showed you in."

Gabriel was shocked. He had no idea that was Victoria, but once he knew, he could easily see why Rill disliked her so. Enos stood there shaking his head in the affirmative or negative to each one of the questions Mr. Marsh had asked them and his neck, was getting tired.

"She's quite the looker is she not?" Mr. Marsh asked as he shook his own head yes and raised his eyebrows several times in rapid succession. "Well, I'll let you boys in on a little secret, ha, ha. She may look good fully clothed, but she looks even better in bed, ha, ha, if you know what I mean, and she can suck and fuck like no woman I've ever known. Why I'd wager she could coax a frightened clam out of its shell with her tongue and she humps like Venus. She's got the sexual appetite of a field mouse too, and at the end of each day I have to fight her off with a stick just so that I have enough skin left on my prick for the next day's escapades."

Gabriel's jaw dropped open in awe and Enos had to reach over and close it for him.

"Might I recommend to you two gentlemen if you are ever given the opportunity of remarrying in your old age, do so with a younger woman. My Victoria is 12 years my junior and you can see all the fun I get to have. Please, gentlemen, don't be getting the wrong idea about her, though. She is the soul of fidelity and the most devout individual I have ever known. She was raised in a nunnery, you see, hence the plain appearance of our home, and her clothing, besides my office, of course, which she permits me to decorate as I wish. To date, she has given me five healthy children and although she can be moody at times, for me it is all worth it in the end."

After he finished his last sentence there was a light but rhythmic knock at the office door. At hearing the knock, Mr. Marsh jumped, regained his composure and then made his way to the door and out of the room. As he was walking out, he spoke to Gabriel and Enos.

"Excuse me, gentlemen, I will be right back. Just give me a moment to go and help Victoria with something."

When he had left, the two of them just stood there, both a little overwhelmed by the reception of their eccentric host and enjoying the brief peace and quiet. The moment however did not last long, as they soon heard a loud banging coming from the room next door. Then there was a sudden crash of crockery, followed by a low but prolonged moan from what appeared to be a woman's voice. When the moan ended, they could then hear footsteps leaving the adjacent room and the opening of the office door to reveal Mr. Marsh. As he walked in, though, Gabriel and Enos couldn't help but notice that his pants were undone in the front and his green corduroy jacket was now inside out.

"Please excuse my absence gentlemen, Victoria needed some help in the other room."

Instead of standing as he had before, Mr. Marsh sat behind his desk and asked his guest to kindly sit down in the two leather cushioned chairs in front of him. He was noticeably less energetic than before, which for some reason seemed to please Gabriel and Enos.

"Mr. Cook, please tell me, how are your lovely wife and children doing?"

Enos was hesitant to respond, expecting Mr. Marsh to cut him off again, but he didn't, so Enos spoke up.

"My wife and daughter are doing well, Sir, they are at home, of course, but my son is currently a prisoner of the Confederate government. He is a soldier with the 10th Cavalry and was captured in Virginia just under a month ago."

Mr. Marsh sat up in his seat.

"My deepest condolences, Sir. May I humbly apologize for bringing up your recent sorrow. Please, Sir, forgive my asking."

Enos quickly reassured him with the wave of his hand that there was no offence taken.

"Not at all, Mr. Marsh. You had no idea, and honestly, I'm at peace with things as they stand. It could be much worse, he may have been killed, so we are just thankful it didn't come to that. I pray daily for him to be paroled."

Gabriel felt awkward. Enos was usually quite private regarding his family, and Gabriel had yet to hear him speak of James's capture. It was also strange now for him to see Mr. Marsh turn so serious, especially after hearing him and his wife in the other room and with his clothes in such an embarrassing disarray, as they currently were.

"As you should, as you should, Mr. Cook, and might I add that he will now be in my thoughts and prayers and in the prayers of my wife and children. I will not mince words with you, gentlemen. I will not lie. I am not a fan of this war. No, gentlemen I am not in the least. I have lost too many friends along Bull Run, down on the peninsula and at Antietam, and I am fed up with it. Too many poor boys going off to die for the rich men in this country, and it's all over nothing but the slaves. Sure, Lincoln says it's to preserve the Union and Jeff Davis says it's to fight off the Yankee invaders, but don't let them fool you, it's over slavery. The Southern plantation owner wants to keep his slaves, because he doesn't have to pay them, and they make him rich. Then you've got the Northern factory owners. They want to outlaw slavery in the south, but it's not because they think it's immoral, or inhumane, they're just jealous that they have to pay for their labor and the plantation owners don't. And don't let them fool you either. They like to align themselves with those looney intellectuals that call them-selves abolitionist. They don't buy into their bullshit, though. They just know they're crazy and will do their dirty work for them. If you don't believe me, look what happened with John Brown. That man was out of his gourd. He was a lunatic and a murderer, but they didn't care, not even when he stormed one of our arsenals, and killed one of our Marines. You know what's ironic is the first person they killed on that raid was a free negro named Heyward Shepherd. The man had a wife and five kids at home, and they blew him away like dust in the wind. Now they make the man into a national hero and write a song about him. "John Browns Body." What a disgrace. Those fucking newspapers are unbelievable. They're filth, only good for getting a fire going or wiping your ass with. That's what I'm gonna do with this one here once I'm done perusing through its lies."

Mr. Marsh pointed to the paper on the floor that he'd tossed in the air when they first arrived.

"Don't get me wrong, gentlemen. I am not in support human bondage. I'm firmly against it, but there has got to be another way to end it than the killing of our boys. Your boy, Mr. Cook, you, Mr. Ballard", he pointed at them. "Those southern streams are running red with our babies' blood. There has got to be another way; there should be another way, but please don't ask me what that is because I don't know. Trust me when I say that I have tried to work it out, though. Let me tell you gentlemen, since after Bull Run last July, if I'm not fucking or feeding when I'm awake, I'm in here trying to solve this nation's problems in my head. It's affecting me, too, gentlemen. I am a happy man. This person you're hearing speak to you now is not the normal James Monroe Marsh. Yes, physically this is me," Mr. Marsh began wildly grabbing himself all over, then he pointed to his head, "but up here, this is not. This up here is another man, a sad man."

As Mr. Marsh paused to catch his breath, another rhythmic knock came tapping at the door. Slowly he stood to his feet, his eyes closed, and he began rubbing his temples with his middle and fore fingers.

"Gentlemen, please excuse me for a moment," he said despondently, and slowly walked to the office door and stepped outside again closing it behind him. Neither Gabriel nor Enos spoke or looked at each other. What Mr. Marsh had just said to them had left them both in deep and serious thought. Their concentration was soon interrupted however, by that same banging sound coming from the room next door. This time though, there was no breaking crockery, instead they heard what sounded like a table collapsing onto the floor, and then a great moan of ecstasy from the voice of a man. Then, like before, they heard footsteps leaving the adjacent room, followed by the office door rattling open and in came Mr. Marsh again. His green coat was now back to normal, and everything else appeared in place as well, other than the fact that his plaid pants were now somehow missing. He still had his long underwear covering his legs and nether regions, but it was outlandish none the less.

"My apologies, gentlemen," he said as joined them again. "Victoria needed some more assistance. You boys understand, I'm sure."

Mr. Marsh appeared to be back to his normal and energetic self. He bounded over to his desk, but instead of sitting behind it he came around to the front and sat on top to be closer to Gabriel. To clear a spot for himself, he simply took his arm and swiped a pile of his papers onto the floor.

"There we go," he said, as he sat down and made himself comfortable. "You two must know my brothers, Rochester and Augustus. They're well known in your area."

They both nodded yes.

"You know, I was born in Cortland County myself, two years after our second war with Britain. Did you know that? Yes, I believe you did. You, Mr. Cook," he said, pointing at Enos again, "you knew because I told you on my last visit. Well, believe it or not, Mr. Ballard, I am in fact a Cortland County native, as is your father's family. Am I correct?"

"Yes, Sir. At least that's where Father was mostly brought up, he was born in New Jersey though," Gabriel was miraculously able to answer.

"Yes, quite right, yes. Well, anyway, I am a native of up there, but I don't quite fit in. They think I'm mad, you see, and after my first wife passed away, the girls and I moved down here. I met with my dear Victoria soon afterwards and hired her to watch the girls while I was at work, but we soon fell in love. These are my people gentlemen. Down here I feel much more at home, and believe it or not I have quite the following for some reason, especially among the young men in the neighborhood. Take my neighbors for instance, the four young men who live next door. The other half of this building is my rental property, you see, but anyway those men adore me, always shaking my hand when they pass me on the street and calling my name from their windows to cheer when I come home. Peculiar boys they are, though. They like to have what Victoria and I call their quiet parties. You see, almost every night they have half the boys in the neighborhood over, even our local patrolman, one of my old tenants attends on occasion. Anyway, they go in there, but they make not a sound, not a whisper. It is the strangest thing, they are young strapping men, they should be raising all sorts of Cain over there, but they don't. They just go in and they're as quiet as the dead. It's almost as if they're listening for something, but I haven't a clue what."

Suddenly there was another rhythmic knocking at the door, and Mr. Marsh looked up.

"That woman," he muttered in an annoyed tone under his breath, then he spoke up in his normally jovial manner. "Yes my dear," he called out to the hallway. "I am coming. Just give me a minute. I'm about to introduce young Mr. Ballard to Holy Peter."

Mr. Marsh turned to give his undivided attention to Gabriel, as a door slammed wildly out in the hall. It startled Mr. Marsh off his seat again, but after realizing it had just been his wife throwing a tantrum, he shot an annoyed glance at the door and sat back down.

"Young Mr. Ballard," he said, "may I ask you your intentions with my daughter?"

Gabriel felt like he was in the spotlight all the sudden. Beads of sweat instantly formed on his brow and he struggled for a moment to answer. Enos sat smiling from his chair. As a father of a young girl himself, he was enjoying the predicament he now found his young friend in.

"Well, Sir," he started to say, "well, I don't know Sir, I…I do like her… if that's what you're asking?"

"Well, of course I know you like her boy, but do you love her?" Mr. Marsh blurted out.

"Well, Sir…why…why yes, Sir. I do," Gabriel answered. An instant wave of relief crept over him.

"Good answer young man, good answer," Mr. Marsh said as he leaned backwards and pulled something from a drawer in his desk. He turned around and in between his pointer finger and thumb he held a long but pencil thin piece of clear cylindrical glass.

"Do you know what this is, Mr. Ballard?" Mr. Marsh asked, while staring him down intently.

"Why, yes, Sir, that looks like a piece of glass to me," Gabriel answered.

"Quite right, quite right, young Ballard. It is a piece of glass, but more specifically it is a stir stick. You see, I use it to mix the sugar into my morning cup of tea. I like to call it Holy Peter, though. In fact, my dear wife Victoria came up with the name. Undoubtedly, you do recognize the religious reference. Holy Peter is actually a multi-use tool, though, Mr. Ballard. Would you like to guess its other use, or just have me explain it to you?" Mr. Marsh asked him.

Gabriel hesitated again, but Mr. Marsh started talking before he could answer anyway.

"How about I just tell you," he said with his infectious smile.

Gabriel nodded his head yes, and he couldn't help but smile back at Mr. Marsh as he did so.

"The stick," Mr. Marsh began to explain, holding Holy Peter up for all to see, "should be lubricated before use with a grease or oil, perhaps heated lard or blubber even. It is then slowly inserted into the urethra, your pee hole if you're unfamiliar with the anatomical term, young man. Next the penis should be place on a hard surface, perhaps lets say the edge of a table or desk would best suffice, and then you just, SMASH! BANG! TWIST! SMASH!"

Mr. Marsh beat his hand on his desk for effect, as Gabriel and Enos instinctively winced and place their hands over their genitals.

"And there you have it boys, a holey peter. Get it?" "Ha, ha, ha, ha, ha," Mr. Marsh laughed hysterically.

"Let me tell you, I've only had to use it once too." "Ha, ha, ha," he chuckled. "A most unfortunate occasion gentleman I can assure you. One day a few years back there was a knocking at our door and when Victoria went to answer it a young thug forced his way in and attacked my dear wife. He tore her blouse in two, exposing her breast and tried to tear away her dress. I was here in my study of course and when I heard all of the commotion I ran out of the room to the hall with a brass candlestick."

Mr. Marsh pointed to a candlestick on the mantel piece above the office fireplace.

"Luckily, the man was too focused with his wickedness to notice my arrival, and a hit him over the head rendering him unconscious." "Ha, ha, ha," he chuckled again. "I was in a rage gentlemen. Can you understand?"

Gabriel and Enos, who were wide-eyed and open-mouthed at this point, vigorously nodded in the affirmative.

"I helped my dear wife to her feet, then drew the man into my office by his hair and flopped him on this very desk I am sitting on now. I was so angry, gentlemen, I didn't know what to do. All I knew was I wanted it to be something despicable. Then for a moment my eyes focused on my cup of tea and the idea for Holy Peter came to mind. Whether sent from God or the Devil, I know not which. Immediately upon my performance of the procedure though, the man regained consciousness and after realizing the condition of his person, he calmly made his way outside and threw himself under the first passing wagon. The wheels popped his belly like a ripe tomato and his guts spilled out all over the street."

The men sat silent as Mr. Marsh stared off into space, apparently still going over the gruesome details of that terrible day in his mind. He then suddenly leapt up from his seat.

"My word, gentlemen, I've left my darling Victoria waiting far too long. Please excuse me," he said as he made his way to the door and shut it behind him for the third time.

It quickly reopened though, and Mr. Marsh popped his smiling face in through the opening.

"My apologies, gentlemen. I almost forgot. You're invited to lunch. We're having sausages. I hope you don't mind. Thank you, I'll be only a minute, just a minute and I'll be back. You two just wait here, I'll be back."

With that Mr. Marsh shut the door, and as those strange sounds emanated from the adjacent room, all Gabriel or Enos could think of is how they were suddenly not so very hungry after all, especially for sausage.

* * * * *

Considering the less than appetizing breakfast they had had, after seeing the Marsh's table brimming with food upon entering their dining room, they quickly recovered their appetites and enjoyed a hardy meal. Mr. Marsh never stopped talking, though, except to put food in his mouth, and once to go and as he said, "help Victoria with something in the kitchen." Strangely they had not seen her, though, since she had let them into Mr. Marsh's office that morning and the only way they knew of her presence was through her occasional moans and the rhythmic knocking system that she utilized to summon her husband. Not once did they see any of their five children either. It was very strange, and Gabriel had a hard time imagining his dear Rill growing up in such a home.

After the meal Gabriel and Enos returned with Mr. Marsh to his office where, for the first time all day, he became the listener and asked his two guests to tell him of their time in the Army thus far, while he smoked a fat cigar. Somehow, Gabriel even gathered up the gumption to tell him of Rill's escape to see him off with the help of Julia Cook, a story Mr. Marsh took great delight in hearing and said that he was looking forward to reading the contrasting letters he would no doubt soon be receiving from his girls.

As the day began to wind down, Gabriel and Enos announced their need to return to their regiment. Mr. Marsh led them to the front door, and they bade him a friendly farewell and thanked him for all he had done for them. The only thing that Mr. Marsh asked in return was a promise from Gabriel that he would write when he had the chance. He said he would do the same.

Upon beginning their journey to their barracks, Gabriel and Enos made a deal not to say another word until they reached City Hall Square, as they had both heard enough talking that day to last them a lifetime. It wasn't long on their journey though before that deal was broken, for about halfway to camp Gabriel spotted Andrew Ferrell and David Ferris strolling across the street in the opposite direction.

"Hey where are you two going?" he called out to them, trying to be heard over the passing carts and wagons in the street between them.

Enos, not seeing them at first turned to see who Gabriel was shouting at.

"What are they up to?" he asked.

They must have not heard Gabriel because they kept walking in the opposite direction, so Gabriel called them by name and shouted a little louder.

"Andrew, David, where are you two off to? We've got to get back!"

Hearing Gabriel this time, both boys looked across the street with startled expressions, then David Ferris, realizing that they had been spotted, took off running.

"What the hell's he doing?" Gabriel thought out loud. Then he looked at Andrew, whose face turned from startled to sullen.

"I'm sorry!" Andrew shouted back. "I hope you'll forgive me!" Then he took off down the street after his companion.

Still unsure what was going on, Gabriel made as if he were going to give them chase, but Enos grabbed hold of his coat before he could take off.

"Wait Gabriel, wait a minute!", he yelled trying to get his attention. "They're gone, they're gone!"

"Gone where?" Gabriel asked, turning to his friend.

"Gone. They're leaving, Gabriel. They've quit. They're done. They're running away."

"Well, why would they do that?" Gabriel asked incredulously.

"I don't know. They're probably sick of being Captain Marvin's whipping boys, I guess. They can't hack it. Soldiering isn't for everyone, Gabriel."

"Well, shouldn't we go after them?" Gabriel asked. "Maybe we can talk some sense into Andrew. I'm sure we can bring him to reason."

"I'm afraid they're long gone by now," Enos said, "We'd never find them in this mess. Besides, we've got to be back soon, or we'll be in trouble ourselves. I'm sure somebody's noticed those two aren't at their post by now anyway, and Captain Marvin's probably on the warpath. We'd better get back quick and tell him what we just saw."

* * * * *

Enos was right. After meeting Lieutenant Moffat at the gate, the three men walked into a camp in chaos. Once it was discovered that Andrew and David had disappeared from their post, Captain Marvin had the rest of the company tearing the camp apart in search of their missing comrades. When the search came up empty, though, it became apparent that the two had likely run off, and Captain Marvin had to go to Colonel Dewitt and report them missing. Now the whole regiment was outside of their barracks doing roll call.

Things got far worse too, especially for Lieutenant Moffat. When he got to Company I's formation, Moffat approached Captain Marvin to report what Enos and Gabriel had seen. After listening to the story, though, Marvin screamed at him and said that the whole predicament was all Moffat's fault. Moffat didn't back down, though. He lost his mind, too, and the two of them got into a vicious argument in front of the whole company. It would have come to blows, if it hadn't been for the quick intervention of Lieutenant George and the company's sergeants, who were able to separate them. Moffat was playing with fire going after Marvin like he did, but in his head, he thought he still had the upper hand.

What Moffat didn't know, though, was that while he was out shopping in the city, Marvin had made an excellent move to check the dirt he had on him. He emptied his trunk of all the liquor and passed it out to the other officers in the regiment, including Major Taft, all his fellow captains, and Lieutenant-Colonel Boughton. He told them that he had bought them as gifts to celebrate their commissioning. Even Colonel Dewitt couldn't turn that down.

"This is highly unorthodox, Captain Marvin," he had said, "but one bottle can't do any harm if its consumed over time. Hell, I'm sure even George Washington must have imbibed from time to time during the Revolution."

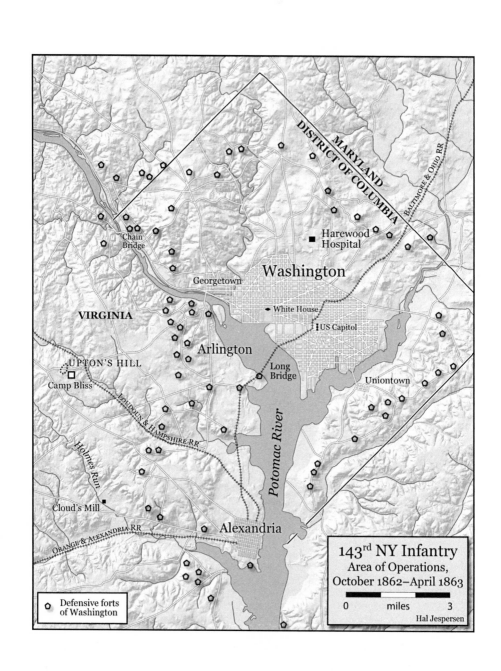

MARYLAND

DISTRICT OF COLUMBIA

BALTIMORE & OHIO RR

Chain
Bridge

■ Harewood
Hospital

Washington

Georgetown

VIRGINIA

White House

US Capitol

Arlington

UPTON'S HILL
□

Camp Bliss

Long
Bridge

Uniontown

LOUDOUN & HAMPSHIRE RR

Holmes Run

Potomac River

Cloud's Mill ■

ORANGE & ALEXANDRIA RR

Alexandria

⬠ Defensive forts
of Washington

143rd NY Infantry
Area of Operations,
October 1862–April 1863

0   miles   3

Hal Jespersen

CHAPTER EIGHT

The day after Andrew Farrell and David Ferris deserted, the regiment left New York for Washington D.C. Company I was, however, another man short, for 54-year-old Lyman Wilcox slipped away when everyone was focused on the Marvin-Moffat row. Captain Marvin was furious, but consoled himself in the reality that Wilcox was far too old and would have likely been lost through attrition in the future. Something was obviously amiss in Company I though, and its growing trend of desertion hadn't gone unnoticed by the other officers of the 143rd New York.

On their journey south, the regiment left Manhattan by boat, floating down to Perth Amboy, New Jersey. From there, they were transported by rail to and through Philadelphia, Baltimore, and finally to the nations' capital. Before leaving Camp Holley a few days before, Gabriel had never been on a boat, nor had he traveled south of the New York border, except for when they passed briefly into Pennsylvania on the train to Cochecton. The trip was an adventure for him, as well as for many of his companions. Of the men from Dryden, only Captain Marvin wasn't enjoying himself. Nine men had deserted from his company in less than two weeks, and he knew that if something didn't change very soon, he was going to find himself transferred, or worse. In fact, Colonel Dewitt had said as much to him before they left Manhattan.

After reaching Washington D.C., around lunchtime on the 14th of October, the 143rd disembarked from their train. Their baggage was loaded onto several wagons, and then they began a march through the city on their way to Arlington, which was across the Potomac River in Virginia. The men were excited, and during their march there were many undisciplined eyes, eagerly looking about with great interest at the sights the capital had to offer.

What intrigued and surprised Gabriel the most, was the large number of negroes going about their business in the city. Dryden had very few folks of color. In fact, it had been years since a black family lived within its borders, and during his lifetime Gabriel had only on a handful of occasions seen someone with a darker shade of skin than his own.

"Just look at them all, Dave," Gabriel said to Dave Nash in a genuinely impressed tone.

They had just turned a corner and were marching past a warehouse with a crowd of negro men laboring about it.

"I know, there's more negroes on this street, than I've seen in my whole life combined," Dave added.

The two sounded grossly ignorant and naïve, but coming from the isolated little northern dot on the map that they did, the diversity of the south was shocking to them at first glance and an eye-opener for Gabriel.

"What are they all doing here anyway? I thought they lived on plantations and such. Do you think their masters know where they are?" Gabriel asked.

"'Course they know," Dave said. "They got slaves in the cities too. Not all of them are farm hands."

Overhearing their conversation, Enos interjected from the rank behind.

"You know you two, they aren't all slaves. They've got free negroes down here too."

"Huh," Gabriel said. "I guess I thought all the negroes were slaves in the slave states."

"Oh, no. Actually, all the slaves here in Washington got freed a few months back. This city isn't even slave anymore. All these folks have got to be free. That, or they're slaves that live outside the city and come into it to work. I'm not exactly sure of the laws. Also, I think I read somewhere that Delaware has thousands more free negroes than slaves and Maryland has more slaves than free, but percentagewise it's almost 50/50."

"Well, I sure learned somethin' today," Dave commented.

"Glad to be of help," Enos responded in surprise, thinking Dave was being somewhat complimentary for once.

"Yes, Sir. I learned who the know-it-all out of the three of us is," he teased, and chuckled to himself.

Enos didn't take it lying down, though. When Dave lifted his right foot on his next step, Enos kicked him in the heel and Dave lurched forward almost tumbling to the ground.

"Damn you, Enos!" Dave shouted. He was just able to keep his balance. Hearing the cry, Sergeant Devaney barked back at the troops, "quiet in the ranks!", in a hoarse and bellowing voice, as the regiment continued along.

Gabriel was quite lacking in regard to his knowledge of negroes and the institution of slavery. Truthfully, he was somewhat indifferent to it all as well. It just wasn't something that was talked about often in his home. Sure, his parents didn't believe it right to own another human being, but they didn't exactly roam the hills of Dryden shouting out their views for all to hear. They were poor farmers, more concerned with raising their crops and livestock and having enough food and money for their family to survive on another year. They lived a tough existence, and the South and slavery was so far away that it seemed foreign to them. In other words, it was very low on their long list of worries. To them, the fight against slavery was a war to be waged by politicians and folks who didn't have to eke their living off the land or with their own two hands.

To cross the Potomac into Virginia, the regiment had to march over the famous span known as the Long Bridge, to Arlington. When they crossed, the fact that they were about to march into the claimed Southern Confederacy did not go unnoticed, even if it was already firmly under Union control.

"Here we go, boys!" Major Taft called out as they began to cross, "Jeff Davis thinks this is part of the Confederacy, but funny ain't it? All I see is the stars and stripes fluttering over there!"

The men broke into cheers and when they reached the other side, scores of them made it a point to sniff, cough and hack up all the phlegm their sinuses had to offer and symbolically spit on the southern soil. Some of the men had terrible aim though and accidentally hit the legs and backs of their comrades marching in front of them. This caused great laughter in the columns, which in turn was met with more calls for "quiet in the ranks!" from the non-commissioned officers.

In Arlington, the regiment was finally issued their weapons, cartridge boxes, and cap pouches. They were given Austrian-Lorenz rifles, with long sword-like bayonets.

"Told you we weren't gonna fight," Dave Nash said upon receiving his. "Fightin' regiments get Enfields and Springfields, not these things."

"A gun's a gun," Enos said, "and if it can shoot, it can kill. We'll get our chance soon enough."

"I'll believe it when I see it," Dave said.

After a very short time in Arlington, the regiment was then sent to what would be their permanent station for the time being, a place called Camp Bliss, on the slopes of Upton's Hill, just a few miles southwest of the capital. The camp was a link in the chain of defensive fortifications surrounding Washington. The most prominent structure on the hill, was Fort Ramsey, whose ramparts bristled with the muzzles of heavy artillery. While at Camp Bliss, which some of the men called Camp Dewitt, in honor of their beloved colonel, the boys from the 143rd were a part of the so-called garrison of Washington, regiments stationed at the capital to protect it in the event of an attack.

The regiment set up their camp in the most tidy and organized manner, and Colonel Dewitt issued a daily drill schedule for his men to abide by. There was still a lot of learning to be done. They had never had weapons before and now had to be instructed in their maintenance and operation. They also had to learn to march with them and how to properly handle, load, and fire them as a cohesive unit abiding to the tactics of the day. It was almost as if they were back at Camp Holley, except now of course they had their weapons, were in a war zone, and although somewhat small, the possibility that they may be called to go into battle at any moment was there.

Interspersed with drill, the men also did picket duty, rotated in and out as camp guards and did fatigue work as well. This entailed going out to repair or upgrade the fortifications in the area. Picket duty was like an advance guard, where the men went and formed a perimeter on the outskirts of the encampment, as a first means of defense and observation. With their schedules full, the men were very busy indeed, but their officers knew that a busy soldier was less likely to get himself into trouble, and a busy mind, at least for the time it was busy, prevented the men from thinking too much of loved ones, and getting ideas of running home.

When they first arrived at Camp Bliss, each company was told where to set up their row of tents, or company street, and the men from Company I were told to choose among themselves a group of four tentmates to live with. In Gabriel's tent, he had Enos, of course, along with Dave Nash and William Baldwin. Baldwin was known as Baldy for obvious reasons or Wee Willy among the Dryden men, because he stood 6 feet tall. They were a good group of friends and Gabriel couldn't have been more pleased. Dave did have his faults, but he was still an integral member of their crew and a good source of entertainment. He also turned out to be the go-to in the company for information, as he was always scrounging about his surroundings in search of drink and unattended goodies. On his searches, he often overheard things that were meant for select ears only.

During the little downtime he was afforded, Gabriel stayed busy by keeping up a lively correspondence with home. The letters he sent back and forth were often filled with the same repetitive day-to-day information, but receiving them was now his greatest source of happiness. Mail call was like a weekly Christmas for him, especially if he was graced with the fortune of getting something from Rill. Letters from her were especially cherished, but came less often, as it was quite an ordeal for her and Gabriel's brother Sam to smuggle them to and from her home. Sometimes her brother-in-law George was able to help if he was out and about on his own, but that was a rare event, as Hannah often accompanied him wherever he went.

When Gabriel first wrote to Rill, he told her of life in camp, his trip south, and his very interesting visit with her father. He left out the wild details of course, of her father's frequent and noisy trips into adjacent rooms with her step-mother, and his introduction to Holy Peter. As time passed, he knew his letters were getting repetitive though, and he worried he was boring her, so he thought he'd surprise her with a gift. He wanted the gift to be something special though, something intimate, something that she would cherish and would always remind her of him: a photograph of himself.

Gabriel had never had his likeness made, so he was excited at the prospect of having it done. He knew Captain Marvin would give him a hard time about getting a pass into Washington though, so he waited for a day when Marvin was away on regimental business. Then, he and Dave Nash approached Lieutenant George, who was left in command of the company, and got one. The trip went well for both men. Dave was able to get drunk and procure enough booze to carry him through the upcoming week, and Gabriel was able to get his photo taken and make the necessary arrangements to have it shipped home. It was expensive. It cost twelve whole shillings, temporarily bankrupting him but he was most pleased with how it turned out and couldn't wait to read Rill's reaction at receiving it in her next letter. During his entire walk back to camp after having it done, all he could think of is how happy she was going to be.

* * * * *

As the weeks progressed into winter and the weather got cold, many of the Dryden boys were surprised and disappointed when it began snowing on occasion. For some reason they thought that they had left the snow behind when they crossed the Mason-Dixon Line. With winter upon them, their A-frame tents were no longer adequate protection from the weather, so they were dismantled, and winter quarters constructed. To do so, the men dug down into the ground about a foot, then they stacked logs, around the sides of the hole for walls. To fill the gaps between the logs they used mud made from their diggings and mixed in straw. A doorway was also cut in one side, and for the roof they simply fastened their old canvas tents to the top of the logs, and a cozy little cabin was made.

For warmth, a fireplace was added, the hearth of which was made with fieldstone, and the chimney two old molasses barrels stacked on end. For sleeping arrangements, they had to make four beds with two placed on each end of the hut, one on top of the other. In Gabriel's abode, they used old hardtack boxes for the bottom bunks and rough-cut lumber for the top. It wasn't exactly like home, but it was far better than sleeping on the ground and quite a bit warmer than their breezy canvas tents.

The men enjoyed constructing their little cabins, too. It was something different to do besides drill and guard duty. Many of them got creative with their construction. Some placed mantles over their fireplaces and drove pegs into the walls to hang their rifles and accoutrements on. In Gabriel's quarters, Dave Nash even installed a secret hiding place for his booze. He dug a square hole in the floor, placed a wooden box in the hole just below ground level and then after the lid was placed over top, he spread a thin layer of dirt over it for concealment.

Food wasn't so bad at Camp Bliss, either. It wasn't just hardtack and salt pork, because they were in garrison and not on the move as troops on campaign. They were stationary, and located next to the massive supply depots in Washington. Quite often they were given fresh beef from cattle that the cooks slaughtered on the outskirts of camp. They were also given rice, potatoes, and beans to eat, and coffee and tea to drink, with a small sugar ration for sweetener. Fresh soft bread was handed out twice a day, after Colonel Dewitt ordered a camp bakery constructed. Sutlers, the mobile merchants that followed the armies, were regularly set up outside their camp, too, where the men could buy all sorts of goodies, pies, canned fruit, canned oysters, candy, etc. Gabriel spent more than he should have at the sutler tents.

For the most part, their time at Camp Bliss was somewhat enjoyable for the men of Company I. Even Captain Marvin and Lieutenant Moffat reduced their feud to a simmer. With the help of large quantities of alcohol, Marvin had eased up a little on the men by stopping his remedial drill sessions. He even tried complimenting them on occasion. It was all part of the changes he knew he had to make to put a stop to the desertions. Through his mannerisms, the men knew he was constantly drunk, though, and could tell that his praise was for the most part disingenuous, but it didn't bother them. They were just happy he'd laid off.

What probably helped the most to ease the tension between the officers was when Lieutenant Moffat's wife, Matilda, came down to Washington at the end of October to visit. Moffat claimed that she had only intended to come for a few weeks, but she ended up staying all the way into mid-March the following year. She rented a small apartment in Washington and sometimes came out to camp and moped around. She liked to put on a big show of being unwell to whomever would listen. Mostly Lieutenant Moffat would go and see her, though. Without a doubt, he was gone with her more often than he should have been, and was neglecting many of his duties. Marvin was too drunk to care, though, and enjoyed not having him around anyway. It was as if the two men had an unspoken agreement. If Moffat didn't turn Marvin in for being drunk, then Marvin wouldn't say anything about Moffat being in Washington all the time. Poor 1st Lieutenant George was the one to get the shit end of the stick, because he had to work extra hard to pick up their slack.

One night in early December, after taps had been played, the boys from Gabriel's mess were enjoying the glow of their crackling fire, while the wind blew flurries of snow around outside their cabin walls. They were all lounging on their bunks in quiet contemplation until Dave Nash, face flushed and bottle in hand, struck up a conversation about the Moffats.

"I tell ya what, boys. When I saw Moffat go toe to toe with Marvin in New York, I thought, now this here is a man I can follow, but after seeing the way he frets over that weakling wife of his I've lost a lot of respect for him."

"She is a bit needy, isn't she?" Enos had to agree.

"A bit? She's a lot of needy. Why, if my Electa complained and carried on like that woman does, I'd a given her the boot long ago," Dave said.

"I just can't believe she's left that daughter of theirs back up to Dryden," William Baldwin chimed in.

"A soldier's camp is no place for an adolescent girl," Enos declared, and he was right about that. "Besides, Matilda is only the girl's step-mother, and I don't think the two of them get along too well."

"That's true," Baldy agreed, "but still, their daughter's been home without any parent for over a month now, and that just doesn't set well with me. Moffat says his wife's been ill, but I don't buy it. I think she just plays sick to try and get attention. If anything, she's sick in the head."

Dave nodded in agreement and reached over to lend his liquor to Baldy. Baldy took a healthy swig and winced as it trickled down his throat.

"Only a mouthful, Wee Willy," Dave said, having managed to corrupt him over the past couple weeks. He looked over at Gabriel.

"You want any, boy?" he offered, but Gabriel shook his head no.

"That's what I thought, but I wanted to be polite. I know old Enos don't want any, he gets mad when I ask him," Dave teased, but Enos ignored him.

"Where is Ella Moffat staying while Matilda is gone?" Gabriel asked.

"With Mr. Burlingame," Enos answered.

"That's right," Dave agreed as he stood up to throw another log on the fire and stash what was left of his bottle in his special hiding spot in the floor.

"Here, boys, I want to show you somethin'," Dave said, as he pulled another bottle out of the box in the ground. "This here is some metheglin my wife sent me from home. It just came in today, but I'm savin' it for Christmas."

He passed it around for the boys to see. Even Enos took a look.

"Pop the cork, Enos. Smell it," Dave said. It was always nice to handle something from home. Enos couldn't pass up the pleasure, even if it was liquor. He took a sniff.

"Woahhh, powerful smelling stuff you've got there," he said to Dave.

"Ain't it wonderful?" Dave said as Enos handed it back. He carefully set it down in his hiding place like he was laying a sleeping baby in its cradle.

"Electa got it from some man over Newfield way. George Teeter I think his name was. They say he makes the best metheglin around."

"That's right," Baldy said, "George Teeter. I've heard the name before."

"How can you know that?" Gabriel asked Dave. "I thought Electa couldn't even write her name."

Gabriel chuckled, happy to give Dave a little taste of his own medicine. He went on.

"Where'd she get the money to buy it anyway, with you blowing all yours on whiskey all the time?"

"Listen here, you little peckerhead. Your daddy wrote the note for her if you must know, and no I ain't spent a penny on my booze either. Other than a few dollars here and there, I've sent every cent I made home to her and the kids."

Gabriel's plan backfired. He felt bad now for having insulted Electa and being completely wrong about Dave.

"Oh. I'm sorry, Dave. I thought…"

"Oh, shut up, boy," Dave interrupted. "I like to dish it out, I think I ought a be able to take it when someone slings it back my way."

"If you're not buying it, how do you get all your whiskey then?" Baldy asked.

"Well, I steal it from the officers of course," Dave answered unabashedly. "Them or the commissary. It's not like they buy it themselves anyway."

"What do you mean they don't buy their own? How do they get it then?" Gabriel asked.

"They get it from our labor, that's where they get it," Dave explained. "Why do you boys think we're always over unloading boxes and supplies at the quartermasters?" Dave asked.

"I don't know. Why?" Baldy said.

"Well, it's because our brigade quartermaster's too damn lazy to do it himself, that's why. So, he asks our officers if he can borrow some of their men. The officers are smart, though. They ask him for somethin' in return, and so he agrees. He gives 'em whatever they want, whiskey, coffee, sugar, candles, extra socks, or blankets. Anything. Then, once they've got their goods, they send us privates over to do the dirty work."

"Is that where Marvin's getting all his booze?" Gabriel asked.

"Sure is, but he's not the only one does it. All the officers do."

"It's like we're their own personal slaves," Baldy commented.

"It's a lot like that," Dave agreed. "That's why it don't bother me takin' from them. I feel like I'm just gettin' my cut of the deal."

* * * * *

December had its ups and downs for Gabriel and the other men in his company. Enos for one, finally got the good news he had been praying for. His son James had been paroled and was sent home on a month-long furlough. It was a great relief and very joyful for him to get the news, but he was also happy for his wife and daughter. They'd have one less thing to worry over and even though he was still away, James would be home with them for Christmas.

There was bad news though, too. On December 5th, Flavell Pattengill, who had been sick in a Washington hospital for several weeks, passed away. It was a sobering event for the men in Company I, for although they had had several desertions, Flavell was the first one that they knew was gone forever. A service was held in his honor, and a collection was taken up to send to his family. Many others were sick in the hospital too, and throughout the month, four of them, Newton Brigham, Andrew Wait, William Hulslander and Clay Knickerbocker, were sent home on medical discharges. After less 4 months of service, the company had already lost 14 men of their original number.

CHAPTER NINE

The new year started out much the same as the last one had ended for Gabriel and the boys of Company I. They continued going on picket, drilling and strengthening their fortifications. Men continued to die and be sent home as well. Philip Mosher passed away on January 11th and A. Ward, John Ferris and Daniel Hollenshied were medically discharged. It was Daniel who the previous summer had ridden to Gabriel's home in Dryden to pass on the news that they were shipping out.

The repetitive grind of being in winter quarters, along with the ever present spread of disease began to wear on the company, but some of the men found some relief to their boredom with their discovery of Washington's booming red-light district. Dave Nash, Gabriel and Enos, stayed far away, but their tent mate, William Baldwin, visited the whores quite often.

"Any of you boys coming along?" Baldy asked them one day in the hut, before taking one of his frequent excursions into the city.

His three friends weren't in the mood to play along, though. Dave had just laid down for a nap, Enos was thumbing through his Bible, and Gabriel was reading a new letter from home with a steaming cup of coffee at his side that he'd just boiled in the coals of their crude fireplace. They ignored him and carried on with what they were doing. Brimming with excitement, Baldy wasn't ready to give in, though.

"Come on now, Gabriel. You know you want to come along and get a little. I'm telling you, this girl we go see, she's got tits down to here." Baldy motioned with his hands to show how low they hung.

"No, thanks," Gabriel said, not even looking up from his letter.

Dave Nash lifted his cap from over his eyes where it had been resting. He was getting annoyed with Baldy, because he always played this game before he went into the city. Mistakenly, he thought he was being funny, but none of them had ever been amused. It'd also been a few hours since he'd had a drink and he wasn't in the mood for tolerance.

"Get the hell out of here, Baldy. Nobody wants to go with you perverts. Besides, I'm willing to wager the only reason that girls tits hang so low, is she's no girl at all. Hell I bet she could have gone to school with your grandmother."

"She is not old, she's a mature lady!" Baldy barked back, noticeably offended at the slight taken to his damsel's honor.

"Ba, ha, ha, ha, ha," Dave roared with laughter, as he went from the supine to sitting. He could tell he'd touched a nerve and wanted to poke the bear some more.

"I'm right, ain't I? She's older than Martha Washington, ha, ha."

Baldy said nothing.

"Tell me, Baldy. Do you all go at her at once?" Dave teased, clearly enjoying himself.

"I'll have you know we take turns and she washes between each suitor," Baldy stated, as if he considered her the pinnacle of sanitation.

"My God, you're actually serious, ain't ya?" Dave said. "Get outa here, Baldy, before I get sick. Last time I ever let you take a swig out a one of my bottles."

In frustration, William Baldwin went for the door and slammed it behind him on his way out. He and his friends made it back from the whorehouse just fine that night, but the next morning at reveille he woke up quite unhappy.

"My word, boys, my groin is on fire with the itch, and there's nothing seems to relieve it," he said as he scratched himself at formation before roll call.

"Serves you right," Gabriel said. "We've told you not to go."

"Are you implying that this has to do with Agatha?" Baldy said, sternly eyeing Gabriel as he continued to scratch.

Dave Nash was standing nearby and couldn't help but speak up.

"Oh, so that's granny's name, is it? Old Aggie Rotten Crotch." "Ha, ha, ha," he chuckled. "Of course that's what Private Ballard's implying, Wee Willy. Are you tellin' me you're too dumb to realize it?"

William Baldwin may not have wanted to believe it, but that was exactly what happened. He wasn't the only one to come to formation with the itch. All of his whorehouse companions had the same complaint and were sent to sick call. While they were gone, their belongings were tossed in piles outside the doors of their respective huts.

"Hey what's the meaning of this?" Baldy called out when he came back to see what had been done.

Gabriel and Dave were home and came out to explain things to him. Dave did the talking.

"Company voted while you idiots were gone gettin' your peckers attended to," Dave said. "You boys can move into one of the empty huts together until the doctor says you're cured."

There were a few empty huts available, as a result of so many men being in the hospital, dead or discharged.

"But that's not fair," Baldy complained. "I helped built this place with my own two hands, I think it's my right to stay here if I want."

Dave wouldn't budge though.

"You waived that right, Baldy, when you went whorin'. Besides, company voted, so it's official."

Realizing there was no use in arguing the fact any longer, Baldy gave in. He made his bed and now he had to lie in it, so he gathered up his belongings and moved along.

* * * * *

In February, the 143rd was reassigned to the 22nd Corps and were to be moved to another camp on the outskirts of Washington on the 12th. Their soon-to-be-new home was at Cloud's Mill and, like Camp Bliss, was in Virginia.

On one of the regiment's last days off before moving, Gabriel was able to procure a pass to go into Washington. He was going to see some of the sights in the city and to pick up a birthday present for Rill who was turning nineteen on the 13th of March. Enos and Dave wanted to stay in camp, so Gabriel asked Cheddiah Arnold to tag along with him. Cheddiah was another young man from Dryden, about four years older than Gabriel.

In the city, he shopped for a while before finally deciding on a green parasol, much like the one Hannah Sweetland had flung at him on the day he enlisted. It was hard for Gabriel to shop for Rill, because her father was always sending her nice things from New York. She had almost everything as far as Gabriel was concerned. Everything except a parasol. He'd never seen her with one and so that's why he chose it.

As he and Cheddiah made their way back into camp after their trip, something seemed off to Gabriel. It was as if folks were avoiding him, and once he'd pass them by it sounded as if they were whispering behind his back. When he got to the door of his hut, Dave Nash came out and caught him as he was coming in.

"Back from your little excursion?" Dave asked with a grin. "Turns out you're not as innocent as you make out to be, are ya?

Gabriel gave him a confused look.

"What are you talking about?" he asked, but Enos popped his head out the door before Dave could answer.

"Shut up, Dave," he said. "Don't say another word."

Dave didn't respond, he just chuckled as Enos pulled Gabriel into their quarters and shut the door.

"What's he talking about, Enos? First I show up and everybody avoids me like the plague and then I hear them…"

Enos held up his hand to shush him and Gabriel obeyed. He was worried, wondering what was going on and if he was in some kind of trouble. Enos told him to sit down and again Gabriel listened. He found a seat on a wooden stool in the center of the hut and started to knead his hands together in nervous anticipation of what Enos had to tell him. Enos picked a letter up off his bunk and handed it to him.

"Read this," he said.

It was still sealed, and the writing on the outside belonged to his mother. He tore open the envelope and nervously unfolded the letter to see what it had to say.

"Please God, please let everything be alright at home. Oh please, Lord," he pleaded out loud as he did so.

When he got the paper open, he read it quickly and with great anxiety. It said ...

January 30th, 1863

My Dearest Gabriel,

Words cannot describe my torn feelings at this time. I want to be mad at you for going behind my back. The thought that not only did you lie to me about going fishing on that terrible day in August, but you also lied to me about stopping by the Sweetland home, disappoints me greatly. The results of your secret relationship however make me happier than I have been since the birth of your baby brother. Martha Marsh is pregnant Gabriel, and we are sending her down for you to marry as soon as we can. We will be providing her with the fare for her passage to New York City, because that is all we have money for right now. From there she is to go to her father and get the rest of what she needs for her trip to you from him. I'll let her explain why below. Remember that we all love you so very much Gabriel. Be careful, pray often, and congratulations on becoming a father.

Your Mother,

Lydia

Hello Gabriel and congratulations. I am so happy for you and for us. Not everyone is though of course. I suppose I have known about this all for a while now but kept it secret until it started to show. I wanted it to be a sure thing, so please forgive me for keeping it from you. It was your happiness I had in mind. I didn't want to get your hopes up and then disappoint you if it went away. George was the first one I told, about a week ago. I wanted his help in breaking the news to Hannah, but as you can guess she didn't take it well. I went to Uncle Gus's place first, but after George came and told your parents what had happened, they went straight to Gus's and insisted I come home with them. I think I will be staying with your parents for now on. They have given me your room and are so very kind. Even Sarah has been pleasant to me in her own way. So now I'm off on the train for Papas and then to you. Hannah will not help in the least and prevents George from doing so as well, so I will go to Papa. I hate it because I feel like a beggar, but he will be happy to help, and we can pay everyone back when we have the chance.

Love,
Rill & Baby

After reading over the letter Gabriel's face lost its color and for a moment he felt as if he may pass out. He tried remaining calm, though. He folded the letter up nice and neat and returned it to its envelope. Enos stood next to him watching for his reaction.

"I take it you know?" Gabriel asked.

Enos nodded.

"Mail came while you were out, and it was in several of the boys letters, mine included."

"I see," Gabriel said. "So am I the last one in the company to know, then?" he asked.

"Pretty much," Enos answered, "you and Cheddiah, but I suspect even he found out before you had the chance to read your letter."

Enos was grinning and when Gabriel stood up he grabbed for his hand and shook it tight.

"Congratulations, Gabriel," he said. "It's a momentous day a man first learns he's to be a father."

"Thanks, Enos," Gabriel said. "It's a lot to take in. Rill's headed for the city to see Mr. Marsh. I guess Mother and Father only had enough to get her to New York. She suspects Mr. Marsh will pay for the rest of her way here," Gabriel explained.

"Oh no, Gabriel, she should have asked Julia. We could have helped. I'm sure Julia would have handed over whatever she needed."

"I'm sure she would have too, but Rill just doesn't feel right taking other people's money. She said so herself in the letter. Besides, I think she wants to break the news to her father in person. At least if Hannah doesn't get a letter to him first. I'm sure she's raising hell around town, telling everyone I ruined her sister or something."

Enos laughed and pointed to an opened letter on his bunk.

"On the contrary. Julia says she's not said a thing. Says she hasn't been seen in Dryden since the word got out."

"Thank God," Gabriel said, happy to hear that his reputation wasn't in complete shambles yet.

"It's strange how everyone's reacting. Mother says it's the happiest she's been since she had my brother George. I would've thought everyone would be ashamed or angry."

"Nobody should ever get angry over a baby, Gabriel," Enos reassured him. "Plus, it's war time, people are so sick of hearing about death and destruction, that any shred of happiness they find they hold onto and bask in for as long as they can."

Enos's words reassured Gabriel. He was such a kind and generous person and with his father at home, he couldn't have asked for a better friend and mentor.

"I think I need to get some fresh air." Gabriel said.

He went and opened the door, but to his surprise the whole company was crowded outside waiting for him to emerge. When he did, they all cheered, shouted and whistled.

"Didn't anybody ever tell ya it isn't polite to fire off your musket indoors Gabriel?" Levi Dodge called out from the back.

"At least not until you've married the girl," Charley Freeman added.

Everyone roared with laughter, while Gabriel's face turned beet red.

Dave Nash was standing just outside the door with both lieutenants. Captain Marvin was the only one not to be seen.

"Congratulations, Gabriel," Dave said as he shook his hand. Lieutenants Moffat and George came up and did the same.

"Well done, Gabriel," George said.

"Yes, well done, well done," Moffat added.

"Gabriel, Matilda and I have talked it over and we would be delighted to have Martha stay with her in the city once she gets here. I trust you haven't made any arrangements?"

"No Sir, not yet. To tell you the truth it hasn't even crossed my mind where she'll stay or how she's going to get to camp. I'll ask her if that's alright though, when she gets here," Gabriel answered him.

"You be sure to, Gabriel. It will be no bother, I assure you. Matilda could use the company. She's been rather melancholy this week and I think she just needs to spend some time with someone of the same sex. Women's business, if you catch my drift."

On the following day, Gabriel received another letter. This one was from Mr. Marsh and it was dated the 3rd of February. In it, he congratulated Gabriel on the "most wonderful news," and expressed his great satisfaction that they were able to meet the previous October. He said that he and Victoria were overjoyed with the "good tidings" and before he closed he informed Gabriel on which train Rill would be arriving on the 12th, the same day the regiment was scheduled to move to Cloud's Mill.

Gabriel felt relieved to finally know Rill's itinerary and to see that Mr. Marsh was taking things so well. These were his feelings at first, however, but after flipping to the reverse side of the letter, he found a most brutal yet childlike illustration of what appeared to be a man using Holy Peter on an unconscious Union soldier. The men were identified above as "me," and "you," and below the illustration were the words, "treat her well or else…" Most disturbing to Gabriel, however, was it appeared that actual blood had been added to the paper to advertise the seriousness of his warning. All Gabriel could do after looking it over was take a big gulp and pray he never crossed his soon-to-be father-in-law.

* * * * *

With few other options presenting themselves, Gabriel decided to take Lieutenant Moffat up on his offer, and with his help was able to procure a pass to Washington on the day of Rill's arrival. The Moffats accompanied him to the train station to welcome her. They had only a day and a night before Gabriel had to return to camp, so they went quickly and were married by the chaplain of an Ohio regiment stationed in the city. The ceremony was short and simple, and the Moffats graciously stood as witnesses to the occasion.

Afterwards, they went to a fancy restaurant for lunch, and then took Rill on a tour of Washington. Because she was so visibly pregnant, they did so by carriage, seeing the White House, the unfinished Washington Monument, the Smithsonian Museum and the Capitol, whose dome was currently under construction. It was cold, but they were dressed appropriately, and the carriage driver provided them blankets for the ride.

It was a happy day and the newlyweds enjoyed themselves immensely. It was surreal for them too, after over four months apart, to finally be able to see and touch one another in the flesh again. Under the carriage blanket they held tightly to each other's hands, sometimes with their fingers interlaced and Rill gently resting her head on Gabriel's shoulder. Each time she would lift her head and turn to catch a glimpse at something of interest, Gabriel couldn't help but look her over. He couldn't believe how lucky he was to be married to someone so gorgeous and kind. She was dressed impeccably in a new dress that her father had purchased during her short stay in New York. Her hair was done up with big brown curls and her cheeks were rosy red from the nip in the air.

Rill's belly however was what he noticed most. It was a glaring change to physique, but he found it most comforting, for he knew that the baby inside her represented an unbreakable bond between them, a bond that they would share for the rest of their lives and beyond.

At the end of the day, after an evening meal, the four of them made their way to Matilda Moffat's apartment. She was staying in a boarding house just inside the city limits and her quarters consisted of two rooms, a small sitting room just inside the door and a separate bedroom. There was, of course, only one bed, which the Moffats took, as Matilda was feeling "feverish" by the time they got in. She retired to it immediately, but Lieutenant Moffat stayed up long enough to borrow a spare mattress from the proprietor for the newlyweds to use. They placed it on the floor in the sitting room. It wasn't perfect, but it didn't bother them in the least. They were just happy to be together.

When they were all situated, Lieutenant Moffat bid them goodnight and went into the bedroom. It was the first time Gabriel and Rill had been alone all day, but since the Moffats were using the only lamp and the only piece of furniture in the room was their borrowed mattress, they decided to get into bed themselves. The day had been long and tiring, but with only a few hours left to spare they had trouble falling asleep. Instead, they spent much of the night holding one another and whispering stories of their time apart in the dark. Private things mostly and things they'd hoped to share but couldn't do justice to in their letters.

They made love as well, ever so discreetly and quiet-like. Rill's belly was too big for them to do so in the traditional way, not to mention they didn't want one of the Moffats catching them in a compromising position, so they spooned, and Gabriel inserted himself from behind.

Time passed quickly and soon after they were finally able to doze off, the morning rays of the sun beat through the window and woke them to the inescapable dread that their time together was drawing to a close. The past 24 hours had been unforgettably pleasant and memorable, but at the same time it had gone by far too quickly. After getting up, they ate a small breakfast provided by the landlady, and then after hailing a coach made their way to the railroad station for Rill's departure. It was an emotional scene on the platform before she boarded the train. Tears flowed freely between them and even Lieutenant Moffat had to dry his eyes after witnessing the pitiful display.

Just as she was about to climb into the train, Rill reached into her pocket, pulled something from it and handed it to Gabriel. It was a tightly braided lock of her hair.

"Here," she said, "if I have to carry around a piece of you in my belly, you can carry around a piece of me too."

She smiled at him as tears rolled down her cheeks and then disappeared into the car. Gabriel held onto the little knot tightly and kissed it as the train pulled away. It was now his most cherished possession, his greatest comfort, his greatest reminder of his darling little wife, his beautiful, kind and caring partner, his Rill.

Part
Two

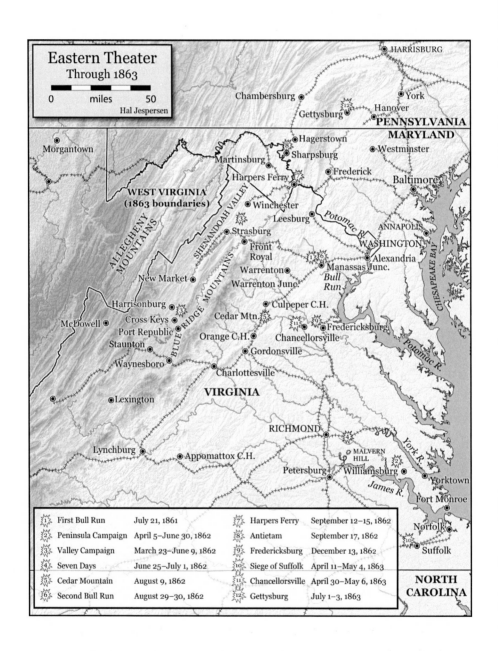

Eastern Theater
Through 1863

0   miles   50

Hal Jespersen

HARRISBURG

Chambersburg ●   ● York
Gettysburg ●   Hanover
PENNSYLVANIA
MARYLAND

Morgantown ●   ● Hagerstown   ● Westminster
Martinsburg ●   Sharpsburg
Harpers Ferry ●   ● Frederick   Baltimore ●

WEST VIRGINIA
(1863 boundaries)   ● Winchester
Leesburg ●   *Potomac R.*   ANNAPOLIS ●
Strasburg ●   **WASHINGTON**
Front   ● Alexandria
Royal   Manassas Junc.
Warrenton ●   *Bull*
Warrenton Junc.   *Run*

Harrisonburg ●   ● Culpeper C.H.
Cross Keys ●   Cedar Mtn. ●
Port Republic ●   Orange C.H. ●   Fredericksburg ●
McDowell ●   Chancellorsville
Staunton ●   ● Gordonsville
Waynesboro ●   ● Charlottesville

VIRGINIA

● Lexington

RICHMOND ●
Lynchburg ●   MALVERN
● Appomattox C.H.   HILL
Petersburg ●   Williamsburg ●   ● Yorktown
James R.   Fort Monroe

CHESAPEAKE BAY

Potomac R.

York R.

Norfolk ●

Suffolk ●

NORTH
CAROLINA

1 First Bull Run	July 21, 1861	7 Harpers Ferry	September 12–15, 1862
2 Peninsula Campaign	April 5–June 30, 1862	8 Antietam	September 17, 1862
3 Valley Campaign	March 23–June 9, 1862	9 Fredericksburg	December 13, 1862
4 Seven Days	June 25–July 1, 1862	10 Siege of Suffolk	April 11–May 4, 1863
5 Cedar Mountain	August 9, 1862	11 Chancellorsville	April 30–May 6, 1863
6 Second Bull Run	August 29–30, 1862	12 Gettysburg	July 1–3, 1863

CHAPTER TEN

Gabriel had been fast asleep, but the sound of rustling sheets and hushed voices woke him. He lay motionless, still very weak, but slightly opened his eyes to survey the scene around him. There was a blue hue coming from the windows, but he couldn't tell whether it was dawn or dusk. The noise he could see was coming from the bed next to his. There were three men standing over it, and two of them were wrapping its occupant up in his own sheets, one at the head and the other at the feet. They lifted him, set him on a stretcher that was on the floor at the foot of the bed, and then proceeded to remove him from the building. Gabriel could tell that the man under the sheets was dead. The third man, still standing next to the bed, watched his companions shuffle away, and then began to gather the dead mans' belongings.

From his blue sack coat and kepi, Gabriel could tell he was a soldier. Many of the hospital stewards and nurses were older, recovering or disabled men, biding their time before getting discharged and sent home or released back to their commands. This man, Gabriel could tell, was just too old for a soldiers' life. His face was slightly wrinkled, his beard had more gray than brown and as he shuffled about, he did so with a slight limp.

"What time is it?" Gabriel asked. The man looked up from what he was doing and then to Gabriel.

"So, you're awake?" the man said, "I'm sorry about your friend," he added, motioning to the now empty mattress.

"No friend of mine," Gabriel said, "I never seen him."

"Oh," he responded. "You two come in together on the same day, had the same symptoms. Figured you were from the same outfit."

Gabriel shook his head.

"How long have I been here?" he asked.

The man was busy stuffing the deceased soldiers belongings into a cotton sack.

"Oh, I don't know, five or six days. Think you come in last Wednesday, that'd be the 19th I think?"

Gabriel was shocked. The last date he could remember was the 17th, when he was lying in a tent at the 11th Corps hospital in Warrenton. After that, it was all a blur. He only had vague recollections of a bumpy wagon ride, the whistle of a train and the feeling of being incredibly overheated. He could also recall waking up at one point in the room he was currently in. Some man was poking and prodding him all over and then a woman tried getting him to drink some sort of nasty concoction he now surmised must have been medicine. Reviewing his memories, he realized he had no idea where he was.

"Hey mister, where are we anyway?" he asked the old man.

"We're in Washington, son. This is ward 6 of the Harewood Hospital and you're in bed number 24."

"Washington?" Gabriel said to the man, with a skeptical look on his face.

"That's right," the man said.

He tied off the sack of belongings and set it on the empty bed, then turned the wooden chair next to Gabriel's bed around and sat down facing him.

"You're in Washington, kid, and you're doing a whole lot better than when you first come in. I thought you were a goner for sure, burning up like you were and talking all that nonsense. Kept screaming 'Rill, Rill, Rill,' all terrified like. Even when you were half coherent, I couldn't make any sense of what you were saying."

Hearing her name, Gabriel suddenly remembered Rill and wondered if she or his parents knew yet what had happened to him. Enos had said he would write them when he dropped him off at the hospital in Warrenton. He had been sick for four days just lying in his tent, while Enos and Dave Nash looked after him. Captain Marvin accused him of faking though, and on the fifth day tried to make him come back to full duty. He was so sick at that point he could barely lift a finger, much less stand.

Furious at Marvin's stupidity, Enos rebuked him in front of the whole company by marching straight to Gabriel's tent, picking him up into his arms and carrying him all the way to the hospital. When he arrived the doctor immediately diagnosed Gabriel with typhoid fever and told Enos he had brought him there in just the nick of time. If they had waited any longer, he said Gabriel would have surely died. The next day he felt worse, though, and developed a rash all over his body. That's about when his memory started going fuzzy.

Gabriel's head ached terribly, but his stomach bothered him the most.

"Say, can I get something to eat? My stomach's growling something fierce," he asked.

"Can't blame it much. All you've had to eat since you come in is a few cups of scalded milk. Have to wait and see what the doctor says when he gets in, though. You look the best you have since you got here, and I don't want to reverse it by giving you something I shouldn't."

The man's reasoning was sound, but it wasn't what Gabriel wanted to hear.

"Well, how the hell long is that gonna be?" he asked in frustration.

"Oh, I'd say about half hour. He's probably up now, but he's got to get himself some breakfast and then he'll be in to do his morning rounds. I'll ask him then if we can feed you something more substantial."

"Well thanks, I suppose," Gabriel said, "and sorry for the outburst. I still don't feel quite myself."

"Not a problem, young man. My name's Isaac by the way."

"Thanks then, Isaac," Gabriel said.

Isaac got up and threw the cotton sack over his shoulder before trotting away down the corridor of beds and out an opening. He was good to his word, and when the doctor came, he got permission to feed Gabriel some ground farina for breakfast. Gabriel scarfed it down in a few gulps and at first felt a little better after eating, but then his stomach turned on him and seemed as if it would burst. The doctor said that bloating was a common symptom of typhoid, though, and said that it would pass.

Over the next few days, Gabriel got slightly better. His rash dissipated, and his fever only spiked on a couple more occasions. He met the doctor in charge of him too, Assistant Army Surgeon Ira Terry. He was a nice enough man, but he prescribed Gabriel with turpentine extract, and Dover's Powder, which he really didn't care for. The turpentine smelled pleasant, but had an awfully bitter taste, and the powder just put him to sleep.

"I'm tired enough," Gabriel told Isaac when he came by one morning to administer him another dose of the stuff.

Most of the time Gabriel just lay in his bunk, as he was still just recovering, and his body had little energy. On one day, he managed to catch up on his journal, though, and write a letter home to Rill and his parents to update them on his condition. Rill had sent him the journal in March so that at the end of the year she could read it and see what he had been up to. He had kept up on it punctually until he got sick. Isaac and another attendant helped Gabriel outside after he was finished with his writing. It gave him a chance to catch a breath of fresh air and get some sun, but the excursion completely exhausted him, and he had to be carried back to his bunk. When they got him there, he passed out and slept the rest of the day and into the next morning.

The hospital was a terrible place to be, but nice as far as hospitals go. Of course, there were all the ill, wounded, and dying men. The smells of excrement, vomit, and putrid flesh were sometimes present, but it was an entirely modern facility, and the many doctors, nurses, attendees, and volunteers on hand, kept it clean and in good order. The building that Gabriel was housed in, was a long and narrow wooden barracks-like structure. It had an open interior, with beds placed every few feet along the side walls and a corridor running in the center from end to end. There were woodstoves in the corridor for heat, although they were not currently running, and lanterns suspended from the ceiling for light. There were windows every few feet on the side walls as well, and each bed had a mosquito net that hung above it, and a wooden chair nearby for the use of the patient or his caregivers. The patients in his ward varied greatly. There were the sick and diseased like him, and then the battle torn men with bullet wounds, broken bones, burns, missing limbs and so on.

* * * * *

On the 30th of August, Gabriel was astonished to see the familiar faces of his Uncle William and Aunt Charity Ballard make their way into his ward after he had finished his breakfast. They were led by his ever-helpful caregiver Isaac, and he was so happy to see the two of them that he was able to stand and hug them both once they reached his bedside. Gabriel lay back down afterwards, and Isaac pulled a couple of chairs over for his guests before returning to his duties, to give them privacy. They were all happy to see one another as they hadn't now in over a year. Gabriel was especially surprised to see his aunt. Aunt "Chat," as he called her, was his Uncle William's wife. She was an attractive woman, about seven years older than Gabriel, and seven years younger than her husband.

Seeing and smelling a woman had become a rare and pleasant privilege for Gabriel, as it was for most soldiers who'd been for so long in the gruff, and often confrontational company of other men. Seeing and speaking with anyone of the opposite sex, was now a novelty, and was always a welcomed and cherished occasion. Just to be in their prescience, and see and experience their often kinder, quieter and softer manner, brought on overwhelming feelings of comfort to most of the soldiers. The female nurses in the hospital were almost always preferred, and beds in the wards with the prettiest ones were the most sought after.

"How the hell are you, Gabriel?" his uncle greeted him as he took his seat dressed in his military attire.

"I'm good, Uncle. I've been better of course, but I've been worse, too. They say I was delirious when I first got here, and I think their telling the truth because I can't remember three quarters of what's happened to me in the past couple weeks."

"So we hear," his aunt said. "Your friend there told us all about it, Gabriel. We're so sorry. You had the typhoid they say, is that correct?"

Gabriel nodded his head. "Yes, it is," he answered her.

Aunt Chat was very kind, and Gabriel had always liked her. In fact, she reminded him a lot of Rill.

"Oh, before I forget, Gabriel, here," she said to him, as she pulled two letters out of the little handbag she was toting and handed them to him. "They're from your parents and Martha. They heard I was coming down and asked me to deliver them to you. They thought it'd be faster than by mail. They got the letter from Enos just the other day, telling of what happened and where you'd been sent."

"That's right," William piped up, "I'd a come over the day you arrived, but I didn't know you were in town until she showed up last night."

"I've seen your baby, Gabriel," Chat added. "She's such a precious little one, so dainty like her mother and helpless as a kitten. You're going to be so proud when you finally get to meet her, and your little wife is doing so well too. She is a natural mother, Gabriel. Such a doting little mama she is. You're lucky to have her."

Gabriel smiled at Chat but said nothing. He was still somewhat bashful about the situation and still getting used to the fact that he was a father. It warmed his heart to hear about Rill and the baby, though, and to top it off he now had a letter from her as well. He bent over and reached under his bed for his haversack. Other than his clothes, it was all that he had of his possessions, and it carried his journal, his letters, and Rill's lock of hair. Enos had made sure it was sent along with him. He tucked his new correspondence in with the rest and decided he would read them once his aunt and uncle had gone.

His baby had been born on the 22nd of June at his parent's home. They chose to name her Martha, after her mother and deceased grandmother. Gabriel was in Virginia at the time and had only just found out about her birth a few days before coming down with typhoid. He was happy to hear that she and Rill were still healthy. His Uncle William congratulated him on becoming a father too, and then turned the conversation to a more somber subject.

"It's hard to believe, Gabriel, that just over a year ago we were all at your folks place for that going away party, and now all five of us are knocked out of the fight. Your Uncle Joseph got discharged back in

April, your Uncle Bill in June. Me, well, my back's all cantankerous. You've got the typhoid, and your Uncle Richard is full a bullet holes," William said. "Joseph's still sick too, even though he's home now. Ma and your Aunt Sarah have had their hands full taking care of him."

"I heard about the others," Gabriel said, "but not what happened to you."

"Most unfortunate Gabriel, let me tell you. Back in January I was workin' as an orderly for our regimental doc. He sent me to go pick up a chest of medicine at headquarters for him one night. I swear the thing weighed more than a pregnant sow, and on my way back I tripped along the road and fell into a ditch. The chest fell on top of me and ruptured my spine something terrible. I couldn't even get up and would have froze to death if it weren't for a passing cavalryman took notice of me. He pulled me out, but I could barely walk. I've been laid up almost all year, but they won't let me out like they did Joseph and Bill. I still don't know what they're planning for me."

"Its been a trying time for your uncle," Aunt Chat added, "he's been in constant pain."

"Yes, and the only way I made it here today is because I took a good dose of laudanum before coming. It's the only stuff can dull the pain."

"I'm sorry to hear it," Gabriel said. "How's Uncle Richard doing though? I heard he was wounded at Gettysburg."

"He's fine," William said, "sent him all the way to Jersey though. Some hospital in Newark. These past couple battles got these hospitals bursting at the seams. Lord knows what they'll do if they get into another big scrap."

"I heard he got shot in the chest. Is that right?" Gabriel asked.

"Shot there twice," William answered. "Once at Chancellorsville and again at Gettysburg."

"I didn't hear about Chancellorsville," Gabriel said, "other than the fact that the 11th Corps skedaddled."

"Not the whole corps," William spoke up in its defense. "The 157th stood their ground. They retreated too, of course, but they did so in good order and killed a few Rebs along the way. Richard got shot right across the front of his chest, but it was a glancing blow and only ripped the skin away. He was well enough to make it to Gettysburg, but that was even worse for the boys than Chancellorsville. Our regiment lost over 300 men of the 400 or so we had present. The Rebs were pushing us back on the first day, and some dutchy general ordered the 157th to go up and hold them off. They went up alright, but got nearly surrounded by a whole Reb brigade. Richard caught one up high on his left front. Luckily the bullet was slowed down by his ribs and sternum and stopped under the skin above his heart. I guess they had to cut the ball out, but he's doing fine now. Broke his sternum in two though, it was hurting him awful to breathe."

At hearing the details of his uncles' injuries, Gabriel could only shake his head and listen in disbelief. William was right. Out of all four Ballards to enlist the year before, they were all knocked out of it for now, his Uncle Bill Neeley included.

"Enough of Richard, though," his uncle said. "We heard you got in on some action down in Suffolk. How'd that go for ya?"

"I wouldn't call it much of any action. We went down there from Alexandria in mid-April to take part in the siege alright, but all we ever did is watch other folks fight. They always had us in the reserve. Sure, we saw the artillery give it to them pretty heavy a few times, and once or twice a shell landed near me, but I never got to fire my rifle. To be honest the most notable event of the whole campaign I'd say was when our colonel resigned on account of ill health and our lieutenant-colonel, Boughton, took his place.

"Did you at least get to see any Rebs?" William asked

"Oh sure, plenty from afar, and they marched a horde of captured ones past our regiment once. I even talked to a few of them. They weren't all that bad, not like I expected. Most of them were just kids like me."

"Well, they may look like you, but they still want to kill ya," his uncle warned, "and don't worry I'm sure you'll get your chance to fight once they send you back. Richard says he's killed a handful already."

"My word…William Ballard," Aunt Chat scolded him. "The Rebels are our enemy, but God-fearing people too. You shouldn't speak of them so coldly."

"Oh, don't get your feathers all ruffled, Chat," William told her. "I never said they weren't God-fearin', just mean they're better off in heaven than down here on earth."

"Well, I can't disagree with that," she said. "We'll all be better off in heaven. That's the truth."

"So, how did you boys get from Suffolk to here?" William continued to inquire.

"Well, after the siege lifted, we went up to the peninsula and poked around there for a while, and then after Gettysburg they transferred us up to help chase Lee. We joined the Army of the Potomac and they put my regiment in the same division the 157th used to belong to. We made it all the way to Warrenton Junction, before we stopped and went into camp. That's where I got sick before coming here."

"Well, I know you're sick, Gabriel," Aunt Chat spoke up, "but it's all for the better. I think that you're a lot safer in here, than out with the Army."

"Oh, nonsense, Chat," William disagreed. "Boy wants to be with his friends. He don't want to be cooped up in here like a chicken. Am I right, Gabriel?" His uncle asked him.

"Sure, you're right, Uncle William. I've got to admit, though, it sure has been nice taking it easy. I need to get my strength back here before I can make any difference with them anyway. If I went back now, I'd just get sick again I think and that wouldn't do them or me any good."

"Quite right Gabriel. See? I told you William," Aunt Chat said trying to get in the last word.

* * * * *

After visiting a while longer, Uncle William and Aunt Chat bid Gabriel farewell, and said they would try and visit again. When they were gone, he went straight for his haversack and tore out the new letters Aunt Chat had brought him. Naturally, he opened Rill's first and was happy to read that mother and babe were doing just fine. Reading on, however, he was shocked to hear of some bad news about his father-in-law, Mr. Marsh.

Apparently, the trouble all happened in July during the New York City riots. The city's residents were upset over the implementation of the draft. It began as a protest, but things snowballed, and the protest got out of hand, and turned into mass chaos. Homes and businesses were robbed and burnt, and people were fighting all over the city. The riot went on for several days before Union troops finally arrived to quell the insurrection.

Due to his anti-war sentiments, Mr. Marsh was radically anti-draft and so when the riots were just beginning, he rallied some of the citizens in his neighborhood with an anti-war, anti-draft speech. People were out and about due to all the calamity going on, and so the crowd he attracted got quite large rather quickly, and there were many strangers in its ranks. Caught up in the heat and passion of the moment, he called on them all to march with him down to city hall to air their grievances. They agreed and cheered him on as he led them down his street.

About to pass by his home, he decided to stop and grab his cane from just inside the door. He thought he'd use it to inspire his followers, much as a drum major would lead his marching band with a baton. Running up his front steps though, the crowd mistook his intentions, and as he unlatched his door, they burst in behind him, thinking he was leading them to ransack the place. Like a dry sponge thrown into a bucket of water the house almost instantaneously absorbed the people from outside, with many more still on the street clambering to get in. The snapping and cracking of splintering furniture and wood could soon be heard, along with the sounds of breaking glass and the beating in of doors. Mr. Marsh tried to call them out, but his voice went unheard in the commotion.

His family happened to be on the second floor at the time, and after seeing the rush of rioters come up the stairs after her, Victoria was able to bar herself, along with their children, in her bedroom. She pushed a wardrobe up against the door to keep them out, but some of the men had brought in clubs and axes and they soon broke it down. Victoria kept a pistol hidden away in the room though, so as the first two men leapt through the opening she shot them dead, both between the eyes. The shots scared the others off and soon the crowd left as quickly as they appeared. The home was in shambles though. In just a few minutes almost everything of value had been stolen or broken and not a window or door was left behind intact.

Mr. Marsh was bruised and abused himself, his coat torn almost in two, his top hat kicked in and he had a large bleeding gash on his forehead. He could hear the children crying upstairs, and made his way to the room he shared with his wife. Stepping over the bodies of the two men Victoria had killed he ran to comfort his stunned wife and children by hugging and kissing them all over.

"Are you all right? Are you all right?" he kept asking them, overcome with emotion.

Turning to survey the dead men, he could tell they meant trouble. They were both clearly members of the Bowery Boys gang, and once word got out to their compatriots of their killing, they would be back and in much greater numbers for revenge.

Quickly gathering up Victoria and the children, he was able to grab a wad of cash, that the mob had luckily not discovered. It had been hidden under a loose floorboard in his office. They also gathered up what little possessions of value they could from their untouched bedroom and made their way out of the home less than ten minutes after the crowd had moved on.

Luckily, they were able to commandeer an abandoned wagon near their home and drive north out of the city and harm's way. From there, they caught a train and made it all the way to Dryden and were now safe and sound in the home of George and Hannah Sweetland. According to Rill they had been over to Gabriel's parents' place to see her and the baby too. Gabriel was happy to read that they had all made it there okay, but he was overjoyed to think that Hannah would now have to deal with seven extra people under her roof. He also wondered if Mr. Marsh and Victoria would be able to keep quiet and behave themselves in Hannah's home or if they were going to carry on like they had when he and Enos visited them the previous October.

* * * * *

After his aunt and uncle's visit, Gabriel's condition continued to improve. On the 1ˢᵗ of September, the doctor began allowing him to eat chicken, greatly raising his spirits. The protein re-energized him and after a few days more he was able to hold down a whole meal without feeling bloated or sick afterward. On the 6ᵗʰ, he decided to go out on his own, and went to the hospital in Washington where his Uncle William was in residence. He returned the favor by surprising his aunt and uncle as they had him. They, of course, were happy for the visit but more so to see him regaining his health. He felt exhausted afterward, but not quite as bad as he thought he would. After a good night's sleep, he was fully rejuvenated the next morning, and on the 9ᵗʰ he was able to procure a pass to do some shopping in the city.

He was without a doubt, on the gain, but in the opinion of his doctor, he still needed more time to recuperate. Because the hospital was daily receiving new patients, the doctor thought it best for Gabriel to go home for a month and be nursed by his own family. It would do him good both mentally and physically, and it would also free up a much needed bed. After his time away, he would be required to return, and the doctor could then decide whether or not he was fit for full duty.

On September 14ᵗʰ, Gabriel was granted a furlough, and made his way into Washington to catch a train home. He was lucky to have been paid that day as well, and had two months' worth of wages, $26, in his pocket. His journey took two days, and on the 16ᵗʰ he arrived in Cortland and hitched a ride home with a man and his son, who had just offloaded a wagonload of goods at the train station.

On the way, he couldn't help but think of the last time he travelled down the same road thirteen months before, with the boys of Company I. He chuckled when they rode by the spot where they had taken their lunch and Dave Nash went missing. The hilarious image of Dave's pale naked body being lugged down the road by Bielby Starr was seared into his mind's eye. Gabriel was very happy to be home, but at the same time, recalling all those memories made him miss his friends, and he couldn't help but wonder how they were getting along, and what they were up too. He hoped he wasn't missing out on too much.

Things had changed in the company over the past year and Gabriel also thought on that some, too. Many of the men he had left Dryden with were no longer with them. He went over their names in his head and after a few minutes of counting he was able to figure that through death, discharge, transfer and desertion, Company I had lost over thirty men of their original number. Also, there was the case of Lieutenant Moffat who had been promoted to 1st Lieutenant earlier that spring and transferred to another company in the regiment. It was done so to ease tension of course, as Moffat and Marvin had never fully reconciled, and the higher ups in the regiment thought it best to separate them. Truthfully, by that point in time the worst of the feud had passed, but it was no secret that the two still disliked one another.

After reaching the Village of Dryden, the man offered to take Gabriel as far as the lake and Gabriel accepted. He wouldn't have minded walking the rest of the way, but his journey had exhausted him, and thinking of his health, he didn't want to push his body that far just yet. After getting dropped off at the outlet of the lake Gabriel graciously thanked the man for his kindness and passed him a crisp Yankee greenback, he had been paid a couple days before. The man tried giving it back, but Gabriel insisted.

Making his way around the east end of the lake was a surreal experience for Gabriel. The thought of returning home had been a dream of his almost since he'd left and now that he was finally back, he couldn't exactly explain how he felt, other than he knew he was happy. He passed the Sweetland's home and then the Cook's but saw nobody about, so he kept plodding along until soon he was in view of his parents' place.

He could see that his father and brother Sam were out front, splitting wood for the stove. Sam looked slightly taller and his father a little grayer. When he let himself in the front gate, his brother was splitting with his back toward him, but his father had seen him come in. He was facing him with a load of splinters cradled in his crippled arm. It took John a few seconds to recognize his son. His time in the Army had given Gabriel a weathered look and the typhoid had reduced him to skin and bones.

Dropping the load of wood to the ground John ran to Gabriel and grabbed hold of him tight with tears in his eyes. When Sam took notice and turned around to see his gaunt looking older brother, he hollered to the house.

"Come out everyone, Gabriel's home! Gabriel's home! Come on, come now, he's home! He's home!"

Sam ran to his father and brother and joined in their embrace. Soon the rest of the family were running out the front door in a great commotion, calling his name, "Gabriel! Gabriel!"

His sisters Sarah and Mary, his little brother George, and then his mother Lydia. They had all grown over the year, especially his mother, who was due to have her 6th child any day now. They mobbed Gabriel, all hugged and kissed him and welcomed him home, tears of joy in their eyes. Even his old foe Sarah joined in the affection. It was a tremendous homecoming, and Gabriel was overjoyed to see them all, but he couldn't help but notice that Rill and his baby daughter were missing.

As he was about to inquire on them, Rill appeared in the front doorway, cradling a bundle in her left arm. Her right hand was placed over her brow to shade her eyes from the sun, and when she was able to make out who it was, she smiled and whispered under her breath, "Lord, thank you."

She was ecstatic he was home but held her composure and stood on the front porch with the baby. Realizing the significance of the occasion the rest of his family grew silent and gave way to him as he made his way up to the house to his wife and daughter. He removed his hat upon reaching them, leaned in and gave Rill a peck on the cheek.

"Hello, Rill," he said to her.

"Hello, Gabriel," she said back.

Then, looking into her arms he saw his baby daughter for the first time. She was precious, a gorgeous little thing, chubby and swaddled in red flannel. She was awake but content, and her beautiful little inquisitive eyes were wide open for her initial inspection of her father's unfamiliar face. For a moment, they stared into each other's eyes and after the baby looked away to her mother, an overwhelming feeling of joy, accomplishment, and devotion crept into Gabriel's soul.

Retreating inside, the family collected in the kitchen. Gabriel held his daughter for the first time, and as Rill and his mother fixed him something to eat, he answered all the questions they had for him, and told them all that he had to tell. When his mother asked why he surprised them like he did, he said that he simply hadn't known about the furlough until a couple days before he left, and he figured if he had written a letter to tell them, he would have beaten it home anyway.

After he was finished eating, Lydia boiled a pot of tea for everyone and they all sat around the kitchen table to drink and talk, while Rill made her way to the rocking chair in the corner of the room to feed the baby. Before long, it was time for evening chores, and Gabriel offered to help, but he was instantly turned down.

"You may have a full belly, Gabriel," his mother said, "but you still look famished and pale. Take it easy for a while."

His father and Rill agreed.

"Thanks all the same, everyone, but I assure you I feel fine and can help," Gabriel said, as he got to his feet.

Not wanting him to start an argument with his parents just as he'd gotten home, Rill interjected with an alternative idea of her own.

"Gabriel why don't we take the baby over and visit with your Grandma?" she suggested.

Recognizing what Rill was trying to do, Lydia agreed.

"That's a wonderful idea," she said. "Gabriel, why don't you go and visit with her? You know how lonely she's been since Grandpa passed. I bet she'd be head over heels to see that you're back."

Gabriel saw that the girls were working together against him, but not wanting to disappoint his lovely little wife, he agreed and the three of them left shortly after on their first family outing.

* * * * *

The baby fell fast asleep in Gabriel's arms on their walk home later that night. He was enamored with her and, other than giving her up to Rill to suckle, he'd hardly let anyone else hold her during their visit. Coming inside, they waved to Sam and his father who were still up, both reading at the kitchen table. Rill grabbed a spare lamp, lit it, and they crept up the stairs to Gabriel's bedroom, or the place that had been Gabriel's room that is, but for the past several months had been occupied by Rill and then their daughter after she was born.

Gabriel was surprised to see how much it had changed. When it had been his room, it was quite plain with a bed, a chair, a chamber pot and a few of his clothes strewn haphazardly about, but now it was overwhelmingly feminine. Lavender hung in bundles on the walls along with a few other dried bouquets of wildflowers Rill had picked for herself in the pasture. There were pictures hung, too, one being the one of himself he had sent her last fall, and there was also a new side table next to the bed and a dresser. Both the table and dresser had white lace tablecloths spread over top of them, along with a vase of fresh flowers.

As they snuck in the room, Rill shut the door behind them. She took the baby from his arms and lay her in a little cradle that sat up close next to his old bed. The cradle was new, too, and like the side table and dresser was made of a fine dark hard wood. The bed was made up nicely as well, its sheets and blankets flat and void of any wrinkles. Noticing Gabriel look about Rill addressed him on all the changes.

"Papa bought it all for me when he came up," she explained.

"That was awful nice of him," Gabriel said.

He had been looking forward to seeing his father-in-law but found out from Rill shortly after getting home that he'd missed him by four days. Mr. Marsh and Victoria had moved to Middletown, New York down closer to the city. He bought a house there and was planning on getting into farming. Gabriel had trouble picturing him as a farmer and Rill had her doubts too. He was also perplexed on how he was able to pay for it all, the new house and all the items he'd bought for Rill.

"How did he get the money to buy all this and his house? Gabriel asked her. "I thought he was only able to save a little wad of cash before fleeing New York."

"Well he was," Rill said, "but it was a wad of $100 bills. Papa also has investments elsewhere and Uncle Roch owed him some money too."

Hunkering down that night in bed with Rill was a dream come true for Gabriel. As small as it was for the two of them to fit in, they slept just fine. Both found the closeness comforting and cozy, and they were lucky to get a full night sleep as the baby was exhausted and never woke up for a feeding. The next day they went to Harford in the morning with his parents to visit with his Grandma and Grandpa Ballard.

Gabriel spent most of his furlough in rest and recuperation. His initial inclinations to go out and help with chores, passed after a couple of days, when the mental high from being home again started to fade. He was no longer sick, but his body needed time to mend and get strong again. His mother and Rill kept him well-fed, sometimes going overboard with their indulgence. The product of their hard work was showing though, as each passing day, Gabriel's face and body began filling out again. In fact, he gained so quickly, that by the time he had to leave at the end of the furlough, he was heavier than when he left the year before.

To keep from getting too restless, Gabriel also took some more trips with Rill and the baby to visit other friends and family. They did some shopping, too. Preparing for the coming winter, he bought himself a new pair of boots as well as a roll of flannel for his mother to make him a new winter shirt. On another day he surprised Rill by buying her a new bonnet and dress. She was thrilled.

One of the visits that they made around town, came as somewhat of a surprise to Gabriel after Rill suggested it to him. She wanted to go and visit her sister Hannah and brother-in-law George. Gabriel declined at first, thinking that even if he wanted to go, Hannah would ask him to leave anyhow, but after some friendly persuasion by Rill one night, he reluctantly gave in and agreed to her request. Gabriel disliked Hannah, and not only for the way she had treated him before the war, but also because she had given Rill the boot after she got pregnant. It didn't change his mind any about her either, when after the baby was born, Hannah half-heartedly offered Rill her old room back. In his opinion, the damage had already been done. Rill kindly declined her anyway.

The visit was awkward of course, not much was said between Gabriel or Hannah, other than the traditional greetings, but it wasn't all that bad. For one, it was the first occasion in years Hannah hadn't seen him in her home only to run him out a moment later. They had a nice meal, and coffee and spent the afternoon talking and doting over the baby.

When it was time for little Martha to nurse, George and Gabriel stepped out the back door to stretch and talk among themselves. The weather was getting to be very autumn-like, and the trees were changing with the season. Red, yellow, orange and brown leaves were scattered about the yard.

"I know it's a little late, Gabriel, but I want to congratulate you on your marriage and the birth of that lovely baby girl of yours in there," George said to him, holding out his hand for Gabriel to shake. He did and was glad to.

"I appreciate it, George, and thanks for everything that you've done for Rill and I. I don't think I'll ever be able to repay you for sneaking her out last fall and smuggling our letters this past winter. I know it mustn't have been easy for you, especially after the time you got caught."

George chuckled at the thought of all the trouble Hannah had given him. "Think nothing of it. We're all family now anyways," he reassured Gabriel.

"Speaking of family," Gabriel said facetiously, "how was it having our father-in-law and his clan here for the past few months?"

Gabriel couldn't help but smile as he asked, because he knew it must have been a nightmare for old George, between having all the extra folks in his house and Hannah complaining about them incessantly. George wasn't one to betray his true feelings, though. He said that it wasn't that bad at first, but knowing how he was, Gabriel pried a little harder.

"Oh really, they weren't at all noisy, were they?" he asked him.

"Noisy, no. Those kids were so quiet half the time I forgot they were even here."

From the way he looked away when answering his questions, Gabriel knew George was avoiding something.

"I wasn't talking about the kids," he said to him.

A smile finally crept over George's face. His tight-lipped defenses had momentarily failed him. Gabriel knew it, and erupted into a contagious laughter, that even George couldn't resist.

"Well, tell me about it. Did they go at it all day and night?" Gabriel asked him.

"All day, every day," George said with a grin.

"My God," Gabriel exclaimed. "They went at it the whole time Enos and I visited them last October, too. He kept disappearing to go and 'help Victoria' is what he told us, but we could hear he was doing a whole lot more than that."

George chuckled. "He said nothing of it to me. We'd all be sitting around and he'd just up and leave every so often to go and well… make some noise with her I guess."

"Unbelievable, and what did Hannah say about it?" Gabriel asked.

"Nothing. She just sat there and ignored it every time. Never said a word to me about it and still hasn't and I don't dare to ask."

Gabriel leaned onto the side of the house and laughed hysterically. It was all just so bizarre and hilarious to him. He laughed so hard that his sides began to ache, and he had trouble catching his breath once he'd finally calmed down. It was a good healthy laugh. George just smiled though and shook his head, half concerned that Hannah would hear what they were talking about.

They both went inside, and Gabriel left with Rill and the baby soon afterwards.

"What was all that giggling about?" Rill asked him as they made their way down the road.

"Oh, nothing," Gabriel told her.

He tried to think of something to divert her curiosity but ended up getting some unexpected help from the baby instead. He was cradling her and started to feel a warm and wet sensation spread over his arm.

"Say Rill hold her for a second," he said as he handed her off.

Rill was somewhat skeptical of what he was up to, but she found out once he took a good whiff of his arm and started retching. She laughed and held the baby out with both arms extended and her head cocked to the side trying not to smell her.

"Dammit, she pooped on my arm, and its diarrhea," Gabriel said in between heaves.

Rill had little sympathy for him, though, and was quick to pass the baby back. She was still laughing, but Gabriel wasn't amused.

"I don't want her now," he said, "she smells rotten."

Rill was adamant, though.

"Maybe so, but she's already soiled your clothes and there's no sense in dirtying mine too.

CHAPTER ELEVEN

Leaving home was another sad and tearful de-ja-vu for Gabriel, but little did he know it would be the last time he would ever have to do so. Word of his upcoming departure spread around town, and on his final week there, he daily received visitors, bearing letters for him to bring to their loved ones. Enos's wife, Julia Cook, was one of the last to see him, and along with a couple of letters, she also brought a hat and mittens for him to take down to her husband. He was more than happy to do so for Mrs. Cook. He would have delivered an elephant for her if she had asked it of him. She and Enos had done so much for him and Rill, and Gabriel made it well-known around town and to his family, that if it hadn't been for Enos he'd be in heaven and his body rotting away in the Virginia soil.

Before he left, Rill and his parents presented some gifts for him to take back as well. As Julia had done for Enos, Rill made him a new hat and pair of mittens and his parents gave him a new and thicker blanket to keep him warm that winter. The hat that Rill made was extra special to him, because it was more than just a hat. It was constructed with the fabric of one of the baby's old blankets, and it was of a unique design. It folded down to cover his face and neck, with a few slits sewn in for his eyes and mouth. She also cut him a new braid of her hair to replace the one she had given him in February.

The train ride back to Washington, was especially lonesome for Gabriel, but he reassured himself with the knowledge that his depressed feelings would eventually pass. He arrived at Harewood Hospital on the 13th of October and was returned to full duty by Dr. Terry the very next day. There was something of a snag, however, for a couple weeks before, his regiment, along with the remainder of the 11th and

12th Corps, had been detached from the Army of the Potomac and sent south to Alabama.

It was an eleven-day journey for Gabriel by rail to get back to his regiment. He left Washington on the night of October 17th with a load of other convalescents returning to their commands. They traveled west through Maryland, and the newly-christened state of West Virginia into Ohio. After passing through Columbus, they continued on through Cincinnati, and then part of Indiana to Louisville, Kentucky. From there, they turned directly south, to and through Nashville, Tennessee and on to their final destination of Bridgeport, Alabama, where they arrived on the 28th.

It had been a long trip, that he started in a melancholy mood, but after making a few friends he loosened up some and made the best of things. Often Gabriel and his new pals would climb to the top of the cars to get a better view of the countryside. They climbed up top in the big cities too, to see the sights and people watch. Some of the boys played a game to see who could get the most girls to wave at them, and a blown kiss garnered extra points. The trip turned into something of an adventure and one of mischief, too. Surrounded by strangers, and with little chance of his deeds ever being passed on to the folks at home, he tried a drink of whiskey for the first time in his life. He found it tasted awful, but he enjoyed its effects, as it seemed to temporarily wash his sorrows of missing Rill and the baby away. In Ohio, he tasted applejack and then in Kentucky he got into some even harder stuff. They quit drinking that though, when one of the boys spit his mouthful out onto the side of a boxcar and its paint began to melt away.

He told himself that this was it. Once he got back to his regiment the drinking would end. He didn't want folks gossiping about him in letters home, and he knew he could never let Enos find out, for if he did it'd disappoint him, and Gabriel would feel crushingly ashamed at having let him down. Enos disapproved of drink entirely, and had up until that point been able to mentor Gabriel away from the indulging influence of some of the other men in their company.

Gabriel also took some of the free time he had to ponder over life and what the future might bring. As the trip neared its end, he thought about his company and was curious to see how much it had changed in the months he'd been gone. He knew there were likely to be more missing faces, men who'd died or been discharged, or were stranded sick in a hospital somewhere just as he had been.

One person he knew would be missing was Captain Marvin. Lieutenant George was now temporarily in command of the company as Marvin was ill and had been sent home on a furlough shortly after Gabriel had been. The two had neglected to see one another, though. Gabriel was happy to know he was gone and hoped he wouldn't ever come back. The stunt Marvin had pulled on him in Virginia was still fresh in his mind, and he knew if it hadn't been for Enos's righteous disobedience, Marvin's loathing and negligence would have killed him.

Truthfully, Marvin was a changed man from the angry tyrant the company had known in the first few months of their service. His public feud with Moffat, and the near loss of his company due to its rash of early desertions, had knocked him down a peg or two. Because of those circumstances, coupled with his ever-growing dependence on alcohol, Marvin had become a bitter and depressed man. His condition further deteriorated with the long and tedious duties that the regiment was constantly being assigned to. Simply put, he desired more action, especially when it seemed that the other regiments recruited around Dryden, were constantly being put in the most vicious of fights.

The desire to prove themselves was one felt by almost all the men of the 143rd, including Gabriel. They all felt unworthy to an extent and as a result, Marvin soon found himself some drinking company among the other dejected officers in the regiment. For the most part, the Dryden boys liked the new Marvin because he was far less demanding of them, even if he had reached the point of being almost too apathetic.

One of the only officers to not take part in their drinking, dancing, gambling and card play, was Lieutenant Moffat. For this reason, Moffat soon came to be known as an outsider among his peers. His reputation took further damage from the constant complaints Marvin was always airing of him, and before long much of the regiments officer corps came to despise him.

It didn't help matters much either that Moffat continued to be captivated with his wife and the procurement of a furlough to go home and see her. The other officers much resented him for this, because during the previous winter his wife had been practically glued to his side in Washington, while everyone else was forced to do without. They thought him weak and arrogant, and that he felt he was entitled to special privileges. They were partially correct, but he was mostly just homesick like the rest of them, and his wife was very difficult to please. She was needy and complained to an extreme, and it drove Moffat half mad trying to make her happy.

Marvin relished in Moffat's downfall, but still held a special grudge for anyone in the company whom he perceived to be Moffat's ally. Gabriel was one of these unlucky individuals, and it was true, too. Gabriel did like Moffat, in fact most of the enlisted men did. They liked him because he showed them respect and was genuinely concerned for their welfare. They also respected him for the fact that he didn't drink, and it wasn't because they were teetotalers themselves. The men saw it as unfair that while most of their officers were constantly getting drunk and partying late into the night, they at the same time had no qualms about punishing their men for doing the same thing.

The event that cemented Marvin's disapproval of Gabriel, was when Moffat had gone out of his way to take him to meet up with Rill and get married in Washington. He thought that Moffat had shown far too much favor with the young private, especially when he heard that he had invited the newlyweds back to his wife's apartment for the night. In Marvin's mind, Gabriel had clearly aligned himself with Moffat in their feud. This made him highly suspicious and bitter toward him and was precisely why he had accused Gabriel of feigning illness at Warrenton.

Had Marvin taken the time to ask Gabriel his true feelings, he would have been told something completely different though, for truth be told if the Devil himself had offered to take Gabriel into Washington to marry Rill that past February, he would have likely accepted. There was no more of a conspiracy against Marvin between Gabriel and Moffat than there was between Moffat and any one of the other enlisted men in the company. Moffat was just being kind as he was to most everyone, and Gabriel took him up on his offer because it was the best chance he had at getting to Rill.

* * * * *

The Union's Army of the Cumberland had been trapped and under siege within the city of Chattanooga, Tennessee since retreating there in September, after their defeat at the Battle of Chickamauga. When it entered the city, the Army had been under the command of General William Rosecrans but on October 19th, as Gabriel's train was entering Ohio, Rosecrans was relieved and General George H. Thomas was named his replacement. General Thomas had been active in the western theater throughout the war thus far and made a name for himself at Chickamauga where his troops held off the Rebels long enough for the remainder of their Army to retreat to safety. This earned Thomas his "Rock of Chickamauga" nickname.

Besieged as they were, Thomas's troops were having a hard go of it. Supplies were extremely limited, as the only route into the city, from the Army's main supply base at Bridgeport, Alabama, was nearly sixty miles long. The route was a logistical nightmare for its length and the fact that large portions of it ran through mountainous terrain where the trail turned very narrow, steep, and dangerous. These conditions, along with occasional Rebel attacks, greatly slowed and cut back on the essential rations his troops needed to survive. Thomas's boys were slowly starving, and their morale was in a downward spiral.

To help save the Army of the Cumberland from destruction, General Joseph Hooker with the 11th and 12th Corps from the east, as well as another contingent of troops from farther west under General William Tecumseh Sherman were being sent to its relief. Placed in overall command of all these converging troops was General Ulysses S. Grant.

Soon after Grant arrived on scene at Thomas's headquarters on the 23rd of October, he not surprisingly felt his first and most pressing need was to open a better route of supply into Chattanooga from Bridgeport. To do so, he made the task a joint operation, utilizing troops from both the Army of the Cumberland and the newly arrived 11th and 12th Corps, who were positioned far outside of the city, around Bridgeport and along the existing supply route into Chattanooga. Not all the troops of the 11th or 12th Corps were chosen to participate, but the 143rd New York was, and they marched out of Bridgeport for the operation on the morning of October 27th.

* * * * *

When Gabriel arrived in Bridgeport on the 28th, he was greatly disappointed to hear that his regiment had left without him just the day before. The excitement that had built at the thought of rejoining his friends quickly subsided. He was angry too, because other than the items in his haversack and the blanket his parents had gifted him, all his possessions were in the regiment's baggage wagons and he had no way to get to them. He had no tent, no knapsack, no poncho, no change of clothes and no canteen. He didn't even have his rifle or its attending accoutrements, and now that he was back in the South and in hostile territory, he felt naked without them.

The next day, rumors began to spread that a battle had been fought upriver and a new supply line called the "Cracker Line" was now open to Chattanooga. Details were few, so Gabriel was skeptical at first, but his suspicions turned to belief when a steamboat and two barges were sent upriver that night loaded with supplies. Folks all about camp were cheerful at the good news, but Gabriel felt left out.

He held out hope that his friends had been held in the reserve, but the next day he was shocked to hear that the 143rd had actually gotten to fight. It was a stunning blow to his pride, and he felt sick knowing that he was now, along with Captain Marvin, one of the few in the company to have never seen battle. He cursed himself for getting sick, and then for not leaving home earlier. He thought that if he had just left a day or two earlier, he would have made it down in time to march off with his regiment. He was consumed with feelings of regret.

Gabriel waited anxiously in Bridgeport for a few days before finally being sent upriver to help along a load of supplies headed for Chattanooga. It took nearly five days to reach their destination, but on November 4th he was finally reunited with his company. Gabriel was thrilled to see them all once again, as they were to see him, especially when he pulled out the stack of letters he'd brought down from home. The men lucky enough to get one quickly withdrew to their tents to tear them open, while the others stood around Gabriel to ask about home, if he had seen their families, how the crops were doing, who was ill, if anyone had passed away or been born and various other inquiries.

Enos and Dave were the last to see him. They had been away on an errand for Lieutenant George when he arrived and when they saw him addressing the crowd on their way back into camp, they ran over to see their dear friend. Enos came up and gave him a big hug, while Dave gave him a nice firm handshake and congratulated him on his return.

"We were beginnin' to think you were never comin' back, boy," Dave said to him.

"That's right," Enos added, "but we're more than happy to see that you did."

Looking over his two friends for the first time in months, Gabriel couldn't help but notice that Dave looked the same as ever, but Enos was strikingly slim, and his skin had paled a shade or two. He didn't mention it, but it worried him.

"Well, I'm happy to see you too," he said to his friends. "Where were you anyway? I've been back for almost an hour now."

"Oh, Lieutenant George sent me over to headquarters with some reports," Enos answered.

"Yep, and I went along with him lookin' for a drink, but they hid it on me good this time. I ain't had a swallow since before we left Alabama."

"Nine whole days. Good for you, Dave. I'm impressed," Gabriel said to him.

"Well, it weren't by choice, little buddy. I'm dying for a sip of somethin'. Why, I'd slurp a drop a whiskey off the ground if it were spilt right here in front of me."

Gabriel couldn't help but chuckle. Dave surely hadn't changed a bit.

"So, I hear you two got to do some fighting?" Gabriel said to them. It still hurt to think about what he'd missed out on, but he thought he'd bite the bullet and get the conversation out of the way.

"Yes Sir, we did," Dave said with pride, his chest puffed out. "We whipped 'em good too, let me tell ya, and all these western boys around here are obliged to us for doin' so. They were starvin' in that city till we come along."

Dave was quite enthusiastic about the battle, but Enos knew it must have upset Gabriel that he hadn't been there and tried downplaying it for him.

"Well, I wouldn't say we whipped them, Dave," he said. "I suppose we won, but Gabriel, it was so dark out we could hardly see where we were going. Some of the boys got lost in a swamp and when we did start shooting it was off into the dark. We had to aim at where we thought we saw the last flash of their rifle fire and then shoot on a whim. It was madness."

"Well, I still wish I was there," Gabriel said dejectedly as he nudged a stone about at his feet. "Was anyone hurt?"

"Six. Five wounded and one killed," Dave said.

"Who died?"

"Oh, one of the boys from Company G. Teller was his name. He was a young buck like you." Enos said.

Gabriel knew exactly who he was talking about. They hadn't been in the same company, but he had talked with the guy a time or two before. He was always friendly.

"He held on for a while," Dave added, "but lost too much blood in the end. Them G boys are awfully shook up over it."

"I can imagine," Gabriel said.

Trying to change the subject, Enos asked Gabriel about home, and it reminded him of the items he still had left to give to them.

"I almost forgot I have these letters here for you two," Gabriel said, as he pulled the envelopes from his haversack and handed them over.

They both thanked him, happy to get their little treasures. Gabriel dug out the hat and mittens Julia had made for him, too. He could see it made Enos a little misty eyed. It had been well over a year since he or Dave had seen their families.

"Looks like your father's handwritin'," Dave said as he looked over his two letters.

"That's right," Gabriel answered him. "We had Electa and the children over for supper one night before I left, and Father wrote one for her and another from your kids. There's a paragraph in there from every one of them too. Electa thought you'd like that."

Dave nodded and smiled, happy to know the Ballards were watching out over his family. He was certainly a rough-around-the-edges character, but he cared deeply for his wife and kids, even if he didn't always outwardly portray it.

"Little devils they are," he said. "Were they well behaved?"

Gabriel hesitated, thinking how he would answer Dave without offending him.

"Well, Dave, lets just say they reminded me a lot of their father," he ended up coming up with. "I didn't see it, but my brother told me when they'd gone, he caught your little John taking a sip of my father's cider."

"Did he, now?" Dave asked with a look of delight.

"That's what Sam claims."

"Well, I'll be. Electa always said he was my spittin' image. Looks and manners alike."

Gabriel found it amusing, but Enos seemed mortified by Dave's reaction. Especially when he gloated that he, "couldn't be more proud of that boy. Takes his first sip at the age of four, while his daddy took his at six. Little rascal beat me by two whole years he did."

After visiting a while longer, Enos excused himself and retired to his tent. He said he wanted to see what Julia had written, but Gabriel could tell he was looking a little peaked too. When he'd gone, Gabriel and Dave went out in search of Wallace Wheeler, the regimental quartermaster, to see about getting his things out of storage. They found Wheeler and he directed them to a wagon full of knapsacks, rifles and other spare items left behind by absent soldiers. They had to dig through half the wagon to find his knapsack, as he had no name on his, and each one they dug out had to be opened to see if it contained anything familiar to him. His rifle was easier to find as Enos had sewn a rifle sock out of an old pair of trousers to protect it during his absence. When they cut it out it smelled to high heaven though and had a greasy substance all over the barrel and trigger mechanism. Gabriel was sickened by the smell.

"What's on it?" he asked looking over his glistening hands in disgust after pulling the rifle out of its homemade sheath. "It smells like death in that bag."

"Quit your bitchin'," Dave said. "It's bacon grease. Must have gone rancid, but nothin' a little soap and boilin' water won't fix."

"How did bacon grease get on my rifle?"

"Well, we knew you'd probably be gone a while, so we coated it in the stuff before Enos sewed it in. Didn't want it to rust."

"Well, why use bacon grease on my brand new rifle, wasn't there anything else available?" Gabriel complained.

The whole regiment had been issued new weapons before departing for Suffolk that spring. Their old Austrian-Lorenz models were turned in and they were given the more modern 1861 Springfields in return.

"No, boy, there weren't. That's all we had. We coulda just thrown it in the wagon as is. How'd you like to be scrapin' three months' worth of rust off the thing?"

Dave was right and Gabriel knew it.

"I suppose you've got a point there, Dave. You two didn't have to do anything but you did, so thank you."

"Oh, shut up," Dave said and playfully slapped Gabriel's kepi down over his eyes.

He was finished being the nice and complimentary Dave that had joyously welcomed him back an hour before.

"Get your shit picked up and we'll go back to camp and melt that slime off," he added before heading off towards where their company was bivouacked.

Hurriedly, Gabriel threw his knapsack on, fastened his belt, and tossed his canteen, cartridge box and rifle over his shoulder before running to catch up with Dave. He instantly wished he'd wiped his hands off before doing so.

"Wait up, Dave," he called out after him. "I want to ask you something before we go back."

Dave slowed down.

"What you wanna know?" he asked.

"It's about Enos," Gabriel said. "What's going on with him? He looks so thin and pale. I thought he was going to pass out before he went back to his tent to read his letters."

Dave stopped, so Gabriel did as well.

"So he looks thin, does he?" Dave asked.

"Oh, for sure. Drastically, compared to when I saw him last."

"Dammit!" Dave said.

"What?"

"Oh I don't know. I thought he was lookin' sickly too, but it's hard to tell when you see him every day. Changes like that are less apparent, and I guess I just kept thinkin' it was all in my mind, but you ain't seen him in months, so it's got to be so."

"Do you think he's okay?" Gabriel asked.

"I don't know. You're the one who was sick, not me. I guess he has seemed to have had less energy lately, though. You saw how tired he looked earlier. Before, he never got sleepy during the day. He was always the first up in the morning, the first to volunteer if anything needed doin', and the last to go to bed. Come to think of it, though, I had to wake him up today, and he almost missed morning roll call."

"How long has he been like this then?" Gabriel asked.

"I'm not sure," Dave said. "Like I told ya, it's been hard for me to notice because I see him every day. I'd guess a month, though maybe more."

Gabriel was worried for his friend. He had thought the anxiety of illness would be all gone once he was back to full duty again, but with

Enos looking so poorly, those worries were back again, and they came on worse than before. He had always been more concerned about his family or friends than he was of his own problems, and he considered Enos to be both.

* * * * *

It took little time for Gabriel to get reacquainted with Army life. In fact, the day after he showed up, he was sent right out onto picket duty. Their camp was located in Lookout Valley, wedged between Raccoon Mountain, the Tennessee River and Lookout Mountain. Most of the land to the east of their position, including Lookout Mountain was occupied by the Confederate Army under General Braxton Bragg. Quite often the Confederates would test their artillery skill on the Yankee camp, and sent shells screaming into their midst on a regular basis. Most of the time, nobody was injured, but occasionally shrapnel from the shells punched holes in their tents and once a solid shot landed right in the middle of Company K's breakfast fire, but it did nothing more than ruin their meal.

The lines of the opposing armies were very close, and quite often men could be seen by their foe, going about their daily business. Consequently, the picket lines were very close as well, and the men had to be exceptionally vigilant when placed in that duty. To make sure he stayed awake while on picket, Gabriel chewed on his coffee beans instead of grinding and boiling them down. He thought it helped keep him more alert. The picket line could be dangerous, and on one occasion, Lieutenant Moffat had a ball pass through his coat while posting a detail from Company G.

The closeness also tempted the two sides into fraternization. On many occasions, the men from both armies would make trade with each other across the lines, and it was in this way that Dave Nash was able to keep himself steadily supplied with spirits. He traded just about anything available, spare socks he'd stolen from a quartermaster, Yankee greenbacks, food, coffee, tea and on one occasion a Dryden newspaper Gabriel had brought from home. Only once was he cheated, when the

Rebs gave him a bottle of river water instead of whiskey. His hooting and hollering after he took the first swig, caused laughter and taunts from both sides of the line, but Dave was none too happy.

"Why, that's a crime close to murder in my book," Dave cried out when he got back to camp. "Them lousy Johnnys are just as rotten as the papers make them out to be. They say God's on their side but what kind of Christian cheats a fellow human bein' as they did me today?" he hypocritically asked out loud to no one particular.

As had been the arrangement before Gabriel was sent to the hospital in August, he returned to being tentmates with Enos again. Enos and Dave had paired up when he was gone, but when Gabriel came back, Dave was kind enough to move back in with Baldy. Unlike the large A-frame tents the men had been issued while on garrison in Washington, they were given the much smaller "shelter half" when they departed for Suffolk. The "shelter half" was a rectangular piece of canvas with a row of buttons and holes running along one of its long ends. Buttoned together with another soldier's "half", these two pieces made a smaller version of the A-frame tent. Back together again, Gabriel tried his best to help Enos out. He always went to get both of their rations when food was issued, he cooked both their meals before Enos could object, and if a detail was being formed, he volunteered before Enos could.

"If only he can make it to winter without getting any worse," Gabriel explained to Dave one night, "then perhaps he'll start to gain his weight back and get better again."

His reasoning was that once in winter camp, there would be much less for the men to do, and more time for Enos to rest and recuperate. Winter was almost always the down time of year for the Army, because the crummy weather usually muddled the roads enough to prevent anyone from moving about. It would, however, be different this year, as Gabriel was soon to find out.

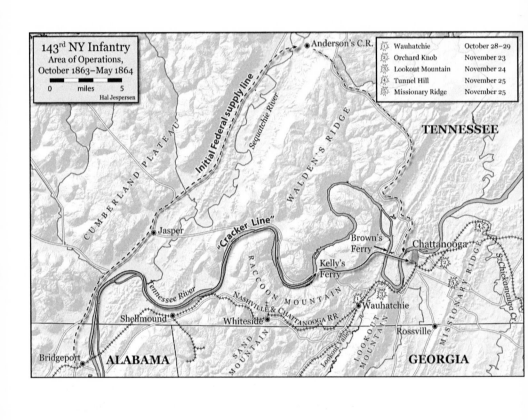

143rd NY Infantry
Area of Operations,
October 1863–May 1864

0   miles   5

Hal Jespersen

Wauhatchie	October 28–29
Orchard Knob	November 23
Lookout Mountain	November 24
Tunnel Hill	November 25
Missionary Ridge	November 25

Anderson's C.R.

TENNESSEE

Initial Federal supply line

Sequatchie River

CUMBERLAND PLATEAU

WALDEN'S RIDGE

Jasper

"Cracker Line"

Brown's Ferry

Chattanooga

Kelly's Ferry

RACCOON MOUNTAIN

Tennessee River

NASHVILLE & CHATTANOOGA RR

Shellmound

Whiteside

Wauhatchie

Rossville

MISSIONARY RIDGE

S. Chickamauga Cr.

SAND MOUNTAIN

LOOKOUT MOUNTAIN

Lookout Valley

Bridgeport

ALABAMA

GEORGIA

CHAPTER TWELVE

On November 22nd, 1863, Gabriel, and his regiment, along with the rest of the 11th Corps, were issued three days' rations, 60 rounds of ammunition, and ordered to pack up their camp in Lookout Valley. They tore down their tents, cooked their food, and loaded everything into their baggage wagons. Even their knapsacks were packed away.

Rumors spread that they had been selected to support the Army of the Cumberland in a major offensive. Usually skeptical of Army rumor, the men became believers when after their camp was dismantled, they were marched out of Lookout Valley and over to Chattanooga. After months of occupation by the penned-up Army of the Cumberland, the town looked bleak and deserted of civilians, but they only saw it in passing, as they marched right through en route to the open table land on the outskirts of the city.

Chattanooga was a river town, the Tennessee River running around a good portion of it, but to the east and south lay the Chattanooga Valley. Beyond the valley stood the prominent heights of Lookout Mountain and Missionary Ridge, where the besieging Confederates were dug in. The Confederates had troops in the valley too at the base of both mountains, and it was there where the opposing armies faced each other.

The next morning, the union troops were roused and formed into line of battle. The men in the 143rd were excited, all of them ready to perform and prove their worth. The nighttime fight, fought a few weeks before, had been their first test, but this was to be much more than that. There were thousands of men in blue assembled and spread out over the land as far as the eye could see. Their foe had the high ground, as well as fortifications directly in front of the Yankee troops on the flats. The Rebel soldiers on the heights looked down on their foe and thought of them as many blue-clad ants, waiting to be squashed underfoot. Gabriel waited about anxiously all morning for the fight to begin, but nothing happened other than a few cannon blasts, and scattered rifle shots from the picket lines.

Around noon, though, the battle began to commence, as two of Thomas's divisions moved forward toward the Confederate lines. As he saw them go, Gabriel looked himself over to make sure everything was belted and buckled snuggly. He was in line with Dave and Enos at either side of him. Unfortunately, Enos had not recovered like he'd hoped, and still looked very sickly, but when Lieutenant George suggested he sit this one out, he refused and found his spot in line.

"I don't know why everyone thinks I look ill. I feel just fine," Enos lied. "Besides, Gabriel," he said to him as they stood about, "if I went to the rear, and something happened to you or one of the other boys I'd never forgive myself."

Gabriel felt uneasy about his friend, but fully understood what it felt like to be left out and couldn't blame him for wanting to tag along.

As Thomas's western troops advanced, the heavy roll of rifle fire and the deafening blasts of cannon pummeled his ear drums. It was louder fighting than anything Gabriel had ever heard, and his heart began beating rapidly in his chest in anticipation, eager to get the order to advance. He waited and waited, and soon the roar of battle began to slacken, its climax having passed. It was only then that the order to move was finally given. Marching forward, a cannon shot or two burst near, and slight rifle fire could be heard again, but there were other men from his division in their front, so the few shots fired from his sector of the battle were far ahead and removed from his position. Soon, the thunder of battle died away again, and an odd sound was heard off in the distance. After a few moments, the men realized it was in fact cheering. The Confederates had been routed from their first line of fortifications and were now scurrying to their hillside lines in front of Missionary Ridge. Victoriously, the Yankees had pushed out much farther from the city than where they had started that morning. Their lines now went out as far as a little wooded hillock in the valley, known as Orchard Knob.

That night, Gabriel and many of the other men in his regiment felt cheated, as they had been held in reserve all day. Enos, encouraged them on, though, correctly stating that the Rebels were far from defeated, and still held the high ground. The following day, the men became even more distraught, though, for as they were sent to work chopping down trees and fortifying their new position, most of the other troops that had come south with them under General Hooker, were now in a victorious fight of their own on Lookout Mountain.

It was more of the same on the third day of the battle. After being used to build a new line of fortifications in the valley, the 143rd was sent north to join up with the troops under General Sherman. It was Sherman's task to attack the Confederate right flank on Tunnel Hill at the northern end of Missionary Ridge. He was to carry that position, and then, once he had broken through, was to march along the top of the ridge folding up the Confederate line as he advanced. Things didn't go as planned, though. Sherman met a much tougher resistance than anticipated, and was repulsed several times, but again the 143rd was held in the reserve. Only after the day was finally won, on a different location on the battlefield, were they finally sent in, and then it was only to mop up. Their only loss was the deaths of two men, Lieutenant Colonel Taft, who was placed in command of a Pennsylvania regiment and died fighting far removed from his own men, and a private, who was shot in the head by a stray bullet, fired from where the real fighting was occurring.

The Battle of Chattanooga was the greatest fight the 143rd New York ever took part in, but it also turned out to be their greatest disappointment. This was especially so for Gabriel, who had been sure it was to be his baptism of fire, his first taste of real fighting, but in the end he saw it as just another Suffolk, for he and his regiment, just as they had that spring in coastal Virginia, just stood around and watched as other men did the fighting for them.

Still, though, the men were spent. With the constant movement and shifting of positions, the building of fortifications and the nervous anticipation of always being on the cusp of battle, the men were physically and mentally exhausted. The pursuit of the retreating Confederates took precedence, though, and in the days following the battle they joined in the chase, following the enemy all the way into Georgia.

On the 29th of November, new orders were again issued to the men of the 143rd. This time, they were to accompany General Sherman and his command to the relief of General Burnside, who was under a siege of his own 120 miles away in Knoxville, Tennessee. They moved off at a fast pace, traveling north along the Tennessee River in a most arduous campaign. Most days they started off before the sun rose and didn't stop until it went down again. On the 4th of December, the 143rd was tasked with building a pontoon bridge across the Little Tennessee River near Loudon. Unfortunately, the river wasn't as small as its name suggested, being nearly 300 yards wide at the bridge site. It was freezing out that day, and it was made worse when the men had to wade into the icy water to aide in the construction. The bridge was made by stringing planks over 50 captured wagons from one side of the river to the other.

Initially, as the men moved towards Knoxville, they were inspired by what they saw as an opportunity to fight in another decisive battle and gain themselves a little more prestige and glory. They simply wanted something good to write home and brag about. That was certainly what motivated Gabriel, but the taxing march was proving too much for his good friend Enos. Each day he lagged behind the main column of the regiment, but he always caught back up to them at night, sometimes over an hour after they had halted. Dave and Gabriel felt bad, so they took turns falling back with him to make sure he made it through each day okay. Lieutenant George begged Enos to ride in the regimental ambulance, but ever faithful and determined to pull his own weight, he refused.

On the day of the bridge build, things for Enos took a turn for the worse, though. While trying to lay a plank across two wagons in the river, he fell into the icy water, soaking himself from head to toe. Luckily, William Baldwin was right beside him and managed to grab ahold of his collar and pull him to shore before he was swept away. He was unconscious, so they stripped him of his wet clothing, wrapped him up in dry blankets as best they could and placed him in an empty wagon.

It was all for naught, too, for the day after, the men received word that they would be turning back toward Chattanooga. The siege in Knoxville had been lifted before they could get there, and the Confederate forces that had been attacking the city were on a full retreat into Virginia. The news was yet another blow to Gabriel and the men in his regiment.

Their dejection made the return march a bitter task to carry out. Not only were they tired and depressed, but the weather was making things miserable as well. It was cold, windy and rained most of the time, and on a few occasions the rain turned to ice, coating the men and wagons, and making the already nearly-impassable roads even harder to traverse. To make matters worse, their provisions were running dangerously low, and they had to make do with what they could find along the way, which wasn't very much in that part of the country.

On the 16th of December, after nearly a month of being in almost constant motion, the 143rd at last reached Chattanooga and on the following day went back into their old camp in Lookout Valley. By this time, the men had reached their limit, some over it. They were famished, and many were dressed in rags or walking barefoot, with blood oozing from their worn out feet at each painful step. Gabriel was lucky to have had the new boots he purchased while home, his footwear was still intact, but considerably worn.

Many were also ill, Enos being the worst among them. After his plunge in the river, he became a permanent resident of the regiment's ambulance, and his condition deteriorated at a steady pace. Each morning, Gabriel and Dave would go and see him before they started the day's march, and each morning he looked a little worse for wear. Noticing this, they shared with him what little they were given to eat. They thought it would give his body the extra nourishment it needed. It worked, but only for a day or two, up until he started having trouble with his bowels as well. He developed a terrible case of diarrhea, and after that it seemed all hope was lost. He could have been fed like a general, but it still wouldn't have mattered. His body couldn't hold anything in long enough to make use of.

* * * * *

On the day Gabriel and the 143rd went back into their old camp in Lookout Valley, Enos was far too ill to accompany them. Instead he was sent to the 3rd Division's hospital and the following morning after roll call, Lieutenant George called Gabriel and Dave aside.

"Listen up, you two," he said to them, "I just spoke with Lieutenant Moffat. He was over to the hospital late last night checking on a couple of the boys from his company. He said he visited Enos too, and that he didn't look good. He thinks it's only a matter of time. I want you boys to go over and see him. You're the two he's closest with, and I think it may give him some comfort seeing you."

By the tone of his voice, Gabriel could tell that Lieutenant George thought the situation dire. He and Dave thanked him for being so considerate and were quickly on their way. As they left, George called out behind them and said to take all the time they needed. He was a good man like that, and easily the best junior officer in the regiment.

The hospital was about a quarter mile from their camp, so it didn't take long for them to reach. After asking around, they were able to locate his tent. Going in, though, they found its condition deplorable. It was colder inside than out, and it appeared as if none of the patients had been seen yet that day. One man was clearly deceased, and from the smell emanating from his bed, they could tell that Enos was laying in his own filth. He was sound asleep, though, so they dared not wake him.

Gabriel felt sick at seeing Enos in such a wretched state. This was nothing like his experience at Harewood in Washington, but then he realized it was an entirely different situation. Dave felt awful, too, but expressed his distaste with anger. Gritting his teeth, he quietly motioned for Gabriel to join him outside.

As they were making their way through the tent flap, a young hospital steward was just walking by and cheerfully gave the two men a tip of his cap and a "good morning." His good mood only added to Dave's frustration though, as he couldn't perceive how someone could be so cheerful while the men under his care were in such a neglected condition. In a fury, Dave leapt at the unsuspecting man and grabbed him by the scruff of his collar.

"Why the fuck haven't the men in that tent been seen to?" he growled, pulling him in so close that their foreheads were almost touching.

In shock, the color instantly drained from the man's face.

"I...I...I," he tried to speak.

"You what?" Dave shouted at the top of his lungs.

"I...I don't know Sir; I just came on duty and am just now making my rounds."

Disgusted, Dave shoved him away.

"Well, tell me why the hell is the stove in that tent cold as ice? Its freezin' in there and there's one man dead and another swimmin' in his own shit."

"I don't know, Sir. Like I said, I just came on duty. I guess the night crew was too busy. We've only got a quarter of the men we need and half the supplies..."

"Oh, bullshit. There's no excuse for what's goin' on in there," Dave interrupted him.

He went for the man again and the man tried to run off, but Dave caught him by the arm and swung him around towards the front of Enos's tent. "Right where I wanted ya," Dave said to him, then gave the man a hard kick in the rear end and sent him flying into the opening face first.

"Now get in there and make things right," he ordered.

As the steward went to work on his patients, Dave went to find some firewood, and he sent Gabriel off to find a bucket of hot water to bathe Enos with. When they got back, Dave got the fire in the tent's woodstove going again, and Gabriel helped the steward remove the deceased soldier's body. That way, Enos could have the man's cleaner sheets and bed once he got cleaned up himself. When everything was as it should be, Gabriel and Dave stepped outside, so that the steward could wake their still-sleeping friend and wash him up with the water Gabriel had fetched. When the man had Enos dressed and tucked back into bed, he stepped outside to let them know Enos was ready to see them.

"Your friend is waiting," he told them.

"Thanks," Gabriel said.

The man had been kind, and was very helpful, despite how he had been treated. Gabriel and Dave could see that he cared, too, and had been truthful when he told them he was just coming on duty when they stopped him. They could also see that the hospital was grossly overwhelmed with patients. Just in the time it took them to get Enos's tent back into shape, over 100 men had come in from morning sick call, with more likely to follow. The Knoxville march had done a number on everyone's health that took part in it.

After realizing he had wronged the young steward, Dave felt so bad that he reached in his pocket and pulled out five whole dollars. It was nearly half a month's pay, but he gave it to the man in thanks and with the understanding that as long as Enos was under his care, he would give him his utmost attention, even checking up on him when he was off duty. The man was more than happy to oblige.

When they went back inside to see Enos, the two men pulled up a couple spare stools to his bedside. He was much cleaner and comfortable looking than when they had seen him earlier. His sheets and blankets were folded prim and proper over his body all the way up to his neck and the hat his dear wife had sewn him was pulled snuggly over his head. It was shocking to look over the frail features of his face though, especially as both men knew the rest of his body looked much the same. The solid, stoutly built man they had known, was now a shriveled-up version of his former self, barely even recognizable to his friends who had known him all their lives.

Enos was awake when they sat beside him and when he recognized who they were a slight smile crept over his face before he closed his eyes again. He felt so weak that it was an exercise to keep them open.

"Thanks for coming to see me off, you two," he whispered to them.

"Don't say that, Enos," Gabriel scolded. "You look much better than you did yesterday. You'll be back in camp with us soon enough. Besides, we're going to need your help in fixing winter quarters."

"That does sound tempting, a nice warm fire and a comfy bunk. Dave, you can make your booze box in the floor like last winter," Enos said.

Dave smiled at him.

"I surely will, Enos. You know I will."

They both sat with Enos all day. When his meals came, they tried very hard to get him to eat, but he refused, telling them he preferred to die in a clean pair of drawers. To make themselves useful, when Enos napped, they helped the hospital stewards care for the other patients in the tent.

Toward the end of the day, William Baldwin, Lieutenant George, Sergeant Hemingway and several other men from the company came by to visit, too. They were only there a short while, though, as Enos was fast asleep. When they left, Dave went back to camp with them. They decided to work in shifts. Gabriel was to stay with him at night, and in the morning, Dave would return to sit while Gabriel went back to camp to get some sleep. There was about an hour left of light when they had gone.

It had been a cold and windy day, and the weather was showing no signs of letting up, so before he went off duty Gabriel's hospital steward friend brought him in a load of wood for the stove, and a few beeswax candles. He was also able to procure a tall-backed chair for him to rest in. It was much more comfortable than the log stool he had sat on all day, and Gabriel soon dozed off.

He didn't sleep long. The wind got heavier after the sun went down and the sound of the gusts and flapping canvas soon woke him to find Enos wide awake as well. He was in a somber mood, though, nothing like his usually optimistic self, but he did seem to have a little more energy and attentiveness than he had earlier in the day.

"You know, Gabriel," Enos said to him still tucked in his bed nice and tight, "I guess I've really let your parents down. I promised them that I would care for you and now look at how things have turned out. Instead of me caring for you, you're here taking care of me."

"That's not true, Enos. My parents said they're indebted to you. I told you. Why if it hadn't been for you, I'd have died back there in Virginia. You know that."

"I suppose so," Enos said as a man a few beds down went into a violent coughing attack.

Gabriel brought the man a cup of water and, after getting his coughing to subside, he returned to his seat. Enos spoke up again.

"I don't think I told you, Gabriel, but before the last battle I got a letter from my son James. He says he intends to reenlist here soon when his first term runs out."

"Does he?" Gabriel asked.

"That's what he writes. You know, Gabriel, I never told anyone this before, but I was often worried about him as a child. He was always so timid and reserved and I thought he was going to grow up to be a shut-in but just look at him now. They say he's one of the best men in his regiment, the best shot and the best man on a horse, and it breaks my heart that I once had such thoughts about my own son."

"I suppose it's only natural to think such things, Enos," Gabriel consoled him. "You know, Rill writes that our baby girl can't even roll over yet, and that worries me. I find myself wondering if she's got something wrong with her, too, but it's not from anger or embarrassment. I think parents just want their children to be perfect sometimes, because it would be less of a burden on their minds not having to worrying about their little faults and whether or not they'll ever be able to overcome them."

The conversation was getting awkward for Gabriel. Usually it was Enos giving him words of wisdom, but the tables had turned. Enos was becoming upset, and Gabriel tried to calm him. He could tell it wasn't doing him any good. It was only draining the life from him that much faster. He wouldn't listen, though. Tears were running down the deep valleys in his shriveled cheeks.

"Oh, Gabriel, what is to become of my dear wife and daughter? How is Julia going to support herself?"

The wind began to pick up again outside, so Enos spoke louder to be heard, almost to a shout.

"Promise me, promise me, Gabriel, you'll write and tell them how much I loved them all," he requested, and as he finished a massive gust hit the tent and for a moment it seemed they would all be blown away. The canvas ballooned, stretching the seams, the door flaps whipped themselves violently against its sides and the candles Gabriel had lit blew out. As suddenly as it had come, the gust then subsided, and all was quiet once again.

"Well, that was something," Gabriel said, thankful they hadn't been scattered in all directions. There was enough light from the stars outside glowing in through the tent flap for Gabriel to make his way over to the stove and relight his blown-out candles. As he did so he spoke to Enos.

"Enos," he said, "I will not write them to tell them that you loved them, I will write and tell them that you still love them and that you're sick but getting all the care you need. You mustn't keep up with this demising attitude of yours. It's unlike you."

As Gabriel approached his seat, though, he saw that his words were falling on deaf ears. Enos was dead, his eyes, still open, were staring off into oblivion and his mouth was slightly ajar. His breathing had ceased, and feeling for a pulse, as the doctors had done to him in Washington, Gabriel could tell that his heart had quit beating. Enos Cook passed away slightly before 9 P.M. on December 18, 1863, in Lookout Valley, Tennessee.

* * * * *

There wasn't much time wasted in laying Enos to rest. The following day his body was transported back to camp in a newly constructed pine coffin. Gabriel and Dave were the ones to place him in and nail down the lid. He was in full uniform, and they also put in several mementoes for him to be buried with. Going with him were his hat and mittens his wife Julia had knitted, photos of his children, and the worn out little pocket Bible he faithfully carried around in his coat and read whenever given a spare moment.

Once in camp, there was a service given in the middle of Company I's street. It was attended by all the Dryden men, as well as the majority of Company D, and several other folks Enos had befriended. Colonel Boughton was there too, and much of the officer corps. Enos was a popular man in the regiment, well known and admired for being a good soldier, who was thankful for whatever he was given, and never complained when asked to do his duty.

After the service, the attendees gathered behind the wagon in which his casket rested and followed it as it drove him out of camp and onto a beautiful little hilltop that overlooked the Tennessee River. It was there were a grave was dug. Each member of Company I, including the transferred Lieutenant Moffat, ceremoniously took turns with the shovel, taking a few scoops each, until the desired depth was achieved. A short prayer was then said, the coffin lowered into the grave, and the newly removed dirt tossed back into the hole.

Back in camp that night, Gabriel lay in his tent and wrote a letter to Julia, Nancy and James Cook. It had been Enos's last request, and Gabriel wanted to make sure he honored it. He wrote and told them of everything that had gone on in the past month. How he'd noticed Enos looked ill after his return from home, how he'd tried to help Enos out by getting his food and cooking his meals, etc. He also told them about the Battle of Chattanooga, the grueling march towards Knoxville that followed, Enos's fall in the river and his rapid deterioration afterwards. He told them of his last day, the last moments of his life, and his dying declaration of love for his family. He also shared how he and Dave had prepared his body for burial. He told of the funeral service that had just recently ended a few hours before and how it was well attended and carried out. He was very detailed, because Gabriel knew there would be so much that they would want to know. They would have so many questions, and he also knew that Enos would have likely kept all his ailments and concerns from them. He wouldn't have wanted them to worry. He was very unselfish in that way.

When he was finished with his letter, he stuck it in an envelope and brought it to Lieutenant George's tent for him to send out in the morning with a parcel of other letters of condolence that the men in the company had written to Enos's wife and children. When he returned to his tent, he found Dave Nash laying inside. He was drunk and had half a bottle of liquor tucked away in the crutch of his arm.

"Since old Enos has moved out I'm movin' in with you," Dave said when he saw Gabriel had returned. "Baldy gets on my nerves, so I told him I was leavin' him again," Dave added, slurring his words as he spoke. Gabriel could tell he was spectacularly drunk but couldn't blame him at all. In fact, he decided to join in. Throwing himself down on his side of the tent, he snatched the bottle out of Dave's arm, and downed it all in one long chug. Dave was stunned silent to witness the occasion. He couldn't believe his eyes, he would have never thought the day would come that he would share a drink with Gabriel Ballard.

"Well, that's no way to treat your new tent mate," he said, just before Gabriel became incoherent. He'd had little to eat in the past 48 hours and the alcohol did quick work on him. Dave wasn't angry, though. He was surprised, but not angry. He knew how much Gabriel was hurting. Enos had been everything to the boy since they left Dryden. He was almost like a surrogate father to him, and Gabriel had meant a lot to Enos, too. He was like a surrogate son, an Army son. They had depended on each other, but all that was over with now. Gabriel was on his own. At least that's how he felt. That's why he chugged Dave's bottle like he did, because, as he had learned on his train ride to Alabama, he knew that it would wash the reality of his situation away and it seemed worth it, even if it prevented him from facing the truth for only a few hours more.

Part
Three

CHAPTER THIRTEEN

Second Lieutenant James Bird was a superb soldier, and it could easily be claimed that there were few men in the Army more deserving of their rank. As was the case with Gabriel, Lieutenant Bird was a son of New York. In August 1862, he and his younger brother, Alexander, answered President Lincoln's call for volunteers by joining the 154th New York Infantry. James signed up as a sergeant, and Alexander a corporal, but both men quickly rose in rank. James made 2nd lieutenant in less than a year, and at the end of 1863 Alexander was serving as the 154th's sergeant-major.

At Gettysburg, their regiment suffered dearly, losing 200 men, leaving them with only 18 soldiers left for duty after the first day of the fight. James was the hero of the regiment that day, for as a horde of victorious Rebels were charging in on all fronts, the regiment disintegrated around him. He, however, remained at his post until the very last. Not until the enemy was just feet away and further resistance would either lead to his death, wounding, or capture did he choose to retreat. As he did so, he managed to save the 154th's New York State colors, preventing them from capture, and giving the few survivors something to rally around for the remainder of the battle.

Although the memory of those days would likely remain with him forever, they were currently not on his mind as he was more concerned with the task at hand. He was now a member of the joint 11th and 12th Corps headquarters staff of General Joseph Hooker, having just recently been transferred there from his regiment. At headquarters he was to command a contingent of enlisted men, who much like himself, were also newly assigned to that department. Lieutenant Bird saw his new posting as a great honor. Being assigned to General Hooker's staff was nothing to bat an eye at. It was a great responsibility and a demanding one, as his actions would be under the watchful eye of one of the most well-known men in the country.

General Hooker himself had been commander of the Army of the Potomac less than a year before, during the disastrous Chancellorsville Campaign. Although that defeat had been a major blow to his reputation, his recent exploits at Lookout Mountain had won back some of his old renown.

Bird had been at headquarters for several days now, getting acquainted with the other officers on the staff, and learning about the new duties he was required to perform. The men that were to serve under him, though, had just recently arrived. They were ushered to the front of his winter cabin as he was having his morning cup of coffee. The door was closed, but sitting inside Bird could hear them milling about in formation and wondering aloud amongst themselves what they had been sent there for. Several men voiced up rumors they had heard, but none of them were entirely correct. Not wanting to waste much time, he downed the last gulp of gritty coffee from his cup, stood up, tossed his light blue overcoat on, and pulled a looking glass out of his pocket to check himself over.

After sweeping a few crumbs from his beard, everything looked to be in order. As he opened the door to head outside and greet the men, he cleared his throat to signal to them his presence. Hearing him, the group stopped their discussions and came to attention. Bird was pleased with this initial gesture of respect, and immediately called them at ease. Physically, he could see they were a good-looking lot, healthy, young, and strong, but their uniforms and equipment were somewhat motley and diverse, the result of bringing together men from so many different regiments and states. Looking over a roster he had been handed that morning, he saw that there were now boys under his command from Ohio, New Jersey, Pennsylvania, Illinois, Indiana, Wisconsin, Connecticut, Massachusetts, Michigan, and New York.

"Good morning gentlemen. How are we doing today, boys?" was his initial greeting to them.

Judging by their blank stares, Bird could see that the men were somewhat suspicious yet, and hesitant to answer, so he continued with his introduction.

"It's cold, I know, and I don't wanna stand out here like a flock of sheep any more than the rest of you, so I'll try and make this as short as I can. My name is 2nd Lieutenant James Bird, and I'll be your commanding officer during your time here. Like yourselves, I'm a new face in this camp. I come over last week from the 154th New York. I'm sure you boys are wondering why you've been sent here. Well, we're all to be pioneers attached to the headquarters of General Hooker. I'm sure you all know by now what the pioneers do. It'll be our job when campaigning to make sure the path of the headquarters wagon train is unobstructed and passable. If there's a road to be widened or cut through a forest or a swamp, a bridge to be build or repaired or any other like situation, we're to do the job."

"Obviously, we aren't currently campaigning, and hopefully won't be until this spring, so in the meantime we're here to do whatever is asked of us by the commanding general or any of the other officers on his staff. Whatever they may need or ask for we are to do or provide. One day, you may act as an orderly for General Hooker himself, and then the next be digging a new shit trench for the officers' latrine. Expect the unexpected gentlemen. You, or we I should say, will be asked to perform a far-ranging number of tasks."

"Looking over our roster this morning, I saw that there are boys here from both corps, 11th and 12th, and ten different states. Be proud of where you're from gentlemen, but don't let it be where you're from that divides us. We're all here fighting for the same flag, and anyone that tries to dispute it will get the boot."

"I'm not stupid, either. I know that may be just what some of you boys want. We're among strangers here, I know. To be honest, I was hesitant myself to leave the 154th behind. All my friends are there, the ones I've marched beside all over creation, and the ones I fought next to in Virginia, Pennsylvania and on Missionary Ridge this past November. Hell, I left my little brother behind to come here, but let me tell you boys this detachment is an opportunity that shouldn't be shrugged off lightly. There's a lot of benefits to being here, as you'll soon find out, and I'll have you know you're among a handpicked crew. General Hooker asked for the best and brightest when he petitioned his two corps for recruits. He told me himself just the other day he wanted boys who could read and write, were in good health and were hard-working. He also wanted tradesmen. I think we've got a blacksmith or two in the detachment, a cobbler, a cooper, a few carpenters, and the rest of you, I'm told, are farm boys, masters of nothing particular, but are known amongst your regiment for having a good working knowledge in just about everything."

"As for what you can expect from me, I like to run a somewhat relaxed command. As long as you boys work hard, and do what you're told, we shouldn't have any trouble. I don't mind if you have a little nip every once in a while, you can even visit the whores if you like. You all know the General's reputation, he won't mind, just do it on your own time and behave yourselves. If you don't, you'll regret it, trust me. There's a lot of high rank around here, too, and I'll expect you to show them their due respect. You will call me 'Lieutenant' and 'Sir' when they're around, but when we're alone please just call me Jim. I'm not much for ego. I was just a civilian same as you a couple years ago. Don't take my kindness for weakness, though. Piss on me or try and pull the wool over my eyes, and I'll fucking take you down faster than you can pull a trigger. Do well by me, and you'll have no better friend or representative. I'll always make sure you're taken care of."

"That all being said, is there anyone here that feels they'd like to return to their regiment? Don't be bashful, I'd much rather have willing participants around here than forced and resentful ones."

Bird's speech was long but spoken clearly and honest, and to his pleasant surprise, not one man out of the lot stepped forward. His words seemed to have impressed them.

"Good," he said with a smile. "How about questions, though. Does anybody have any questions for me?"

Only one man in formation raised his hand.

"Go ahead, Private. Tell us your name, if you please," Bird requested of him.

"It's Robertson, Sir," the man said. "Sir, I was just wondering where we're to make our camp while we're here?"

"Good question, Robertson. Actually, that's our task for the next couple days. We need a company street of huts built here, strung out to the left side of my quarters. Make them nice and square, too, boys. I want the door ends all flush and in line with mine," he told them, motioning how he wanted them laid out with his hands.

"We'll get started just as soon I dismiss you, but first I have one more thing to do before we break formation. Whichever one of you is Private Ballard, step up front here with me so everyone can get a good look at you."

* * * * *

Gabriel was shocked to hear the Lieutenant call his name. For a moment, he thought he may have misunderstood the man or that there was another Ballard among them. Looking over the crowd he saw no one else move, though, so he figured that he must actually be looking for him, but he didn't have the slightest idea why.

Nervously, he squeezed his way through the crowd of men to answer Lieutenant Bird's call. Like everyone else, he was still weighted down with all his gear, and he jingled as he moved. Stopping in front of Bird, he came to attention and raised a salute. Bird returned it, then told him to turn around and face the other men. He put his hand on Gabriel's shoulder as he turned to face his peers and seeing that Gabriel's face was red with embarrassment, he told him not to worry and that he'd done nothing wrong.

"Believe it or not boys, but other than myself, Private Ballard here is the only New Yorker in this detachment. I couldn't believe it when I glanced over the roster this morning, considering us Yorkers account for at least a third or more of both corps, but I can assure you that it's true. Anyhow, in keeping with my call for unity amongst all the different factions we're made up of here, and also to squash any ideas in your little pea brains that I'll show Private Ballard any favor, I'm putting him in charge of the first task, other than building your huts, that's been requested of us."

Bird stepped away from Gabriel with a smile on his face and looking directly at him said aloud that he was to be up all night keeping a fire going outside of General Hooker's quarters.

"The General sent me a note this morning with the request," Bird told them all. "He says he'll be having company over and wanted somewhere to retreat to if he needed a breath of fresh air. As I said, boys expect the unexpected."

To Bird's satisfaction, his gesture had the desired effect on the men. They seemed pleased with his effort and even though he was the butt of the joke, Gabriel found it amusing, too. He liked Bird. Initially, when he was on his way over that morning from his regiment, he was having second thoughts about agreeing with Colonel Boughton to make the move. Much of the other men felt the same way, but after hearing Bird's speech those second thoughts had passed. They decided to give the man a chance, and were especially impressed with him, when after dismissing them to construct their huts, he went to work right alongside them. It was inspiring, and they worked twice as hard at their task, even through their noonday meal, and by the time the sun was going down, they were just stretching the last bits of canvas roof over their huts. They finished the job in half the time they'd been given, and Bird was likewise greatly impressed and pleased with them.

* * * * *

As were his new companions, Gabriel was exhausted at the end of the day. After finishing their huts, the men ate a quick meal of beans and hardtack and went straight to bed in their cozy new quarters. Gabriel didn't have that option though. Duty called, so after supper he bundled himself up as best he could and made his way through camp to were Lieutenant Bird instructed him the General's quarters were located.

He kept busy at first, gathering wood, building the fire and watching various officers and young ladies arrive for the evening's festivities. It'd been a while now since he'd seen anyone, though, and with the cold wind picking up, he soon found himself hovering close to the fire. The warmth felt good, but it also brought on feelings of sleepiness, and although he managed to keep his eyes open, his mind began to wander. He thought of home and wondered how much snow was on the ground up there, if the lake was frozen over and if so, had his father and brother been harvesting any ice. He also wondered whether Rill and the baby were in bed by now. He hoped that she missed him as much as he did her. It had been just over a month since Enos's death, but time had passed rapidly since then. So much had happened over those few short weeks that Gabriel hardly had any time to process it all, so as he sat by his lonesome, he tried doing so.

It had been just about three weeks prior, on the last day of the year, when Colonel Boughton's orderly was taken ill and Gabriel was sent to fill in for the man until he returned to duty. It was Lieutenant George's idea. Gabriel had been terribly depressed ever since Enos passed away and George thought working for the Colonel would divert his attention from the way he was feeling. He put Gabriel's name in for the job and after explaining the situation to Colonel Boughton he took him up on his offer.

To George's credit, the plan was a success. Working for the Colonel kept Gabriel busy and kept his mind from wandering. He liked the work too because most of it was done inside. Usually he preferred to be outdoors, but not right then in the dead of winter. The Colonel's office was always warm, and he was happy to miss out on the fatigue and picket duty that his friends were being forced to endure.

The Colonel enjoyed having Gabriel around, too. He was a quick learner, efficient with his paperwork and worked hard to please. The Colonel was especially impressed with his handiness. Before Gabriel showed up, there was a long and neglected list of things that had broken and needed fixing around the office. Soon after his arrival though, he had it all taken care of. For instance, he fixed a pair of broken hinges on the Colonel's field desk, he repaired a folding camp chair that had been tripped over and snapped in two, he replaced almost all of the chinking in-between the log walls of the office, as it had been shoddily mixed and applied when built, and he also rehung the door, as that too had been improperly installed and was never able to fully close.

It was to the Colonel's great displeasure when, after three weeks of being in the hospital, his former orderly recovered enough to come back to full duty, and Gabriel's services were no longer needed. The day before he was to return to his company, the Colonel received the request from General Hooker's headquarters looking for good, handy, and hard-working soldiers to be sent on detached service there. He was sorry to see Gabriel leave the regiment, but after getting to know him over the past few weeks, he thought him perfect for the job.

"When I read the General's request, you were the first soldier to come to mind, Gabriel. Honestly, I'm sorry to lose you, young man, but I think you're just the type of soldier they're looking for, and I know you'll represent us well and make the regiment proud," Colonel Boughton had said when informing him of his transfer.

Naturally, Gabriel was flattered with the Colonel's praise, but he was also unsure if it was really something he wanted. He was torn. Leaving all the Dryden boys behind would be tough, but at the same time he recognized it as a good opportunity to do something different, something more exciting than what had become a daily schedule of repetitive drudgery. The lull of the end of campaign season, along with the relatively poor health of the regiment thus far that winter, had resulted in a serious dip in morale. There was also a significant amount of infighting going on among the officers and things were getting out of hand. Lieutenant Moffat for instance had confided in Gabriel that he was seriously considering tendering a resignation, and in fact, a few weeks after Gabriel's transfer he did just that.

"First Enos and now you. The hell am I supposed to do?" was Dave Nash's response upon hearing the news of Gabriel's transfer. He was most upset.

"You'll be fine, Dave. You've still got Baldy to tent with, and it isn't like I'm leaving for good. First Enos and now me? What's that supposed to mean, anyway? Enos is dead. I'm not dying, I'm just going away for a while."

"You don't know that. Could be permanent, and to hell with Baldy, I'll sleep by myself from now on. I've been down that road before and won't try it again. You remember how bad his feet smell, and his guts are rotten. I swear he breaks wind about every minute and it only gets worse after he falls asleep. No Sir, I'd bunk with a grizzly before I ever pitch a tent with him again."

Gabriel had to admit Dave was right. Even if he was a good friend, Baldy wasn't exactly the most hygienic man in the company.

"You know, Dave, I'll be at Hooker's headquarters. They say he likes the booze just as much as you. I bet if you come and visit you could find yourself a bottle or two laying around."

Gabriel remembered that that had shut Dave up right quick, and he soon had a new-found opinion on his departure.

"I suppose you've got a point there," Dave admitted. "With general's pay I bet he likes to drink the good stuff, too. Ya know, Gabriel, this transfer business may not be so bad after all."

* * * * *

Another bracing wind blew through the camp and sent sparks flying in Gabriel's direction. Tiny little embers pelted his face and quickly brought his mind back to reality. He forgot all about his reminiscing when the door to the General's quarters whipped open and out stepped a tall and well-built figure from the glowing and rambunctious atmosphere inside. He had dark, knee-high riding boots on, a tall black slouch hat, and although he left his blue coat inside, Gabriel recognized him as an officer and snapped up off his rear to salute the man as he approached the fire.

"Good evening, Sir," Gabriel shouted nervously.

From the fire's glow he could see that the man was none other than the handsome, blue-eyed Major General Joseph Hooker himself. He had never laid eyes on him before in person, but recognized him from sketches he had seen in the newspapers. The General ignored his greeting, though, and reached over to Gabriel and forcefully threw his still saluting hand and arm back down to his side.

"No need for that now, Son," he said to Gabriel before taking a swig from a bottle he had carried out from the party. His cheeks were rosy red and reminded Gabriel of his father. Whenever John drank, his face would get all flushed too.

"You can toss another couple logs on, though. Some whore's in there running around bare-assed with my coat on. I tried to catch her, but the little she-fox was too fast for me, God damn her," Hooker said with a chuckle.

Gabriel obeyed and tossed a few splintered logs on the fire until the General told him that was fine.

"Here, Son, take a couple swallows for yourself," Hooker said handing his bottle over to Gabriel. "It'll warm you up some."

Gabriel hesitated, not quite knowing what to do. The encounter had been very informal, and he couldn't tell if the man was serious or not, and wondered if it was a test or a trap. He thought Hooker may not have realized he was speaking to a lowly private, too. Hooker grew impatient with his hesitation.

"Grab the blasted thing and drink, Son," he barked at Gabriel. "Privates are supposed to follow their general's commands, are they not?" he added.

That answered his speculation. Nervously, Gabriel snatched the bottle from his hand and took two big swallows before handing it back. It tasted awful and burned like fire going down.

"Sorry, Sir. I'm not much for drinking," he said, but it seemed to disappoint Hooker.

"Well, you'd better take to liking it. I'll have no teetotalers at this headquarters. I tried to put down the bottle once last year, young man, and I lost the Battle of Chancellorsville. Won't do it again."

The General sat down in a chair next to the fire and directed Gabriel to take a seat as well.

"I spoke with Lieutenant Bird this evening and he told me why he put you on the job. He's a good junior officer, that Bird, and I'm happy to have him around. He's a fighter, and I like a fighter. Headquarters always seems to draw in all the pencil pushing cowards, but I won't have it so in my command. How many battles have you been in?"

Gabriel cringed at the question. He still felt awful about having missed out on Wauhatchie in October and after hearing Hooker's opinions on nonfighting men, he was afraid that his answer was going to send him over the edge.

"None, Sir," he shyly admitted looking away over his shoulder ashamed.

"Did you just say none, not one? Are you kidding me?" Hooker asked him incredulously. There was an undeniable look of appalment on his face.

"Where did you come from anyway? What regiment?" he asked Gabriel. He was acting as if it were a great mystery that he suddenly needed to get to the bottom of.

"The 143rd New York, Sir. I'm sorry, Sir, but we've only actually fought in one battle, the night one at Wauhatchie before Chattanooga. I was on sick leave though, and didn't get back until they'd already marched off. I was at Suffolk and Missionary Ridge, but we never got to fire a shot in them battles on account of us being held in the reserve."

"I see," said the General, still disappointed but accepting his answer. "My apologies, young man. I was concerned I had a coward in my midst, but I suppose it's none of your fault. If you're still with us in the spring, though, it's something we'll have to remedy. I'll make sure of it. The first chance we get, I'll have Bird take you to fall in line with someone. I suspect young Mr. Bird would like that anyway."

"Thank you, Sir," Gabriel said, "I'd greatly appreciate it."

He was feeling less on edge. Hooker's open and talkative manner helped to relax the initial shock of being in the presence of such a famous and powerful man. It now felt almost as if he were sitting around the campfire talking to another private he'd just met.

"Think nothing of it. Like I said, young man, I need fighters in this command anyway and fighting is what we're going to be about. I've got a reputation to fix. Lookout Mountain was a good start, but it's going to take more than that. I'd like to go back east with my two corps, but for some reason I don't think it's gonna happen. They fucked me when they took the Potomac away from me and fucked themselves too, if you ask me. Unlike that old turtle Meade, I wouldn't have let Bobby Lee get away after Gettysburg and this war would have been over in July. Chancellorsville wasn't my fault either. I told that idiot Howard to watch his God dammed flank for just such an attack, and he ignored me. He was probably too busy reading his fucking Bible or praying, and because of it he got slaughtered and ruined my plans. My God, they were marvelous plans too. They were perfect."

Gabriel could tell they were covering a touchy subject, so he decided it best to just to be quiet, nod his head and ride it out. He added another log to the fire and the General took another swig out of his bottle.

"Here, have some more," Hooker said holding out the bottle again.

Gabriel didn't hesitate this time and got his fair share. They still had halfway to go on it, but he was already feeling its effects. He hadn't been drunk since the night Enos was buried. Hooker continued with his venting once Gabriel handed him back the bottle.

"Nope, I think we're stuck out here. I've just got a premonition. It's too bad, too, because I hate being around these western sons of bitches. They all think they're so much better at fighting than us easterners, but they've never faced Bobby Lee. They can't admit that they needed us to come out here to their rescue, either. They act as if we never came. I took a mountain and Sherman couldn't even take a hill and then Grant acts like he's some big hero. Makes me sick. We'll show them, though. We'll show them all come spring."

General Hooker seemed to be thinking out loud more than talking directly to Gabriel. Gabriel was surprised by his openness in speaking of such matters with the mere private that he was, but he suspected it was the whiskey that was doing most of the talking. Hooker peered into his bottle to see how much was left. There was still a good amount, but he decided he'd had enough and handed it over to Gabriel for a final time.

"Here, I've had enough for one night, my treat."

Gabriel graciously accepted. The cork was missing, but it was no bother, he'd find something to plug it with. He decided he'd have a little more anyway and then save the rest for Dave. Admittedly, he'd been craving a drink but considered it too risky to try around any of the men in his company. He was scared of gossip making its way back home, but now that he wasn't with them anymore, he thought it safe to do as he pleased. Gabriel wasn't scared of Rill finding out, just his mother. He'd written to Rill and fessed up about the train ride to Alabama, and the night Enos was buried. She wasn't overly concerned, as long as he was honest with her and didn't make a habit of it, she said it was fine. Her faith in him was unwavering. She knew he was a good boy, or a good man now, that is, and she couldn't ever imagine him letting himself get out of hand or doing something to get in trouble.

The wind picked up again and it showed no signs of stopping, so Hooker decided he'd about had his fill of fresh air. He stood up to ready himself for his return to the party by re-tucking in his shirt and adjusting his pants. Gabriel instinctively stood up too, ready to act on any request the General made of him.

"Throw a couple more logs on and then you can dismiss yourself. I'm going to go back in there to find that whore with my coat and sneak off to bed with her now anyway".

"Yes, Sir," Gabriel said.

"Also young man, I forgot. Before I go, do by chance happen to have a pair of drawers?" the General asked.

"Drawers, Sir?" Gabriel looked confused.

"Yes, drawers. Undergarments. You know, the things that go on under your trousers." Hooker explained.

"No Sir, I'm afraid not," Gabriel answered, "that is I don't have any other than the ones I've got on now."

Hooker shook his head in disappointment.

"So I suspected," he said. "Well, no bother, I was just wondering, but if you happen to come across a pair send them my way and I'll make it worth your while. I enjoy a nice pair of drawers you see. This wool gives me the worst chaffing and I can't have that if I'm to be entertaining the ladies, if you know what I mean."

Gabriel nodded his understanding.

"I do, Sir," he said.

"Women have the best drawers young man. Theirs are always the most comfortable. I'd often take the best pair I came across. I'd pay the girls extra of course, especially if they were made with silk. That was up in Washington and Virginia, though. The girls down here don't wear nothing at all to cover their bottoms. They're considered a luxury, so they tell me. The only benefit that I can tell of the practice is it's easier to undress them. Have you noticed a lack of drawers from the girls you've come across?"

"No, Sir, I haven't," Gabriel said, neglecting to mention that he had never visited a brothel, nor did he ever intend to.

"Well, take notice next time, and you'll see I'm right." Hooker said.

"I will, Sir," Gabriel lied. "I'll see what I can do about finding you a good pair, too."

"You do that," Hooker told him.

The two men stood for a moment in silence. Then the General spoke up again.

"What happens to be your name, young man?"

"Private Ballard, Sir," Gabriel answered.

"And your first?"

"Gabriel, Sir,"

"I see. Private Gabriel Ballard of New York. My sister lives in Watertown, you know. Are you from anywhere near there?"

"No, Sir, at least I don't think so, Sir, but then again I've never heard of it. I'm from Dryden myself."

"Dryden, eh? Never heard of it. Well, enjoy the rest of your night, Private Ballard. Don't forget my drawers now, and I'll make sure you get to do some fighting."

General Hooker returned to his party, and Gabriel, after carrying out the General's last request, headed back to his cabin for some much-needed sleep.

CHAPTER FOURTEEN

In March 1864, Ulysses S. Grant was promoted to lieutenant-general, and made overall commander of the whole Union Army. For his replacement as commander of the troops in the western theater of the country, he chose his good friend General William Tecumseh Sherman. Sherman's official title was Commander of the Military Division of the Mississippi. Grant's grand plan for the coming spring was to go to east and keep an ever-watchful eye on the Army of the Potomac's spring offensive toward Richmond, while in the west, Sherman would be on his own, in a push to capture Atlanta, Georgia.

Atlanta was a major rail hub, manufacturing center, and supply depot for the Confederacy. It was Grant's hope that along with capturing the city, Sherman's offensive would prevent the Rebels out west from reinforcing General Lee's Army of Northern Virginia in the east. As of yet, it still remained undetermined where the troops under General Hooker, the 11th and 12th Corps, would end up. Whether they stayed out west or returned east was a subject of great interest and speculation, especially among the men whom it mattered to most, the common soldiers of those two corps, like Gabriel.

* * * * *

Things couldn't have gone better for James Bird in his first two months overseeing the pioneers. It took no time at all for him to organize the men. It was easy really, because the detachment was small, and the men all worked exceptionally well together. To his delight, they were also quite well-behaved, even during their down time, which they had a lot of being it was still winter, and the off-season for campaigning.

Bird's leadership style was very appealing to his men. They enjoyed serving under him and they didn't want to jeopardize their place as one of his pioneers by making trouble. He was firm if he needed to be, but fair, and a natural leader who was true to his word. He lived up to the speech that he greeted them with to the best of his ability. When they worked hard, which they always did, he rewarded them. Not with gifts, but by allowing for a relaxed atmosphere in camp, and making sure they were always well fed, clothed, and equipped. He was also honest with them and kept the men well-informed on whatever rumors he heard swirling around among his fellow officers. It was this, his trust, that most endeared the men to him, and they worked hard and behaved well, not just to stay in his good graces, but also because they didn't want to let him down.

After having dealt with Captain Marvin's antics for so long, Bird was a breath of fresh air for Gabriel. Bird and Marvin were opposite ends of the spectrum in almost every way, and although he initially missed the Dryden boys, after a while Gabriel wasn't sure if he ever wanted to go back to his old company, especially if Marvin ever returned.

Marvin wasn't the only factor drawing Gabriel away from his old regiment either. After having spent a few months at headquarters, he had developed new friendships and a strong sense of belonging with the other pioneers. He enjoyed the perks of being at headquarters too, most notably having access to all the paper, and envelopes, he could ever want. At headquarters, he was able to write Rill at least two and sometimes three times a week. Mail, official dispatches and reports were constantly coming and going, so it was no problem at all for him to get his letters posted quickly.

It was on a night in early April that Gabriel made up his mind on what group he wanted to be with, after a visit from his old friend, Dave Nash. Dave's visits were usually a treat for Gabriel, because the 143rd had been stationed in Bridgeport since the end of January, while Hooker's headquarters remained in Lookout Valley. The only time the two saw each other was when Dave could get himself put on the escort of one of the loads of supplies that passed back and forth between the two places.

Dave was in a foul mood when he burst into Gabriel's hut. Gabriel was seated on his bunk perusing through old letters from Rill when he came in and Dave's sudden entry startled him.

"Marvin's back!" he blurted out as he burst in with a small satchel tucked under his arm.

"Son of a bitch," Gabriel swore to himself, half from being startled and half from the news. Being out of the watchful eye of old friends from home, he'd taken more to cussing lately.

"Are you sure Dave? Are you sure he's back?" Gabriel asked hoping it wasn't true.

"Hell yes, I'm sure. The bastard's been here almost two weeks now."

"Well, I'm sorry to hear it," Gabriel said, genuinely disappointed.

"I knew you would be."

Dave sat down on an empty hardtack box they were using as a bench and lifted his leg up to show Gabriel the sole of his right brogan. It was near torn off and Gabriel could see Dave's muddied sock on the inside.

"Tore the damned thing open on the way over," he explained, wiggling his toes for effect. "Well, give it here Gabriel, I'm fuming mad and parched, need somethin' to calm my nerves."

Gabriel knew just what he wanted. He reached under his bunk and pulled out a green bottle and handed it to Dave.

"Oh, boy," Dave cried with excitement, his mood instantly improved. "So, what's on the menu tonight?" he asked.

"That there is wine," Gabriel answered.

"Wonderful," Dave said. "I'm impressed. Is it any good?" he asked.

"General Hooker says it's the best," Gabriel told him.

Dave popped the cork and inhaled the pleasant aroma.

"Smells like wine," he said. He took a sip. "Tastes like wine, too. Delicious! Give old Joe my compliments next time you see him, Gabriel. Tell him Private Dave Nash says he has impeccable taste."

"I'll be sure to do that," Gabriel said sarcastically.

Dave had forgotten all about his damaged brogan and mooned over his new bottle while Gabriel got up to poke at the fire in his earthen hearth. He stared blankly into the flames after adding another log and subconsciously let out a long sigh. Dave picked up on the hint of unhappiness in his demeanor.

"Sorry to be the bearer of bad news, but I figured you had to find out sooner than later."

"Thanks, but I'm fine," Gabriel said. He put the stick he had been poking the fire with in the corner and went back to his bunk to sit down. "I'd just been hoping we were done with Marvin, that's all. You know that, though. You've got to deal with him more than I do now, at least until I get sent back to the company."

"Who's this Marvin you two keep blabbering on about over there?" a voice called out. It came from under the blankets of a bunk at the back of the hut. It was one of Gabriel's tent mates, John Spencer. He was a good man, and Gabriel got along with him first rate.

"Sorry, John. Didn't mean to wake you," Gabriel said.

"Sorry about that," Dave added.

"No bother. I was just dozing anyway. Who is this Marvin, though? Is it that ass of a captain you've told me about, Gabriel?"

"He is one and the same," Dave answered him.

"I see," Spencer said, as he tossed aside his covers and sat up on his bunk. "You know, my cousin had a captain like him in his company. I've told this story to Gabriel already, but I'll tell you, too," he said to Dave. "His captain was a real tyrant, a lot like yours. The man was constantly placing folks under arrest, making them ride the wooden horse and putting them on double duty, nonsense like that, you know? Just a bully with bars on his shoulders."

Dave nodded his understanding.

"They got even at Shiloh, though. Put ten bullets in his back when he stepped out in front of the company in the thick the fight. Took care of him good, they did. Looked like holey cheese, Frank said, when they went back to bury him after the battle."

"Tarnation!" Dave exclaimed. "Not sure we could pull that off on Marvin, but it sure sounds appealin'. What happened to your cousin and his friends, though? Hell, their heads must have rolled after that."

"No, why would they?" Spencer said. "They got him in the thick of the fight. There were no questions asked. The other officers just figured he'd turned around as a squad of Rebs were drawing down on him. Everyone likes to take a shot at an officer. You know how it is."

Spencer swapped stories with Dave and Gabriel for a while longer, before he stepped out to "spread some manure," he said. Taking advantage of their new-found privacy, Dave decided to tell Gabriel why he'd really come to see him.

"Ya know, Gabriel, I didn't trudge all this way just to tell you about Marvin."

"Well, why did you come then? Drink Alabama dry, did you?" Gabriel picked.

Dave ignored him. He was trying to be serious.

"I come to tell ya that I'm gonna be leavin' for a while."

"That's great news, Dave," Gabriel said, happy to hear of his friend's good fortune. "Sure wish I was going on another furlough, but I'm glad for you all the same. You haven't been home in almost twice as long as I have."

"No, they didn't give me no furlough. I'm just takin' off for a while that's all."

Gabriel couldn't believe what Dave was saying. It angered him to think his friend could be so foolish.

"You can't just leave, Dave. You know they're liable to shoot you if you get caught. Make an example out of you."

"I've got no choice," Dave tried to tell him, but Gabriel wouldn't hear it.

"No choice? Of course you've got a choice. Spring's here, we're about to go on campaign. It can't be that bad. I know Marvin's an ass, but he can't be worth getting shot over. Let me talk with Lieutenant Bird, I'll see if he can pull some strings and get you transferred."

Dave got angry that Gabriel wasn't letting him explain.

"Now calm down boy, calm down and let me fuckin' explain myself!" he shouted. "Ya don't think I know all that. Ya don't think I know the risks, or that the boys are gonna call me a coward and say that I run just before the fightin' started? God damn it all, Gabriel, ya know I wanna fight just as much as the rest of the boys, but it's my wife and kids. They're sick."

Gabriel's eyebrows lifted. He was stunned by the sad news.

"All of them. Very sick, too," Dave went on. "God damn it, I knew I shoulda' dug a new well before we took off. I know that's what done it, it has to be. I'll never forgive myself if any of them die," Dave chided himself.

"That's terrible, Dave," Gabriel said. "How did you find out?"

"Electa wrote me with the help of your pa about a month ago. She mentioned they were ill, but it didn't sound too serious. Then Marvin come and he told me that when he left they were all in rough shape. May not make it, he said. Pulled me aside, he did, and tried to play it off like he was all concerned and apologetic about it, but I know he just wanted to watch me squirm. He's an evil bastard, he is."

"Why run, though, Dave? What about a furlough? Won't they give you a furlough?"

"That's the first thing I asked him," Dave said, "but no he couldn't do that he said, not with campaign season just around the bend. He couldn't do that when there was fightin' to be done. I told him that if my wife and kids died, I'd have nothin' to fight for anyway, and do ya know what his response was to me? Do ya know?" Gabriel shook his head. "That bastard told me we must all make sacrifices for the good of the country. I said to hell with the fuckin' country. The country means nothin' to me without my wife and kids in it. I'm just one man, Gabriel. One man don't mean squat."

"I can't believe he said that to you," Gabriel said. It made him angry, almost vengeful towards Marvin.

"Well, he did, Gabriel. He did, and he's a piece of shit for it, too. I have no respect at all for the man, not an ounce. He's gone over six months, sittin' on his ass at home, and he has the nerve to tell me I can't go see my sick wife and kids, and after he'd just made it a point to tell me they may be on their death beds, mind you. Hell, they may all be dead now for all I know. God help me if they are. God help Marvin, too, because I'll kill him if even one of them has passed away after I asked to go home, I'll murder the son of a bitch."

Dave lifted the bottle of wine to his mouth and downed the remainder in a long pull.

"So that's why your leaving, then?"

"That's the reason," Dave said. He tossed Gabriel the empty bottle and wiped his mouth with the sleeve of his coat.

"Well, I can't say I blame you then. If Rill and the baby were sick, I'd probably take off, too."

"I've been mullin' it over since I found out," Dave said. "Waitin' for another letter and wonderin' what to do. I'm sick of pacin' around and wringin' my hands, though. I finally found the gall to say fuck it and go home the other day. I just hope I'm not too late."

"That's a far way to go, Dave. You know that every train station between here and New York is crawling with men looking for runaways like you," Gabriel warned him.

"I'll be fine. I got a nice suit of civilian garb in here that I lifted off a sutler," Dave said, patting the satchel he had showed up with. "I'm a reporter for the Dryden Herald, see?" Dave pulled a pencil and a tiny pocket diary from inside his coat. "Come down to visit my local regiment and write a story on their war experiences."

"So that's your story," Gabriel said.

"Yes Sir, that's my story and I'm stickin' to it."

After Dave spilled the beans, the tension seemed to die down in the room. Gabriel pulled out a hunk of cheese he had stashed away, along with a wooden bowl of butter and a fresh loaf of soft bread baked just that morning. Dave was impressed and could see why Gabriel enjoyed himself at headquarters so much. The men sat silently, taking in their fill before Gabriel struck into conversation again.

"How's the company?" he asked. "What's their take on Marvin's return?"

"Oh, they're doin' alright. As well as can be expected. Henry Fitts died of course, think I told you that last time I was here. Peter Bessey too, and I heard someone say Isaac Overacker wasn't long for this world. He's up home now, so at least he can die in his own bed if he does. You know how it is. Nobody trusts Marvin, but there ain't much they can do about it. Most of the boys just try and stay out of his way and ignore him. Then of course there's always those few that try suckin' him off every chance they get."

"Well, if you're leaving Dave, I don't want to go back," Gabriel said. "I've got it too good here, as you can see. I really like these boys, and this Lieutenant Bird is the best officer I've ever met."

"I'd suggest against it," Dave said. "Marvin seems to still hold a grudge for anyone that was ever friendly with Moffat. He won't shut up about him, either. He's happier than a pig in shit that he resigned. Takes jabs at him whenever he can get a word in."

"I suppose that's the price he's gonna have to pay for resigning," Gabriel mentioned, in reference to Moffat.

"I can only imagine what he'll say about me when he finds out I run off," Dave said.

Gabriel nodded in agreement. He knew Marvin would relish defaming Dave. He was that kind of man. He loved to tear others down behind their backs, and was always ready to pounce when someone was at their lowest. He did so just to draw attention away from his own glaring faults.

"Whatever happens, you'll be fine," Dave reassured him. "If Electa and the kids get better, I'll come back right away, and we can take on Marvin together. Just don't be drinkin' too much while I'm gone."

Gabriel's face flushed with embarrassment.

"What do you mean?" he tried to lie, "I haven't had a drink since the day we buried Enos."

"The hell you haven't," Dave taunted him. "Every bottle you've had for me is half full or watered down, like that bottle of wine tonight, for instance." He laughed. "And don't think I can't smell the pipe smoke on you, either," he added.

Gabriel's face turned cherry red. He knew he'd been caught, and he felt mortified.

"Oh, don't worry. My lips are sealed," Dave said with a chuckle.

Dave spent the rest of the night with Gabriel, and when Gabriel woke up the next morning he was already gone. In a pile next to his bed was Dave's neatly folded uniform coat and pants with his worn out old brogans on top. Wedged into the flap of the torn sole was a piece of paper and Gabriel snatched it out to see what it had to say.

> *Thanks for the new boots Gabriel. You know I couldn't pull off my newspaperman act with torn up old brogans on. Anyone looking for deserters would see right through me. I'm sure your precious little Lt. Bird can find you some new ones. In the meantime feel free to use mine, my treat. -Dave*

"Damn him," Gabriel whispered under his breath, and tore the note in two.

* * * * *

Fortunately, Gabriel didn't have to worry about serving under Marvin again for very long. Shortly after Dave's visit, Lieutenant Bird called his pioneers together after morning roll call and informed them of some major changes that were coming.

"As I've always done for you boys, I want to pass on what I've been hearing from the top. Now keep this under your caps because nobody else knows about it yet, but I've been told that the 11th and 12th Corps are to be consolidated to form a new corps, the 20th, and General Hooker's to be in charge."

A unison gasp emanated from the gathered soldiers.

"Old Prayer Book Howard's getting sent to command the 4th Corps, and Slocum is going to stay behind and guard some railroads here in Tennessee."

Bird was reading from a notebook and stopped to turn the page. Gabriel and his comrades listened intently because he'd said nothing on their status at headquarters yet.

"The new corps is to be one of the largest in the Army and will utilize the old 12th Corps five-pointed star as its identifying insignia. Generals Williams, Geary and Butterfield will be in command of its three divisions respectively and contrary to recent rumor we will not be returning east, we are to remain here in the west and march with Sherman towards Atlanta."

Having read the rest of his notes, Bird snapped the book shut in his hand and placed it into the inside breast pocket of his coat.

"As for us, gentlemen, I am happy to say that we are to remain here at Hooker's headquarters, or shall I say 20th Corps headquarters, and will serve under him in the upcoming campaign as his own personal pioneers."

The men were grateful to hear the news. They were all smiles, shaking hands, and patting each other on the back. Bird was happy to see their positive reaction, but he held up his hand to silence them.

"Remember, boys, not a word to anyone. I'm not even sure all the generals are aware of it yet."

After Bird released the men from formation, he waved Gabriel over for a chat.

"How are you today, Gabriel?" Bird asked him. "Are you pleased to hear the news?"

"I'm doing good, Sir, and yes, I'm very pleased."

He was more than pleased, he was delighted and also relieved.

"I'm glad to hear it. We've got a great group of boys here. I know some of them were hoping we'd go back to the Army of the Potomac, it's closer to home, I understand, but I feel like we still have something to prove to these western troops. I wouldn't feel right going back east just yet, I'd feel like we had unfinished business we were leaving undone here, and I know they'd jeer us to no end and say the "paper collar soldiers" couldn't handle it out here. Do you know what I mean, Gabriel?"

"Yes Sir, I think I know all too well what you mean," Gabriel told him, and he did. Gabriel felt that way every day, inadequate and that he still had something to prove to all the battle hardened veterans he now served with.

"I thought you would," Bird commented. "Something else, though, that I wanted to speak to you about in person. Tell me, Gabriel, I didn't know you were such good friends with the General. He wanted me to give you his personal thanks, something about a pair of drawers. Now, what's that all about?"

Gabriel smiled.

"Well I wouldn't call us friends, Sir," he said.

"Jim. Please, as long as there's no other officers around, you can call me Jim."

Gabriel nodded. Lieutenant Bird was always correcting the men for calling him 'Sir', but they felt awkward calling him by his first name. It was unnatural to them.

"Okay. Well, Sir... or well, Jim, no I'm not friends with the General. We just spoke once, and he made a request of me. I just honored his request, that's all, Sir. Sorry, Sir, that's all, Jim."

"I see," Bird said, still curious as to what the connection was between one of his privates and his commanding general.

Gabriel could tell he was looking for a more in-depth explanation but didn't exactly know how to tell the man.

"It's an awful long story Sir."

Bird knew Gabriel was holding back on him, but didn't push the subject other than to say he'd like to hear it sometime, to which Gabriel agreed.

What had happened is that in one of his letters home to Rill, he told her all about meeting General Hooker and his conversation with the man, including the bit on women's drawers. Naturally, Rill had found the story most amusing, and told Julia Cook about it the next time she saw her. Being the great seamstress that she was, Julia decided to make a pair of drawers for Gabriel to give to the General. She made them out of light cotton but sewed a silk insert in the groin and inner thigh portion of the pants to help combat the General's chafing. Gabriel was surprised to have received them in the mail the day before, and at first thought them for himself, but after reading Julia's note he was soon aware of their intended recipient.

He wasn't sure just how to deliver them to the General, though. The two were just acquaintances, and due to their vast difference in rank, the only time Gabriel spoke to the man is when Hooker acknowledged him first. He knew it'd be highly unethical to approach him outright, so he decided to wrap the drawers back up in their packaging and place them at the General's doorstep. Worried they'd be considered trash or free for the taking, he pinned a note to the package that read, *To General Hooker from Mrs. Julia Cook, by way of Private Ballard of Dryden, NY.* Apparently, they had found their way to Hooker and were well received.

* * * * *

Martha Marilla Ballard was surprised but happy to read in her husband's letter that Dave Nash was on his way home to be with his family. She knew that it would likely mean trouble for Dave down the road, but that it was the proper and righteous thing for him to do. Gabriel had also warned her in his letter to stay away if she could.

"There's plenty of other folks in town to help, Rill. Let them bear the burden, and keep yourself healthy," he wrote, concerned for her wellbeing.

Rill had no such intentions though. She was too kind and caring to stay away. Gabriel's letter was far too late anyway, for she and the other women in the neighborhood had been working in shifts at the Nash home for weeks, trying to nurse the beleaguered family away from death. Rill went to help, as well as Gabriel's mother and his sister Sarah. His aunt Polly Purvis went too, Julia Cook and her daughter, and even Rill's older sister Hannah Sweetland managed to lend a hand. They cooked, cleaned and nursed. They emptied chamber pots, scrubbed sheets and clothes and gave Electa and her children the many doses of medicine that Doc Montgomery had prescribed them.

The doctor was unable to make a full diagnosis, and so it was a mystery as to what ailed them. Electa had told him that she suspected it was the well water. She remembered Dave thinking the well was going bad before he'd left, but he'd never got around to digging a new one. She told this to Lydia Ballard too, so Lydia got the bright idea to send over Gabriel's father John and his brother Sam to dig them a new one. Hearing about it from Hannah, George Sweetland showed up to help too with several other men from the neighborhood. They had it dug and laid up in a week, hitting water fourteen feet down. When Dave finally made it back home, Electa and the kids were still sick, but far better than they had been, and well on their way to a full recovery.

Since Gabriel had gone back to the Army the previous October, Rill had been busy raising her infant daughter Martha. She also helped her mother-in-law Lydia care for her two youngest, Gabriel's brothers, 3-year-old George and baby Edward, who'd been born in October shortly after Gabriel left. With a house full of young ones, Lydia was more than thankful for the extra help. She loved Rill, too. How could she not, as kind, pretty and thoughtful a girl as she was? She thought her an excellent mother to her little granddaughter, and over the past year had grown to consider her one of her own. Gabriel's whole family had adopted her as such, his mother, his father, his siblings, his aunts and uncles, and his grandparents, too. They all grew to love the girl, and saw her as an integral member of their extended clan.

Rill's side of the family was doing well, too. Her father was settling into his new home nicely and wrote her often. He claimed he was considering opening a hotel. Her sister Hannah was the same as ever, stubborn and demanding, but Rill could see she was making attempts to be nice at times and seemed to have forgiven her for getting pregnant. She hardly ever spoke of Gabriel, though. Every Sunday, Rill and the baby would go visit her and have supper at her home. On one of their Sunday visits in January, Hannah even offered a second time for Rill and the baby to move back. Rill was grateful, as she had been when Hannah first asked the previous summer, but respectfully declined. She loved her sister and her brother-in-law George, but she'd been down that road before, and didn't want to repeat the experience.

She knew that initially Hannah would have treated her well, but that eventually things would have ended up like they had been before, with her doing all the chores around the home while Hannah feigned injury or illness. She wasn't afraid of the extra work. On the contrary, she enjoyed it, and toiled awfully hard to help out around her in-laws' home. It was different with the Ballards though. There, she felt appreciated and everyone pulled their own weight equally, even the older children, and they were always willing to help one another.

With the assistance of the Ballards, Rill was getting along just fine. She still missed Gabriel, of course, and longed for the day when he'd come home. She lay awake most nights wondering how it would be when he got back, when they could finally start living together as a happy little family. She knew they would have to stay with Gabriel's parents or rent at first, but that in a few years if they worked hard, and scrimped and saved, they could buy a farm of their own. Nothing too big, fifty acres would do, just enough to raise crops and have a place to pasture their livestock. They would build a small house at first but build it in a way where it would be easy to add on to in the future. She would have a kitchen garden and little Martha would help her plant the seeds, water, and weed it. Gabriel would work the fields, and care for the animals. He'd gather firewood to cook with and keep them warm in the winter. She wanted apple trees and a grape vine and a strawberry patch so that she could make jam. They'd mail some to her father because strawberry jam was his favorite treat. On Sundays Gabriel would hitch their horse to its buggy and they'd ride to church together as a family. She wanted more babies, too, some more little girls and a couple of boys, so that Gabriel would have someone to hunt with and teach to run a plow, mow a field and saddle a horse. She wanted all that and more, and every night before she fell asleep, she would pray that the war would be over by morning.

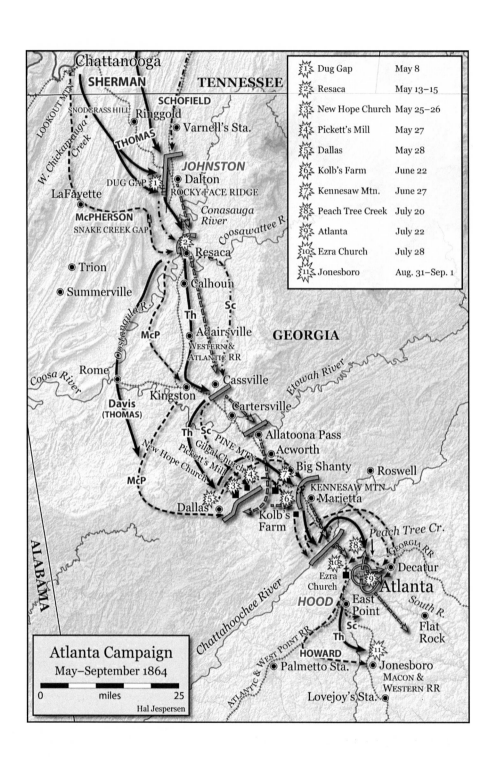

❋ 1	Dug Gap	May 8
❋ 2	Resaca	May 13–15
❋ 3	New Hope Church	May 25–26
❋ 4	Pickett's Mill	May 27
❋ 5	Dallas	May 28
❋ 6	Kolb's Farm	June 22
❋ 7	Kennesaw Mtn.	June 27
❋ 8	Peach Tree Creek	July 20
❋ 9	Atlanta	July 22
❋ 10	Ezra Church	July 28
❋ 11	Jonesboro	Aug. 31–Sep. 1

Atlanta Campaign

May–September 1864

0   miles   25

Hal Jespersen

CHAPTER FIFTEEN

As final preparations for the spring offensive were being buttoned up, an air of excitement was emanating throughout Sherman's army. The troops knew that their winter hibernation had come to an end and they were raring to get the war going again and perhaps, if they were lucky, force some kind of conclusion to the misery they had endured for far too long.

It was an especially exciting time for Gabriel, as he'd never been a part of something so grand and so promising before. Since the beginning of his military career he had spent most of his time in camp, or sick and the few times that he was actively soldiering, it was in comparatively minor operations. It was true that Chattanooga had been a significant Union victory, but due to his regiment's minor role in the fighting and the fact that he had missed out on Wauhatchie, he didn't feel that he'd contributed much to its successful outcome. He felt unworthy of being labeled a victor, and saw himself more of an observer than a participant.

Things were different now, though. This time, he was starting out the campaign at its very beginning and all signs were pointing for it to be a hard fought and bloody affair. His first taste of battle was fast approaching, and he was eager for the test.

Sherman's invasion force, his Military Division of the Mississippi, that he planned on pushing into Georgia with, consisted of three separate armies. The Army of the Cumberland, the Army of the Tennessee, and the Army of the Ohio, and they all varied greatly in size. The Army of the Cumberland, by far the largest of the three, was commanded by General George H. Thomas, the hero of Chickamauga. It consisted of four corps, the 4th, the 14th, the 20th, of which Gabriel was a member and then a separate corps of cavalry. The Army of the Tennessee, second to the Army of the Cumberland in size, was commanded by General James B. McPherson. It consisted of two corps at first, the 15th and 16th but was joined by a third, the 17th, later in the campaign. The smallest army, the Army of the Ohio, was commanded by General John M. Schofield. It consisted of only one corps, the 23rd, and a division of cavalry. Together, all three forces combined to around 110,000 men to start out the campaign. Disproportionately, around 70,000 of these men belonged to General Thomas, as his three infantry corps were fat with over 20,000 men apiece.

Facing the northern troops in their invasion of Georgia, was the far smaller Confederate Army of Tennessee, commanded by the talented yet cautious General Joseph Johnston. Johnston had led the Confederate Army in Virginia during the first year of the war, but after his wounding at Seven Pines in 1862 he was replaced by General Robert E. Lee. At the start of the campaign, Johnston's army had only around 53,000 souls, less than half of his northern opponents. These men, however, were resourceful, hard-fighting and battle-tested troops, and although they had lost the majority of the battles they'd taken part in, it was mostly due to poor leadership and missed opportunities.

Johnston had no delusions about the odds he faced. He knew the cards were stacked against him, but was determined to play his hand well by taking advantage of the terrain, attacking only when the odds were in his favor, and eventually slipping away to fight another day when he felt he was about to be surrounded or cornered into a disadvantageous fight. When Sherman's troops embarked south during the early days of May 1864, most of Johnston's army was centered around the town of Dalton, Georgia. Located behind a screen of mountains and along the Western & Atlantic Railroad, Dalton offered Johnston an easily defended and supplied position. To defend the city, he placed his troops, in the valley to the north of town, and on the mountainous terrain to the west. Others were left available to plug any gaps through the mountains that the Yankees might try and use to their advantage.

Naturally, Johnston's troops were Sherman's main target. If they could be defeated and swept away, he would have a clear path to Atlanta, and free reign on Georgia and much of the deep south. A victory would also free up troops that he could send east to assist the Army of the Potomac in capturing Richmond.

To attack Johnston, Sherman planned on sending his massive Army of the Cumberland and Army of the Ohio, to demonstrate against Johnston's main lines outside of Dalton. If they somehow broke through that would be wonderful, but Sherman knew that taking those positions with full-fledged assaults would be far too costly and have a low chance of success. Instead, the move was more of a feint, meant to divert Johnston's attention, while Sherman sent General McPherson and his Army of the Tennessee south and then east through the undefended Snake Creek Gap. There Sherman wanted him to attack Resaca, a town in between Johnston and Atlanta and, like Dalton, also located on the Western and Atlantic Railroad. If Sherman could capture it, he would have cut off the main supply line to Johnston's army and his easiest route of retreat. If McPherson succeeded, Johnston's army would be sandwiched between two Union armies and could be captured or destroyed in just days.

* * * * *

Gabriel and his comrades in the 20th Corps, moved south of Chattanooga and into Georgia on the 3rd of May. On their first day out, they traveled over the old Chickamauga battleground where the remnants of that fight were still strewn about the landscape. Bits of canvas, clothing and uniforms, the splintered spokes of a shattered cannon wheel, a horse harness here, a bullet pierced canteen there, a broken rifle stock, and so on. What most caught their notice, however, were the bones of the fallen. Some were from bodies that still lay where they fell the previous September, but most had been rooted from their shallow graves by hogs, dogs, and other wild animals in search of food. From the bits of blue, gray and butternut wool that still cling to some of the bones it was apparent that they belonged to men from both sides, North and South.

It was an eerie and foreboding site for many of the men, and even managed to catch the ever-eager Gabriel off guard and remind him, if only for a moment, that it wasn't all glory and adventure that he was about to partake in. There would be death, destruction and great suffering as well.

Gabriel didn't dwell on it for too long, though. As they rode beyond the old killing fields, his excitement returned. He was more than ready to get out of camp, and like many of the other men, had trimmed his possessions by mailing home to Rill his old letters from her, and the various knickknacks he had accumulated over the winter. He also included in the package a small bouquet of southern wildflowers he'd collected and dried for her. He knew she'd love them and would hang them on the wall in their room with all her others.

Gabriel was excited for things to finally be in motion, but he was also happy because he was traveling in style. A few days before their departure, Lieutenant Bird informed the men that a number of them would be issued mounts for the campaign. This was done with the idea that if there was a problem with a road or bridge ahead of the column the pioneers could gallop up and fix it before the wagons arrived, thus cutting back on delays. The men without mounts, the tradesmen and a few others, mostly the big city boys who were fearful or ignorant of handling the four legged beasts, were to stick close to the wagons, to care for and guard their extra tools and equipment.

To the men who were to be mounted, Bird gave a stern warning that the horses didn't give them the right to ride off as they pleased. They too were to stick close to the wagons like the other men, where they could be quickly dispatched ahead when their services were needed. He also reminded them that the horses didn't belong to them but were U.S Government property, and that they shouldn't get very attached. He said that he was informed if anyone else at headquarters, any officers, orderlies or messengers needed a spare mount they were likely to come and take them from the pioneers.

Gabriel's mount was a chestnut mare quarter horse, that he guessed was around six years old. She was well built and one of the largest in the lot, but quite stubborn and unruly at first. She actually reminded him of Rill's sister Hannah, and he named her so accordingly, a detail he chose to omit in his next letter home. It still went without saying though, that having a horse had its perks. Gabriel much preferred to ride than walk, especially when the roads were rutted, wet and muddy.

He found that towering over the men on foot made him feel somewhat exalted, too. As an infantryman, he had previously had a natural disdain for those with mounts, especially the cavalry, but now with one of his own he had to admit that most of that was due to jealousy. When he rode past his old company on the first day of the campaign, they reminded him of that and jeered him mercilessly. Most were joking and having fun with him, but some, frustrated and tired from their first march in many months seemed downright angry. Captain Marvin was especially envious to see one of his former underlings mounted up above him. Gabriel was riding with Bird when he passed Marvin and it was the first time he'd seen the man since the previous summer, so he greeted him as he passed. Marvin pretended not to have heard at first, but after Gabriel tried a second time, he felt forced to acknowledge.

"Any word from that slithering friend of yours, Private Ballard?" Marvin snarled at him.

Gabriel pulled back on his reins to slow to Marvin's pace.

"Who might that be, Captain?" he said, trying to look as oblivious as he could.

"Don't give me that. I know you're in league with that drunken bastard Nash. He's run off, scared to fight I suppose. I'm surprised to see you haven't gone with him."

"Can't say I knew about that," Gabriel lied, "but I did hear from home that his family was sick. I'd guess he's gone back to care for them."

"He has not. He's yellow," Marvin shouted, but Gabriel didn't hear. He'd spurred his horse to a gallop to catch back up with Bird before Marvin could open his mouth, knowing it would irk him not to get in the final word.

"Who was that crotchety old badger?" Bird asked him when Gabriel returned to his side.

"Oh, him? He's just my old captain from home, Harrison Marvin," Gabriel told him, trying to brush it off.

"What was he so angry about, then? He didn't seem to care much for you," Bird inquired.

Gabriel was embarrassed that he'd detected Marvin's low opinion of him.

"That's another one of those long stories, Jim," he answered, finally managing to call him by his first name without being reminded.

Bird turned his head left and right, like he was looking for something.

"Don't see any Rebs, no wash outs, no swamps or torn up bridges. We've got nothing going on that I can see but putting road behind us, so lets hear it."

Gabriel was hesitant. He knew he was in the right in regard to his problems with Marvin, but was nervous that Bird might think otherwise or not fully believe him. There was no escaping it, though. He could think of no excuse to avoid the conversation and was forced to relent to Bird's pressure.

As they rode along, he told Bird everything from beginning to end, starting off with signing up in Marvin's store, and the early troubles Marvin had had with the men. He told how their company was transferred to another regiment, the desertions that followed, and Marvin's bitter feud with Moffat. He also told about finding out he was to be a father, how that all came about, and getting married in Washington to Rill. How he got sick after Gettysburg and how Marvin would have let him die if Enos hadn't scooped him up and carried him to the hospital. He ended by telling of Marvin's most recent wickedness involving Dave Nash and his ailing family.

Bird was quiet the whole time and listened intently to what Gabriel had to say. When he'd finished, he felt bad for him and all his old friends too, but he wasn't surprised. He'd heard of and seen many examples of incompetence or injustice over the past couple years, but made sure to let Gabriel know he was on his side.

"It's a wonder, Gabriel, there's anyone left in your old company.

Sounds like that captain of yours doesn't deserve to be a soldier, much less an officer. Never mind what he thinks of you. His opinion clearly isn't worth squat anyway. Honestly, I'd be more concerned if the man had liked you. Think I'd send you back if he did."

Bird knew just what to say and Gabriel smiled. He had always known Marvin was in the wrong, but it made him feel good to hear it from someone outside the company.

"And Gabriel," Bird added, before closing the matter, "if he gives you any more trouble you come straight to me and I'll take care of him. I don't care if he outranks me or not, you're one of mine now, and I'll make sure he knows it."

* * * * *

Initially, Sherman's plan was executed well. His troops under Thomas and Schofield were in place outside of Dalton by May 7th. Then, on the 8th they made a series of small attacks at Rocky Face Ridge, Dug Gap and Buzzard Roost Gap, Confederate positions in the mountains to the west of town. Also on the 8th, McPherson's troops began making their way down Snake Creek Gap toward Resaca. McPherson emerged from the gap on the 9th, and successfully advanced his troops against the Rebel positions outside of town. His lead troops made it to within a couple hundred yards of the railroad, but then things began to go askew.

Fearing he was outnumbered and about to be ambushed, McPherson got cold feet and made a huge mistake by cancelling the advance and pulling his troops back into Snake Creek Gap. His concerns that persuaded him to fall back were unfounded, however. He was the one who outnumbered the Rebels, not the other way around, and he was walking into no ambush. What could have been an easy victory turned into a missed opportunity. The railroad remained open and subsequently Johnston's supply line south did as well.

Hearing of McPherson's misfortune the next day, Sherman, who had already sent some troops to his support, decided to transfer Thomas and Schofield's men toward Resaca too. Only Thomas's 4th

Corps, commanded by, "Old Prayer Book" General Howard, and a portion of cavalry were left behind, outside Dalton. Sherman hoped to get his troops between Johnston and Resaca and force a battle.

Johnston's movements prevented this, however. Although the Yankees outside of Dalton continue to pester him, after hearing about McPherson's push toward Resaca, he began dispatching troops toward that town, too. At first, he was unsure as to Sherman's true motive and only sent a few troops, but he soon made up his mind and sent them all. He decided that the Yankee numbers to his rear were growing and posed the greatest threat. On the morning of May 13th, Howard's 4th Corps walked into Dalton unopposed. By now the majority of both sides had arrived at or are near Resaca, and throughout the day and into the evening they moved into position for battle.

On the morning of the 14th, their positions were as follows: Johnston's troops were dug in and strung out on high ground in the shape of a giant fishhook. Their left flank was anchored on the Oostanaula River and in front of Resaca and the fort there, protecting the railroad bridge over the river. From there their line stretched north for roughly two miles and then curved back east across the road, running into Resaca from the north. Behind them ran the railroad.

The Yankee position nearly mirrored that of the Confederates. Their right was anchored on the Oostanaula and then their line ran north and curved east. They too were positioned on high ground, and in between the two sides was an open valley with a small waterway, known as Camp Creek, running through it. Both hills were wooded in areas, but there was also a lot of bare and brushy ground, especially in the valley. The Yankee position had a flaw, though, as their line ended just short of the road north out of Resaca, while the Confederate line went beyond the road. It is here where they were at most risk of being outflanked and overrun by the Rebels.

* * * * *

The shooting started early in the morning, while Gabriel was up tending to his horse and enjoying a cup of coffee. Nothing too substantial, just skirmishers and a few intermittent cannon blasts at first, but then around 11 A.M. heavier firing could be heard to the north and word soon passed through camp that the 14th and 23rd Corps to their left were making an attack on the Rebs. Smoke was seen in the valley and on the ridgeline opposite where Confederate rifles and cannon were firing into their advancing comrades. For hours the fight went on and then died away.

"Well, that didn't quite go our way," Bird said to Gabriel as the sounds of battle began to slacken.

They were watching from the ridge, where the 20th Corps was positioned near the center of the Union lines.

"How can you tell?" Gabriel asked him.

"That strong Reb line on the far ridge never moved. Our boys may have pushed back their skirmishers, but nothing more," Bird explained.

"I see," Gabriel said, looking unamused.

He was frustrated. It felt like Chattanooga all over again, watching other men do the fighting, while he sat by idle. It'd been the same a few days prior even, when Geary's troops from their corps attacked Dug Gap outside of Dalton. It was worse, though, for his friend Jim. Bird's old regiment, the 154th, was in Geary's division, and he was sick with guilt watching them go into battle for the first time without him. He paced back and forth like a caged lion the whole fight, and when the casualties started making their way back and told him his regiment was getting hit hard, Gabriel saw tears in his eyes. Remembering what Hooker had said about Bird, Gabriel knew the man was a fighter, and that it must have hurt his pride even more than it hurt Gabriel's, to be out of the action.

Thinking the fight may be over for the day, Gabriel and Bird rode back to where the other pioneers were lounging about next to the cluster of headquarters tents. They were eating and a few men were tossing a ball back and forth. Bird disappeared into one of the tents and Gabriel went over to his friends to tell them what he'd seen.

Cannon fire began to pick back up again and went on for a while. Most of it was coming from the Yankee guns. Dispatch riders kept coming and going from the tents, and then Lieutenant Bird emerged from one and jogged over to his men. Seeing the eager look on his face those of the boys that were sitting stood and they all gathered round when he reached them.

"Hope you boys are ready, we've finally got a job to do," he said, unable to conceal his joy. "Williams' division is marching north to the left flank of our line. Apparently the Rebs are massing for an attack up there and Howard's pissing his pants. Thinks he's got another Chancellorsville on his hands."

"What's that mean to us, Jim? We're not part of Williams' division," one of the men asked.

"I'm getting to that," Bird said. "Hooker's going up there with them and he wants twelve of us to tag along, twelve mounted men. The rest will stay here and if headquarters needs to be moved, you're to help tear it down and escort it to its next destination."

Bird hand-picked twelve men. They each were to sling their rifles around their bodies and attach a spare spade and axe to their saddles.

"We're to help clear the way if anything obstructs the route," he told them, "and once the division goes into the fight Hooker wants us sticking close to him in case one of his orderlies needs a new mount. Might use us to run dispatches, too."

Williams' division was already in line ready to take off when Bird and his men approached. They rode to the head of the column where they found Hooker in an excited mood. Bird saluted the General.

"Lieutenant Bird, I see you've arrived with your men," Hooker said as he returned the salute. "Ha, ha," he chuckled. "Do they have the spades and axes I requested?"

"Yes, General Hooker, they most certainly do," Bird answered.

Both men were over the top with enthusiasm and good humor and Gabriel, who was on his horse just behind Bird, couldn't help but smile at their giddiness.

"Something funny there, Son?" Hooker asked staring over Bird's shoulder at Gabriel.

Gabriel gulped thinking he'd offended the General.

"No Sir, just excited to get into a fight," he managed to squeak out.

"As you should be, young man," Hooker said. "This will be your first, Private Ballard, will it not?" he asked.

It still astounded Gabriel to know that the famous General Hooker knew him by name.

"It will be, Sir. That's right," Gabriel answered.

"You see, Private, I'm a man of my word," Hooker said to him. "You found me these wonderful undergarments I'm wearing, and I kept you around here long enough to go into a fight with this dashing lieutenant of yours," Hooker said with his hand held out and open towards Bird as if he were a showman presenting his next act to the crowd.

"When we get into position, Lieutenant, you and Private Ballard are to leave your horses with one of my aides, and I'd like you to accompany the young man into the fight. Show him how to soldier, as I know you know best," Hooker instructed.

Bird nodded his approval.

"Consider it done, Sir, and thank you, Sir, for the opportunity."

Hooker held up his hand.

"Think nothing of it, Lieutenant, and don't worry about your other men. They can ride with me until the Rebs are beaten."

Bird agreed and turned to his men to make sure that they had heard the General.

"Oh, and one more thing before we take off," Hooker said, looking to Gabriel. He reached into his pocket and pulled out what looked to be a coin that shined bright in the afternoon sun. "Here Private, I won't send a man off to meet his maker knowing that I owe him money."

Gabriel tried objecting the offer.

"Sir I couldn't accept…"

"You can, and you will," Hooker interrupted and shoved the coin into Gabriel's hand with force. "Now that's a $20 gold piece. Half goes to you to buy a first rate whore with after this is over, and the other half is to go to that Mrs. Cook. You can tell her there's more where it came from, too, if she's willing to make me another pair."

Twenty dollars! Gabriel was astonished, General Hooker had just handed him a month and a half's worth of pay for a pair of drawers.

"Tell her I suggest she open up an establishment of her own," Hooker recommended. "Why, if she moved to New York or Washington, she'd make a killing. Will you do that for me, young man?"

"I'll mention it, Sir, but I don't think Julia will be leaving Dryden anytime soon."

Unknown to Gabriel, however, was that Julia Cook had done just that. She'd recently gone to Washington D.C to work as a nurse in an Army hospital but got dangerously ill and was forced to return home after only a few weeks of service.

* * * * *

As their column traveled toward the far left flank of the Union line, Hooker rode up and down the road beside his marching troops cheering them on and shouting that Sherman was in a pinch and needed the eastern men to come and bail out his westerner boys. The men were elated to see their commander so confident and boisterous, and they cheered him on just as much as he did them. It wasn't lost on Hooker, either, that he was going to the rescue of the 4th Corps, now commanded by General Howard. Howard was the man he blamed most for his disaster at Chancellorsville the year before, and he knew it must have irked him to no end that Sherman was sending Hooker to his rescue. Hooker relished in the thought of that.

"If only I had my Potomac with me today, I'd know we were invincible," Hooker said riding up to Gabriel as they were nearing the sound of heavy firing.

"What's a Potomac, Sir?"

"Potomac's my old war horse," Hooker explained. "Poor thing's gone blind."

"Sorry to hear it, Sir," Gabriel said.

"Some things can't be helped, Private. Lookout here will have to do, though," he said, patting the neck of his new horse.

"I've decided these drawers your friend made me will bring us good fortune as well."

"How's that, Sir?" Gabriel asked, curious to know the reasoning behind the General's claim.

"Luck, Private Ballard, luck. I've decided, or I get the feeling rather, that these drawers are lucky, and I intend to wear them until their luck runs out."

"But how will you know when that happens, Sir?"

"When we lose, or I am shot of course."

Gabriel didn't quite understand the General's logic on such matters. He had never been a very superstitious person, so he said nothing more. They were coming into view of the fighting anyway, and Hooker was soon shouting orders.

It was nearing dark when Williams' division finally arrived on scene. The Rebs had already hit the Yankee flank once and captured the first line of rifle pits, sending their occupants scrambling to the rear. Wounded and bewildered-looking men were passing Williams' troops as they formed for the attack. Some officers, Gabriel could see, were trying to rally their demoralized commands, many of which couldn't be persuaded. He saw one man walking to the rear, his lower arm mangled beyond recognition and hanging in red ribbons of flesh at his side.

Gabriel's heart was pounding and felt as if it were working its way up through his throat. Bird called him off to the side of the forming troops, where they both dismounted, and slung on their cartridge boxes as one of Hooker's aides gathered up the reins of their horses and led them to the rear. Hooker was still out in front of the troops cheering them on. Gabriel's old brigade, Robinson's, was to lead the assault. It was formed up in line of battle on a wooded ridge overlooking a great open field.

"Load your rifle now," Bird ordered him.

Gabriel obeyed. He pulled out one of his cartridges and tore the folded end of paper off the tube with his teeth. After pouring the powder down the barrel he nervously rammed the bullet home. He was shaking so bad he dropped three brass firing caps in the grass before he could finally place one over the rifle's nipple. Bird was cool as a cucumber, though. He didn't even appear to be excited, just focused and absorbed in what was happening around him.

"Come with me," he said when Gabriel had finally finished loading. He took off and Gabriel followed closely behind him to the front rank of one of the regiments in Robinson's brigade. There was another regiment behind them, and Gabriel could see the battle flag of the 143rd farther down the line. They both squeezed themselves into the rank of men next to each other, but the captain of the company saw them and tried shooing them away.

"Lieutenant what in the hell are you doing, falling in with my men?" the man shouted. Before Bird could explain General Hooker appeared in front of their line.

"Lieutenant Bird is here on my orders," he told the captain.

The man immediately came to attention and saluted the General.

"Yes Sir. For you, General Hooker, we'll be happy to have them."

Hooker nodded his approval to the man, then spoke to Bird.

"I knew I'd find you up here," he said. "Knew you'd be spoiling for a fight."

Bird smiled up at him somewhat bashfully, then General Hooker rode off and the order to advance was given. The clang of canteens, bayonets and cartridge boxes bouncing off one another and the unison thump of thousands of marching feet filled the air. Smoke from the fighting ahead was blowing back in clouds and enveloped the formation as it marched forward down the hill and into the open ground at its base.

In front of them, a Yankee battery was pounding away with canister at an oncoming horde of Confederates, canister being nothing more than a steel can with dozens of small leaden balls on the inside. When fired, the can tore open and the balls spread out in all directions. The farther they went the more they spread. Gabriel could see the blast were tearing great holes into the Rebel ranks, but they kept coming, screaming their horrible Rebel yell. The blasts of the cannon were deafening, and Gabriel could barely decipher the orders the officers were giving. As they closed in on the rear of the Yankee battery, the Rebs were just yards away, almost ready to sweep into its guns and viciously slaughter the men who had been doing the same to their own lines.

Suddenly, the Yankee formation halted. Gabriel looked around, not quite sure what was happening as he could hear no orders. Bird saw his look of bewilderment.

"We're firing by volley!" he shouted at the top of his lungs.

The order to 'present arms' was given, then 'aim'. Gabriel, lifting his Springfield Rifle into his shoulder, looked down the barrel and placed the front sight in the chest of a gray clad man out to his front. The man's coat was barely visible through the smoke and fading light. "Fire!", an officer directly behind him shouted, Gabriel pulled the trigger and felt the rifle butt kick into his shoulder. He tried to see if he hit his mark, but the smoke was too thick. Then, he felt a hand slap his back, grab the belt of his cartridge box and pull him down to the ground. It was Bird.

"Get down!" he shouted as a volley of rifle fire erupted from behind them. It was the regiment to their rear.

Gabriel closed his eyes and hugged the earth. What once had been a field of tall grass was now downtrodden and littered with men and debris. The firing began to slacken and Gabriel could hear an angry cheer erupt from the men around him. They stood and the order to reload was given. His shaking had ceased, and he had no problem ramming the bullet down to the base of the barrel as he had before. The call to advance was then given and the men resumed the attack.

As the smoke cleared and blew away Gabriel could see why the men had been cheering. The Rebs were falling back, the Yankee volley fire being too much for them after having taken such a pounding from the battery. They were retreating to a tree line in the distance, some in an organized withdrawal, and others in a full on sprint for safety. Passing over the ground in their front, Gabriel had to step over the bodies of dead and dying men, many of whom were whimpering for help.

At one point, Gabriel was shocked to see a pair of legs lying on the ground still in pants and boots but missing everything above the waistline. He slipped and almost fell as he passed them but caught himself. He saw that the grass was covered in a dark and slippery slime, then a terrible stench hit him a few paces beyond. It was then that he realized what happened. A canister blast had disintegrated the head, chest, and gut of the man the legs belonged to, spreading a jelly of excrement and tissue over the ground like warm butter on a slice of bread. Gabriel recognized the smell from when he and his father butchered hogs at home in the autumn. He felt like vomiting, but the call to halt was given, and they went through their motions of firing once again. Luckily, Gabriel had a clean patch of ground to lay on, but he knew that some poor bastard would be forced to take refuge in the gory smear behind him.

After firing a few more rounds and advancing a short distance further, the bugles sounded, and the call to halt was given. There was no sense in pushing forward any farther. They had accomplished all that they had come to do. After their timely arrival on the battlefield they had stopped the Rebel attack and saved the left flank of Sherman's army from being overrun. They were the heroes of the day.

Because they weren't members of the regiment they had fallen in with, Gabriel and Bird broke away from it after the fighting had ended and found themselves a clean spot under a thick pine in the rear to rest and catch their breath. They drank from their canteens and shared in what little victuals they happened to be carrying in their haversacks. Gabriel couldn't conceal his excitement. He was shaking again, but not out of fear, but because the adrenaline from the fight was still pumping through his veins.

After nearly two years in the Army, Gabriel had finally passed the test of a true soldier by firing his rifle in battle. He was unlike Bird had ever seen him. Usually, Gabriel was reserved and kept to himself, but now he was loud and boisterous and couldn't stop talking about the fight. He kept asking Bird questions about what he'd seen and thought. Bird knew it was a special moment for him. He smiled and politely answered his questions and acted surprised at what Gabriel had to say, even though he knew it was a minor affair compared with Chattanooga the winter before and the battles he'd fought in back east. In the fight that evening they'd only gotten off a handful of shots and had hardly been fired on by the Rebels. Bird did have to admit though, it still felt damn good to win.

It was well past dark when Lieutenant Bird decided they should try and catch back up with his other men. Most of the troops were sprawled out on the battlefield for the night, so it took some time to find anyone affiliated with headquarters. When they did finally run into one of Hooker's aides, the man informed them that their horses had been temporarily commandeered, and that the other pioneers were sent to help bring up the headquarters train. He also informed them that the remainder of the corps, Geary's and Butterfield's divisions, would also be coming up to join them, and that they would be making an attack on the Rebels sometime the next day.

With no horses and none of his other men to look after, Bird decided it was safe to call it a night. He and Gabriel replenished whatever ammunition they had shot away that evening and returned to the spot under the pines where they had rested earlier. It was a cold and fitful night, made worse by the fact that their knapsacks and blankets were tucked away in one of the headquarters wagons. They knew they were lucky though, for their comrades would be on the road all night and would likely get no sleep at all.

At sunrise, when they woke up, the other two divisions of the corps were still arriving. According to Sherman's plan, the 20th Corps was to be between the 4th and 23rd Corps, with the 23rd being the extreme left of the whole Union line. As a corps, the 20th was laid out with Williams' division on the left, Butterfield's in the middle and Geary's on the right. When the attack began around 1:30 though, Geary's and Butterfield's divisions were the only ones to advance, as the 23rd Corps hadn't completely arrived, and Williams' was forced to hold in place and guard the left flank.

By the time of the attack, Gabriel and Bird had been given back their mounts and reunited with the other pioneers. Unlike the previous evening though, Hooker wouldn't let them take part directly in the fight. Instead, he held them back behind the infantry, where they could be easily found. Hooker knew that if the Confederates were defeated and withdrew south towards Resaca, they were certain to obstruct the pursuing Yankees' path. His mounted pioneers would be desperately needed if that happened. On their horses they could ride ahead of the pursuing troops with their axes and spades to quickly clear the route of fallen trees and overturned wagons or whatever else was thrown in the way.

Seeing his old regiment march into battle again without him was painful for Lieutenant Bird. Gabriel watched the man, visibly agitated, pace back and forth with his horse as they moved off.

"Should have rode over and wished Alex luck. Don't let me forget to do that again," he said to his men, as the blue columns began their push forward.

Each mounted pioneer had a shortened spade and axe strapped to their horse, and a rifle slung around their backs. Even Bird had one. Lieutenants didn't typically carry a rifle, but he had successfully argued that with so few men in his outfit the extra firepower was a necessity. The unmounted men in the group sat by in a supply wagon with their collection of tools and some spare rations, ready to follow the horsemen wherever they were instructed to go.

The 20th Corps attack was a failure, however. They never broke through the Confederate lines, only pushed them back in a few places, and so Gabriel and his fellow pioneers were never summoned to do their duty. It was a similar story for the other Union attacks made that day as well. They were all failures.

As the firing died down, it wasn't long before Gabriel saw the wounded begin streaming back towards them through the fields and brush. He thought about riding up to help some of the worse-off ones, but before he could suggest it to Bird, a rider galloped up to their little group. He seemed agitated, and Gabriel recognized him as one of the men from General Williams' staff.

"I'm looking for General Hooker. You men know where he's at?" The man asked urgently.

Lieutenant Bird spoke up.

"Haven't seen him since the attack began," he said, pointing off to where a few scattered shots could still be heard. "Why, what's happening? You look worried."

The man started to ride on before Bird finished, but he shouted an answer over his shoulder before going out of view.

"Rebs are massing to our left. Got to find Hooker and let him know."

"They're trying to flank our line like yesterday, Jim," Gabriel said.

Bird ignored him, though. He took a deep breath and twisted his face, exhaling out his nostrils. He seemed to be mulling something over.

"Too bad der General tells oos to shtay her," one of the men they called "Dutchy," commented. He was one of the many Germans the old 11th Corps had been so known for.

"Shut up, Dutchy," Bird told him.

He took another deep breath and sighed.

"Shit," he said. It appeared he'd made up his mind. "We ain't doing no good standing around here," he said. "If they needed us, they'd have sent a rider by now. That attack's been defeated, I'm sure of it. Look at all the men coming back."

Hordes of Yankees were now retreating toward them. He trotted his horse over to the men in the wagon.

"You boys stay here, let them know where we've gone off too. I'm gonna ride over with the boys and see if we can't lend a hand."

The corporal with the reins nodded his understanding.

"Will do, Jim," he told him.

Then, Bird turned his horse around to face the rest of them.

"Von't der General be vangry?" Dutchy asked.

"He'll be even more angry if his flank gets turned," Gabriel retorted, not wanting Dutchy's apprehension to ruin his prospects of getting into another fight.

Bird wasn't listening anyway. He was getting ready to make his move. He shouted, "follow me!" then kicked his heels into his horse's side and took off in the direction of Williams' division.

* * * * *

When they reached Williams' men, they were adjusting their position to face the coming threat by spreading out along a wooded ridgeline. In front of them was a massive open expanse of field, brush, and stunted pine saplings. The Rebels were off in the distance yet, still on the far side of the Western & Atlantic's tracks, mingling at the edge of a taller wooded area. Bird had the men dismount behind the ridge and left a couple of them to guard the horses. The rest unslung their rifles and joined on the far end of the closest union regiment. To Gabriel's delight it happened to be his own 143rd. The pioneers fell in with Company A, but Gabriel asked Bird if he could go down and stand with the Dryden boys instead. Bird consented, but warned him not to get separated from the pioneers if things went bad.

His friends were happy to see him. "There's a sight for sore eyes," "Gabriel!", "hey Ballard decide to join us?" they called to him. Some of them harped on him too and asked where his horse was and why he was falling in with them and not the cavalry. Gabriel smiled, waved, and shook hands. William Baldwin came up and gave him a big hug.

"I'll fight next to you, Gabriel," he said.

Sgt. Hemmingway came over, too.

"Gabriel, we're pleased to have you," he said. "Will you be staying for long?"

"No, Sergeant, we're just falling in for the fight," he answered pointing down the line to where Bird and his other friends stood.

Hemingway smiled at him.

"Well, we're pleased to have you all the same."

Gabriel was pleased, too, to be back with his old friends again. It felt like he had never left. He didn't see Captain Marvin though, and wondered where he was at.

"Sergeant Hemmingway, where's the Captain?" he asked.

"Oh, he's around here somewhere. Last I knew he went off to see about having an extra box of ammunition sent over."

"Damn," Gabriel whispered under his breath. He'd hoped Marvin had gone home again or something.

Baldy heard him.

"Don't worry he won't be back any time soon. Tried the same thing yesterday. Said he was going to fill canteens for the men right before we stepped off down the hill. He walked away without a canteen on him though and we didn't see him till the fight was over. He said he fell in with a regiment behind us, but I know he was lying."

Gabriel laughed at the thought of Marvin cowering somewhere in the brush to avoid the fight. As with Gabriel, it had been Marvin's first time going into battle the day before, or at least it would have been.

The chatter among the men began to pick up, and Gabriel looked out to see that the Rebs were moving forward out of the woodline and over the railroad tracks. Their blue-crossed red banners were out front and waving brilliantly, and the ominous beating of their drums could faintly be heard. Soon it would be time to go to work.

"Sure wish Dave was here," Baldy said, trying to strike up a quick conversation before it got too loud to even think.

"Enos too," Gabriel added.

Being with the Dryden boys again made Gabriel think how things had been before he'd left the regiment. As the order to load was given, he thought about Rill and the baby, and then about Enos dying, and he wondered how it would be if that'd never happened. He wished that his old friend could have been there to greet him, just as the others had. Strangely, he felt his presence still, and imagined he was there in spirit, watching over him and Baldy and the rest of the company, even Captain Marvin, who he correctly guessed was off on the other side of the hill hiding out of sight.

The Rebs came on at them that afternoon, screaming their unnerving Rebel yell, but like wheat in a hailstorm they were mowed down by the clockwork firing of the 20th Corps. When the Rebels were first closing in on the regiment, Colonel Boughton ordered them down the hill to where a field opened up, and they began to fire. The world seemed to explode around him, but like everyone else, Gabriel stood his ground and kept loading and firing his rifle until its steel barrel was too hot to handle, and his face was painted almost black with powder residue.

The fight was much different than the one he'd been in the day before. The Rebs came at them in waves this time, once getting as close as 75 yards before being blasted away. The cannon and rifle volleys were deafening, and not less than a few times Gabriel heard the zip of Rebel bullets passing by or overhead. Some men felt the bullets too. Harry Conklin, one of the boys from Company I, got shot in the stomach after the Rebs fired their first volley. Another man from Company E caught one in an eye and died instantly, while over a dozen more were wounded and carried to the rear.

Despite their losses, the Yankees were still winning. They refused to be moved and when the last of the Rebels retreated away, the Union line erupted with cheers. With his old townsmen at his side, Gabriel shouted until his voice went hoarse and it was too painful to yell anymore. They'd done old Dryden proud that day.

* * * * *

The next morning it was discovered that the entire Confederate Army had slipped away over the Oostanaula during the night. They did so quietly, so as not to risk detection, and left their dead on the battlefield where they'd met their end. Men were sent out in burial parties before they moved on in pursuit of the retreating Confederates. Gabriel and his comrades were among the unfortunate few to be assigned the task. They were given a small section of the battlefield to take care of. Lieutenant Bird divided them into two groups, one to dig the long trenchlike grave and the other to find the bodies. Gabriel was one of the searchers. It was terrible work, especially when it came to handling the mangled corpses of men who'd had been torn apart by the artillery. Luckily, the bodies in their section had only been dead less than a day so they hadn't begun to smell too awful bad yet.

After collecting the corpses and neatly stacking them in the grave, Bird sent the men out for one last search before they tossed dirt over top of the hole. Gabriel went off by himself into a thicket that he didn't remember seeing anyone search yet. Pushing his way through the brush he found that there was a little clearing in its center, and in the grass there he caught sight of a young man in gray wool laying on the ground. The man was on his back with the brim of his cap pulled just down over his eyes, his arms crossed over his stomach and his rifle resting neatly by his side. At first, he thought he'd found a Rebel deserter, or a man who had fallen asleep and was never awakened by his retreating comrades.

Not being currently armed himself, Gabriel snuck towards him, hoping to snatch up his rifle before the man came to, but as he approached, he saw that his skin looked a slight shade of blue, and noticed a bullet hole between the buttons on his coat. He was dead. It seemed strange to Gabriel how neatly the body was arranged though, and he couldn't decide if the man had fallen that way by chance or been kindly placed there by his friends.

Suddenly, there was a rustling in the brush on the other side of the clearing. Gabriel thought it was another searching pioneer at first but was surprised to see that the men who emerged were in fact strangers. There were three of them, a tall and well-built but filthy-looking sergeant, and two smaller privates about Gabriel's size.

"How's it going?" Gabriel said to them in greeting, but none of them answered. They just walked up, looked at him and then at the dead Reb on the ground. The sergeant was gnawing on a plug of tobacco and spit a stream of brown juice down onto the Reb's face before focusing on Gabriel.

"Robbing the dead, were ya, boy?" he said.

Gabriel looked at him surprised and embarrassed by the accusation. He tried to set the record straight with the man by telling him the truth, that he was part of a burial party.

"Horse shit," the sergeant said, disbelieving. "Don't lie to me, boy. I don't care. Nothin' wrong in it. We just want our fair share, that's all."

"I swear, Sergeant, I…"

"Shut your fucking mouth, boy," the sergeant yelled to silence him.

Gabriel gave him a dirty look but obeyed. He was infuriated, though.

"Search him," the sergeant ordered his two cronies as he bent down himself to tear open the Reb's coat and rummage through his pockets. Oddly the hole in the man's chest had hardly bled.

It hadn't occurred to Gabriel that the sergeant was referring to him, so he was surprised when the two men approached, one per side. "They're just a pack of thieves and see me as easy pickings," he thought to himself, but was unsure whether he should give in, or make a run for it. He froze in indecision.

"Check his brogans too, boys. The dumb ones always hide their goods in there, and he looks a few cards short of a full deck, if you know what I mean," the sergeant added with a raspy chuckle.

His men laughed too, but the insult was just the spark Gabriel needed. The anger he felt at it thawed his frozen instincts, and he reacted accordingly. He'd been in his fair share of schoolyard scraps over the years, and he wasn't about to go down without a fight. As the man on his right bent down to go for his brogans, Gabriel grabbed the back of his greasy head and drove his knee into the man's face as hard as he could. The man let out a yelp and tumbled over backwards onto the ground, clutching his wounded face. Gabriel then turned on the other man who had stepped back when he attacked his partner. He was about to take a swing at him but was stopped by the distinctive click of a revolver hammer being drawn backwards.

"Hold it right there, Private," the sergeant calmly ordered, as he leveled his revolver at Gabriel from where he stood next to the corpse.

His nose gushing blood, the man Gabriel had kneed stood up off the ground with a knotted stick in hand. He raised it over his head to take a swipe at Gabriel, but the sergeant stopped him.

"I don't think so, James. It's your own damn fault. You should've made sure old Willy had ahold of him before you checked his brogans, you idiot."

"But John, he..."

"I said no!" the sergeant shouted.

James backed down begrudgingly, and the sergeant told the other man, Willy, to search Gabriel, which at gunpoint Gabriel had no choice but to allow. Almost instantly, Willy discovered the $20 gold piece on the inside pocket of his coat, the sudden loss of which made Gabriel seethe in anger and kick himself for having gone off out of sight on his own.

"Lord almighty John, look at what I've found. A gold coin," he said, holding it up for all to see.

His partner with the bloody nose reached up to grab it for a look of his own, but the sergeant stopped him.

"Give it here, you two," he barked as he eagerly tucked his revolver into his belt.

With his enemies engrossed with his gold coin, Gabriel slowly started to back away, thinking he would make a run for it, and go get help. He was stopped by a hand lightly taking grip on his shoulder, though. It startled him at first, but turning he saw it was the hand of Lieutenant Bird, and a wave of relief instantly washed over him.

"Excuse me, gentlemen, but what's going on here?" Bird interrupted them.

Too busy looking over their treasure, the other three men hadn't noticed Bird's presence and, like Gabriel, were surprised to see him.

"What the hell," the sergeant said gruffly as he looked up.

Once he realized he was talking to an officer though, he completely changed his tone and demeanor. His two minions played along and stood at his side while he did all the talking.

"Oh, sorry Sir. Didn't see I was in the presence of a superior," the man said, trying to flatter him.

"That's fine, Sergeant."

"Sergeant John H. Reed, Sir, 101st Illinois. I apologize for not introducing myself."

"I didn't ask, Sergeant Reed. I was just wondering what you boys were up to," Bird questioned him, waving his arm at the unusual scene.

There was a dead Reb on the ground with his blouse undone, pockets turned inside out and tobacco juice on his face and standing nearby was a living man with a crooked and still bleeding nose.

"Well Sir, you see, my men and I, these two here beside me, were out and about looking for a missing comrade of ours when we came across that private there," Sergeant Reed said pointing at Gabriel. "He was busy plundering this poor dead Reb here, Sir. We know it ain't exactly against no laws to go through a Reb's pockets, Sir, but being the good Christians that we are, we decided to set him straight."

As he listened to the sergeant tell his lie, Gabriel felt the anger build in him again, but kept quiet, knowing Bird would be smart enough to see through the man's deception.

"I see, Sergeant. How noble of you," Bird commented.

"Well thank you, Sir," Reed said with a smug looking grin.

"But why's this man's face bloodied, Sergeant Reed?" Bird said pointing to the man named James.

"Well, Sir, like I told you, we confronted the private there, but he wouldn't pay us no mind, so James here tried to stop him and the private went wild, Sir. Grabbed him by the hair, Sir, and drove his knee into his face?"

"Is that true, Private?" Bird asked turning to Gabriel and giving him a wink.

"Well, Sir, the part about me driving my knee into that thieving coward's face, that part is true."

"You can see his insolence now, can't you, Lieutenant?" Sergeant Reed said to Bird in an agitated tone.

"I can Sergeant, I can," Bird answered him, "But what's that gold coin you've got there? Did the private find that on the corpse?"

Sergeant Reed looked down into his hand, wishing he'd tucked the coin into a pocket and out of the lieutenant's view. Now he stood the chance at having it taken from him.

"Why, as a matter of fact, Sir, no. This be mine," Reed said defensively.

"Is that so, Sergeant Reed?" Bird questioned him.

"It is, Sir."

"Well, Sergeant, what if I told you that I know this man?" Bird said pointing to Gabriel. "That he's under my command at 20th Corps headquarters, and not two days ago I saw General Hooker himself personally gift that coin to him?"

The color drained from Reed, and his face turned sour. He thought Bird had been eating right out of his hand, but instead he'd been making a fool of him and he didn't like it. He knew he'd been caught in a lie, but he wasn't about to give up so easy. His cronies,

James and Willy, looked to have accepted their fate though.

"Well, Sir, I'd say you were a lying son of a bitch," Reed growled as he reached for his revolver.

Bird suspected the move though, and had his own revolver pointing at Reed's head before Reed's hand even made it to his belt.

"On the contrary, Sergeant Reed, I am being completely honest, and if you want to get out of here without a hole in your head, or me bringing you up on charges then you will do as I say."

It sounded like Bird was letting them go, and Gabriel couldn't believe it, but he didn't say anything, he just followed orders.

"Gabriel, go over there and relieve the sergeant of his sidearm, and retrieve your coin from him as well," Bird told him.

Gabriel approached the man, took his revolver from his belt and snatched the gold coin back out of his hand.

"I'll get even boy, you can count on that," Reed whispered to him as he did so.

Gabriel paid him no mind though. He got what he was after and returned to Bird's side. Next, Bird had the sergeant's companions, Willy and James, grab their two rifles and the dead Rebs and smash them against a boulder that lay on the ground nearby. They tried to object, but before Bird could prod them along it was Reed who told them to listen.

"Just do as he says you jackasses, he's letting us go. I can get you new ones when we get back to the regiment."

He was right too. He could. There were lots of spares available now after the battle. Next, Bird had the three thieves make the dead Reb presentable again. He made them replace his pockets and button up his coat, and he also had Reed wipe the tobacco juice from his face. Then he ordered them to respectfully lift and carry the body out of the thicket and to the trench, where they placed him in with the other dead Confederates. After that, Bird told them to get and they ran off without hesitation, pleased to have been spared the harsher punishment they deserved.

Gabriel and Bird stood next to the grave as the others filled it in. They thought it odd when Gabriel and their lieutenant had emerged from the woods leading three men at gun point, but kept quiet for now, knowing they were sure to hear all about it soon enough.

"Thanks for that, Jim," Gabriel said. "But how in the hell did you ever come across us?"

"Everyone else had come back but you, so I went looking for ya. Saw where you walked into that thicket over there, so I followed your trail."

"Why'd you let them go, though? That Sergeant Reed would have shot you if you hadn't drawn on him so fast?"

"He wouldn't have shot me," Bird said. "He just wanted your coin, that's all. He thought I was trying to rob it from him. Thought I was lying about knowing you and all. Army is full of men like that, Gabriel, crooks, thieves and murderers, you know that. It's bound to happen. You can't enlist over a million men in three years and expect them all to be preachers."

"I guess you're right about that," Gabriel said, "but still I think you should have arrested them."

Bird shrugged. "Too late now," he said.

Not knowing what to do with the revolver he'd confiscated off Sergeant Reed, Gabriel tried handing it over to Bird, but Bird wouldn't take it.

"No, you keep it, I've got one already," Bird said. "They're a good backup to have, especially when you're mounted like we are now. A sidearm's faster to deploy than a rifle slung around your back."

Gabriel was thrilled, and happily looked over the gun. It was a 36. caliber Colt revolver, slightly worn, but glossy with oil, and there wasn't a speck of rust on it. Reed was a dirty and sloppy looking man, and Gabriel suspected it must have been something he'd recently stolen or scavenged.

"Thanks," he said to Bird.

"I've got something else for you, too," Bird said. He walked over to their wagon nearby and pulled out a slouch hat like the black ones all the western troops liked to wear. This one was dark brown though. He tossed it to Gabriel.

"Try it on," he said.

Gabriel caught it and pulled it onto his head. It fit perfectly.

"Where'd you get this?" he asked.

"Don't you remember? The Rebs had them on," Bird reminded him.

Gabriel snatched the hat back off his head in disgust. Bird was right, the dead Rebs they'd gathered had been wearing them. He thought it looked familiar, but didn't notice why at first. Taking a closer look, he saw dried blood spatter on part of the brim and tossed it on the ground.

"I can't wear that," he told Bird.

"The hell you can't," Bird said.

"Well, why do I gotta wear a dead man's hat?"

"Not just you, we all do, I've got just enough for everyone." Bird lifted a canvas tarp up off the back of the wagon to reveal a pile of the things.

"Well, what for, then?" Gabriel asked.

"For uniformity," Bird said. "I need to tell you boys apart from the rest. I realized it when we fell in with your regiment yesterday, and I couldn't tell my own lot from theirs. These hats should fix that."

"Well what about General Hooker? Do you think he'll allow it? They're brown, not black like all the western boys have. We'll stick out like a sore thumb," Gabriel argued.

"That's the point," Bird said, "and never you mind the General. You know he loves me. Once I explain my logic behind it, he'll have to say yes."

And he did.

CHAPTER SIXTEEN

After the Battle of Resaca, Gabriel and his comrades joined in the pursuit of General Joe Johnston's army across northwest Georgia. Sherman was desperate to catch Johnston before he reached the Etowah River, as the land beyond it was less developed, with poor roads, and rugged, heavily-timbered terrain. If Johnston could reach that country, it would help his smaller army, which had just recently upped its numbers to around 70,000 men. From there, they could have their pick of an almost endless array of easily defended positions to fight Sherman from. It wouldn't make him invincible, but Sherman's men would pay a hefty price in casualties trying to defeat him. Sherman also knew that beyond the Etowah, his supply line would be stretched nearly 100 miles from its main base in Chattanooga, making it extremely vulnerable and difficult to defend.

Johnston was willing to fight, though. He wasn't on a dash for the river, but he would only do so, of course, under favorable conditions. At Adairsville, and then Cassville, the two sides formed up across from each other in line of battle, but on both occasions Johnston decided against a full-fledged fight and retreated further east. Sherman failed to catch him, and he eventually crossed the Etowah on May 20th, and went into camp at Allatoona for a brief respite. Sherman's army did likewise, and for three days caught up on sleep, letter-writing and bathing.

General Sherman used the brief break in the campaign wisely. With Johnston now across the Etowah, he knew that supplying his troops would be substantially more difficult. To remedy this, he ran the trains day and night to ship supplies south from Chattanooga, and made several stockpiles closer to his army. He also issued orders to his commanders to begin supplementing and saving their rations by sending their men out to forage off the local inhabitants. On May 23rd, Sherman and his troops resumed the campaign. Their next objective was to reach the City of Marietta, but the route he chose had them converge on the hamlet of Dallas on their way there.

* * * * *

The almost constant toil that Gabriel and his fellow pioneers withstood in the days immediately following Resaca had greatly drained their strength and morale. They went almost entirely without sleep, except for a few sporadic minutes here and there when they were able to doze off in the saddle. They were busy day and night mending bridges, widening roads, and helping the long line of wagons creep deeper into Georgia.

The break they were afforded after Johnston crossed the Etowah couldn't have come sooner. They spent the first day of it asleep, and on the second they damned up the little creek near their camp and bathed for the first time in nearly a month. While they did so, Bird also had them boil their clothes in sudsy water to clean them and kill the lice they were all infested with. Gabriel sent a small box home to Rill, too. Inside, he placed his old kepi, along with the $20 gold piece Hooker had given him stitched into its fabric. He included a letter as well, telling her all about the campaign thus far, and the fighting he was in near Resaca. He also instructed her on what to do with the coin. He told her if there was nothing she was in dire need of for the baby or herself to give the whole thing to Julia Cook.

"It would be nice to tuck it away for ourselves Rill, but with Enos gone and James still in the Army, Julia needs it awfully more than we do." He wrote.

After everything the Cooks had done for them, Gabriel knew that Rill would be happy to do so. Julia had had the idea for the drawers anyway. She was the one who designed them, made them, and paid for the fabric and shipping cost to send them to Gabriel.

When they resumed their march on the 23rd, Gabriel felt like a new man. He was rested, fed, clean, and happy to be on the move again.

His horse was happy and rested, too. Despite her initial stubbornness, Hannah had recently grown to trust Gabriel, and was now a relatively obedient follower of his directions and commands. She didn't remind him much of his sister-in-law anymore, and Gabriel even considered renaming her. He appreciated her change in attitude and went out of his way to find her apples and carrots or any other kind of treats he came across. She loved sugar, and whenever he got it from the commissary or found some along the way, he happily let her have it.

On their third day out after their rest, the pioneers found themselves in front of the 20th Corps with General Hooker and General Geary. Geary's division was in the lead that day. The trees thickly lined the road, but the path was wide enough for the wagons and artillery to pass unencumbered, so they weren't very busy. Gabriel was riding beside his friend John Spencer, and they were both having a good time listening to General Hooker boast loudly to Bird about all the beautiful senoritas he had wooed while fighting in Mexico.

"Hell, Bird, I didn't have to pay a one of them. Those girls would line up outside my tent just for the chance at seeing me, much less bearing me their goods. Beautiful girls too, beautiful girls they were. Hair black as coal, bronze satin skin and tits like melons, every one of them."

Gabriel detected a faint scent of smoke in the air and thought nothing of it until they rounded a bend in the road and saw that the Rebs had set fire to a bridge up ahead. A couple of them were still tossing dead branches and logs into the flames, and when they saw the Yankees come into view they scrambled to their horses and rode away. A few men ahead of Gabriel fired at them, but without any success. Then Bird called out to his men, "come on boys let's save that bridge!" and took off down the road with Gabriel and the others in tow. They were determined to put out the fire, because they knew if it burned, it'd be their job to build a new one.

When they got on scene, Gabriel and John Spencer hopped down off their horses and stumbled into the creek. They used their new brown slouch hats as buckets to shuttle water up to the flames, while the other men tossed wet blankets on the timbers and used their spades to fling the burning debris the Rebs used to set the blaze off the bridge and into the water below. The situation turned especially hazardous when, perched on a hillside above the crossing, a few Rebs opened fire on the toiling pioneers.

They leapt for cover, but luckily the flames had been mostly extinguished by then, and General Hooker led a squad from his Illinois Cavalry escort across the charred decking and toward the smoke of the Rebel guns. They opened a fire of their own as they went, and the enemy soon scattered.

With the bridge still intact, the march resumed, but the incident had stirred the men considerably, and they were especially vigilant afterward, and on the lookout. Lieutenant Bird told his men to be ready to fight fire again because the Rebs were likely to try the same tricks on any other water crossings that lay in their path.

Not too much farther ahead, they reached a fork in the road. The path off to the right wasn't on any of their maps, but Hooker figured both paths must eventually lead into Dallas, so he split his corps in two and sent it down both roads to save time. He went to the right with Geary's division, while Williams' and Butterfield's divisions went off to the left. The pioneers accompanied General Hooker.

As they traveled down the uncharted path, the trees got thicker than before, and the branches started rubbing the sides of the wagons. Gabriel was skeptical that they had perhaps taken a wrong turn and was waiting for the command to be given to dismount with their axes and widen the way, when shots began to ring out. They were scattered at first, a pop here, a pop there, but then whole volleys could be heard followed by shouts for assistance to the troops on the road. The fire was coming from up ahead, where a skirmish line had fanned out about fifty yards in front of the column to prevent an ambush. Gabriel could see nothing of the fighting though. The forest was far too thick with trees, brush and shrubs.

As the infantry hurried forward, Lieutenant Bird ordered his pioneers off to the side of the road next to where Generals Hooker and Geary were conferring on what to do. After a short conversation, they seemed to come up with a course of action. General Geary began shouting orders for his troops to spread out and prepare themselves in case the Rebs made a full-on attack. He rode away to help place his men, while Hooker scribbled off notes and handed them to riders that kept coming and going from Thomas and Sherman and everyone else he was communicating with.

Taking advantage of the temporary inactivity, Gabriel pulled out his revolver and looked it over making sure it was capped and ready for action. He assured that all his pouches were firmly closed as well and reached into his haversack for an apple he'd stored away in there. After taking a couple healthy bites he tossed the rest on the ground for Hannah to nibble on. She did so readily, seeming to take no notice of all the shouting, shooting and troops rushing bye. Gabriel gently combed her mane as she ate.

"Good girl," he soothed, "that's a good girl."

Then, General Hooker, who was looking around for another rider, having sent his last orderly away, shouted over to him.

"Private Ballard, get over here!"

Gabriel was so eager to make haste, he spurred Hannah a little too hard and she almost bucked him off when she shot forward. He was quickly by the General's side though, and was handed a note.

"Get this to General Williams. Tell him to bring his division on the double quick. You know where he's at, don't you?" Hooker asked him.

"Back down to the fork and up the other road, Sir," Gabriel answered.

"That's right, now hang on and ride that horse as fast as she'll take you. Christ knows how many pesky Rebs we're facing here. Tell him it may be the whole damn Reb army, and all I got right now is one division to fight 'em off with."

Hooker then slapped Hannah's haunch with an outstretched hand and she and Gabriel were on the move. It took him a bit to work his way through the infantry that still clogged the road, but after he got past them and the wagons, things opened up and he found himself alone. He knew the fork wasn't much farther ahead and that there would be other riders and troops along shortly, so when he saw a group of horsemen trotting toward him four abreast, he didn't think much of it. As they closed in however, he saw that they appeared to be wearing gray uniforms, so he pulled up on Hannah's reins to slow her down. As he did so he heard snapping twigs and turned around to see two more gray clad horsemen trot up onto the road behind him. He was in trouble now, and he knew it.

"Oh Lord help me," he whispered.

He stopped and so did the men behind him. The four in front drew closer and stopped as well, except for one who Gabriel guessed was their leader. That man kept riding until he reached Gabriel. A thousand thoughts rushed through his head. He wondered to himself how these men were even on the road with all the Yankees about, and he couldn't believe that with that being the case, there wasn't anyone around to help him. He knew grabbing for his revolver would only get him killed, as they well outnumbered him and a few of the Rebs already had their carbines pointed in his direction. For a moment he thought about turning off into the woods and making a break for it, but the lone Reb seemed to read his mind, and as he reached for Hannah's reins, he warned him.

"No use going into the scrub, Yank. I got men in there, too, that'll blow your head off if you so much as sneeze."

At that moment, Gabriel knew he was doomed and had failed General Hooker. He felt the muscles in his throat begin to tighten and started to panic.

"Nice horse you got here, though," the Reb told him.

He was a young-looking man, about his age or younger, Gabriel figured. He could see that he barely had enough whiskers to shave. The Reb smiled at Gabriel, then tried to pet Hannah's nose, but all of a sudden Hannah reared up onto her hind legs and with her front hooves hit the Reb under the chin knocking him backwards off his horse and into a pile on the road. His companions on either side of Gabriel shouted, but before they could shoot or rush him, Hannah charged off into the woods. Gabriel instinctively ducked and held onto her neck, not wanting to be dismounted by a passing limb. He held on for dear life, as she snaked her way through the trees. Gabriel was surprised he wasn't being shot at, but figured the Rebs wouldn't have done so unless it were absolutely necessary. Any shots would surely bring more Yankees than they could handle down the road on top of them.

After a couple minutes had passed and Gabriel could hear nobody behind him, he tried to get Hannah to stop, worried she'd lead him into the arms of another group of lurking Rebs. She wouldn't pay him any mind though and it was all for the better, because before he knew it, he found himself emerging onto another roadway and into the path of an oncoming column of Yankee troops. Hannah had known all along where she was headed. Gabriel thought she must have smelled that they were near and led him directly to them. By the look of the long mustachioed man at the head of the column, Gabriel instantly recognized the troops were none other than those of General Alpheus Williams, with their leader riding out front ahead of them. The very man Hooker had sent him to find.

Gabriel galloped up to General Williams and, after saluting the man, gave him Hooker's message.

"Thank you, Private, but I have already been made aware of General Geary's predicament and am on my way. Tell me though, Son, why do you look as though you've been wrestling a shrub?"

Gabriel looked himself over. He hadn't taken the chance to yet and saw that after his ride through the woods he was covered from head to toe in leaves, twigs and sticks. He tried to explain.

"I'm sorry Sir. I ran into a group of Rebs on the other road and took off into the forest to get away."

General Williams looked impressed.

"Good for you young man. I'm sure I needn't tell you how fortunate you are. You tag along with us so nothing of the sort happens again. We'll be happy to have you, and when we get up to the action you can fall back in with General Hooker."

"Thank you, Sir. I'll do just that," Gabriel answered, and found himself a spot in line.

General Williams was an excellent soldier and had led troops in some of the toughest fighting the war had to offer. He was well-liked by his men and they affectionately called him "Pap" Williams to show it. Gabriel had never met the man, but after his short conversation with him a moment before, he decided that he liked old "Pap" too.

* * * * *

Once they'd retraced the route back to Geary's position, Gabriel went off with "Pap" Williams to find General Hooker. Hooker was pleased to see Williams' troops arriving with Butterfield's men close behind them. After conferring with Williams, he told Gabriel that Lieutenant Bird and his friends were busy clearing cannon emplacements for the artillery, but for him to stick close so that he could use him as a courier. He ended up running dispatches to Generals Geary, Butterfield, Ward, Knipe, Ruger and Colonel Robinson that afternoon. It was hard work tracking the men down, and with the heat and humidity only rising as the day went on, Gabriel found himself soaked through in perspiration. Hannah was sweating profusely as well, and Gabriel worried for a time she'd overheat.

Around 5 P.M., the bugle call to advance was given. Not entirely convinced that Hooker was facing anything substantial, Sherman ordered him to make an attack on the Confederates in his front and push them out of the way. Hooker staged his troops with Williams' division out front making the main assault, Geary's division behind them in reserve and Butterfield's off to the left to protect that flank. Williams staged his three brigades in as many lines for the attack, one behind the other, with Robinson's brigade out front, followed by Ruger's in the middle and Knipe's in the third line to the rear.

Gabriel found himself next to General Hooker and General Williams when the troops started forward. They were on their horses just behind Robinson's men and for the second time Gabriel found himself going into battle next to his old regiment. As they first stepped off, he rode down to where they were on the left of the brigade and cheered them on. Hooker was putting on a show of his own too, hooting and hollering and calling to his troops as he often did to show their western friends how Potomac men fight.

Before he lost his voice, Hooker retired to the side of General Williams again, with Gabriel in tow.

"Your division looks splendid, Pap," Gabriel heard him compliment Williams.

They did, too. Gabriel was impressed with how straight their lines were, even through the almost junglelike undergrowth that covered the forest floor they were marching over.

It wasn't long before the familiar sounds of rifle fire were heard. The pop, pop, pop as the skirmishers from both sides ran into each other. The Rebs quickly gave way at the sight of the impeccable Yankee columns and Gabriel found himself weaving Hannah through the rifle pits they had recently vacated. Up and over the rolling terrain and back and forth down the lines of men Hooker rode, and like the other men on his staff, Gabriel was having a time of it trying to keep up with him. Bullets were whizzing by as he went, and occasionally he could hear them slapping into the trees to his left and right. He felt exposed being up on the horse, and shuddered at the thought of being shot, especially as he passed men laying on the ground with mangled arms and legs. He saw one man prodding a group of ragged looking Rebel prisoners to the rear with the point of his bayonet. It didn't appear to Gabriel as any guard was needed though, for the Rebs were all smiling and looked pleased to have been captured. "Now we'll have ourselves a proper meal," he heard one of them say.

After successfully advancing nearly a mile through small ravines and thick forest, Robinson's brigade ran into a virtual wall of lead spewing from the Rebels in their front. Shot, shell and canister tore through their lines and they took whatever cover they could find. To the rear of the brigade, Gabriel was sitting atop his horse when a courier rode up to General Williams with a note. He read it and handed it to Hooker.

"Colonel Robinson says the Reb resistance is stiffening. He thinks he's closing in on their main line and he's got a couple prisoners that claim Hood's whole corps is dug in up ahead."

"Damn," Hooker said.

He pulled out his watch. It was getting close to dark and he knew that any minute Sherman would start pestering him with notes asking why they weren't advancing faster. He looked about and then back towards Williams. A shell exploded above them, but he paid it no mind.

"Get some fresh men in there, maybe they can break 'em. Send Ruger in in place of Robinson. I'll send a courier to Massa Sherman and let him know he was wrong, and that I am facing more than just a handful of fucking bushwhackers," he said sarcastically.

"Private Ballard!" Hooker shouted to summon Gabriel. He planned on having him run the note to Sherman, but as Hooker turned to face where Gabriel had just been, he found him kneeling on the ground next to his horse, and she was dead.

* * * * *

When the shell exploded above them, Gabriel instinctively ducked his head. He was quick to regain his composure though, and after looking himself over saw that he was fine, but then Hannah's front legs suddenly folded and she flopped over onto her side. Gabriel was just able to jump off before she rolled on top of him. Blood was spouting out of her head where a shell fragment had caved in her skull between the eyes. Gabriel knew she was already dead, and when General Hooker called for him all he could do is look up and shrug his shoulders. He felt awful. Although he'd only had her for a short time, he found the situation almost as sad as when Enos had passed away, especially after what she had done for him a few hours before.

Completely numb to the sight of such things, Hooker called on another courier and sent him on his way before turning his attention back to Gabriel.

"Take off your saddle, young man, and set it aside. We'll find you a new mount when this fight is over. Without your horse you're no use to me anymore though, so unsling your rifle and fall in with Ruger's troops when they pass by."

Gabriel followed his instructions and set his saddle under a tall pine nearby with a round shot lodged in its trunk. When General Ruger rode up with a few of his regimental commanders, Hooker called back out to him.

"Private Ballard, over here, fall in with Colonel Crane's men, they're some of your fellow New Yorkers."

The colonel looked down at Gabriel and gave him a nod.

"You're more than welcome, young man."

Crane's regiment was passing by around the group of gathered brass, and Gabriel squeezed himself into the line of strangers as he and Bird had done on the first day of Resaca. Scores of men passed through their formation as they marched to the front. Some were wounded, some were dangerously dehydrated and searching for water, some for more ammunition, and a few had simply had enough fighting for the day and were in search of a safer location. Gabriel thought he spotted the heavily-bearded face of Captain Marvin when he passed by one particularly thick growth of briars, but he wasn't certain of it.

When they reached Robinson's troops, the tired men stepped aside and let them pass through. They were an exhausted-looking lot, drenched in sweat, their faces black with dirt and powder residue. The trees around where they had been fighting were shot to shreds, some even toppled over or shot in two farther up the trunk where they'd been hit by an artillery shell.

Once they were on their own, Colonel Crane gave the order to close in on the enemy, which they did with great courage, loading and firing away as they went. The Rebs in their front retreated quickly, and then for a moment went out of sight. As they moved forward, Gabriel could see a long line of mounded red Georgia soil through the trees and knew they were closing in on the main Rebel breastwork. Some of the enemy began shouting insults at them, trying to entice them in closer, then Gabriel heard a Reb officer screech, "Fire!" at the top of his lungs, and the air in front of him instantly erupted in a soup of flames and smoke. A collective moan emanated from the regiment and Gabriel heard bullets and shells go shrieking past. The peculiar thud of lead as it tore into flesh and bone could be heard as well, and Gabriel saw men falling all around him.

Instinctively, he winced, and reached for the top of his head and held down his hat as if he were walking headlong into a brisk winter wind. Peeking out his left eye down the line of soldiers to make sure he wasn't alone, he saw a shell land at the feet of an unlucky man several yards away. Gabriel closed his eye for an instant as the shell burst, and when he opened it again the poor soul was rolling about on his back in the dirt like an overturned turtle, his legs and groin blown into oblivion. The man didn't struggle but a moment before all the life had left his body.

"Find cover!" Colonel Crane called out to his men. He'd come to quickly realize they didn't stand a chance out in the open.

Gabriel eagerly leapt to the ground and crawled forward in the direction of a large boulder he had seen before the Reb volley enveloped them. Instead of finding the stone though, he felt himself falling headfirst into a hole. He shouted as he fell, but the hole wasn't very deep, and he landed on something soft, a body. He righted himself and picked up his rifle.

"Sorry about that," he said, nervously wondering in the back of his mind if he was talking to a Reb or a fellow Yankee.

"No use in apologizing to him, he's dead," a familiar voice said from the other end of the hole.

Gabriel could see now that he'd fallen into one of the Rebs' small rifle pits that they'd dug ahead of their main line of breastworks. It was about three foot by twelve, and four deep. Gabriel had fallen in the center, but was now on one end while the living man who spoke to him was on the other. Rifles were erupting above them, but they were safe for now in the hole.

"Willy there's lost his head, and James is lying up top. He's dead too, he is," the man spoke up again, and Gabriel instantly realized who he was.

It was Sergeant Reed, who had tried robbing him after Resaca. He said nothing, but adjusted his hat to hide part of his face from view.

The light in the sky was fading, and in the shadow of the hole he thought that maybe if he kept quiet the sergeant wouldn't recognize him.

If he already hadn't, that is. Taking a better look at the supposed Willy, he could see that the man had truly been decapitated, so there was no way of properly identifying him. His head and neck were completely gone above the clavicles. He also noticed that neither of them had rifles and wondered what they were doing so far ahead of where Robinson's brigade had been fighting. Eventually, he came to the conclusion that there was no way around revealing himself, and with the knowledge that he was the only one armed, Gabriel decided to confront him.

"So, Sergeant Reed," he said, "what brings you so close to the Rebel lines? Deserting to the enemy were you?" he asked, suspecting he had guessed correctly.

He was wrong, though.

"Hell no. I ain't no traitor," Reed said. "Got captured, we did, and made a break for it when we saw you boys so close. They shot us down though as you can see. That is, everyone but me. I got lucky."

"You don't remember me, do you Sergeant?"

"Oh, I do, I do. You're my wealthy little friend," Reed laughed. "Wasn't positive at first, seeing you with that brown hat on. Still got my sidearm though, I see," he said pointing at Gabriel's waist. "How about that gold coin of yours? Don't have that, do ya, boy?"

"No, you're right. I don't," Gabriel answered him honestly.

"Ha, I knew it. I knew that bastard lieutenant was lying. He stole it from you after we left, didn't he?"

"No, I sent it home to my wife," Gabriel said.

"Like hell you did. He took it from you once we left. That, or he made you split it with him."

"Think what you want, you son of a bitch. I told you the truth," Gabriel said.

He felt vulnerable and was annoyed that not only did he have to worry about the Rebs assaulting him, but a man from his own side too, and one with superior rank, at that. He despised the man, but not just for the obvious reason that he was a crook and had tried to rob him, but because it appeared that he thought all men were as crooked as him. Reed was quiet for a moment, then spoke up.

"I out to kill you right now," he said, sounding nasty and full of hate. Gabriel leveled his rifle at him.

"Try if you want," he dared him, half hoping the man would, so he could be done with him.

Reed thought about it but didn't like his chances. He waited for the next Reb volley to erupt overhead then hopped out of the hole and ran for the rear.

"This ain't over," he said to Gabriel just before doing so.

After Reed had gone, Gabriel went right to work. Other men joined him, once they noticed him firing from a more concealed position than the thin trees they were hiding behind. He was happy to have company. They would kneel down and load in the hole, then pop up and get off a quick shot before ducking their heads again. Gabriel helped one of them lift the rigid corpse out of the trench and onto the ground above them to use as a bullet stop. They loaded and fired, loaded and fired again and again. They couldn't see much of the Rebs as they were well hidden behind the dirt and head logs of their breastworks, so they aimed at the flash of their volleys instead.

Gabriel had powder in his mouth from tearing open so many cartridges. It parched his throat and crunched between his teeth at first, then dissolved and left a terrible taste in his mouth. Soon he was out of rounds and water and had to borrow from the other men in the pit. Then they all were out, and one of the men went searching above for more off the dead and wounded that littered the ground around them. He had trouble finding any because everyone else was running into the same problem and most of the dead and wounded had already been picked clean. Gabriel remembered he had his revolver and shot that off, too. It went quick, though.

It was almost dark when they were relieved. Robinson's brigade returned and sent them back to rest and resupply. Gabriel was happy to be out of there. He helped the men that had been in the pit with him carry one of their wounded corporals to the rear. They were friendly fellows, and after talking with them learned that they were from the 107th New York, and that many of them were from Schuyler, Chemung and Steuben Counties, just to the west and south of his own, Tompkins County. One of the men, who introduced himself as Manley Crane, said he was at Antietam and Gettysburg, but never had he been under fire as heavy as that night. The 107th paid a hefty price for it too, losing over 160 men.

Gabriel got his canteen filled and his cartridge box resupplied before stepping out in search of the spot were Hannah had been killed. He needed to recover his saddle. He had forgotten all about her death during the fighting, but when he saw the officers riding around on their horses behind the front lines he was sadly reminded.

"Poor girl," he thought to himself.

It was fully night now, pitch dark and to top it off rain had started coming down in torrents. Miraculously, he was able to find Hannah's carcass in the dark, but the saddle was gone, and he had to ask around for where the 20th Corps headquarters had hunkered down.

It took him a while, but eventually he found it, too, and was relieved to see that his saddle and other belongings were safe and sound in their supply wagon. His friends, excluding Lieutenant Bird, were all asleep, sprawled out in the muck and mud under a few filthy strips of canvas. Bird was still up though, hunkered down out of the rain under a small shelter he'd made out of sticks and pine boughs. Despite the weather, he had a little fire going and was puffing on a cigar when Gabriel approached him. He was a sight to see in his sopping wet uniform, with water streaming down over the brim of his hat in little waterfalls and his rifle, gear and accoutrements hanging heavy at his shoulders. It seemed as if he might topple over and Bird couldn't help but crack a smile. He could tell Gabriel was almost delirious with exhaustion.

"Look like you had a hard go of it today," he said to Gabriel.

Gabriel grunted in affirmation.

"You have no idea, Jim," he answered him. "This is one hell hole of a place, let me tell you."

"So I've heard it said. Can't win them all, though. Hooker told me he sent you into the fight after your horse got shot down. We got your saddle."

"I saw. Thanks," Gabriel said, still standing out in the rain.

"Come on under here and get some shuteye, if you can," Bird told him. "I got orders to have you boys up in four hours. Sooner, if the Rebs give us anymore trouble."

Gabriel came in and had barely stripped off his gear before he was fast asleep. It'd been a long day, a stressful day, a sad day, a day he would likely never forget. The Battle of New Hope Church was a loss for the Yankees, but for Gabriel it was more than that.

Before Resaca he'd had a deep desire to go into battle. He wanted to experience it and to prove himself that he was worthy of being called a soldier. After that fight he felt relieved and confident, and was eager to get into another scrap. His experiences at New Hope Church were much harsher than what he'd went through at Resaca, though. They were sobering. On a scale of size, it was a much smaller battle, but the fighting, the violence and the carnage he witnessed was far more terrible. Not to mention, his horse had been shot out from under him and he'd narrowly escaped capture earlier in the day.

New Hope Church changed the way Gabriel felt about battle, and after it he no longer had the desire and longing to get into another scrap. He didn't see it as a great and unknown adventure anymore, he'd been there and done it. For him now, going into battle would be a terrible yet necessary task that when called upon he was willing to perform. He hadn't turned coward. On the contrary, his sense of duty was as strong as it had ever been. He was still eager to do his part, and fight alongside his brothers in blue. It's just that rolling the dice of life was no longer a game to him anymore.

CHAPTER SEVENTEEN

For over a week, the 20th Corps simply endured the nightmarish conditions around New Hope Church. Immediately after their fight on the 25th of May, they started digging-in, in case the Rebels decided to make an attack of their own. Bird's pioneers were constantly helping to dig trenches, construct log breastworks, and clear fields of fire so that any enemy who tried advancing on their position could be more easily shot down. They did countless other minor jobs, too. For instance, Gabriel and his friends built pine bough shelters around headquarters and outside the field hospitals, to provide shade and protection from the almost daily rainstorms that rolled through the area.

Rainwater became almost as hated as the Rebs. Like their lice, it was always present, either falling from the sky or in puddles on the oversaturated ground. Gabriel felt as though he'd never be dry again. Rain wasn't the only thing that soaked them, either. They found themselves drenched in sweat, too. It poured from them, drawn out by the oppressive heat and humidity they were forced to toil in. Everyone stank awful, and there was no real way to rid themselves of their filth. The rain was a cleanser, but at the same time it only made the ground and works they inhabited muddy and when they were forced to move about and carry on with their duties, they were soon filthy again.

Not only did the living smell, but the dead as well. Many still lay where they had fallen in the dangerous strip of land between the two sides. Their putrefying corpses were black and bloated, and their stench permeated the air all throughout the works of the 20th Corps. Even the ones that had been buried fouled things. Rain runoff washed the thin layer of cover dirt from many of their graves, exposing them to the air and exacerbating the lingering stench of death. When Gabriel was busy building pine shelters at the hospital, he was also tasked with recovering some of these exhumed corpses that had been buried nearby. It was a horrendous job that he especially despised. To help lessen the intensity of the odor, he spread pine sap on a rag and tied it over his face. It wasn't a cure all, but it helped some.

*　*　*　*　*

Fortunately, the Rebels never made any full-scale assaults on the 20th Corps' position, nor did the 20th Corps attack the Rebels again, but skirmishing was constant between the lines, and Gabriel saw wounded men being stretchered to the rear quite regularly. Scattered rifle shots and the occasional exploding artillery shell became the norm, and he grew to pay them little mind. The sounds were almost as uninteresting to him as the pitter patter of rain.

Skirmishing went on all the way up and down the Union lines, in fact. During and after Hooker's attack on the Confederates at New Hope Church, Sherman was busy bringing the other elements of his army up along either side of the 20th Corps. When they were all in place, the Yankee earthworks stretched for miles, with one end anchored at Dallas and the other near a place called Pickett's Mill. New Hope Church and the 20th Corps were near the center of the Yankee line.

On the 27th, Gabriel and his companions could hear the sounds of a tremendous battle being waged off to their left. It was the Battle of Pickett's Mill, where General Sherman had sent the left wing of his army in another offensive thrust at the Confederate breastworks. It was horrendously executed though, and met the same fate as Hooker's attack, in a lopsided defeat. On the following day, they heard the same sounds, but off to their right this time. This was the Battle of Dallas, where the Confederates made a push of their own on the Yankee right. The assault, like the two the Yankees had attempted, was easily defeated.

The two sides found themselves in a stalemate and the lack of progress greatly annoyed General Sherman, for he wasn't getting any closer to Marietta, or his main objective of Atlanta. His lines there weren't in direct contact with the railroad, either. This further complicated the already difficult task of supplying his army and as a result, his troops and horses were short on rations.

In an attempt to ease their suffering and get the campaign going again, Sherman tried shifting his army toward the railroad and Marietta in the first days of June. He was able to reach the railroad, but Johnston pursued and blocked him from Marietta by digging in on the mountains outside of town. Sherman was forced to dig in across from him, and the miserable stalemate was resumed. Slowly but surely though, with a series of chess-like troop movements that threatened the Rebel lines, he was able to force Johnston backward.

By June 19th, Johnston's army was placed in a wide arc around the western approaches to the city. It was known as the Kennesaw Line, named for the twin peaks, Big and Little Kennesaw Mountain, that the line passed over. Sherman's troops mirrored the arc, and were dug in themselves opposite of it. On the 22nd of June, the Confederates made an attack on the portion of the Yankee line where the 20th Corps was located. It was known as the Battle of Kolb's Farm, and ended in defeat for the Rebels. Hooker's troops held their ground and fought off the attack with ease, inflicting heavy casualties on their enemy and sustaining relatively few of their own. A few days later, on the 27th, Sherman decided to attack part of the Confederate position with a portion of his army, but like almost all the other attacks in the campaign thus far, he was defeated, and suffered horrendously lopsided casualties, losing roughly 3000 men to the Rebels' 1000.

Sherman persisted though, and kept up pressure on Johnston, forcing him out of Marietta on July 2nd, then over the Chattahoochee River on the 10th. The Chattahoochee was the last natural barrier between Sherman and Atlanta. By July 17th, Sherman had crossed most of his army as well, and it seemed it would be only a matter of time before they took the city.

Johnston's superiors in Richmond were furious at this. They were sick of his defensive approach to warfare and feared that he would retreat even further and leave Atlanta to the Yankees without a fight. Trying to prevent this from happening, Confederate President Jefferson Davis sent him a telegram on the night of July 17th, relieving him as commander of the Confederate Army of Tennessee. His replacement, he was informed, was one of his corps' commanders, the offensively-minded yet recklessly aggressive General John Bell Hood.

* * * * *

The weeks following their withdrawal from New Hope Church seemed to Gabriel an endless blur of dizzying fatigue. Through rain, mud and oppressive heat, he dug, chopped, or sawed every day, and his labor was always interspersed with the brief yet agonizing episodes of pushing, pulling and prying the headquarters wagons over the nearly impass-able roads on which they were forced to travel. He'd been relegated to the wagons ever since his horse was killed, and had yet to be reissued another. Just as with the soldiers, horses were having a tough go of it surviving the campaign, and there weren't a whole lot of extras to go around.

Because of this, when all his friends rode off with Lieutenant Bird to help repel the attacking Rebels at Kolb's Farm, he was left in the rear with the wagons. At first, he tried telling himself it was a blessing to be left out, but when the battle got into its full fury, he felt rocked with guilt, and afterward vowed to never be left behind again. He'd grown to appreciate peace after New Hope Church, but not peace for himself while his friends risked their lives.

Before passing over the Chattahoochee River on July 17th, Gabriel had quite the surprise. He was on the driver's seat of the pioneers' supply wagon, reins in hand, when he saw the familiar face of Dave Nash in the crowd of men waiting their turn to cross over on the pontoons.

Through a letter from Rill a few days before, Gabriel knew of the Nash family's recovery, and Dave's eventual return to the Army. He didn't at all expect to see him that quickly though, so when he did, he leapt down off his seat in excitement and tackled his old drunken friend. They rolled around on the ground tussling, Dave a little less playfully than Gabriel, while the other boys from Dryden stood back and had a good laugh.

When he was finally able to break away, Gabriel hopped to his feet and lent his friend a hand. Dave accepted, but as Gabriel heaved him up, he had a few choice words for his young friend. Gabriel worried he'd gone a little too far with Dave, but once on his feet Dave wrapped his arms around him and squeezed until he was unable to draw a breath.

"It's good to see you too, you little shit, but if you ever do that to me again, I'll knock your fuckin' teeth out," Dave had said.

* * * * *

It was just three days after Gabriel and Dave's reunion that the Rebels made a surprise attack on Thomas' Army of the Cumberland just north of Atlanta. It was well into the afternoon, and Bird's pioneers were among Williams' troops picking blackberries when the sounds of the attack were first heard. They had moved across Peach Tree Creek that morning, but afterwards had stacked arms and lounged about, so when the heavy firing erupted off to their left, it took them by surprise. The Rebs were attacking in echelon, so as they advanced, they hit the troops on Williams' left first, and then rolled down the Yankee front like an angled wave hitting the shoreline. The warning sounds of fighting gave General Williams just enough time to form his men from column into line of battle before the wave reached them. He placed his troops on a high piece of ground, with ravines running along both ends of his position.

As Williams' division was deploying, the pioneers stuffed what berries they had gathered down their throats and congregated in the rear, waiting for instructions. They watched for a few minutes, but the chaos was making everyone anxious, even Lieutenant Bird, for the threat of being overrun was very real. The stress made Gabriel's stomach churn, so he stepped away into some bushes to relieve himself, but when he returned, it was to the sound of pounding hooves as Bird and the other mounted men were galloping away. Gabriel was still without a horse, and grew frantic as he saw them ride off. All he could think of was that he was about to sit out on another fight.

"Wait for me, Jim!" he called out, but the thunder of battle overpowered the sound of his voice. He wouldn't be so easily defeated, though. He felt angry for being left behind. Storming over to the back of the wagon, he reached in and pulled out his rifle and cartridge box. His belt with his cap pouch and pistol was already fastened around his waist.

"What are you doing?" one of the other wagon-bound pioneers asked him as he gathered his things. "Jim said to wait. He's going to send word back if he needs us."

"I'm not waiting, I'm going up there with everyone else," he told the man.

"But Jim and the boys are mounted, you'll never catch up."

"Well, I'm going to try," Gabriel said as he took off after them.

Bird was halted with his other horsemen behind the infantry when, out of breath and gasping for air, Gabriel jogged in among them.

"What in the hell are you doing, Gabriel? What if we got to ride away on a job? Then what are you gonna do?" Bird asked him.

Gabriel shrugged, then bent over with his hands on his knees desperately trying to catch his breath. "Run along behind you," he managed to say.

Bird rolled his eyes.

The division was still in the process of moving into line of battle and were taking fire as they did so. General Hooker was on scene now though, riding about and shouting orders to his subordinates to help and place his men. He was full of energy and looked almost possessed. When he caught sight of Bird and his boys quietly watching from behind, he rode over in great haste with a few of his aides in tow.

"Lieutenant Bird!" he shouted, "your pioneering services are no longer needed, not until this contest is decided. Get your men and fall in, before we're overrun!"

"Aye, General!" Bird eagerly answered with a shout. It was just what he had been hoping for.

He hollered like a madman at the top of his lungs in a great outpouring of passion, before hopping down off his horse and unslinging his rifle. He began to load, and his men followed suit. His enthusiasm was infectious among them. Gabriel's heart was thumping, too. The Rebs were coming, and he felt scared and excited all at the same time.

"To the far left boys. Far left is where they'll hit first. Let's go!" Bird called out to them. The group took off at a sprint down the line of Williams' infantry, to where the 143rd New York was anchoring its flank.

When they reached them, Bird had Gabriel take them to his company, which he quickly did. The regiment was tiny now. Only a few hundred men were fit for duty anymore. The rest were dead, sick, or had gone home. Company I was pathetically low on men. Little more than a score of them remained of their original number. They'd just gotten into position when the pioneers fell in. Gabriel was surprised to see Marvin standing behind the company as he ran past. Marvin was surprised to see him too, and tried calling out, but Bird was upon him before he could say so much as a word.

"Lieutenant Bird, of General Hooker's staff," he said as he held out his hand for Marvin to shake.

Marvin turned to face him but didn't take his hand. He knew who he was and wasn't pleased to see him.

"What do you want, Lieutenant?" he asked Bird curtly.

"Only to kill some Rebs, Captain."

"Well, why don't you find another place to do so, Lieutenant? You're crowding my company."

"Like hell I am," Bird shot back at him. "I've been ordered here with my men by General Hooker himself, so if you want to send us away, you'll have to take it up with him."

Marvin was flabbergasted by his quick insolence and didn't know how to respond. If Hooker had ordered it, he had no business sending them away, so he crossed his arms in frustration and kept quiet as Bird moved on.

Gabriel squeezed himself between Dave Nash and Albert Kizer. Baldy was on the other side of Al. They were happy as hell to see him.

"Just like old times," Baldy said.

Gabriel was still breathing heavily. He'd essentially run there all the way from his wagon in the rear. Nash said nothing, though. He just flashed Gabriel a smile and gave him a pat on the back. He was nervous, this being only his second real fight, and his first since Wauhatchie the year before. He'd missed out on a lot since he'd gone home to care for his family, and had gotten awfully lucky when, on his return, he'd been welcomed with little reprimand. The regiment had shrunken so much by that point, and Colonel Boughton didn't want to lose another to a court martial, so it was brushed under the rug. He'd come back on his own accord anyhow.

Gabriel lifted his canteen and took a healthy swallow. His stomach was still growling, even after eating the berries he'd picked, and he thought he'd ask around for another quick bite. Just as he was putting the cork in his canteen though, the regiment was given the order to advance. Their objective was to link up with Geary's troops, who were busy fighting across the ravine to their left. The forest was thick, though, on that end of the line, and they couldn't see very well where they were going.

The Reb fire started to pick up in its intensity as they advanced. A few men went down from stray bullets, but they couldn't see well enough to know where exactly the fire was coming from. Then, Gabriel heard shouting and could see other men in blue sprinting for their position. Looking terrified they scrambled behind the regiment. Some were wounded and others were without weapons, having thrown their rifles away in their mad dash to safety.

"Geary's boys are breaking, we've got to hold!" Bird shouted from behind the men. He ignored the fact that he was a guest among them. Marvin was in a daze anyway it seemed and was stumbling along behind the line silent as a church mouse.

Down the hill in front of them, the sound of marching feet could be heard. It was an eerie sound as there was no talking, shouting, or orders being given, just the echo of a mass of men snapping and crunching their way through the forest. Gabriel guessed it must be Rebs, but no one was positive of that yet. He tried hard to catch a glimpse of them, but the brush was too thick in their front. As they waited, their anxiety mounted, until finally Dave Nash thought he saw a flash of butternut from an opening in the foliage.

"Johnnies!" He shouted at the top of his lungs.

He was right. Moments later the whole Reb line came into view.

They stopped about twenty yards in front of the New Yorkers. There was a moment of silence before Colonel Boughton gave the order to make ready and aim. The Rebel officers mirrored him and when the final command to fire was given both sides opened up on each other, simultaneously spewing smoke, flame and lead into the faces of their foes. Severed sticks, twigs and leaves rained down on them as well, and men fell rapidly on both sides.

Next to Gabriel, Albert Kizer took a bullet to his right thigh and went down hard. The fat hunk of Rebel lead had splintered his femur nearly in two and as he dropped his rifle and hit the ground, Albert cried out and grabbed for his leg in agony. Glancing down to see what had become of his friend, Gabriel saw a small fountain of blood spouting up from the new hole in Albert's trousers. The leaves and pine needles underneath him were already covered in blood, but before Gabriel could reach down to help, Sergeant Hemmingway and Lieutenant Bird grabbed Albert by his arms and pulled him behind the firing line. Producing a long thin rag from his haversack, Hemmingway handed it to Bird, and Bird smartly tied it above Albert's wound to staunch the flow of blood. Albert shrieked as he did so, but Bird paid him no mind.

"There, now you won't bleed out," Bird said to him, before returning his attention to the fight. So far, he had taken a few shots here and there, but mostly he was playing officer by tending to the men and directing their fire.

The sight of Albert's mauling had a maddening effect on Gabriel. He was angry with the Rebs for coming again. Coming to try and kill him and his friends. Trying to deprive his wife and daughter of his love. He was sick of it, sick of the fighting and he felt mad at them for wanting to go another round. Dwelling on their audacity, he felt vengeful. He wanted to punish them for picking another fight. He wanted to shoot them, kill them and maim them, cause their families the grief that they wished on his. As the fight wore on, he kept on loading and firing and with each trigger pull, he felt better and better.

The Yankee fire was rapid and well-placed, and the Rebs were getting the worst of the exchange. Soon it became too much for the them, and they started to pull back down the hill. Gabriel and his friends cheered as they did.

It went unnoticed by most of them, but the 143rd had advanced a bit farther ahead than the rest of their brigade. When the Rebs first hit them, they were left to fight on their own. Realizing they were lucky to have survived the mistake, Colonel Boughton ordered them back up the hill before the Rebs made another charge. They were quick to obey. Grabbing their dead and wounded, they scrambled to the rear. Gabriel helped carry Albert Kizer. He held the wounded leg and Baldy the other, while Corporal Hildebrandt and Sergeant Hemmingway took a hold of his upper extremities. Gabriel tried his best to be gentle so as not to cause Albert any added pain.

Albert was in a daze though, and seemed not to mind at all how he was being carried. His face looked white as snow, and his eyes were glazed. His leg had an old shirt wrapped around the wound below Birds makeshift tourniquet, but blood was still seeping through and dripping onto the ground, leaving a speckled trail up the hill. Despite his best efforts to avoid it, Gabriel hands were covered in Albert's blood. It felt tacky and, as it dried, weakly glued his fingers together. He was horrified by it, but his adrenaline kept him going.

"He'll lose a leg, at least," Dave said as he trotted up beside them. Gabriel gave him a dirty glance, as if to tell Dave to shut up. Dave chuckled.

"Oh don't worry about him, Gabriel. He's in shock. He can't hear a things bein' said."

After reaching their new position and setting Albert down in a leafy spot, they were ordered to throw together a hasty barricade. There was no time to cut down any trees or dig in, so they gathered dead logs, branches and rocks, anything that could stop or deflect a bullet.

"I'm surprised to see Marvin here," Gabriel said to Baldy as they piled debris in front of them.

"We are, too. This is two in a row for him, though. After he disappeared at New Hope Church, Boughton had a talking with him, and he hasn't missed a fight since."

"I thought I caught a glimpse of him hiding back at the Hell Hole," Gabriel said. It was the name they'd adopted for their old lines about New Hope Church.

"That was him," Baldy answered.

"How'd he finally find the courage?" Gabriel asked.

"John Barleycorn," Dave said butting into their conversation. "I had half a canteen full, and he took it from me just before you showed up. Sucked it down like it was water, and now I've got nothin' for myself, damn him," Dave explained in disgust.

"Did the same thing at Kolb's Farm. He was so drunk, Lieutenant Hill had to take command of the company," Baldy added.

"Just look at him now." Dave said pointing behind them.

The whiskey had finally taken hold and Marvin could barely stand. His arms were wrapped around a skinny oak trying to stay on his feet. He looked pathetic, and Gabriel actually felt sorry for him. Some men just weren't cut out for battle he thought.

Lieutenant Bird came up behind them and asked how they were doing. He was sweating and covered in dust and debris but looked happier than Gabriel had seen him in weeks.

"We're fine now, but we may need some cartridges here before long," Gabriel told him.

"We're working on it," Bird said. "Guess Hooker got a little worried. Thought we were lost or worse down there, but your Colonel sent him back a note telling him we were fine. He requested some ammunition too, so it should be coming along shortly."

Gabriel introduced Dave and Baldy to Bird. They shook hands and exchanged pleasantries, then Bird asked them about Captain Marvin.

"What's the matter with your Captain anyway? He's acting drunk."

"He is," Gabriel admitted.

"Looks asleep to me," Dave said, pointing again over to Marvin who was now on the ground next to the tree he'd been propping himself up with. His eyes were closed, and he was snoring obnoxiously loud. Sergeant Hemmingway ran over and crouched down over his body to check on him.

"Everything okay over there, Sergeant?" Bird asked.

"Uh… yes Sir, at least I think it is. Captain Marvin… he uh… I think he's gone down from the heat."

"I see," Bird said.

It was obvious that the sergeant was lying, but he couldn't blame him. To have your very own captain pass out drunk in the midst of a battle was a humiliation. Hemingway was only trying to save face for the regiment. After directing Corporal Hildebrandt to stay with Marvin, he came over to Bird.

"Lieutenant, sorry to bother you, but Captain Marvin is far too sick to remain in command. Lieutenant Hill is with division headquarters today and we have no other officer to command the company. Seeing as your pioneers almost outnumber our own, I think it only proper that you take charge until the fight is over, Sir."

Bird happily agreed to the sergeant's suggestion but thought it strange he'd come to him and not another officer in the regiment. When he was out of earshot, he asked Gabriel why Hemingway had done so, and Gabriel explained.

"Well, Jim, you see we here in Company I, and D also, are from Tompkins County, but the rest of the regiment is from far to the east of us in the Catskills. We all get along just fine, but there's still a slight sense of mistrust between some of us. Hem's just trying to keep this from the Sullivan County boys. That's all."

Bird didn't like taking part in the deception. He knew Marvin's behavior should be reported and dealt with accordingly, but he decided to bite his tongue for Gabriel's sake. He didn't want to cause any trouble between him and his old company.

Men were still adding to the barricade when the Rebs came at them again. They weren't quiet as they had been before. With a fierce Rebel yell, they attacked in a full on charge up the hill, firing indiscriminately as they went.

The Yankees scrambled for cover. The barricade wasn't big enough for them to stand behind, but they could kneel and have enough in their front to provide some protection. When the Rebs got within thirty yards of the line, Colonel Boughton gave the command to fire. Once again, their rifles erupted in flame, smoke and lead, and scores of the enemy fell to the ground writhing in agony. The volley was so effective it stopped the Rebel charge in its tracks, but they stood their ground too and started pouring a deadly fire of their own into the New Yorkers.

Soon almost all the foliage between the two sides was shot away and they could see each other very clearly. Once looking into the Reb lines as he loaded his rifle, Gabriel caught sight of a young color bearer. The boy looked almost identical to his brother Sam, and Gabriel did a double take to make sure he wasn't seeing things. The young man was bravely standing, his Confederate battle flag held high and waving back and forth in defiance of his foe. Even though he was the enemy, Gabriel couldn't help but be inspired and it pained him when he saw the young man go down with a bullet to the face. It was a horrifying sight, but he shrugged it off, lifted his rifle to his shoulder, and fired at the next man to pick up the flag.

After another vicious exchange, the Rebs retired down the hill again, and again the men went to work to improve their hasty barricade. A few even dragged some Reb corpses up to add to the pile in front of them. Gabriel shook his head in disgust, thinking it disrespectful to a gallant foe. He said something to that effect, but Dave Nash disagreed and let him know how he saw it. His nervousness had gone after the first shots were fired, and he was in rare form.

"Fuck them fuckin' Rebs. They'd do the same to you," he growled. "Hell, if I had the time, I'd go down and drag them all up here to hide behind, even the ones ain't dead yet."

After the last Rebel charge, everyone's ammo had about been depleted, so some of the boys started poking around in the dirt with their bayonets in search of good throwing stones to pelt the Rebs with if worse came to worse.

"Look at this one!" Gabriel called out, excitedly displaying his find for Dave and Baldy to see. The stone was about the size of a baseball, but with sharp points on its exterior, almost resembling the head of a mace an ancient knight might have wielded.

"I bet that'd send a Reb scurrying for the rear if you landed it on his forehead," Baldy said genuinely impressed.

"Sure would," Dave added.

The three of them collected a good sized pile, but luckily the rocks weren't needed because fresh cartridges soon arrived, and Lieutenant Bird went about passing them around. There was enough to give each man twenty more shots, which pleased them greatly.

The final Reb charge came with much less enthusiasm than the first two had, and they were beaten back in no time at all. Dave had a close call when they first came, though. He dropped a cartridge to the ground and bent over to pick it up as two bullets passed overhead and slapped into a tree directly behind him. The sound scared the hell out of him, but he made light of it when he looked at Gabriel and said, "gonna need a change of trousers after that one."

Gabriel got off twelve shots before the Rebs retired down the hill for the final time. Dave and Baldy only had a few left, too. When it was clear that the Rebels wouldn't be returning, some of the men ventured forward to search for wounded and to take prisoners. Lieutenant Bird said that it was time for the pioneers to go though, so Gabriel shook hands with all his old friends before taking off. Marvin had since regained consciousness, but was still in no condition to walk, and Gabriel wondered if Hemingway would be able to keep his secret much longer.

* * * * *

The Rebel attack at Peach Tree Creek had come close to breaking the Yankee line, but in the end, it was a failure. The following day was much quieter. The Yankees sent men forward of their lines to see if the Confederates had pulled away. They hadn't, but both sides were content to lick their wounds. Other than digging a few graves and a pit for all the severed arms and legs the surgeons were busy sawing off, the pioneers relaxed some too.

Dave Nash had been right about Albert Kizer. Gabriel payed him a visit at the field hospital and saw that his wounded leg had been amputated high up on the thigh. He was no longer in shock and was able to talk some, but not much, as he was still in great pain and was extremely exhausted.

"They took my leg Gabriel." Albert said pointing to his bandaged stump when he saw that his old friend had arrived and looked troubled at the sight of him. "I've resigned myself to it though, it's no bother. Other than my prick, an arm's the appendage I'd have the most trouble parting with. Unlike some of the other boys around here, I can at least still pick my nose and wipe my own ass."

That afternoon, Gabriel and Bird were lounging about, conversing under a tree, when they heard cheering erupt from a crowd of troops in front of them. Curious as to what all the racket was over, they got up and approached the mob to see General Hooker mounted up on his horse, with officers and enlisted men alike surrounding him. It was him they were cheering, and he was slowly moving his way among them, laughing and reaching down to shake their hands, talking to the boys and telling them all how proud he was of them. They cheered and cheered him until they went hoarse. It was their collective way of letting him know how much they loved him too.

"Just look at that," Bird said. "What a sight."

"He is awfully inspiring isn't he," Gabriel agreed.

"He's magnificent. You know, I've got to admit, after Chancellorsville I didn't exactly have a flattering opinion of old Joe, but now I think I love the man."

"I'd say we all do," Gabriel said.

"He's done so well by us. He's always up amongst us in a fight. He makes sure we're well taken care of and he's personable with everyone, even the lowest of ranks like yourself, no offense," Bird said.

"None taken," Gabriel assured him.

"He's a true soldier, you know? Likes to fight and fuck and have a drink, but never gets out of hand, like that captain of yours."

"That he does," Gabriel admitted. "He's awfully fond of you too, Jim. Whenever he's taken the time to speak to me, he always makes a point of it to say how great of a fighter you are, and that I'm lucky to be under your charge."

Bird smiled.

"Well I don't know about how great I am, but I'll admit I do like to get into a scrap."

"How come?" Gabriel asked him curious to know. It had been something he'd been pondering on of late.

Bird thought about it for a moment before answering.

"I'm not too sure, Gabriel. Guess I just like the excitement of it, the uncertainty. There's nothing like being in battle. For me, it's almost as good as sex, but in a different way. Don't you like to fight? You do just fine at it, from what I've seen."

"Well I did, or I thought I did at first. Not now, though. I know what you mean by the excitement, I feel that, and I'm happy when we win, but it's just… I don't know. It's just so damn awful seeing men get shot down and torn apart, especially when it seems like half of these Rebs we fight have been robbed from the cradle or the grave."

Bird nodded his head in understanding. He knew combat affected people differently and was happy to talk about it with his men. He thought it did them good to speak their mind and be listened to.

"Just yesterday, Jim, I saw a Reb looked the spitting image of my little brother. Couldn't have been more than fourteen, but he was standing across from us waving his flag as proud as could be, and then next thing I know his face is caved in like a rotten pumpkin. It was just a moment, a flash of an image in front of me, but it felt like I watched him standing there dead for a minute or more before he finally crumpled over. He was so young, and I thought what if it was Sam, or what if Sam was with us and got killed and how horrible that would be. I know if we're gonna win this war it needs to be done, so I trudge on, but it scares me to think about dying, too. I don't know what Rill and my baby daughter would do."

"I know what you mean, Gabriel. I agree it is terrible, but I guess it doesn't bother me as much. I don't have no wife and kids to worry about like you do, either, so you've got a little more on your plate than me."

"Oh, that's not true. You've got loads more to worry about. Think about all us boys you've got to care for and lead."

"That's different, though," Bird disagreed. "Wife and kids are a different kind a worry."

"They'll come. You're older than me. There's got to be some homely looking girl from wherever it is that you're from that you can trick into marrying," Gabriel joked.

Bird took a playful jab at his arm.

"It's Ellicottville, you idiot, and are you kidding me? There's more than one. Lot more than have your fancy over in Dryden, ha, and not a one of them is bad looking. Girls from my part of the state are prettier anyway."

"I respectfully disagree, SIR!" Gabriel said with a smile.

"Oh, shut up with your Sirs, you fool," Bird told him. "I don't know. I'll probably marry someday. I've no plans for it yet, though. After this war's over, I think I might go west to the territories. I want to see the great plains and the buffalo. Maybe try and find a little gold or silver in the mountains, too. We'll see. Could even marry a squaw and live with the Indians for a while. I've heard say there's some real pretty ones."

"You won't go back to New York?"

"Sure, I will at first maybe, to see my folks, but I won't stick around. I've got things I want to see and do before I settle down and start a family."

Gabriel nodded. "Well I do, I want to go back and settle down and have a big family with Rill. Live on a nice little farm, somewhere near my parents. I think about it all the time."

As Gabriel and Bird stood contemplating over their futures, General Hooker continued to mingle with his men. He felt on top of the world, and when he saw their familiar faces watching from the distance he waved and lifted his hat to them before carrying on. Little did he know that this would be his last hurrah, for his time in their charge was quickly dwindling away.

CHAPTER EIGHTEEN

General Hood's attack on the Yankees at Peach Tree Creek was his first in a series of attempts to drive the Union army away from Atlanta. General Sherman had his troops positioned to the north and east of the city with General Thomas' men on the right, General Schofield's in the middle and General McPherson's on the left of the Yankee line. After failing to dislodge Thomas at Peach Tree Creek, Hood made another attack on McPherson and Schofield's men two days later in the Battle of Atlanta. This contest was fought to the east of the city and ended up being the costliest battle of the campaign, with over 9,000 casualties. As at Peach Tree Creek, the Confederates were defeated though, and afterward retreated into their ring of fortifications surrounding the city. The one bright note for Hood was that during the attack General McPherson was killed, depriving the Yankees of one of their most well-liked and ablest commanders.

* * * * *

On July 22nd, the same day as the Battle of Atlanta, 20th Corps pickets discovered the Rebel works in their immediate front abandoned. Venturing south, beyond the empty fortifications, the Yankees discovered their foe in a new, yet equally-defended position, closer to Atlanta. Taking advantage of the ceded ground, they too moved in closer to the city as the sounds of battle could be heard raging to the east.

For the next few days after, Gabriel and his friends were put to work again, helping to fortify their new line with breastworks and trenches. After one of those days, much like he had on his first night with the pioneers, Gabriel was tasked by Bird with keeping an all-night fire going outside General Hooker's tent. Things were slightly different now, of course, than that cold January night months before. Gabriel was now a seasoned veteran and no longer felt the stranger. Headquarters was his home. He knew the whole cast of characters about it and was on speaking terms with all of the officers. It seemed to him as if he belonged there, perhaps even more so now than with the 143rd.

As he sat around the fire, Gabriel's thoughts drifted to home as they did almost every night, or during any spare moments of leisure he was afforded. It was nearing midnight when General Hooker emerged from his tent. His hat and coat were off, but due to the heat this time, instead of a playful prostitute. He approached the fire and Gabriel stood and saluted him as was customary, but the General wasn't in the mood for playing soldier.

"Relax, young man. There is no need for that right now but thank you all the same. Sit. Please, sit," he requested.

Gabriel obeyed and took a seat. He sensed an air of melancholy from the General though, that put him on his toes. It was odd for General Hooker to appear so sullen and devoid of his usual vigor. His face looked sad, and his arms were drawn behind him, his hands clasped together at his back.

After several minutes of awkward silence, General Hooker spoke up.

"How have you been, Private Ballard? Have you heard much from your family in uh … Dryden, is it?" he asked.

"Yes, Sir, that's right. Dryden. I've been well, Sir. Still living, at least. I've heard from my family too, yes, Sir, I got a letter from my wife a few days ago. She's doing fine, and my little girl is, too. My wife's been boiling and mashing vegetables from the garden and mixing them with butter for her to eat. She spits most of them out though, Rill tells me."

Hooker chuckled at the thought.

"Still wants mother's milk, does she? Ha, ha," he chuckled again. "Can't blame her for that, can you?"

Gabriel blushed at the General's insinuation. He had to agree with him, though.

"Good to hear though, young man. I didn't realize you were married, or a father for that matter. You look too young for that. How long have you been together?"

Gabriel had to think about it for a moment.

"We've been married almost a year and a half, Sir. Had the ceremony in Washington, last February. It was a hasty ordeal. We wanted to be married before the baby was born."

General Hooker chuckled again. Gabriel was happy to see him livening up.

"Oh, I see. Ha, ha, ha. A little roll in the hay before you left got you into some trouble, did it?" Hooker asked him with smile.

"Something like that, Sir," Gabriel answered.

"No shame in it, Son. Lord knows, I've probably got some young'uns out there under my belt. I'd venture to say there's a few in Mexico, not much younger than yourself. Maybe even some in California, too."

Perhaps it was a moment of misjudgment, but seeing how General Hooker's mood had improved, Gabriel tried to politely inquire of him, too.

"How about you, Sir? How have you been?"

At hearing the question, though, Hooker's face instantly reverted to its solemn look from before, and Gabriel knew he'd made a mistake by asking.

"I've been better, young man," Hooker told him in a deep and worried voice. He seemed to wait for Gabriel to question him further, but Gabriel didn't dare push the subject. He was already regretting speaking out of turn. He should have known better, he thought, than to question a general. The usual rule in regard to higher-ups of that caliber, was to speak only when spoken to.

"Just should have kept your mouth shut, you dumb bastard," he thought to himself.

"You've heard of General McPherson's death, I'm sure?" Hooker finally spoke up.

Gabriel said he had.

"Well, General Sherman has to fill his position now. Logically, I should be his choice. I commanded the Army of the Potomac once, mind you, but I have heard rumor that he is going to choose General

Howard to take McPherson's place, and if that happens, my boy, I will be forced by honor to resign as commander of the 20th Corps."

Gabriel was astounded by what Hooker had said, and he had a hard time hiding the look of shock on his face. General Hooker resigning his command, after all they had been through together, and his great victory less than a week before at Peach Tree Creek. It defied logic.

As Gabriel was processing what he'd been told, Hooker turned away and went into his tent for a moment, before emerging once again with a pencil and paper. He had a camp chair in his other hand and he placed it next to Gabriel and sat down.

"If I go, Private Ballard, I should still like to purchase a new pair of drawers from your friend there that sent me the ones I am wearing now. You know I have worn them almost every day since you left them for me, except the day we made our assault at New Hope Church. I took them off to have them laundered and they were still drying in my wagon when the battle began. I was never able to retrieve them. It was a fateful mistake, but I vowed to never repeat it, and would you believe we have won two more fights since then, and during both occasions I had my lucky drawers on. I told you they were good luck, didn't I?"

"You did, Sir. I remember you making mention of it," Gabriel agreed.

"Well, would you be so kind then to write down your friend's information so that I can write her to place another order?" Hooker asked, holding out the pencil and paper he had brought from his tent.

Gabriel took them from him and wrote Julia's name, *Mrs. Enos Cook* and *Dryden, New York* on the paper, and handed it back to Hooker. He glanced it over before stuffing it into his vest pocket.

"Thank you. I will be in touch with Mrs. Cook shortly, I'm sure."

Hooker then picked up a stick that was lying nearby and started to poke at the fire like a child. As he played, he carried on with their conversation from before.

"I know what you're thinking young man. I must be mad to consider a resignation, especially after the success we've had of late, but let me tell you, it is a matter of principle and honor, and it would be a disgrace for me not to resign. You enlisted men, you volunteers may not see the logic in it, but I would lose much of my credibility among the officer corps if I did not. It is something I will have to do if the situation is thrust upon me, but believe me, it will be with a heavy heart. It won't be a happy occasion, that's for sure."

Hooker tossed his stick aside and lit up a cigar. He offered one to Gabriel, but Gabriel declined so he tucked it away for later.

"What do you think the men will say, Private Ballard?"

"They'll be devastated, Sir," Gabriel answered him honestly, and without hesitation. He felt his emotions getting the better of him.

"Why General Howard though, Sir? Didn't we have to rescue him at Resaca? And then he got whipped at Picket's Mill too."

"Don't forget he fucked me over at Chancellorsville, the bastard, and then almost lost it all at Gettysburg on top of that," Hooker added. "Yes, Sherman is aware of all that. How could he not? He just hates me, young man, and that's all there is to it. Howard, though… Howard! How the hell he could choose Howard over anyone else just boggles my mind. If not me, you think he'd promote one of his western friends. A man that has served with this army since the beginning, but Howard? I don't know, I almost want to think he's just doing it to get rid of me. He knows I'll be forced to resign then. You know what, young man? I think I know why he's chosen Howard. He's jealous of my success thus far and he doesn't want me stealing the limelight. If I had to bet on it, I'd say that's it in a nutshell."

Hooker's jealously theory seemed rather far-fetched to Gabriel, but he had to admit some of his reasoning did make sense. Sherman clearly wasn't a fan of the man.

On the following day, when word began to spread that General Hooker had resigned, the men of the 20th Corps were devastated as Gabriel had predicted. To a Christian, Hooker was not the best of men. He was a notorious womanizer, a drinker, a schemer, and a self-promoting braggart at times. To the common soldier though, men like Gabriel, Dave Nash, Lieutenant Bird and his fellow pioneers, Hooker was a God. They loved him. He was fair, cared for them as well as he was able, and when they were in a fight, he was always right there beside them, leading from the front. He was inspiring and entertaining. His boasts and aggressive nature stimulated confidence and a fighting spirit in his men, and his faults made him seem all the more human. He also spoke and joked openly with his boys, even the lowest of ranks. He wasn't like many of the other officers in the Army who were reserved in their emotions and carried themselves as if they were an aristocratic elite. He was one of them. He was one of the men.

* * * * *

To replace Hooker as commander of the 20th Corps, Sherman chose General Henry Slocum. Slocum was stationed in Mississippi at the time of his appointment, so until his arrival General Williams was made interim commander. In the weeks to follow Hooker's departure, there were a few more battles fought around Atlanta, but the 20th Corps did not participate. They remained in their lines on the northern outskirts of the city, dodging the occasional artillery round and trying their best to keep out of view of lurking Rebel marksmen. Gabriel and the pioneers worked steadily during that time alongside the infantry to improve the earthworks the corps inhabited, and they ran errands around camp for the headquarters staff.

On August 25th things changed though, for the 20th Corps pulled out of its lines and retreated to a new position just south of the Chattahoochee River. Sherman placed them there to guard his railroad and its bridges over the river, while he traveled off to the south with the rest of his army to destroy the Macon & Western Railroad. That railroad was still under Rebel control and their last remaining supply line into Atlanta. If Sherman could cut it, which he did after defeating Hood at the Battle of Jonesborough on September 1st, the Confederate chances of holding Atlanta would be naught.

Huge explosions could be heard coming from the city on the night after Jonesborough, that shook the ground and filled the sky red with flame. Gabriel watched in awe from afar, with Lieutenant Bird and the other pioneers, as the glow above the city grew and grew. It was unlike anything they had ever seen. Afterward, word passed rapidly throughout the ranks that the Confederates were destroying everything of military value in the city before retreating.

As expected, the next day it was discovered that the Rebels had evacuated Atlanta, and the 20th Corps were the first troops sent in to secure the prize. Bands played, and the soldiers sang and cheered as they marched in. Those of the civilians who chose to stick around watched quietly from their windows and doorways, praying that they would be left unharmed. Headquarters was at first set up at the Trout House, a large four-story brick hotel on Decatur Street in the middle of town. Gabriel helped to move field desks, supplies and General Slocum's personal baggage inside when they first arrived. Slocum had taken command of the corps just a few days before, on the 27th of August.

After everything was in its place and the pioneers were no longer needed, Lieutenant Bird and his men ventured out to explore the city. Bird warned them to leave everything as it lay, and to take nothing, even if it was abandoned or left unguarded. Despite that, they saw many other less-controlled or discipled Yankees stealing anything that wasn't nailed down. Scores of hungry civilians, white and black alike, were also out and about scavenging for whatever they could find. Gabriel found it very satisfying to witness folks, recently unshackled from the chains of bondage, move about on their own free will.

The destruction of the city was great, and on a scale unwitnessed by many of the soldiers thus far in their short military careers. Every house and building Gabriel saw seemed to have some sort of damage from the Yankee bombardments unleashed on the city over the past month. Some were worse than others, but one house Gabriel saw left a most memorable impression on him. The second story wall along the street side of the home had been completely shot away, exposing the interior to anyone who walked by. Inside though, the room it exposed was surprisingly still set as it had been when the house was whole. The bed was neatly made, the nightstand still in its place with a full wash basin on top. Still on guard of its masters' home, an abandoned lap dog even sat on the bed and barked incessantly at the soldiers as they passed. Some of the men shot in its direction for a little fun and when it scurried under the bed they cheered and cheered. "You'd make a fine Reb soldier," one of them called out in jest.

In the yards of many of the homes were dugouts or makeshift bomb shelters that the citizens scratched out of the ground to survive the bombardments. Gabriel crawled into several of the holes and thought them worse than some of the trenches he had dug outside of the city. He cringed at the thought of Rill and the baby being subjected to such hardships and prayed the day would never come that the war reached upstate New York.

Another place they visited was the sight of the explosions the night before. It was just to the east of the city where General Hood had ordered his 81-car ammunition train, with five engines, destroyed. It was an amazing sight to behold. Gabriel thought it looked like Hell had existed there for a time. All the buildings surrounding the site were damaged with shrapnel, not a window was left in any structure, and some were on fire or in smoking piles on the ground. Nothing was left of the cars but their steel wheels, most of which were still on the rails, bent and twisted as they were. Around where the former train had been, the ground was still smoking and hot, and the stone fill the tracks sat on was inundated with hardening pools of melted lead, bits of exploded ordinance, and ash. The smell was nauseating, and Gabriel was obliged to escape the area when Bird suggested they move on.

There were other places they sought out, too, spots that hadn't been destroyed yet. Most impressive to many of them was the Car Shed, a train depot located across the State Square in front of the Trout House. It was a massive building, 300-foot-long and made of brick. The inside was cavernous, and Gabriel imagined he could fit forty or more of his parents' barns on the inside. They also visited the concert hall across the street, the locomotive house down the tracks, and city hall.

When they went back to the Trout House toward dusk, they climbed to the roof and discovered that it had a spectacular view of the city. From it, they could see for miles around in all directions. They were only at the top of a hotel, but for Gabriel and his friends they felt on top of the world. As they looked out over the shattered Rebel city with thousands of scurrying blue-clad soldiers moving about, it finally sunk in on them that they had made it. They had fought long and hard since the first days in May, but they had finally reached their objective. They had finally taken Atlanta, and they were victorious.

* * * * *

During the first nights of the occupation, the pioneers managed to commandeer a couple unclaimed rooms in the Trout House for themselves. They were happy to sleep indoors for the first time in as long as any of them could remember. Their luxury didn't last long though. They soon overstayed their welcome and Lieutenant Bird was ordered to have them set up camp in the square across the street.

After months spent living out in the open, they were determined to live in relative comfort though, so they constructed themselves huts, very similar to the ones they made the winter prior in Tennessee. There weren't many trees to be had in the city, so they gathered their building materials from the leftover debris and scavenged abandoned and destroyed houses for boards, and brick to build themselves proper chimneys. They made themselves bunks, and some of the men even stole mattresses to furnish them with. Gabriel wasn't so lucky in that regard, but he was able to find himself some clean straw and made one of his own out of a pair of fancy curtains he found in the rubble of some skedaddled Reb's former home. As he had during the winter, he bunked with his two friends, Spencer and Robertson, and they had a good time together.

As many other soldiers were doing, the pioneers hired a couple newly-freed slaves to do their laundry and cooking for them. They were a father and son duo that had been sent to the city from a plantation down the Chattahoochee to help build the ring of defensive fortifications prior to the Yankees' arrival. When the Rebs evacuated, they hid in an empty carriage house and came out free men when the Yankees marched in. They all chipped in and payed them each ten cents a day, which wasn't much, but they figured it was more money than they'd ever had.

With no more wagon trains to help along, ditches to dig, or breast-works to build anymore, the pioneers found themselves with little to do as far as hard labor went. Mostly they kept busy performing menial little chores for the officers around headquarters. The ones with horses still had the chores associated with the care of their animals, too. They had to be fed and watered and brushed down. Bird had the men ride them to the outskirts of the city every day in search of fresh grass and to keep their riding skills sharp. At first, Gabriel didn't participate, but halfway through September he was finally issued a new horse and found himself going off on the daily jaunts. She was black in color, and good-sized like Hannah had been, but very mild mannered and easy-going. She could get up and go if she needed to, though. He named her Eva after his old schoolteacher from Dryden, Evaline Sweetland.

On his downtime, Gabriel continued to explore the city with his friends. They played baseball some, too, and he would go over to his old regiment every few days to visit with Dave, Baldy, and the rest of the boys. He liked catching up on the latest gossip from Dryden. He posted several letters home and a couple to Mr. Marsh, who was very much caught up in the upcoming election. Rill's father was a strong supporter of General McClellan and wrote exceptionally long letters to Gabriel listing the man's, *"many good qualities."*

> *"Surely my boy you see why you must vote McClellan. The sooner he takes office the sooner the war will be over, and you can be home to care for my dear Martha and adorable little granddaughter."*

Gabriel, however, wasn't so easily persuaded. He planned on voting for Lincoln. Sure, the Democrats may end the war if elected, but what then of all those who'd been lost or mangled over the past few years? Their sacrifices would have been in vain, and Gabriel would never support such a thing. It would be like spitting on Enos' grave, as far as he was concerned. He didn't admit as much to his father-in-law, though. He just thanked him for his advice and said he would think on it.

After abandoning Atlanta, General Hood regrouped his army to the south of the city at Lovejoy's Station to rest. He had certainly put up a fight, but his losses were lopsided when compared to that of the Yankees, something the dwindling Confederates could ill afford. At the end of September though, after meeting with Jefferson Davis, Hood decided to get back to work and struck out on a new campaign, with roughly 40,000 men. His objective was to travel over the ground they had fought and retreated over that spring and summer, to destroy the Western and Atlantic Railroad, General Sherman's main route of supply and communication. By doing so, he hoped to draw Sherman out of Atlanta and into the open where he could be attacked and destroyed.

Sherman was no idiot. He knew what Hood was up to, but since his supply line was essential for the survival of his men, he was forced to go after Hood. He didn't fully evacuate Atlanta, though. He left the 20th Corps behind, and General Slocum was put in charge of the city. Naturally, being left alone in the middle of enemy territory worried Slocum, so during the first couple weeks of October he put his men to work strengthening the city's fortifications. No longer were there over 100,000 men to man the walls, and he needed to make them defendable with the few he had been left with.

* * * * *

As with the other men of the 20th Corps, Bird's pioneers were tasked in early October with helping to strengthen Atlanta's network of fortifications. With their supply line under constant attack by General Hood's army, they were forced to do so though on half rations, which made the backbreaking work all the more exhausting.

To help alleviate the grumbling bellies of his troops, General Slocum decided to send some of his boys out on a massive foraging expedition into the countryside. Colonel Robinson, Gabriel's old brigade commander, was put in charge, and gathered 700 wagons to haul their spoils. A brigade of infantry from each of the three 20th Corps divisions was also sent along to help protect and fill the wagons.

Gabriel was excited when Lieutenant Bird informed them that they'd be going, as well. He was sick of wielding the pick and shovel and was looking forward to exploring and finding some good things to eat. His horse had been living on half rations too, and he wanted to treat her to some fresh fodder.

Gabriel was no stranger to foraging. He had done some in Virginia the year before, and regularly entered homes along the path to Atlanta in search of food. He was excited, as was everyone else. There was also a mood of competition among the men. Whatever the pioneers brought back would end up on General Slocum's plate, so Bird brought along their own wagons from the headquarters train and intended to fill them with the best of supplies. To do so, he told his men to keep their eyes peeled for undisturbed homes along the way, for if they were the first in the door, they could have the choicest pick of the spoils.

Unfortunately, Bird's instructions were easier said than done. There were just too many other soldiers about, and it seemed they were always left to sift through the scraps. On the third day of the expedition, at a place the locals called Flat Rock, Gabriel was working in a cornfield with over 100 other men, chopping down the crop and loading it into the wagons when they heard shouting beyond the still standing stuff. At first, Gabriel thought a group of Reb cavalry was sweeping in for a quick strike, but then after some rustling in the corn, a frantic herd of bleating sheep charged out, with a collection of laughing soldiers behind them. Seeing the fun they were having, the corn gatherers joined in the chase too, and it soon became a free-for-all. Soldiers were running and pouncing here, there and everywhere, trying to tackle the frightened sheep, and the sheep were doing their best to get away. Gabriel and a couple of other men followed several into a stand of trees. They dispersed in different directions and the men split up themselves to capture them. Gabriel tracked down two relatively quickly. They were laying quietly together in a dip in the ground, so he snuck up behind them with his revolver and shot them dead before they could take off again.

As he was preparing to drag their bodies back to the cornfield, he caught sight of a house through the trees. It was down a slight hill and in a little meadow surrounded by the forest. Thinking it looked pristine and untouched, Gabriel decided to go have a look for himself before anyone else noticed its existence. If he ever had a chance at being the first into a place, he thought, this was it. Making his way to the edge of the woods, he came to the little clearing the house sat in and walked up to the front door. The house was small and modest, but it was well kept, and Gabriel was impressed to see that it had a fresh coat of white paint on the siding. He could hear the other men talking from up on the hillside behind him and knew it wouldn't be long before he had company.

As he approached the front door, he saw an old negro woman sitting on the steps. She had on a wide brimmed straw hat, and wore a weathered-looking gray dress, with a white apron over her lap. A basket of potatoes sat beside her, and she was busy peeling them. When she saw Gabriel approach she stood up and called into the house.

When Gabriel reached her, the front door swung open and two more women stepped out from inside. These two were white though, both thinly built, well dressed and pretty, with blond hair and greenish-looking eyes. One looked to be in her fifties, and the other around Gabriel's age. Gabriel surmised they were a mother and daughter pair. The negro woman was obviously their slave he thought, but it confused him that she was still hanging around with all the Yankees in the area. In fact, she seemed to scowl at Gabriel with more indignation than the older white woman behind her. The young girl seemed to be friendliest of the trio. She was chewing on one of her fingernails, with a half-smile on her face.

"What do you want, Yank? Your horsemen already cleaned us out yesterday," the older woman said to him from the top step. She wasn't very inviting, but then again, he couldn't blame her for that. He didn't believe her, though. The Sesech always cried poverty, but most of the time the soldiers could still find something hidden or tucked away in an unsuspecting place.

"We just showed up here today, Ma'am. I know I'm the first to come here. Now, why don't you just let me in to have a look-see?" he said to her.

"The hell you are, Yank. Can't you see they've already robbed us?" she said pointing at an open-doored smokehouse in the side yard. "All we've got left to eat is these here spuds my woman's preparing for supper."

Gabriel could see that the smokehouse was empty and noticed an array of hoofprints in the yard.

"Dammit all," he said in frustration. "Damn cavalry always spoils it for us."

"Easy for you to say, Mister," the younger girl said with some sass, trying to egg her mother on. At the same time though, she kept smiling at him and gave him a teasing little wave without her mother noticing. Gabriel pretended not to have seen.

"You stay out of this," the older woman scolded her.

Gabriel was annoyed with the old woman's obstinacy but didn't want to leave without a more thorough inspection of the place.

"How about cornmeal? Do you have any meal to be had? I know you grow it hereabouts. I just helped chop about ten acres of it up the hill there."

"Oh Lord," the woman shrieked. "Our corn, no doubt. I was counting on selling that to General Hood's men to help get us through the winter. Now we're doomed!" she cried.

Gabriel laughed at her.

"General Hood? I guess you haven't heard, Ma'am, but Hood and his army are well away from here. They went north of the Chattahoochee almost three weeks ago."

"You're a liar!" the woman shouted at him.

Gabriel was surprised some by her outburst. She had tears of frustration in her eyes, and her slave seemed to be getting upset, too. The young girl kept watching from the top step, though, and hadn't taken her eyes off of Gabriel. He realized he hadn't seen any men about and questioned her on it.

"How about your husband, Ma'am? Do you have a man about the place?" he asked.

The woman was wiping tears from her eyes and her slave was now at the top of the steps with her arms around her master, trying to comfort her. Gabriel was confused by the whole situation.

"My husband, my husband is around here somewhere, Yank. Pray he doesn't show up when you're still here," she told him in a foreboding tone. Her daughter gave her lie away though and shook her head in the negative, again without her mother seeing.

"How about sons, Ma'am? Do you have any sons about?"

The young girl shook her head again, but this time her mother didn't lie.

"My sons, no they're not about, they're up north in Virginia with General Lee. All five of them are and they've killed more of your wretched kind these past three years than they can even count. Soon I hope they too can travel into your land and rob your family blind, maybe even kill them if they so please, dirty mongrels that I'm sure they are."

The woman's comments had finally crossed the line for Gabriel. He was fed up going back and forth with her anyway.

"Well, Ma'am, if you've got five sons in the Virginia Army and they've killed as many of my friends as you claim, then I'm afraid I'm going to have to search your house whether you like it or not."

He started up the steps and was going to push her out of the way when he noticed that the old woman had something concealed up her sleeve. It was a hatchet, and before she could deploy it, he grabbed her by the wrist and pulled it out of its hiding place. The woman fell back into the doorway on top of her slave, then reaching into the shadows she grabbed something. It looked like a stick at first to Gabriel, but when she stood up in the sunlight, he saw that it was an axe, with a newly sharpened edge that shown bright in the light. Acting quickly, Gabriel jumped down off the steps, tossed the hatchet off into the yard and drew his revolver on her.

"Drop it!" he ordered.

Even the young girl was scared now. "Put it down, Mother, and let him search the house," she pleaded. The negro woman had been frightened inside, and Gabriel could hear her crying. The old woman stood for a moment, thinking over her options before she dropped the axe. Gabriel ordered the daughter to grab it and toss it on the ground beside the stairs. She obeyed, and once she had done so, he finally made his way up the steps and into the house.

After making sure they were unarmed and there was nobody inside waiting to ambush him, he put his revolver away. It was modestly furnished on the inside, an oak table with four chairs, a woodstove and cupboard in the main room. There was an old portrait of George Washington on the wall and another of a man Gabriel didn't recognize.

"Who's this?" he asked them, trying to defuse the situation some.

"General Francis Marion," the older woman grumbled.

"He's a hero around these parts," the young girl added, inviting his attention. "Haven't you ever heard of him?" she asked.

Gabriel shook his head and said he hadn't. There was something strange about the young girl, but he couldn't exactly put his finger on it.

It was an odd feeling for Gabriel standing there in the presence of the three women. He hadn't been in an occupied house since he left his own in New York a full year ago. He knew he was the enemy, and they wanted him gone. He was robbing them, for crying out loud, and the old woman had just tried to hack him down a few moments before, but for some reason it still felt comforting for him to be there.

"You have a beautiful little place," he told them. "It's very clean and tidy."

"What did you take us for, swine?" The old women was quick to question. "We southern folk may be poor, but we're not lazy like I've heard your girls are up north."

"Easy for her to say, she's got a slave to help her with everything", Gabriel thought to himself. He saw an open barrel in the corner and walked over to see what was inside. To his astonishment it contained at least a half a bushel of cornmeal. He reached and sifted through it with his fingers to make sure they weren't hiding anything else in it.

"I thought you said you had no meal?" he asked.

"That's all we've got, but take it if you must. We'll just sit here and starve, no bother," the older woman answered him sarcastically.

Gabriel laughed. "Well, I won't take it then, but if I find anymore it's coming with me."

"Oh dear me, Yank, you're so generous. Will you permit us to keep any more of our property?" she answered him back with some more sarcasm.

Seeing that there was nothing he wanted in there, Gabriel went into the next room. He saw that it was one of family's bedrooms. The door opened to the right, and behind it was a bed in the corner covered with a number of neatly folded quilts. Off to the other side of the room was another doorway leading outside, and on either side of the door sat a pair of trunks on the floor. They had no locks, so he walked over to see what they contained. There was nothing good, no food or gold at least, just old men's clothing, mostly hats, homespun chore pants, and shirts that Gabriel guessed must have belonged to the woman's Confederate sons.

He stood up and turned around to leave but saw the three women had returned and were blocking him in at the door. The young girl still had the queer smile on her face and longing in her eyes, but the older women, the slave and her master, were showing their teeth like growling dogs and all three of them now had an axe in hand.

"Come any further and I'll split your brains out, Yank!" the older woman shouted at him.

Gabriel was shocked that they had come back to try at him again. He wondered if the old woman's husband had been about after all and had finally come to their rescue. He pulled out his revolver and drew back the hammer. At this, the older women got frightened, so they tossed down their axes and ran out of the house shouting and carrying on as best they could. The younger girl still stood in the doorway, though.

Gabriel walked up and easily jerked the axe from her hands and tossed it to the floor behind him. Then, before he could react, the girl leapt onto him and wrapped her arms around him like a baby monkey does its mother. "Oh take me, Yank. Just take me!" she cried. He almost fell backwards. He didn't want to accidently shoot her, so he pointed his revolver in the air and tried prying her free with his other arm. She wouldn't budge though. Gabriel's hat fell to the floor and he told her to let go but she latched on even tighter and started sucking on his neck with sloppy wet lips.

"Ugh", he cried. It was all the girl's doing, but it still made Gabriel feel as though he was being unfaithful to Rill. He got mad at her, and since his prying had no effect on her tight grasp, he dug his thumb into her side as hard as he could. Finally, she let go to grab at her ribs, and when she did Gabriel tossed her onto the bed beside them.

"I said get off me!" he shouted at her, but she seemed unfazed and sat up to plead with him.

"Oh, take me, Yank. Take me right here, right now. I ain't been with a man in two years Yank. Just take me. I'll tell them I let you."

Gabriel couldn't believe the woman. She was out of her mind.

"What is the matter with you lady? Are you crazy or something? I'm not screwing no one. I got a wife and a baby girl at home," he told her.

The woman didn't take his rejection very well, though. She tossed herself back on the bed and cried out to the heavens. Gabriel was about to make his escape, but he heard footsteps quickly approaching the room, and braced himself for his enemy's return. To his surprise he was happy to see that instead of the axe wielding women or a protective father the footsteps belonged to a fellow Yankee.

That is, he was happy until he realized that the fellow Yankee was none other than Sergeant John H. Reed of the 101st Illinois Infantry.

CHAPTER NINETEEN

"Well look who it is. My wealthy little chum, and I see he's made a friend. Save any for me?" Reed said to Gabriel, with a disgusting grin as he arrived.

"It's not what it looks like," Gabriel told him. Reed was the last person he expected or desired to see, and he wanted out of there, so he holstered his revolver and pushed him out of the way to leave. The girl sat up and started wiping the tears from her eyes, trying to make herself look presentable again. Reed looked her over. She was a pretty little thing, he thought, and if circumstances were any different, he might try and get with her, but they weren't. There were too many others about, so he tipped his hat to her. "Ma'am," he said, and went out after Gabriel.

"What's the matter, Private? You don't look too pleased to see me." he called from behind him.

When Gabriel made his way outside, there was a whole passel of folks mingling about the front door. The older woman and her slave, Mr. Fichehurst, a civilian wagon driver for the 20th Corps headquarters, and two other familiar faces Gabriel immediately recognized. They were Reed's two minions, Willy and James, who'd tried robbing him after Resaca. They were alive, not dead as he had been told in the rifle pit at New Hope Church. For some reason he had been lied to, but he didn't exactly understand why.

Reed followed him out the door and called to his two friends.

"Hey boys, fine lookin' young lady in there looking for a new suitor. If you ask politely, I bet she'd let ya have a turn. Our old friend here just bit off a piece for himself."

"My daughter! My daughter what have you done to my daughter?!"

The old woman screamed and lunged at Gabriel. Luckily Mr. Fiche-hurst and her slave grabbed ahold of her and held her back before she reached him.

"Had his way with her, Ma'am," Sergeant Reed said, trying to pro-voke her.

"I've done nothing of the sort," Gabriel cried out. "What's the matter with you?" he shouted at Reed, who erupted into laughter. The situation was rapidly getting out of hand, and Gabriel was starting to wish he'd never seen the house at all. He wondered where Bird was, and hoped he'd show up soon to set things straight. The old woman was going berserk though, and his friend wasn't in sight.

"Where is my daughter, you scum? What have you done to her?!" she shouted again, while trying to free herself.

Reed and his friends were standing by with huge grins on their faces, enjoying the trouble he'd stirred.

From inside the house the younger woman finally emerged, though. She was prim and proper-looking again, and her tears had been dabbed away. She had heard everything that had been said and seeing her mother in hysterics walked over to calm her down.

"Oh, my daughter. My God, what did he do? What did he do?" she sobbed.

She hugged her mother and Mr. Fichehurst let go. The slave moved to the old woman's side and rubbed her back to comfort her as well. Gabriel didn't understand why the negro woman seemed to be showing such devotion and empathy toward her owner. Why she hadn't run off the instant she set eyes on him he hadn't a clue.

"Mother, he did nothing. It was my fault, Mother. Don't believe what that other man has been telling you." Gabriel felt relieved to hear the girl clear his name.

"Thank God," he whispered to himself.

"What do you mean? That man with the stripes said you'd been assaulted. Are you sure he didn't touch you? You mustn't be ashamed if he did. We'll tell no one, but if he did, he needs to be punished."

The girl laughed. The slightly crazed and attention-starved young woman Gabriel had tussled with a few moments before had regained her composure and Gabriel was happy for it.

"No, Mother, believe me, if he had harmed me in any way I wouldn't hold back, but it wasn't his fault. It was mine. I don't know why, but when I saw him come up, I just got a little carried away. Besides those horsemen who made off with the goods in our smokehouse yesterday, it's been so long since we've seen any handsome-looking men about. I just...you know Mother... I've been so lonely having only you and Izzy about, and when I had him alone in there a few minutes ago I let my desires get the best of me. I guess I was a little too fast with him."

"I see," the mother said understanding now what had occurred. "So he didn't touch you, then?"

"No, not in the least, only to push me away after I'd made my advances."

"Hmm," the old woman grunted, and looked toward Gabriel. "What's the matter, Yank, my daughter ain't good enough looking for you?" Gabriel blushed. She obviously wasn't a woman easily pleased and it didn't surprise him any to hear that all five of her sons went off to the war, if that was the truth.

"No, Ma'am, your daughter is very pretty, but..."

"But he's got a wife and a little baby girl at home, Mother, and he's true to them," the girl said and smiled at Gabriel.

"He's got a wife and baby at home, and still he robs us before our very eyes. Now where's the sense in that?" The old woman said. Gabriel bowed his head in shame knowing she was right.

"Orders are orders, Ma'am," Mr. Fichehurst spoke up. He'd been watching the whole scene play out and was happy to see Gabriel come out on top and innocent. He liked the boy. He was always very kind to him, polite, and helpful, unlike some of the other soldiers that he had to work with.

Sergeant Reed and his two cronies weren't very happy, though. They watched on, stone-faced and silent. Their fun was over, and it looked like Gabriel was getting away again. Fichehurst saw their disappointment, and suspected they might try a few more tricks, so he spoke up to Gabriel.

"Come, come, young man, it's time we were on our way. Column's about to move out, and Lieutenant Bird is still up in the field holding onto your horse. He saw you go for them sheep and sent me down after you."

Gabriel nodded in agreement. Seeing that he was about to leave, the younger woman walked over to Gabriel and held out her hand, while her mother was being helped back indoors by Izzy.

"I'm sorry about all that in there, Mr. Yank. I hope you won't hold it against all southern girls. I can assure you we typically aren't so forward with our cravings."

Gabriel smiled bashfully. She was a pretty girl, but he was eager to part ways with her. He shook her hand.

"No, I don't think I will Miss. I won't hold it against you, either. We all have our moments now and then, don't we?"

"That we do," the girl agreed, and Gabriel turned to walk away.

Sergeant Reed tried calling after him, but he didn't even acknowledge the attempt. He just stuck close to Mr. Fichehurst and followed him back to the field. He didn't even bother to stop and fetch the sheep he'd killed. He just wanted to be gone from there, and in the back of his mind he hoped that the three women would find them and have something good to eat before they left as well. They'd have to leave, he thought, because other than their half bushel of cornmeal and the few potatoes on their front steps, there was nothing left to eat for miles around their little farm. He and his friends had taken it all.

* * * * *

The next day, the foraging party rolled back into Atlanta with their long train of wagons bursting at the seams with plunder. The pioneers had done especially well on their last day out and returned triumphant. They had live chickens and ducks tied at their feet with twine and hanging off either side of their saddles. A few fat pigs and sheep were crammed into the back of one of the wagons, and several cows were being led along behind it with rope. In the other wagons they hauled their produce, corn, sweet potatoes, and squash to be roasted, peaches and apples to be eaten raw, along with every other kind of crop that could be grown in the Georgian soil. One of the pioneers had even found a stash of honey hidden in a hedgerow the night before. They found enough fodder to feed their horses for a long while too, on top of all the grass they had gotten to munch on along the way.

When they got back, Lieutenant Bird directed the headquarters wagons to the front of the Trout House to be unloaded. As they began to take their spoils inside, Gabriel was surprised and annoyed to see the dastardly Sergeant Reed walking down the street toward them, leading a lieutenant and two armed privates. Gabriel set down a box of potatoes he had just picked out of one of the wagons when he saw the sergeant point in his direction and turn to say something to the men behind him. Then Reed caught sight of Lieutenant Bird as he emerged from the main entrance of the Trout House and approached him with his followers. Again, Sergeant Reed pointed toward Gabriel and they all looked at him now. Gabriel could see Bird was angry and arguing with the men, but the lieutenant behind Reed seemed to get angry, too. Gabriel stood still. He knew something was terribly wrong. Bird nodded his head at the lieutenant, and then started walking toward Gabriel. When he reached him, he took off his hat and kneaded it nervously in his hands. Gabriel could tell now what was happening. He figured it out. Sergeant Reed had found a way to take his revenge and was doing just that.

"Gabriel, I'm sorry to do this, but I'm afraid you are being placed under arrest."

Tears slowly welled in Gabriel's eyes as he was being told, tears of anger and concern. The other pioneers were walking by oblivious to what was going on, their arms full of goods on their way to the storeroom inside. Gabriel watched as the men who had come for him approached closer. Reed was in tow, his yellow teeth glowing and exposed in sheer satisfaction.

"What for, Jim?" Gabriel asked him before he was taken into custody. Bird hesitated to say.

"What for, Jim?" he asked again slightly louder.

Bird exhaled with a sigh then told him. "Your being charged with attempted rape. I'm sorry Gabriel."

Gabriel felt his legs go weak and he dropped to his knees. His surroundings seemed to spin around him, and he was unable to stand when the two provost guards came over and placed his wrists in cuffs.

* * * * *

It wasn't until his second day under lock and key that he had any visitors. Lieutenant Bird came by with two chairs and a stack of paper stuffed under his arm. The guard had just dropped off his breakfast and emptied his slop bucket. Gabriel was lying in the pile of straw and blankets on the floor that served as his bed, when Bird arrived. It was the only thing in his makeshift cell, other than the wooden bucket he had been given to relieve himself in. His hardtack and salt pork breakfast still lay uneaten on the floor next to him. Bird sat down and set his papers on the floor as the door was shut and locked behind him.

Gabriel was fortunate to have what he did. At first, they were going to take him to a house near the 1st Division headquarters where he was to be held with all the common drunks, thieves and brawlers, the provost guard had rounded up over the past couple of days. Bird pulled some strings though and had him jailed in the Trout House, in a spare room on the 4th floor. They'd taken all the furniture out and kept him locked in with a guard at the door, but it was a better alternative. Bird wanted it that way, so he'd be able to keep a better eye on him.

"Sorry I haven't come by sooner, Gabriel, but I've been awfully busy trying to help you out. I hope you like the accommodations I was able to procure."

Gabriel didn't say anything. He hadn't even acknowledged Bird's presence. He just lay on the floor staring up at the ceiling in a mute indifference.

"They tell me you haven't eaten. I know it's shit, but you can't starve yourself," Bird told him. Gabriel continued with his silence.

"You know, I can't help you if you don't speak to me. Things could be worse you know. You could be dead."

Gabriel rolled over to face the wall. He could feel tears welling in his eyes again, and he wanted to hide his face from Bird's view.

"I'd rather be dead, Jim. Besides, what's the use? It's all over with. I'm done for."

"What's over? Nothing's over. You need to stay strong, Gabriel, and if not for yourself then for your family. Your wife and baby girl. Your court martial is still eight days away, and I think if we work hard, we've got a good chance at winning. I think we can have your charges dropped."

"How so? It's my word versus that of a sergeant's, simple as that."

"Bullshit, there's Fichehurst, too."

"He's a civilian," Gabriel argued.

"That doesn't mean anything. He's well-respected around here, even if he is a civilian. The officers talk, and the men that'll hear your trial will know of his reputation and that of Sergeant Reed's."

"What of Sergeant Reed?" Gabriel asked. He rolled over and sat up. He'd been in a self-pitied sulk for two days, but Bird's persistence was reviving his spirits some. At least he no longer felt like crying that is.

"Come, sit up here and eat something," Bird said to him slapping the other chair he'd brought in. "It's nice and comfortable, I'll leave it here for you when I go."

Gabriel heaved himself up on his feet and grabbed a piece of hard-tack before taking a seat. He adjusted the chair to face Bird, as he took a bite and choked it down. His depression spoiled his appetite, but he knew he had to eat something.

"Did you send the letter?" Gabriel asked him.

"I did, I sent it out first thing the next morning."

"Thank you," Gabriel said.

As they were hauling him to his room on the day of his arrest, Gabriel asked Bird to write a letter to Rill and his parents, telling them what happened. He knew once the boys in Company I found out, they'd write home about it, and he wanted his family to know before anyone else in town. He wanted them to be prepared.

"So what's this about Reed?" Gabriel asked.

"Well I've been asking around and apparently he was once a first-sergeant, but got busted down a while back. That friend of his too,

James, he was once a sergeant but now he's a private. They've both got a terrible reputation in their regiment."

"How does that affect me?" Gabriel asked him.

"I'll tell you how. It affects you because the Judge Advocate for your trial, the man who will be basically running the whole thing, is 1st Lieutenant English of the 101st Illinois. He's from Reed's regiment, and he's a good man, I hear. He knows all about Reed and his sordid past. He's bound to mention it to the men on the jury, and guess who one of those men is. Guess."

"You," Gabriel hopingly answered him.

"No, not me, but Hezekiah Watkins, your lieutenant-colonel from the 143rd is, and that should help you, too."

"Really?" Gabriel asked him, surprised. Bird nodded his head and picked the papers up that he'd set on the ground next to him.

"I've taken some notes here. Now, the reason I've been gone for the past couple days is I've been asking around. I spoke with the men of Reed's regiment, of course, but I also talked to some of the officers from my old regiment, the 154th. I know a few of them who've sat on a courts martial before and they've told me all about how it's run, and what we'll need to do to win. You'll be representing yourself, for one thing, have they told you that yet?"

"Representing myself?" Gabriel asked.

"Yes, you'll be handling your own case. With my help you'll need to round up witnesses and make sure they know when and where your trial is. You'll also need to come up with what questions you'll want to ask us."

"Us, what do you mean by us?"

"Me and Fichehurst. Marvin, too."

"You and Marvin?"

"Yes, my friends say to get a couple of officers that know you and will come and say something nice about you. You know, that you're a good soldier and do your duty, short and sweet like that."

"Even though you weren't there at the house?"

"That's correct," Bird said. "And then when Fichehurst comes up, you can ask him all of the specifics about the incident and everything to discredit Reed and show that he's lying. Reed, I hear, is the only witness for the prosecution, and he'll go first before your witnesses."

It all sounded promising to Gabriel, but he had reservations about Marvin.

"Marvin will never come and help me. Why even bother asking?"

"Because technically he's been in charge of you for longer than I have, and he knew you before the war."

"But he won't."

"He might. I've spoken with that Watkins, your lieutenant-colonel, and he said that he'll send him over to speak with you later today. You can ask him then, and if he says no, maybe I'll have a little talk with him myself. I know a few tricks I think would persuade him to comply," Bird said with a mischievous smile.

They sat for an hour more discussing his case and composing the questions Gabriel would ask. He also made Gabriel write down a statement in his own words of what had happened that day. He explained that after he had called all his witnesses, it would be best if he read the statement to the jury before they went in to deliberate.

"Questioning doesn't always paint a clear picture, but if you write a good statement that tells them what happened from beginning to end, the jury will have a better understanding."

Before he left, Bird promised to be back in the morning to continue going over the case.

"I'll have someone bring you up your meals from our camp, too," he told him. "I didn't know they we're feeding you this slop," he said motioning towards Gabriel's plate.

Gabriel thanked him.

"You've got to eat, Gabriel. You've got to keep positive, too. We'll beat this, I promise you, but you've got to stay focused."

Gabriel nodded, and said that he would.

"The boys miss you too, and they send their regards. I'd like to say something to you too, Gabriel," Bird said looking down to his feet then back up to Gabriel. "I just wanted to say that I'm sorry."

"What for?" Gabriel asked him.

"You were right. I should have dealt with that bastard Reed after Resaca, but I never did. I let him slither away and now it's bitten us in the ass. You, mostly. This is all my fault."

Admittedly, Gabriel had thought back on that day several times since his arrest and wished Bird would have brought Reed up on charges. He didn't blame him for his trouble now though and wanted him to know it.

"No, Jim this is Reed's doing, not yours. I blame myself, too. I never should have taken off on my own like I did. I should have learned after the first time he tried giving me trouble, but I didn't. If there is anyone else to blame other than Reed, it's me."

* * * * *

As Bird had informed him, Captain Marvin showed up that evening. It went just about as well as he expected, too. Marvin was stupid drunk, of course. He'd had more than he could handle again, and Gabriel was astonished the guard even allowed him to enter the room. He was rude and insulted Gabriel when he came in, but Gabriel ignored him, trying to be the better man. He showed him his due respect and greeted him appropriately. When he asked Marvin if he'd make a statement in his defense during the trial, Marvin erupted into laughter.

"Say something nice about you? Are you insane?"

"Nothing too detailed Captain, just a short sentence or two describing my character," Gabriel tried to explain.

"Your character. You're a weasel. You're a conniving conspirator, Ballard, and if you call me to the stand, I will tell them as much."

"Conniving conspirator?" Gabriel questioned him.

"Yes," Marvin said.

"How so?" he asked.

"You and your little group there, Nash, Baldwin, and Cook. Everyone who was friendly with Moffat conspired against me, you did, but look now how the tables have turned. Moffat has run away home with his tail between his legs, Enos is dead and you're rotting in jail about to be sent to prison for a decade with hard labor, or worse."

"That's not true," Gabriel told him.

"Oh, yes it is, and it's only a matter of time before Nash screws up again, and then I'll get rid of him, too."

Gabriel was furious, especially after Marvin had insulted Enos. Enos was one of the most loyal men he'd ever known, and he had rarely said anything against the despicable Marvin.

"Captain, we never conspired against you. Moffat may have, but we never did, and yes, we were friendly with him but only because he was friendly with us. Everyone else in the company liked him, too," Gabriel argued.

"Maybe so, but look where it's gotten them. There's almost nobody left. Just a handful that I can count on my fingers and toes."

"And you take pride in that?" Gabriel asked him, disbelievingly.

"If they went against me, their captain and rightful leader, so be it," Marvin said in a bitter tone.

"That's insane. You're delusional. Half the company went to your store and signed up with you don't you remember? If we hated you so much, why would we have done that?"

"That was all before Moffat poisoned your minds," Marvin reasoned.

Gabriel could see there was no use arguing. Even if he was clearheaded and sober, Marvin would never listen to reason. He quit trying, so Marvin happily left.

The next morning, Bird came back, and they worked on the case. He told Gabriel not to worry about Marvin. He'd go and have a talk with him, but if he couldn't be persuaded, he thought that with Fichehurst and him and then Gabriel's final statement at the end they would be fine. Gabriel still hadn't been given the chance to write a letter of his own to his family, so Bird had him do so, and took it with him to mail out when he left. It was hard for him to write. He didn't know what to say. Bird had already voiced Gabriel's innocence to them in his letter, so he decided to just tell them all how much he loved them and asked them to pray for him.

Bird ended up stopping by every morning and evening until the day of the trial to go over notes with Gabriel on what he was going to have to say and do. They did practice runs too, where Bird would pretend to be himself or Fichehurst and Gabriel would ask the questions he'd come up with. He had other visitors, as well. His two bunkmates Robertson and Spencer brought up his meals twice a day, and Dave Nash and Baldy came by several times as well.

On their first visit, Dave smuggled in a fifty foot length of rope, by wrapping it around his waist and stomach.

"Now here, Gabriel," Dave had said as he removed his coat, after the door was shut and locked behind them, "Baldy is going to unwind this from me and we'll wrap it around you. Then, tonight when the guards are all asleep and the coast is clear, you can throw it out the window and slide to safety."

Gabriel had to laugh at their harebrained idea. He greatly appreciated their concern and desire to assist him, but much to their disappointment he declined the offer.

"Thanks, you two, but even if I did get away, it'd only make me look guilty, and I'd never be able to show my face in Dryden again."

As he lay on the floor of his room the night before his trial, that was something Gabriel thought on deeply. His reputation, and what the folks in Dryden would do and say once they found out he'd been arrested and why. He knew it'd cause a big uproar, and the townspeople would likely take sides on whether they thought he was guilty or not, even though they knew nothing about the true facts of the case. They'd still gossip about it and pass false rumors around. It was only natural, and Gabriel knew it. It's what people did, it's how society operated. He also knew that even if he ended up winning in the morning and was acquitted, there would still be the doubters. Folks that, no matter what happened, would always think that he had gotten away with it. He imagined his sister-in-law Hannah would be among that faction. In the end, he realized his reputation was likely beyond full repair, and it was just something he was going to have to accept.

Sadly, he knew that his family would be subjected to the same ridicule. He hadn't accepted that. He knew that whenever Rill and the baby went to town, people would say things behind their back. The same with his parents and his siblings. It was the harsh reality. He felt as if he had let them down. He was their pride and joy, their hero, their husband, their father, their brother and son. He was the one they spoke of among themselves, and to anyone else who would listen.

Whenever one of his letters arrived, they would all gather around the kitchen table and his father would read it aloud for everyone to hear. Then they would take it to Grandma Rummer and his Aunt Polly's, so they could read it, too. His father loved to brag about him. In her last letter, Rill had told him that he was telling everyone in town that his son rode with Hooker and was one of his trusted confidants. *"He is so proud of you"* she wrote *"we all are."* All that was over now. If they hadn't already, they would be getting Bird's letter any day and the bragging and pride would cease. He knew that his arrest would crush them, it would bring shame and hurt to them. Knowing that, hurt him the most.

He realized, too, that there was still hope. There was still a chance to reverse some of his misfortunes and clear his name. He'd have to be near perfect, but if he trusted in God and told the truth, he thought there was a chance he could win over the jury in the morning.

In the event that they weren't, he'd taken some precautions. He'd written a letter that night to Rill before the sunlight disappeared from his window. It was terribly difficult to do but in it he gave her his farewell and his apologies. He had come to the conclusion that if he was found guilty, it would be best if they just moved on and forgot about him, for once his prison term was up, he planned on never returning home. His shame, he knew, would be too great. *"I love you and the baby infinitely Rill, but it would be unfair of me to ask you to remain my wife,"* he wrote. In the morning he planned on handing the letter to Lieutenant Bird, with instructions to mail it if he was unsuccessful.

* * * * *

As Gabriel was busy pondering his uncertain future, Lieutenant Bird was on his way to an uninvited visit with Captain Marvin. He had done everything in his power to help Gabriel since his arrest. He'd gotten him his own lodgings, wrote his family, assured that he was well-fed and cared for, and also worked tirelessly to prepare him for his trial. He even tried to get some cavalry friends of his to bring the young Sesech girl in while they were out on patrol, but they found her house deserted, the family having set out to find refuge at the home of relatives, far out of the Yankees' reach. The only thing that he had failed to do was convince Captain Marvin to testify in Gabriel's defense. He had told Gabriel, that it wasn't a problem if Marvin didn't testify, and he thought so too, but with the trial almost at hand, he wanted to leave no stone unturned. He hadn't told Gabriel about it, but he had already gone to Marvin a few days before, and Marvin vehemently objected.

"No, and you can go to hell with him, Lieutenant," Marvin had said to Bird when he asked.

He wouldn't be taking no for an answer this time though, even if it took some unconventional persuasion to change his mind.

It was dark out, just after midnight, when he entered the camp of the 143rd New York. He snuck through it, so as not to be seen, and made his way to the Captain's lodgings where he had come a few days before. He heard talking and saw that Marvin had company, so he lay down outside and waited for the other man to leave before crawling to the entrance and letting himself in. Marvin was just getting ready for bed when he did so. He heard Bird come in and turned to see who it was. It startled him to see the unfamiliar figure of Bird standing in the shadows.

"Who's that? Who's there?" he asked.

Bird said nothing but stepped forward in the candlelight. Marvin recognized him. He was a short man, shorter than Marvin at least, but stout and powerful and Marvin could tell he wasn't one to be crossed.

"Oh, it's you. You're that pain in the ass little Lieutenant. I know what you want, and I already fucking told you no, so get the hell out of here!" Marvin shouted.

Bird cringed, he didn't want Marvin making a racket, or he'd draw attention to them and ruin his plans. He pulled out his pistol and pointed it at Marvin's face. He had to quiet him down, and this was the quickest way he knew how. On seeing the gun, Marvin stepped back. He certainly wasn't expecting it.

"What are you doing?" Marvin asked him angrily.

"Be quiet, Captain," Bird whispered, and cocked the hammer back on his pistol to show him he meant business. "Sit down," Bird said, pointing with his free hand to a chair Marvin was standing by. Marvin quickly obeyed. He didn't know Bird that well and wasn't sure what he was capable of.

"What do you want from me?" he asked in a quieter tone.

"I want you to listen," Bird said

"Okay, then talk."

Bird took a deep breath and spoke. "There is a soldier of yours that's in need of your assistance, Captain. Why won't you help him?"

"I've already told you both why. Because he's a fucking traitor. He's a conniving bastard, and he and his friends have gone against me ever since I raised the company back in New York."

Bird rolled his eyes.

"That isn't so, Captain. He told me himself."

"It is so."

"No, it's not. There was never any conniving or grand scheme against you. It's all just been in your head since the very beginning. Sure, they may not like you, but that's from your own doing. They gave you your chance to lead them, but you blew it."

"They did not. They never did, and that's beside the point. It doesn't matter anyway how I've treated them, I formed the company, I signed them up, they owe me their loyalty."

"Owe you? Owe you, for what? For denying them proper medical care, for marching them on the parade ground until they could barely stand because you didn't know your proper commands. I know all about it. You won't even go into battle with them."

"That's not so. I've been in every battle they've fought since Resaca."

"What, you think just because you were there, makes you present? They say you hid at Resaca and New Hope Church and were drunk at Kolb's Farm. I was at Peach Tree Creek with your men, can't you remember? You were so drunk during that fight I had to take control of your company while you lay unconscious for more than half the battle."

"I went down from the heat."

"The hell you did. You were drunk off your ass, and the whole company knew it. You're lucky I didn't turn you in too, you owe me for that."

"I owe you nothing," Marvin shouted, "and I will not be testifying at his trial. Gabriel Ballard was one of the worst men in my company, and I won't lift a finger to help him."

"You will so."

"I will not, and you can't make me. I've listened to what you have to say, now leave!"

Bird moved closer to Marvin, his pistol still pointed directly at his face. His eyes were flaming mad and Marvin could tell he'd touched a nerve.

"You won't fire that at me. If you shoot, my men will come running," he tried to reason with Bird.

"They'll come running because they'll hope to see that you've killed yourself, not out of loyalty you cowardly bastard." Bird placed the muzzle of his pistol between the Captain's eyes. Marvin was frightened and Bird was shaking with anger.

"You're right though, they would come running and I'd be arrested, wouldn't I?"

"That's right, that's right. You'd be arrested, and hanged or shot yourself," Marvin said nervously, sweat rolling off his forehead.

"I thought so," Bird replied, "that's why I brought this along." From behind his back he pulled out a long and sharp knife from his belt with his left hand, and placed its point into Marvin's neck just hard enough to break the skin. Marvin whimpered and squeezed his eyes shut, scared that Bird was about to end him. Bird holstered his pistol with his other hand.

"There, that'll do. Nobody will hear you die if I slit your throat."

Marvin groaned. He was too scared to talk, worried that if he did so the knife would cut deeper into his skin.

"Let me tell you, Captain, I've worked awfully hard over the last several days trying to help Gabriel out as best I could. Do you know why?"

"No," Marvin managed to say in a strained voice.

"Because I am his superior, just as you are, but for now he is under my care. It is my job to care for him and he is my friend. Being an officer doesn't entitle you to respect. Respect must be earned. You can't walk about throwing your weight around all the time and making your men grovel at your feet, and then expect them to respect you. You need to show them that you care. Help them, care for them, show them respect and maybe you'll start to get some back."

Marvin was silent, he listened to Bird somberly. He couldn't figure out why, maybe it was the threat of death, but Bird's words were hitting home.

"Contrary to what you may think of him, Gabriel Ballard is one of my finest men and I have a hand-picked crew, mind you. He's pleasant to be around, he does what he's told without complaint, he works hard, he's honest, he's intelligent and he fights splendidly. He's been dealt a bad hand with this rape nonsense, and I'm partially to blame myself for it. It's all a bullshit lie, though. He's innocent, the victim of a vengeful low-life sergeant, that's probably not much worse of a man than yourself. I want you at your division headquarters tomorrow morning 9:30 sharp, the trial starts at 10:00. Be prepared to testify, and God help you if you're not there, or you sabotage his case, because I promise I'll hunt you down and cut you to pieces. I'll kill you slowly, and draw it out as long as I can, as long as your body can endure. You won't be the first man I've killed, and probably not the last, but you'll be the most tortured, I give you my word."

Seeing that Marvin had ceased with his belligerence, Bird pulled the knife away from his throat. Marvin instantly put his hands to his neck and let out a sigh of relief.

"I'll be there, 9:30 sharp," he gasped.

"Good, I'm glad we were able to come to an agreement," Bird said as he backed his way to and out the door. He was away into the night as quietly as he had come. Marvin remained sitting though. He didn't attempt to give chase or sound the alarm. When Bird had come into the room he was filled with anger and hate and thought he could shout and order him away. Even with the gun pointed at him, he thought so, but when he had the knife to his throat something clicked in his brain. It got his attention, and for the first time in a long time he had an honest view of himself and what he'd become. It was an epiphany of sorts. He finally realized how wrong he'd been and that he'd have to make a change somehow. He knew that if he carried on like he had been, and continued the poor relationship with his men, they'd never forget it or forgive him, and once he got home he'd be one of the most hated men in Dryden.

* * * * *

Although Gabriel was detached to the 20th Corps headquarters, he still technically belonged to the 143rd New York, so his peers in the 1st Division were the ones to judge him. The trial was held in a house next to division headquarters, and Gabriel had to be brought there by wagon under guard. Mr. Fichehurst drove, and Lieutenant Bird rode in the back with him, along with the Provost Marshal. Gabriel had already given Bird his farewell letter to Rill. When they got to the place of trial, Dave Nash and several other men from Company I were there to wish him luck as he was led indoors. He wasn't permitted to stop and talk, but he gave them a nod and wave. Hearing their good wishes gave him some confidence. To Lieutenant Bird's credit, Marvin kept his word and was waiting outside at 9:30 just as he'd instructed him to.

The house was large and had been a family home before the Yankees came to Atlanta. Now, some of General Williams' staff officers lived upstairs, and the parlor was turned into a courtroom. The family's massive dinner table served as the jury's bench, and across from them sat Gabriel. Behind him was a line of chairs on the back wall of the room, where Bird, Marvin and Fichehurst sat on one side of the room and Reed on the other. Gabriel was surprised to see that Marvin looked sober and appeared to be well-groomed. Bird was, too, and Fichehurst as well, but Sergeant Reed looked dirty and hung over. Gabriel, on the other hand wore a brand new sack coat and trousers, with a new brown slouch hat that Bird had given him to wear that morning. His face was freshly shaven, and his hands were washed and clean. "A good appearance will go a long way," Bird had told him when he came to his room earlier that morning, bearing the gifts.

When he made it into the makeshift courtroom, the orders appointing the court were read, and Gabriel was asked if he was opposed to any of the members of the jury. He said "no," and then the Judge Advocate swore him in, having him place his hand over a Bible. He felt nervous on the ride over, but now that things were underway, he was focused and mindful of maintaining a professional appearance and using good manners. After the Judge Advocate was sworn in by the President of the Court, Lieutenant-Colonel Hezekiah Watkins, Gabriel's charges were then read as written by the Provost Marshal who had arrested him. After this was done, Gabriel was asked what he pleaded. "Not guilty," was his answer.

Sergeant Reed was then called up to the big table to be questioned by the Judge Advocate, 1st Lieutenant English. The two men knew each other and based on the disgusted way in which English looked at Reed as he approached, he could tell that he had little use for the man. He was also slightly embarrassed by Reed's appearance, for they both belonged to the same regiment and Reed was making them look like slobs. An unpleasant odor drifted through the air when Reed came to the table, and the few members of the jury who were seated across from where he stood, pulled handkerchiefs out of their pockets to cover their noses. They were disgusted with him as well, and Gabriel was pleased to see it.

Despite his appearance, Reed was, however, somewhat well-spoken and charming with his testimony, and gave an accurate description of the events at first. It wasn't until toward the end of the questioning that he started in with his lies. Gabriel wasn't very surprised when he did. He said that the women were overjoyed when he came along and were happy that there were still "real men around." This was a complete fabrication, along with his claim that Gabriel had given him a false regiment when asked which command he belonged to. Of course, he completely neglected to say anything about how he had tricked the mother into thinking he had assaulted her daughter, and didn't say anything of how the girl had come to Gabriel to apologize and wish him well when he had left. It frustrated Gabriel to witness him spin his web of lies, but all he could do was keep a straight face, watch, and wait.

When it was his turn to call his supporters to the stand, Lieutenant Bird and Captain Marvin came up first, and testified to Gabriel's reputation of being a good soldier, that was hard working, obedient, and dedicated to duty. Their testimony was short and sweet as planned, but being that they were both officers, it had the desired effect and held great weight in the eyes of the jury. Mr. Fichehurst came to the stand next. He was Gabriel's main and only witness who was at the house in Flat Rock when the alleged assault took place. He, unlike Reed however, told the truth. Gabriel only hoped that his telling was more believable to the jury than Reed's.

What sealed the deal for Gabriel though, was his prepared statement at the end. He gave it smoothly, with conviction and honesty and his story matched up perfectly with that of Mr. Fichehurst. The jury recognized this, they found him to be extremely well-prepared, well-groomed and honest, and after the courtroom was cleared for deliberation they quickly came back with a verdict of "not guilty."

CHAPTER TWENTY

As Gabriel prepared for his trial locked in the confines of his Trout House room, General Sherman was busy chasing after General Hood northwest of Atlanta. There were a few minor scraps in the pursuit, Hood tore up some railroad and captured a few small Yankee garrisons, but his attempt to destroy Sherman's supply line and force him to abandon Atlanta was unsuccessful. The Yankees were able to repair their track almost as quickly as it had been destroyed, and ironically it was General Hood's men who were forced to retreat out of Georgia to rest and resupply.

With Hood having escaped, Sherman was left with a dilemma. He knew that he had to keep an eye on Hood but didn't want to give up all the progress he'd gained over the spring and summer. He also wanted to march his troops deeper into Georgia and eventually to the sea, in a campaign against the southern populace. Sherman knew that it would have a crippling effect on southern morale if he could show that he could march about virtually unopposed in the heart of their country.

To accomplish both tasks Sherman split his army in two, by sending General Thomas north to Nashville with the 4th and 23rd Corps, to keep an eye on Hood, while he returned to Atlanta with the remainder of his men. There, he began preparations for his famous march to the sea, the plan of which was approved by General Grant on November 2nd, the day after Gabriel's trial.

In Atlanta, Sherman formed his downsized army into two wings for the upcoming campaign. The right wing was made up of the 15th and 17th Corps, and commanded by General Howard, while the left wing, consisted of the 14th and 20th Corps, and was commanded by General Slocum. With Slocum in control of one of Sherman's wings,

General Williams was put in charge of the 20th Corps, as he had been after Hooker's resignation in August.

Before departing Atlanta, Sherman had all buildings and infrastructure of military importance destroyed. The massive Car Shed across from the Trout House and in view of Gabriel's cell was even leveled. The railroad tracks were torn up too and placed over bonfires made of ties. When sufficiently heated in the middle, the soldiers wrapped the tracks around trees and poles to render them useless. Sherman wanted nothing left behind for the Confederates once they returned to the city after his departure. He also sent all his surplus supplies north on his own supply line, and before stepping off had that destroyed as well, its tracks pulled up, its bridges and trestles leveled, and so on.

Sherman knew that stretching a supply route any deeper into Georgia would be nearly impossible. Instead, he decided on feeding his troops off the fat of the land. They would eat what could be gathered along the way, and each command was tasked with sending out foraging parties as they went, to procure food and fodder. Not only did this serve to provide for his men, but it further depleted and demoralized the enemy.

* * * * *

Gabriel was overcome with joy upon hearing the court declare his innocence. He was required to stand and hear the verdict read, and when it was, he knelt down onto the table in front of him and with tears in his eyes gave his thanks to God. He was happy for himself, but most of all for his family, his parents, Rill and the baby. Sergeant Reed, upon hearing the courts findings, immediately exited the room in disgust, but Bird, Fichehurst and even Marvin remained behind to congratulate him. Bird was the first to come forward and gave him a hug. Through teary eyes, Gabriel thanked him for all that he'd done for him and his family. Fichehurst was next, and then Marvin. They both shook Gabriel's hand, and to Gabriel's surprise Marvin even managed to say something nice to him.

"Well done, Gabriel. You did a marvelous job conducting yourself," he told him before leaving. When his friends outdoors heard the verdict from Marvin, they erupted into cheers, making Gabriel feel all the happier.

Needless to say, he was awfully surprised when the provost guard came up and informed him that they were there to take him back to his cell. Apparently, he couldn't be released until the case was reviewed and approved by General Williams. After a few reassurances from Lieutenant Bird and the Judge Advocate that all was normal procedure, Gabriel reluctantly agreed to go, but it would be another week before he was set free. General Williams didn't get around to signing off on the decision until the 8th of November. It was a tough week of waiting. Gabriel's mind went wild with anxiety, over the possibility of General Williams rejecting the court's findings and having him retried.

He also got his first letter from home with Rill's reaction to his arrest. It wasn't as reassuring as he had hoped. She made sure to let him know of her unwavering support and belief in him, but he could tell that her characteristic optimism was being tested. She couldn't help but express her concern for his well-being, and her frustration with the Army for, "*allowing such an injustice to befall one of its most noble soldiers,*" as she saw him. She also alluded to the anxiety she felt over what would happen to her and the baby if the unthinkable happened, and he was found guilty. He wrote home, of course, to tell her and his parents of the trial, but knew that a response to the good news could be months away, as the supply line north was already being dismantled and there would be no way to receive mail until they reached the coast, if they ever did.

The uncertain concern he knew his loved ones felt at home depressed Gabriel, and even when he was finally released on the 8th, much of the relief and happiness he felt after the trial had seeped away.

* * * * *

It had been nearly two weeks since they'd left Atlanta in ruins. They were making their way through the countryside in a northeasterly direction in search of food. It was their main task now, there being enough escaped slaves laboring for the Army that their pioneering duties were less needed. Robertson and Spencer were in the lead wagon out of three, while Gabriel and Lieutenant Bird rode ahead on the lookout.

Most of the homes and barns close to the route of march had already been picked clean, but after about three miles out they came across an old negro man, who promised to take them to an untouched plantation a little further down the road. He said that it was hidden down a long and abandoned-looking laneway. All he asked for in return was that afterward they take him back to the Army, so that he could join with the other emancipated refugees tagging along behind it. Lieutenant Bird agreed.

As the man had told them, the path looked to be abandoned, other than a few fresh footprints in the dirt. It was exceptionally overgrown, more of a tunnel of vegetation than a road. Leaves covered the ground in all directions and the wagons could barely fit down it without branches and brush scrapping at their sides. Alertly scanning ahead, Gabriel led the way, with his revolver at his side and his rifle slung around his back, not fully trusting the old man's story.

His suspicions were soon relaxed though, when after going around a sharp turn, the path began to widen and opened into a well-cared-for wood of towering live oaks, smothered in Spanish moss, and a few waxy-leaved magnolia trees. At the end of the path, through and just beyond the grove, there stood a large red brick home, with two large brick chimneys at either end and a portico entranceway with four massive white pillars. The house had a wide face but was not too awful deep. There were five windows with black shutters on the second story and four on the first, two on either side of the door, centered in the middle of the pillars.

Upon seeing the home, the men grew restless at the thought of all the goodies they were sure to find.

"Looks virgin to me," Bird said to Gabriel as he rode up front alongside him.

"Sure does," Gabriel agreed. "I think we'll be the heroes in camp tonight."

The men eagerly made their way down the path under the trees to the beautiful home. Gabriel directed the men where to park, while

Lieutenant Bird hopped down off his mount and approached the door. Something was amiss though, for as he made his way up the front steps, he noticed the door was slightly ajar, and there were a pair of nicely polished leather shoes sprouting up from the ground just inside the opening. Bird sharply turned around and caught the attention of the others. He shushed them with his finger and motioned for Gabriel, Robertson, and Spencer, to come over with their rifles.

Gabriel quietly slid down off his mount and tied her to the wheel of the lead wagon, while the other two retrieved their weapons that were laid in its bed. Once they reached Bird, he turned back to the front door, and with the point of his sword nudged it in ever so slowly, not wanting it to squeak. As it opened, the light from the outside revealed that the pair of shoes were attached to the newly-dead corpse of an old, yet well-dressed negro man. He was tall and thin, with short-cropped white hair. His eyes were closed, but a look of grief and pain remained etched in the expression on his face. At his belly could be seen the obvious cause of his death. A massive and deep laceration, with bloody and protruding bowels poking through the interruption in his skin.

There was more to behold too, for beyond the corpse, sat an older white woman. She wasn't sitting for pleasure though, she was fastened to the chair with a thin hemp rope. Her legs were tied to the wooden ones, her back to the back of the chair, and her hands together under the seat. She was crying, but not noisily, only with her tears. Her left eye was red and swollen shut, and her mouth, gagged with a smaller length of rope, was bleeding from a corner, along with her nose.

"My God," Lieutenant Bird whispered to himself as he took in the scene.

Suddenly there was a noise. It came from within an adjacent room and sounded like the clanging of pots and pans. The animated voices of a couple men could also be heard. The door to the room was closed, located just beyond the head of the dead man. Upon hearing the noise, the woman motioned with her head to the group of Yankees towards the door, as if to say, "they're in there." Bird took the hint, and with his foot he rolled the corpse out of the way, and went for the handle as Gabriel and his two companions prepared to charge in.

Slowly, Bird opened the door to the adjacent room, and after moving it about a foot he poked his face into the opening to inspect the interior. Gabriel couldn't see anything from his location, but Bird was able to view it all. The room was large and well-furnished, with tables and cushioned chairs. There was also a large fireplace on the other side of the room across from the door, with a marble mantle and a large brass framed mirror above it. At a table in the center of the room, stood two men, with their backs to the door. One was a short and scruffy-looking man, with a scraggly red beard and a weathered Confederate uniform, while the other was tall and black, a muscular and powerful looking specimen of man, in tattered homespun rags. Each had a large cotton sack laying on the table in front of them, and they were both busy looking over the contents inside.

As he continued to peer in, Bird noticed a third individual, but this one was much smaller. He wasn't exactly black or white, but a color in between and couldn't have been more than ten or eleven years old. He was also quite an agile little lad, for he quickly hopped onto a stool next to the fireplace and lifted himself up onto the mantel to go after a pair of shiny-looking candle holders mounted to the wall on either side of the mirror. After taking down the first holder, he shimmied his way to the other side of the mantel, but as he was going past the mirror, he caught sight of Lieutenant Bird in the reflection and let out a cry.

The boy jumped down off the mantel and shot out a door on the back wall of the room that led to a patio outside. Lieutenant Bird and the two men were startled by the boy's reaction. After seeing him run out, the taller man of the two turned around and caught sight of the Yankee soldier behind him. He then bent over, picked up a chair next to the table, and with all his might flung it across the room at the surprised looking man peering in. It all happened within a moment, and Lieutenant Bird was barely able to react and shut the door before the chair crashed into the place where his face had just vacated. When it hit the door, the sturdy built chair exploded into a multitude of splinters, and the two men took the time to quickly gather their spoils and high-tail it out of there. They were just clearing the back door when Bird and his crew came charging in. Gabriel, Spencer, and Robertson sprinted across the room, dodging the numerous pieces of furniture, but Bird knocked his right knee on the corner of a granite topped side table and so was the last to make it outside.

When they got out back, the three thieves were sprinting across the back yard, which was wide open field to a woodline about 100 yards distant. The young boy had just about made it to safety, but the greedy men, weighted down by their plunder were not so far off.

"Shoot them!" Lieutenant Bird shouted as he limped his way out the back door.

Robertson was the first to take aim and fired quickly. His bullet hit home, and a piece of skull from the head of the taller man on the left, went up into the air and landed in the grass, hair side down. The man, instantly killed, fell flat on his face and skidded to a stop, while his cotton sack tumbled to the ground beside him, spilling the silver tableware it contained in all directions. The shorter man, seeing he was in for it, dropped his sack to pick up speed but it was too late. Gabriel and Spencer, fired at him almost simultaneously, but Spencer slightly before Gabriel. The first bullet, hit the man high up on his back, severing his spinal cord and rendering his legs useless. His body began to fall, but as it did it twisted, and that's when the second shot, Gabriel's, hit, carrying away most of his lower jaw and tongue with it. The man, still alive, landed on his back with a thud in the browning vegetation below. By now the young boy had made it to the safety of the tree line and was out of view.

The three Yankees were happy to have all hit their marks. They made their way out to the bodies to inspect the results. When Robertson reached his kill, he nudged the man with the barrel of his rifle, and after confirming him dead, began to gather up the spilled silver, strewn about the body.

Going a few yards beyond the first man, Gabriel and Spencer, came to their victim. It wasn't a pleasant scene, as the man's legs were flopped and folded around each other very unnaturally. His arms were writhing about strangely too, but the man's face was his most noticeable ailment. Blood, torn flesh, bits of bone and teeth were all that was left of his mouth. The hinge portions of his lower jaw were still attached though, and the two pieces of bone could be seen moving about, along with a small piece of muscle, the remnants of the man's tongue. There were strange sounds coming from his throat, too.

"I think he's trying to talk," Gabriel said. Spencer couldn't bear to answer, though. He quietly walked away, the gruesome sight of the man's suffering being too much for him to handle.

Lieutenant Bird had finally made it out to the scene and was standing next to Gabriel, looking over the mangled man.

"Shoot him, Gabriel. Put the poor devil out of his misery," he said to his younger subordinate.

"Shoot him?" Gabriel asked, initially appalled at the request.

The man was in noticeable agony, and with his face half shot away, the only signs of emotion could be seen in his eyes. They were wide, and although he couldn't physically call out, they clearly expressed the tremendous amount of fear and pain he was feeling.

"Yes, I'm serious," Bird said. "Man's a goner. Just get it over with. I left my sidearm on my saddle, and I see none of you boys brought your cartridge boxes. You're the only one here with a loaded weapon."

Gabriel felt wrong. The man had been stopped. He was apprehended. Shouldn't they help him out, even if he was a lost cause? Bird saw the reluctance in Gabriel's demeanor.

"Shoot him, Gabriel. He didn't give that old man at the door a chance. They must have gutted him as soon as he answered the bell, and Lord knows what they would have done to the woman, had they not been disturbed."

Picturing the dreadful scene of the poor old man and woman in his mind, Gabriel realized that Bird was right. No, he had to die, Gabriel agreed, for his own sake and for his crime. Without a second thought, he pulled out his revolver, aimed and then fired one last shot into him. The force of the bullet jerked his head violently to the side and made a small hole above his right eyebrow from where blood and bits of pulverized brain matter began to pour. His pupils, which had been staring at Gabriel as he prepared to execute him, rolled into the back of his head, and the sockets looked as if they had ivory marbles placed inside.

After gathering up the silver, Gabriel and his three companions made their way back to the house. Upon seeing that the shootout had ended, the other men in their party made their way to the captive woman and cut her loose. As the Yankees went to work rounding up her food and valuables, she dropped to her knees over the old man, kissed his forehead, and wept over his body. They were later able to pry out of her that he had been their butler, and the man Robertson had killed, one of her former field hands. After the death of her husband from cholera a dozen years before, the old man and her had become the best of friends. She had been a city girl, raised in Savannah, and knew little of farming, so when her husband died, her friend helped advise and assist her in running the plantation. He was also put in charge of her slaves. She, of course, owned it all, even he, the old man, but without any children of her own, she had nobody else to turn to. By the way she was responding to his death, it was clear to Gabriel and his comrades that she had feelings for the old man too, black as he was.

The men found the house full of provisions and other valuables, and robbed her thoroughly, without much concern for her future or current misfortunes. With the old man dead and her slaves recently run off, she wouldn't be needing much now, anyhow. She tried in vain to convince the old negro that had led them to her home to stay on and work for wages, but the man declined. He belonged to another farm in the area and was scared that his former owner would track him down. He made the right decision to go.

The Yankees weren't completely devoid of human compassion though, for at the request of the old woman, they did her a favor before departing. They buried her old friend out next to her husband, but they did so leaving enough space between the two men for her own body to be deposited when the inevitable came. That was how she wanted it.

The bodies of the two thieves, however, were left where they fell for the crows and wild hogs to pick apart.

* * * * *

After piling the wagons up close to bursting with provisions, and having a short meal to themselves, Lieutenant Bird ordered the men to mount up. It was time to leave. He would lead the party back to the main road but posted Gabriel to bring up the rear. Although they had killed two of the thieves, the little one was still around somewhere and for all they knew there may have been others they hadn't seen.

Loaded heavily, the wagons moved much slower than on the ride to the plantation, so Gabriel held up a few minutes and let them get a head start before he followed. He sat on his horse admiring a set of silver teacups he took from the old woman. They were old, but polished beautifully and he planned on sending them to Rill as a Christmas present once they had the chance to post mail again. When the wagons made it through the grove of trees at the front of the house, Gabriel put the silver away, gave his horse a slight nudge and moved along.

Half an hour after leaving the plantation, the column had yet to reach the main road, and was still moving down the thick and abandoned-looking laneway. Gabriel had been riding close to the rear wagon for some time now, so he stopped to let them get ahead of him again. He wanted some quiet to listen for any movement other than their own, and to watch behind him for anyone that may be trailing them. He was thirsty too, so he popped the cork on his canteen and took a good swig. Before taking off, all the men had filled up from a well at the back of the house. The water was clean, cold and refreshing.

After setting still a few minutes, he was satisfied that no one was in the area and decided to catch up again. Halfway to the rear of the last wagon though, there was a slight movement in the bushes at the side of the road a few paces ahead of him. He immediately drew his revolver and rode to where he had seen the disturbance. As he closed in, he looked down into the thick brush and soon found the cause. Standing in the mess of branches and twigs was the light-skinned negro boy he had seen sprinting out across the field at the plantation house. An angry look grew over Gabriel's face, and he brought his revolver up to bear down on the boy.

"Get the fuck out here before I blast you away," he called out. The boy instinctively put up his arms and walked out of the brush and into the laneway. Gabriel kept his gun pointed at him the whole time. He could see that the boy's eyes were wet with tears, and that he had been crying for some time now. There were streaks of clean skin on his cheeks, where the tears had washed the dust from his face.

"What are you crying for?" he said to the youngster. "How do you think that man back there felt after you and your partners run him through? What's two negroes tagging along with an old Reb for, anyway?" Gabriel asked.

The boy wiped the tears from his eyes and spoke up.

"Those two weren't no partners of mine, and the cracker weren't no Reb neither. He don't deserve the title. The cowardly trash run off the first chance he got, and the hand run with him."

"Bullshit!" Gabriel shot back at him angrily, "I saw you in the field running ahead of them. You'd better quit lying lie to me or I'll kill you, too."

The boy was adamant though.

"Yank, those men weren't my friends at all," he said. "They kidnapped me a few days back, and I haven't had the chance yet to get away. I'm happy they're dead, I swear it."

"Why would you run, then?" Gabriel asked him.

"Because," the boy said, "I was scared. I saw that other Yank there in the mirror and thought there was about to be some shootin', so I got out of there."

By now the men at the rear of the Yankee column had noticed Gabriel's company, and Lieutenant Bird started trotting towards him.

"What's going on, Gabriel?" he shouted from afar.

Gabriel held up his free hand for him to stop.

"Hold on, Jim," he said, "I'm just figuring things out."

Bird halted, but kept his attention directed at his friend and the stranger.

"There ain't no escaping now," Gabriel said, "so you'd better explain things quick and believable, or that other man up there on the horse is liable to come up and shoot you before I do," he lied.

The boy looked terrified but pushed his fear aside and explained.

"Like I said, Yank, them other men kidnapped me a few days back. They come to my house askin' for somthin' to eat, and once I let them in and fed them, they threatened to kill me and my daddy's wife if I didn't go with them."

"Now why would they do that?" Gabriel asked, skeptical of the boy's story.

"Because I'm small. I can fit in windows to unlock the doors of places folks have fled from. Saves from having to bust them down. They was scared your folks might be about to hear and come and investigate. They've been shadowin' your army ever since you left Atlanta."

His story was wild but based on everything he'd seen over the past couple years, it seemed believable to Gabriel. He'd come to learn that the two sides weren't as well defined or unified as he'd previously supposed, and both had their fair share of criminals. To the boy's relief, Gabriel dropped his revolver to his side, but continued with his interrogation.

"Was there anybody else with you three?" he asked.

The boy shook his head. "No, Sir. Just us."

"Where was your daddy when those men come and took you?" Gabriel asked.

"My daddy's with General Lee in Virginia," the boy said, "Hill's Corps."

"What is he, some kind of servant?" Gabriel asked, not very surprised. It wasn't uncommon for officers in the Confederacy to bring along a slave from home. The boy puffed out his chest seemingly offended by the question, though.

"I'll have you know, Yank, my daddy is a captain in the infantry, and he's fought with your people in over a dozen battles."

The boy stood proud and defiant, forgetting all about how upset and scared he had been just a few minutes before. Gabriel smiled. He was impressed by his bravado but didn't believe him in the least.

"There ain't no negro officers in the Rebel army," Gabriel challenged him, "not even in ours."

"I know that, Yank. My daddy isn't a negro though. He's white, like you."

Gabriel shook his head and began to raise his revolver again, but the boy went on, realizing he had better explain himself.

"My daddy's white and my mama was black. Daddy got married to his wife, and he bought my mama to help her out around the house. Mama was beautiful, though. The most beautiful woman my daddy had ever seen, he told me. It wasn't long before my daddy and mama fell in love. Mama got pregnant and she had me."

"Your pa's wife didn't mind?" Gabriel asked.

"She did, but not at first. She thought Mama had gotten pregnant by Daddy's field hand Felix, but Felix was dark like my mama and I was light, and not getting any darker. After a few months, Daddy's wife got suspicious. She confronted him one day after breakfast, and Daddy admitted everything. She was angry, though. She got Daddy's gun and came out to the barn where Mama was milking the cows. I was in a basket next to her, but Daddy's wife shot her. Killed her and was going to shoot me too, but the first shot shook up all the animals and she got trampled as they run out of the barn. I was fine, but she got her legs broke so that the bones come through the skin and the doctor had to saw them off and sew them up."

"And she lived after that?"

"She lived, yes, but she has an awful time getting on by herself."

The boy's story was almost unbelievable, but he told it so quickly and without hesitation that Gabriel thought it must be true. He felt bad now after having been so cruel to him at first. He asked him where he was headed, and the boy said he had to get home. His father's wife depended on him. She had other ailments too, and he didn't know if she'd have been able to pull herself about the house. He thought it likely she'd not eaten in the four days he had been gone, and the animals would have all went without as well. They lived alone in a remote area, and Felix hadn't been seen since he'd been sent to Atlanta to help build the fortifications before the siege.

Pitying the boy, Gabriel pulled him up onto his horse behind him. The least he could do was give him a ride to the main road. From there, they would have to go their separate ways, the boy to home and he and his companions back to the Army. Knowing the terrible scene the boy was likely to encounter on his arrival home, he reached into his haversack before their parting and pulled out one of the silver cups he had intended to send Rill.

"Take this," he said. "If you can find a good person to bargain with for a ride, it may get you home a mite quicker."

* * * * *

On the way back to the main column of troops, Gabriel resumed his place at the rear of their little detachment of marauders. The couple hour trip was uneventful, and although they had no idea before they left that morning of the Army's itinerary, its trail was easy to follow, as it was littered with debris, footprints, and wheel tracks left by the artillery and its supply wagons. Eventually, they caught back up just after sundown.

The ride was a quiet one for Gabriel, and one of deep thought and reflection. As engrossed as he was, he was lucky there were no enemy about as it would have been easy for him to have been overtaken.

The events of the past couple months, the past couple years even, lay heavily on his mind. Nothing made sense to him anymore. When he had joined up back in '62, it was at one of the North's darkest hours, and he did so with the intention of helping to preserve the Union and the Union only. Mr. Marsh had spoken to him of slavery being the deep-seated cause of the war, but Gabriel hadn't taken his ravings seriously. The Emancipation Proclamation brought the issue to the forefront though, and as contentious a subject as it was, even throughout the ranks of the Union Army, Gabriel was forced to admit that Mr. Marsh had been right.

During his first days in the Army and before, Gabriel had been for the most part somewhat indifferent to slavery. After seeing it practiced first-hand over his time in the south, however, he had to disagree with Mr. Marsh on whether or not its destruction was worth the bloodletting. Its evils were just too obvious, and this became especially evident to him during their campaign to Atlanta and now beyond. The sight of thick keloid whip scars on the backs of some of the negro men he encountered best showcased the practice's brutal inhumanity. What saddened Gabriel the most though, were the countless rag-covered and hungry-looking children he came across. It sickened him to see and then to think of his own dear daughter having to live that way, with no real prospects of life ever getting much better.

Admittedly, he had also seen well-dressed and cared-for slaves, as well as many freedmen, some of whom were far better off financially than the multitudes of poor white trash he had also encountered. In Gabriel's mind though, the suffering of the former heavily outweighed the luck of the latter, and these observations made him an ardent supporter of emancipation.

His arrest had changed things though and muddied his mind some. Not in regard to slavery, but in the war in general, and the politics of the country as he thought he knew them. Things weren't so clear to him now. The slave woman at Flat Rock had attempted to run him out just as earnestly as her owners. This all when Gabriel thought she should have been siding with him. His arrival should have marked the beginning of her freedom, yet she was against him and stayed on, and Gabriel couldn't understand why, then or now. Had she truly enjoyed her life in bondage, he wondered, or was it her ignorance of the alternative that made her stay? Was she kept in the dark of the outside world, too sheltered and restrained to know any better? Perhaps her owners had frightened her of the Yankees, creating a false prejudice. Even if they had influenced her though, Gabriel recognized there was still no denying her devotion or concern for them.

Gabriel was also having trouble processing what had happened at the plantation that day. Meeting that negro boy, a proud son to a Confederate officer. How could that happen, and how could that boy have cared for his father's wife as he did, after what she had done to his mother and attempted to do to him? There was also the old woman and her obvious love for her slave, and then his death and her beating at the hands of a fellow southerner and one of her former people. It made him sick trying to imagine what other horrors they could have imposed on her if he and his friends hadn't come along.

He and his companions were contradictions, too. Sherman's whole invasion force was, for that matter. They marched to war waving the flag of unity. They didn't call themselves the Union for no reason. Yet, here they were out stealing from those whom they were trying to entice back into the fold. Those whom they claimed they wanted to call their fellow countrymen. And they not only stole food and provisions, but personal items and valuables as well. Even he himself was guilty of that.

Gabriel was sure he would never forget the face of the man he shot, the sheer look of terror in his eyes as he leveled his revolver to finish him. He had fired hundreds of rounds over the past several months, but only once could he confidently and without any doubt say he had killed a man, and it wasn't even in battle. It was an execution of sorts.

What of the man's black partner, too? Had he deserved to die? Sure, they had found the bloody knife used to disembowel the old man tucked in his belt, but perhaps the old man wasn't that innocent either. Perhaps his murder was payback, retribution for years of abuse when he worked as overseer to his fellow slaves on the plantation. If that were the case, Gabriel thought, then maybe he couldn't blame him for the killing. Who knew, though? Gabriel certainly wasn't going to go back and ask.

Nothing made sense anymore. What he had once seen as black and white, good versus evil, was all gray now. A confusing and never-ending mess of extenuating circumstance. In the beginning, he had expected to see death, destruction and sadness, but he had now come to learn that contradiction and confusion also reigned supreme. Uncertainty was now a certainty of the war in his eyes. That, and his desire for it all to end. His hope for peace.

The war was just about over. The writing was on the wall. They were on a nearly unopposed free-for-all through the heart of the south, acting as if they were the reincarnated legions of ancient Rome. Surely, the war was nearing its end and Gabriel was happy for that. He was happy that all his friends might not have died in vain. His greatest worry now, his ultimate goal, was managing to survive to the end with his honor intact and making it home to Rill, the baby, and all the other loved ones of his he had left behind.

EPILOGUE

Gabriel went on to finish the March to the Sea, reaching Savannah with Sherman's horde shortly before Christmas of 1864. From there, he participated in Sherman's push into the Carolinas late the following January. He fought at the battles of Averasboro and Bentonville in March, and was with the Union troops that pressured General Joe Johnston to surrender his Confederate Army at Bennet Place outside of Raleigh, North Carolina on April 26, 1865. The over 89,000 men the surrender encompassed was the largest of the war.

Peace needed to be a sure thing before the volunteer army could begin the long and drawn out process of demobilization. Because of this, after marching to Washington D.C. and participating in the Grand Review, Gabriel and his friends from Dryden were required to wait around the capital for two months before they were finally mustered out of service on the 20th of July. He didn't make it home until sundown on August 1st, 1865.

Soon after getting home, Gabriel and his parents made an agreement that he would work for them on their farm for room and board and $20 a month in cash. He and his father also started a side business called John Ballard & Son. They owned a threshing machine and a portable sawmill and would thresh crops all over Dryden and the surrounding area during the harvest. When they weren't threshing or farming their own land, they used the sawmill to saw logs into lumber for paying customers.

Gabriel and Rill didn't live with his parents forever. In the years following, they rented several different places, and Gabriel held a number of different jobs. He worked as a farm hand, a lumberman, and also for the railroad when the South Central was run through town. In 1869, they were finally able to afford their own place. They purchased a house and 68 acres of land on Blackman Hill in the town of Caroline and started a little farm of their own.

Gabriel and Rill had four more children after their first child, Martha, came along during the war. Frank was born in 1866, Charles in 1868, and their second daughter Emma in 1871. Their fifth and final child, the author's great-great grandmother, was born June 12, 1874, and they named her Julia, after Enos Cooks' wife, Julia Cook.

Sadly, Gabriel never got the chance to see his children grow up. Along with his Springfield rifle, numerous memories and life lessons learned, Gabriel came home from the war with disease as well. At some point during his time in the Army, he'd contracted consumption, known today as tuberculosis, and died from it on March 24, 1875. He was only 31 years old, and was laid to rest in the Harford Cemetery, not very far from his parents' home in Dryden where he'd grown up, or the farm that he and Rill bought and lived on together with their children in Caroline.

After Gabriel passed away, Rill was left with all five kids and no job or way of supporting them. At first, she and the children moved in with Gabriel's parents, but in 1877 she remarried and, as was customary in that era, the children were bound out and adopted by local families. Only Frank was able to stay with a relative. He was raised by his uncle, Stacy Ballard, known as Sam in this book, while Martha and Charles were bound out. Martha was sent to live with Julia Cook, to learn dressmaking, and Charles to a farmer. The two youngest daughters were adopted, Emma to the Lamont family of Virgil, and Julia to the Boice family of Caroline. Julia was not even a year old at the time of her father's death.

Although the children and their mother were separated, they still stayed in touch throughout the remainder of their lives. They visited each other often, and as they grew old and had families of their own, met yearly for reunions and picnics. Emma and Julia even married a set of brothers, Lyman and Henry Watros.

ACKNOWLEDGEMENTS

There are so many people to thank. Too many to be honest. My parents, grandparents, aunts and uncles, a select group of my former teachers from Newfield Central Schools, and anyone that ever encouraged my interest in history as a child or teen.

More specifically, I'd like to thank my cousin, Bob Watros, for introducing me to Gabriel, and the Ballard brothers of Canada: Rick, Mike, and Mark, for providing me with copies of Gabriel's journals, his portrait, his photograph, and his enlistment papers. Thanks to Hal Jespersen for the wonderful maps he designed and provided, and thanks to Jessika Hazelton of The Troy Book Makers for her expertise in putting it all together.

I would also like to thank Bob Mrazek, for his guidance and encouragement over the past couple of years. A stranger at first, he certainly wasn't obligated to lend a hand or to even respond to my request for assistance. He kindly did, however, and his vast expertise as an accomplished author has been invaluable to me throughout this process.

My 8th grade Social Studies teacher, Charley Githler, deserves my hearty thanks as well. Charley always encouraged my love of history in the classroom and has been a supporter of this book since I first contacted him for advice early on in its writing. When I had a completed manuscript he graciously worked as my editor and did so free of charge, despite my insistence to the contrary. He has been an unbelievable help and mentor throughout this project, and I will be forever grateful to him for that.

Lastly, and perhaps most importantly, I'd like to thank my lovely wife, Brittany, for her steadfast ability to put up with and endure my side historical pursuits. In our nearly thirteen years of marriage there isn't a vacation we've taken, and we've been on many, that she hasn't been forced to stop at some sort of museum, fort, battlefield, or out of the way historical site or marker. That's not to mention the several excursions I've taken with one or both of our boys, while she was forced to stay at home to work or care for a baby. Granted, they were to places she had no interest in visiting, but the unfairness was there all the same. She's spent many a Saturday at home alone with the kids while I was off researching at a library or historical society. Of course, there is also the fact that much of this book was written during the raising of our three young children, most notably through two pregnancies. I remember many nights with Britt languishing up in bed, too big to move and in pain, while I sat about downstairs happily drinking a cup of tea or coffee while typing away on one of my cheap PC's. She's a trooper, let me tell you, and deserves all the credit, thanks, love and appreciation I have to offer, and much more. I'm a lucky man, for sure.